What readers are saying about The Box

'A gripping tale of lust, greed, innocence, sadness and poetic justice. The author shows a good knowledge of the plot area. A compelling read.'

Mrs B, Cheshire

'A powerful story of a young woman's struggle against a painful family tragedy and of an unspeakable crime but through it all love and hope that kept me glued to each page.

This is one of those books that drags you in and keeps you on the edge of your seat. If you like mysteries, love and hope then you will love this book.'

Lisa D, Oxfordshire

'I'd been looking forward to reading the third book in The Lighthouse Series, and it didn't disappoint. Captivating storyline and intriguing characters. Another great read!'

Tina C, Oxfordshire

AJ Warren worked as Head of an Early Years setting for 18 years. She lives in Oxfordshire with her husband, and her two grown children and her grandson who live nearby. When not in Lockdown, she spends her days spoiling her four-year-old grandson, keeping a close eye on the family youngster, a 17th month female Romanian crossbreed rescue, swimming and working out new plots for her novels. Her books, The Lamp-post Shakers and The Ghost Chaser are available on Amazon in both E-reader and book format. The books are part of The Lighthouse Series and can be read alone or as part of the series. The Box is the third instalment of the series.

A short word from the author:

'Hello, I'm Andrea, alias AJ Warren. I started working on The Box in August 2019, and it soon became one of the most enjoyable books I've written so far. In fact, despite some short notes on characters profiles, and a working title– I had no idea what I was going to write each day! It soon fell into place and I began to work to the strengths/weaknesses of the characters and began to add a variety of story arcs. I hope you enjoy The Box, and if you do, please let me know, share on social media or write a review on Amazon or Goodreads. Thanks.'

You can contact Andrea via her website: https://ajwarrenauthor.wordpress.com

or via her Facebook page

Other books by AJ Warren

The Lamp-post Shakers (The Lighthouse Series)

The Ghost Chaser (The Lighthouse Series)

The Box

AJ Warren

This book is dedicated to a shining star who was taken from us much too soon. For the memory of Lauren, and those who knew her. Shine bright, beautiful girl.

The Box

Part 1

Jenny

The hot sun beats down on my warm swimsuit clad body, as I sit on the beach and stare out into the gentle surf in front of me. I close my eyes briefly in a bid to memorise the moment. Turning to look across at my friend Lottie, I can't help but give her the biggest smile.

'This is the life,' I dig my toes into the soft sand.

Lottie shrugs in companionable appreciation, her glorious natural red curls bouncing lightly onto her golden freckled shoulders. She clinks her bottled water to mine. The distant look on her face falters momentarily, before she leans closer, holding my gaze.

'I know, but you need to wake up, Jenny.' Her voice deepens with concern and a note of fear. 'You can't stay here!'

I stare at her in confusion. What was she saying? My head begins to hurt when I try to make sense of her words. Momentarily, I close my eyes, block out the world and listen to the calming sounds of the surf.

'Open your eyes,' Lottie touches my shoulder lightly. 'You need to go back.'

'But I don't want to,' I whisper.

'Wake up! Wake the hell up!' A loud voice screams in my head.

My eyes shoot open, I can't breathe. Panic sets in, alongside a fear that seizes every fibre within me. I can't move. The world is black. Oh God! Now I remember where I am. I'm in a place so far from the beautiful sandy beach and the hot fresh air. So far from freedom, cold water and the sun, that it hurts.

I'm in hell.

If hell is the coffin-shaped, long wooden box I find myself imprisoned in, then yes, I'm there. I draw air into my lungs, to calm myself, but the burn stings like crazy scorching my chest, until I close my eyes again and count to ten. Finally, my breathing settles.

Shuffling my damp, pyjama clad bottom until my bare feet are touching the end panel, I bend my legs as far as I can, and kick hard with my heels. I wince as my toe catches on splintered wood, splitting the skin. God, that hurt! Bloodied knuckles crack, as I force my hands into fists, the agony is almost too much. I kick again. Pain sears through my feet and ankles, and jolts up to my knees, making me wonder how much more of this constant kicking my damaged feet can take.

The box is far too strong for me to make any progress. Wrapping my arms around myself to stop my body from shaking, I resign myself to the fact that I am going to die in this damn place. Frustrated tears slide down my cold face at the possibility of never leaving this cool, dark prison. I ignore the soreness, telling myself to simply lie still and wait for the end to come.

'Please God, let me fall asleep and never wake up,' I whisper into the dark silence. Of course, there is no reply, no one is here, no one is listening. I close my eyes and wait. For how long, I'm not sure. I imagine the ticking of a clock. Tick tock.

'Jen?' A voice, deep, intense and as familiar to me as my own, calls out. For a moment I am convinced that I am imagining it, and my heart beats so fast, I think it's going to burst from my chest.

'Jen?' The voice shouts again. It's Stuart. He's here.

At last.

Please find me. Warm tears of hope follow those of despair, and I put my arm over my eyes, and hold it there, to force them to stop. For a moment, my eyes blur.

'Stuart!' I shout, my voice hoarse from lack of fluids and constant shouting. I bang my fists on the lid above me, and wince as pain shoots up my aching arms. 'Stuart!' I can't believe he's here, that he's found me.

'Jenny?' His voice sounds closer, frantic and breathless as though he's climbing the stairs.

'In here. I'm in one of the upstairs bedrooms. In a long box.' I half-shout, half-cry, as I lie helplessly in the dank darkness. I use the palms of my hands to bang any part of solid surface I can reach, trying to make as much noise as I possibly can.

'Keep talking. I'm going to find you,' his voice tries to reassure me, but I can hear the sound of desperation in his tone. He's usually so calm, so confident.

'I'm in a wooden box of sorts. I'm not sure what it looks like or where I am,' I shout. 'Please hurry!' I start to panic. What will happen if he can't find me?

'Jenny, I've checked all the bedrooms, and the bathroom. I can't find you.'

'Noooooooo...' I scream so hard, that my head begins to pound. 'No… keep looking, I'm here.' I can hear my voice rising in panic, feel my body stiffening. I'm going to be locked in here forever. I'm never getting out.

‘I won’t give up. I can hear you,’ he’s saying, desperation in his voice. ‘I just need to… wait a minute,’ his words sound clearer, louder.

Heavy footsteps move closer, until I hear the sound of something being lifted from the top of the box. I hold my breath. Waiting. Hoping. A fumbling sound above my head, is followed by a sharp click sound, as the lid creaks and begins to lift. Strange, but I never noticed the lid creaking before. I haven’t seen daylight in two days, and sadly my eyes have become used to the black void of nothingness. The only light I’d seen was from a small lamp in the corner of the room, and the artificial brightness that filtered through the material of my rough hessian hood on my bathroom visits.

The lid of the box is fully open, and the first thing I see is a strip of sunlight streaking across the darkened room, through a large gap in the partly drawn curtains. The light hurts my eyes and sends a sharp pain to my head, so I quickly rub my forehead and use my arms to cover the top half of my face, giving my stressed eyes time to adapt.

When my eyes eventually stop stinging and my vision clears, a mop of short, mousy hair moves towards me. Hair belonging to someone very dear to me. Stuart’s angular chin, and brown half-closed eyes stare back at me and his lips form a grim line of concentration. He leans over me, stroking my matted blonde hair away from my face, as the moment freezes in time. I’m going to live.

‘Holy mother of God! I can’t believe I found you,’ Stuart’s voice is strained with relief and fear. He reaches into me with warm, steady hands and tries to pull me up into a sitting position.

‘Are you OK sweetheart?’ He asks, his dark brown, almost black eyes meeting mine – full of concern.

'Yes, I think so,' I nod, but my nerves are shot, tears are falling down my face and I can't stop sobbing. The relief of being found, being rescued - it's almost too much. 'It was Felix,' I mutter, 'he did this to me.'

'I know,' he answers, looking at me, his words are clipped as though he's trying to control his temper, 'I figured it out.'

'Do you know where he is now?' I tremble over the words, there's no mistaking the fear in my voice. I grab the front of his blue jumper and hold tight.

'He's gone,' he says, his voice void of emotion as he covers my hands with his. Then his hands carefully take my arms, to help me to stand.

'Just give me a minute,' I say in a low weak voice. 'Let my legs and arms get their circulation back, they've cramped up. He hasn't been back for a really long time.' I wipe the salty wetness covering my stinging red face with the arm of my sleeve. My emotions are all over the place.

'I don't know where he's gone,' he says in a harsh tone, lifting his thumb to gently brush away a tear, 'but the police had better find him first.' He holds me with care, one hand under my elbow and the other around my waist, waiting patiently until my legs stop shaking.

'Ready?' he asks, holding my gaze.

I give him a trusting nod before he bends slightly, places his hands under my thighs and scoops me effortlessly out of the box. His jumper is soft against my cheek when I shift my gaze to look up at his stern profile, 'because, the next time I see him, I'm going to fucking kill him.'

Part 2

Stuart

I can't forgive myself for not finding her sooner. I scoop her in my arms and hold her tight. What kind of monster would kidnap a young woman and imprison her like that? I look at the dark circles under Jenny's blue eyes, the nightwear consisting of a dishevelled long-sleeved, red top and purple pyjama bottoms, which felt a little damp against my hand, when I picked her up.

Her long blonde hair is mussed and tangled, not surprisingly considering what has happened to her. I take in her bloody knuckles, the scrapes on her hands and her bloody jagged fingernails, where I guess, she's been trying to push the lid open. My eyes stray to her bare feet. Bloody toes and scratched, bruised heels. She never stood a chance. I am so mad.

'Stu?' her quiet voice interrupts my frantic thoughts.

'Yes, sweetheart?' I say, taking the stairs carefully but swiftly. I need to get her to the hospital and call the police. In what order, I'm not sure. It depends who I meet on my way to the main house.

'I thought I was going to die,' her voice sounds so sad.

'I know, baby. I've got you now and I'm going to keep you safe. Hold on to me.'

She closes her eyes and begins to sob quietly. After a few seconds, she looks up at me, her lovely face frowning with embarrassment, 'I wet myself.'

'Don't worry about that Jen,' I say, staring into her face. 'You did what you had to do. You had no choice. I'm here now. Let me take care of you.' It's killing me to see her like this. I kiss her forehead gently as I carry her out onto the white veranda of the Summer House and into fresh air. I take a deep breath, savouring the untainted air, the only thing that Felix hasn't managed to poison with his worthless life.

Henry Dean, the estate manager comes out of the stables and immediately catches sight of me striding towards the main house. The look of shock on his aged weather-beaten face is understandable. His usually smart appearance of blue trousers, a white shirt, a dark blue tie and a blue and black checked jacket, is marred by the slightly kinked collar of the jacket and the tie that sits askew his neck. His shoulders are slumped on his tall, thin frame and his short grey hair is untidy, he's been worried since Jenny went missing.

Henry and his wife, Rose have cared for Jenny for most of her life. From what she's told me, they'd been there when she'd taken her first steps as a toddler. Routinely, her parents had spent the majority of her youth, attending important meetings in their respective offices, situated within the main house.

'Oh my God! Is that Jenny?' He shouts with a rough edge to his voice.

'Yes!' I yell back, watching him as he begins to run towards me. 'Call the police and get an ambulance.'

With a nod of his head, Henry turns around and runs to the main house. I keep talking to Jenny to reassure her that she's safe and that everything will be all right.

'Will they find him? I don't want him to come back to the house,' she asks quietly.

'They will, one way or another. I can't see him coming back to here, but if he does there will be police officers guarding the house. And, I'm going to make sure that you're not left alone.'

'Thank you,' her eyes hold mine in appreciation, as though I am some kind of hero. Shit.

'Don't fucking thank me, Jenny' I say harshly, angry with myself and hearing the harshness to my tone. This was on me. She'd done nothing wrong. 'I should never have left you alone with him. You had your suspicions about him. I should have insisted you stayed with me.'

'It's not your fault,' she says carefully, her sad eyes holding mine. She's trying to let me off the hook.

'That's debatable,' I grind out, more to myself than her.

As I reach the dark oak front door of the main house Rose comes running towards us, in her black low-heeled shoes, scrunching along the gravel driveway. Her bright green cooking apron is flapping in the wind, a blue striped tea towel dangles carelessly from her hand. She is clearly distraught.

'Jenny! Oh, my darling girl,' her deep voice full of concern as she strokes Jenny's face with the hands of a loving mother. Her eyes are shining with unshed tears.

'Let's get you in the house honey, the Red Room will do,' Rose mutters, then looks swiftly at me. 'Henry says the police and an ambulance are on the way.'

I nod my thanks and continue through the Great Hall and into the Red Room, I don't think I'll ever get used to visiting Gateshead. The grey stone manor house oozes opulence, money and power.

I carefully lay Jenny down onto a red velvet sofa and Rose gently pushes a black silk cushion to support her head.

'I'm fine. Really I am.' Jenny begins.

'No, you're not,' Henry walks into the room staring at the tableau of panic and relief in front of him. We're not out of the woods yet, old chap, I think carelessly as I collect a grey cashmere throw from the arm of the sofa and spread it over Jenny's lower body, to keep her warm. I hear the faint sound of sirens fill the background and look at Henry, silently asking him to get the door. He nods, before moving through the hallway to wait in the Great Hall for the emergency services.

I think back to last night. I couldn't sleep. Rose had made up the Garden Room for me, but I had found myself tossing and turning well into the early hours, worrying about where Jenny was and what was happening to her.

***

Memories of our last moments together on Friday night, snuggled on the sofa drinking wine and waiting for our pizza to be delivered before we watched the Bruce Willis film 'Red' on Netflix. I'd made fun of her pizza choice. Jen's favourite was ham and pineapple. It's one of those toppings you either love or hate. People constantly argue whether it is acceptable to have fruit as a pizza topping, I personally wouldn't have it, and I couldn't help teasing Jen as she added her choice to the online order. We had a lovely evening, nothing out of the ordinary had happened to indicate that she was worried or in trouble.

Finally, at 2am, I'd dragged my grey jeans onto my tired legs, yanked them over my bottom, pulled the zip, threw my dark blue jumper over my head and went in search of the kitchen. Dark shadows followed me as I walked along the corridor to the staircase. Light from the moon streamed through the glass arcs that sit on the top of the front wooden doors, sending sharp shaped patterns along the dark carpet of the hall.

A moment later, I had found myself in her room. The room smelled of Jenny, the subtle notes of her perfume with its rose, vanilla cream and light musk scent. As I looked at her things, the make-up left haphazardly on her white French dressing table, her glass jewellery box and silver necklace tree stand, covered in an array of brightly coloured necklaces, it broke me apart. I placed my hot mug on her matching white bedside table and fell to my knees. Leaning over the soft blue paisley covered duvet, I had put my hands together and quietly start to pray. 'Please God, let her be all right, bring her back to me.'

I wiped my wet eyes and climbed into her bed, ignoring the hot drink. Jenny's scent soothing me into oblivion.

Some hours later, I heard movement in the house. Every bone in my body ached as I stretched my limbs and focussed on what was happening. I sat up and stared at the red digital numbers on the clock on the table next to me, the one sat next to my mug full of chilled tea. The clock said, 9am. Shit. I must have slept for longer than I thought. What day was it? Sunday.

I made my way back to the Garden Room to splash water onto my face and collect my phone from its charger. Stuffing it into the back pocket of my jeans, I headed downstairs to find Rose and Henry. I found Rose in the kitchen, making a pot of tea. When she saw me, she pushed a mug of hot, milky tea across the counter, and I nodded my thanks, added sugar and walked to the table when I felt my phone buzz in my pocket. The screensaver showed a text from Lottie.

'Any news?' She asked.

'No. Nothing.' I typed back.

'Bugger. Where is she Stu?' Came her quick response, before she added a sad emoji.

'I wish I knew.' My fingers flew over the letters on the phone screen.

'Text you if I hear anything. X' I told her.

'Ditto,' she finished, as I put my phone on the table.

'Anything from DCI Carter?' Rose had asked with red eyes.

'No. Nothing,' I'd said flatly, it was hard trying to hide the cloud of depression that was hanging over me. I'd put the mug to my lips to take a careful sip. It felt heavy, like it was made of stone.

Everything had seemed such an effort and I was dog-tired, due to my lack of sleep. I'd grabbed my phone and skulked around the numerous rooms of the house, checking cupboards, the garage block, anywhere I could think of, for signs of my girlfriend.

I'd forgot to go back for lunch, instead I'd sat in a silent daze on Jenny's bed. I must have dozed because when I'd woke the clock had said 3.10pm and I was bloody annoyed with myself. *Jesus! Pull yourself together man! You need to focus.* The sudden rumble of my empty stomach had reminded me that I was hungry, so I'd pushed myself to a standing position. Time to go in search of something to eat.

I was sat at the kitchen table, spreading butter on to a slice of wholemeal bread, when Rose had wandered into the kitchen carrying a laundry basket. 'You know,' I'd said to her, almost talking to myself. 'I don't think that this is a ransom thing. I mean, we would have heard from them before now, wouldn't we?'

'Yes,' she'd said, putting the basket onto the floor and slumping into the chair next to me. She was wearing a bright green cooking apron tied over a dark blue dress. 'I can't help but think that there's a connection between Jenny's disappearance and Felix's absence.'

'I agree,' I'd said. We'd sat in silence for a moment, until the shrill ring of the house phone echoed through the house. Without thinking, I'd pushed my chair backwards with some force, ran to the Great Hall and grabbed the receiver from the mahogany console table.

'Gateshead?' I'd said quickly, my voice full of hope.

'Hello, is Miss Gloverman there?' A deep, brisk voice had said down the phone line.

'No, I'm afraid she's not,' I'd replied, feeling deflated that the voice didn't belong to Jen. 'Can I help you? I'm Stuart Greyson, her boyfriend.'

'I don't think so,' replied the rough voice. 'It's Ellis Sykes from Sykes Builders. Miss Gloverman has commissioned us to renovate the Summer House. We're due to start work in a couple of weeks and we came over first thing yesterday morning, around 9am to discuss last minute details. We arranged this meeting last week, but when we arrived, she never turned up. I tried calling her, but there was no answer. So, I thought I'd give her a quick call to let her know we hadn't forgotten to come.'

'I see. When you were at the Summer House, did you see anyone hanging around?' I'd asked carefully.

'We met the old man. The one with curly hair, and a moustache, wearing a Rolex. His blue car was parked next to the house and he was about to leave when we arrived.'

'Really?' I'd answered, now that's interesting. He was describing Felix Gloverman. In my mind, a small idea was beginning to take root. ‘Did you get the impression that the man had been in the house?’ I’d asked.

‘Couldn’t tell you,’ said Ellis Sykes. ‘But it was a bit strange that he was outside the house, I mean, what other reason would he be there for?’

‘It does sound strange,’ I’d muttered, agreeing with him. What an utter bastard you are, Felix. If you’ve done, what I think you’ve done, I am going to kill you.

‘Thank you, Mr Sykes,’ I’d said as calmly as possible, as I watched Rose move around in the kitchen. ‘I appreciate your call and I’ll be sure to pass on your message to Jenny when I see her.’

I’d thrown the receiver down on to the table, not bothering to disconnect him. I’d ran to the front door, yanked it open and rushed out onto the gravel driveway. Straight to the Summer House. She couldn’t be down there, could she? I’d argued with myself. Right under our noses, all this time.

***

Like a statue, I stand rooted to the spot on the expensive red patterned Persian rug, and stare at the floor. If Ellis Sykes hadn’t called, I would never have found her. I vaguely remember her saying something about renovating it, but I didn’t realise that she’d planned to do it so soon.

A soft sob breaks my silent thoughts and I roll my head from side to side to bring me back to the present. The sob comes from Rose as she strokes Jenny’s hair trying to soothe her. Jenny lies back on the sofa, totally still, with her eyes closed.

‘Stu?’ She opens her eyes suddenly, looking for me.

'I'm here, sweetheart.'

'Don't leave me,' a painful looking red cut on a purple bruised hand creeps out from under the throw and she reaches out to me. I kneel beside her, taking her cold hand gently, but firmly.

'Never,' I grind out helplessly.

The arrival of the ambulance and police car is announced by the piercing sirens that are immediately both unsettling and reassuring. Two paramedics, rush in carrying backpacks, a case and a stretcher.

I let go of Jenny's hand, stand and motion to them with my arms.

'Jenny,' I explain, 'I found her about twenty minutes ago. She's been held captive in a large chest in the dark for almost three days.'

Immediately they stoop to Jenny, talking to her quietly and pulling back the throw to begin their assessment and examination of her before taking her to the hospital.

A tall brooding figure looms in the doorway. Detective Chief Inspector Brian Carter, in his standard black raincoat, blue shirt, brown tie and brown corduroy trousers. He's not bad looking in a rugged, brooding sort of way. Probably in his early forties. He's staring at Jenny, his face thoughtful yet relieved that she has been found after being missing for nearly three days.

'DCI Carter, I told you she was missing,' I feel the accusation in my voice but the relief and acknowledgement of finding her overshadows the negative tone. 'I know you were sceptical because of the note she left, but I knew in my gut that she wouldn't leave without talking to me.'

'I know. I know,' he gives in, holding his hands up in resignation. 'Do you still think it was Felix Gloverman behind this? I've put a warrant out for his arrest.'

‘Sorry,’ one of the paramedics cuts in, the one named ‘Bob’, the short, bald-headed man, with a black goatee beard and a tiger tattoo peeping out from the folded over cuff of his green uniform. “But we need to get Jenny to the hospital.”

‘Sure,’ Carter watches Jenny closely. ‘We’ll take a statement later, when you’re up to it. Are you able to confirm that it was Felix who kidnapped you?’

Jenny looks at him. She has a fearlessness about her, but I know what it takes for her to show this defiant, strong side. I see the pain behind her eyes, the cuts, the bruises, the fragility.

‘Yes. It was him,’ she replies, her voice husky with emotion. ‘I could see some things through the hessian hood he put over my head, when he took me to the bathroom. There’s no doubt it was him.’

Carter nods and walks forward, staring out of the window across the manicured lawns of the top terrace. He takes out his phone, presses a button and starts to speak.

‘I’ve got confirmation that it was Felix Gloverman who took Jenny Gloverman. I want people placed around the entrances and exits at Gateshead, and in the main reception and on her door at the hospital. We’re heading there now. The John Radcliffe?’ He asks the paramedics and waits for their confirmation nods, before continuing. ‘Yes. Any sign of Gloverman’s car? Let me know if you find anything.’

‘I want to walk,’ Jenny’s firm voice tells the paramedics. The Asian, dark-haired paramedic with the name tag ‘Kate’ looks at Bob and they both give a nod and begin to help Jenny to her feet.

‘If you’re sure,’ Kate says, keeping her arms close enough to Jenny to catch her if she falls.

'I want to come with you,' I say, as Rose hurries into the room with Jenny's slippers and helps her to shuffle her feet into them. 'I promised Jenny I would stay with her.'

'That's fine,' says Bob.

Carter finishes his call and looks across at us.

'I'll meet you both at the hospital. Good to see you're safe Jenny.'

Jenny tries to smile. I follow her as the paramedics gently walk her to the ambulance.

'I'll call Lottie and lock up the house. Henry and I will meet you at the hospital.'

'Thanks,' I say, wondering where would we be without them? The glue that has kept this family together for God knows how many years.

'Look after her Stuart,' Rose calls.

'I will.'

I wave them off as I sit in the ambulance waiting for Jenny to be secured and a blood pressure cuff to be wrapped around her arm. Bob starts to put a cannula into Jenny's hand.

'I'm just going to push some fluids into you,' he reassures her. 'Rest up, as much as you can. We'll be there in about fifteen minutes.'

The blue light starts as we set off for the hospital.

I can't help but think that under different circumstances this may have been quite an exciting way to travel. Running the red traffic lights and zooming in and out of traffic. Then, I'm brought back to the reality of the situation that we're in.

'Stu,' her voice sounds frail as she puts out her hand to take mine.

'It's OK, sweetheart, I'm here. It's going to be OK,' I say, taking her hand and stroking the bruised and cut tender skin lightly.

An hour later we're at the hospital and have been moved to a private room. White walls and storage units fill the room, alongside a bed made with white cotton sheets and a blue knitted blanket folded neatly at the bottom. There are two wooden, green cushioned chairs either side of the bed and a wheeled metal overbed tray for patients to use. Two folded dark grey metal chairs are balanced against the windowsill. A petite female police officer with short jet-black hair, stands unsmiling in the corner of the room and a male officer has been placed outside the door. DCI Carter looks broodingly at his phone.

I'm sitting next to Jenny, watching over her sad frame as she lies in the hospital bed. She's still wearing her nightwear, having refused the offer to put on a gown, lying on the bed with her eyes closed. I'm holding her hand, the one that's not attached to the drip.

A tall brisk female doctor walks into the room. Maybe in her forties, she has her dark brown hair pulled back into a ponytail and has a silver stethoscope draped casually around her neck. She is followed by a young slender nurse, late twenty something with short dark curly hair and a grim determined look on her face.

'Hello Jenny. I'm the Senior Trauma Registrar, Dr Sam Tracker. This is Staff Nurse Lisa Skinner. Please call me Sam.'

Dr Tracker briefly makes eye contact with Jenny and there is a sudden air of discomfort as she leans in closer to Jenny.

'We are going to need to give you a full examination, to record and assess your wounds and current state of health. I am also going to do a more thorough examination to determine if you have been sexually assaulted,' the doctor continues.

She gives Jenny time to process what she is saying. Jenny looks confused, her mind trying to remember exactly what had happened throughout every minute of her last three days in captivity.

'To your mind, do you know if you have been sexually assaulted?' She asks Jenny, bluntly.

Jenny looks at me and then looks away. Shame is shadowed throughout her face. I am holding my breath. My mind wants to float away to a happy place, so I don't have to deal with the situation in this room.

'No. I don't think so,' she says quietly.

I slowly release my breath. Thank God. I don't know what I would have done if she'd said yes. Well, of course I would have dealt with it, that goes without saying. Baby steps. Let's just get through each second, each moment, each stage as it happens because if we start thinking of the long-term repercussions of what Jenny has been through. Who knows, it may cripple her for life.

DCI Carter looks at Jenny and the doctor. I can tell by his face that he wants to ask questions but understands the need to wait until the examinations, observations and assessments have been done.

'I'll give you some space. I'll go and grab a coffee, while I chase a few leads. PC Leadbetter will stay here and document your injuries.'

I nod at his comment and watch him leave the room.

'Can you stay with me?' Jenny asks me. 'During the exam, I mean?'

'Of course. Whatever you want,' I say, momentarily wishing I could follow Carter – but knowing my place is here by Jenny's side.

I am worried about controlling the burning temper that's building inside me. It's hard enough seeing her hands and feet bloody and bruised from what that bastard did to her, but if there's more, I'm likely to lose it. My fists are itching with the need to punch something hard, like Felix's head.

'Right. If everyone can leave apart from Mr Greyson, Staff Nurse Skinner and the female officer. We'll start the examination.'

I look at the Registrar, she acts with such detachment. A job needs to be done and she needs to do it to the best of her ability. Swiftly Dr Tracker detaches Jenny's line from the saline drip and watches her carefully to make sure she doesn't feel disorientated or unwell. Without speaking I walk to the windowsill, collect a folded grey chair, carry it to the corner of the room and quietly sit down. I lean forward with my arms on my knees, clasp my hands together and let my chin dip so that it rests on my knuckles.

'Can you stand Jenny? We'll help you,' Staff Nurse Skinner asks, taking one side and Dr Tracker the other as they gently support Jenny to stand. When she's standing the women stay close, almost on sentry duty covering Jenny's personal space. Staff Nurse Skinner snaps on gloves, collects evidence tubes and rips open a sterile swab pack.

'I need to swab your mouth and nose and take samples from your fingernails,' the nurse explains, 'to collect any trace evidence from your kidnapper.'

Jenny nods and opens her mouth. The room is silent, as the swabs and samples are taken and safely stored into tubes. I held my breath as Jenny's winces during the scraping of her cracked nails.

‘Well done, ‘the nurse says, offering a small smile. Dr Tracker steps forward and asks Jenny in a low voice, ‘ready?’

Jenny dips her head and stares at the floor.

Slowly they slip her long top up her arms and over her head until she’s standing topless. PC Leadbetter picks up the police iPad and moves forward. The doctor and nurse move around Jenny’s standing form.

‘There is finger-mark bruising to her upper sternum. Consistent with being held down. On her back, there are contusions, cuts and bruising,’ the doctor says. The officer walks around Jenny, positions the electronic tablet and records the injuries.

They move to the drawstring on Jenny’s pyjama bottoms and for a second, her eyes catch mine and her hands move to stop the intrusion and humiliation that this examination is causing.

A single tear escapes my right eye. My fingers are clasped so tightly that my knuckles hurt, and my head feels heavy as it sits on my clasped hands. I give her the briefest nod. For God’s sake, let’s get this nightmare over and done with.

Jenny slowly releases the string and allows the medical staff to lower her pyjama bottoms, she uses their outstretched arms to balance each leg as she steps out of them. The stark reality of seeing her completely naked is overwhelming. I’ve seen her naked before, but never like this. Never in a room of professionals while she’s being examined. Never seen her so fragile and vulnerable.

I watch as she closes her eyes.

‘Fingerprint bruises to the upper thighs. Red marks to the buttocks,’ the nurse speaks quietly, the doctor and Leadbetter swiftly glance at each other, before continuing the examination.

Those marks had better not mean what I think they mean. I close my eyes, trying to still my frantic thoughts. *Please don't make this any worse for her. She's been through enough.* I silently pray.

More photos are taken, until the doctor is satisfied that they have enough.

'You're doing really well, Jenny. Let's put this gown on you and get you onto the bed. The internal examination will take just a few minutes.'

A gown is swiftly draped over Jenny's still form and she's ushered to the bed where Nurse Skinner gently encourages Jenny to lie down. When she is lying on the bed the nurse reattaches the saline drip.

'Take a deep breath, dear. It will be over soon,' she tells Jenny, trying to reassure her.

Dr Tracker collects a sterile kit from the trolley next to the bed. Staff Nurse Skinner lifts Jenny's knees, and carefully opens her legs, letting the hospital gown falls softly to her thighs.

'Try to relax, Jenny. I'm going to examine you for evidence of sexual assault.'

Jenny's eyes close tightly, her face winces in concentration, and she starts to shake.

'I feel cold. So cold,' her voice whispers across the room. I cannot stand this. Cannot stand the feeling of helplessness. I need to do something to help her, to comfort her. There's not much point in me being here if I can't help her. So, I stand and walk quickly to the bed. I take Jenny's hand firmly in mine and rub warmth into her.

'Look at me,' I stare at her closed eyes. 'Look at me Jen,' I repeat.

It's as though she can't face me, her head turns to the side. She's too ashamed. Why? She's got nothing to be ashamed of. I want to tell her that I don't care what's happened to her, what she's been through, that she will always be my girl, my woman.

Please God, just give me five minutes in a room with that bastard and I'll feel better. I'd like to torture him to within an inch of his life. Dark thoughts, of cutting his balls off with a bread knife and watching him bleed to death, suddenly cloud my vision. *Shit, rein it in Greyson, get a grip. This is not helping Jenny.* I take a deep breath.

'Sweetheart,' I gently cup her cheek, turning her to face me. Those deep ocean blue eyes, full of shame, hurt and pain. They look at me. Hold my stare.

'Stu.'

'Keep looking at me. I've got you.'

'Stu,' tears spill down her cheeks.

'I've fucking got you babe. Stay with me.' I hold her hand tightly, I never want to let her go. Her gaze never leaves mine.

'What did he do?' She asks quietly, with such a look of utter desolation on her face, it almost brings me to my knees.

'I don't know baby. We'll find out. Then we'll deal with it.'

Finally, the doctor finishes her examination. She adds an assortment of swabs to test tubes and clear evidence bags.

'I'm sorry Jenny,' Dr Tracker begins, 'so sorry, but there are signs of a sexual assault.'

'No!' Jenny screams, pushing me away. 'That's not possible! I would have known.'

PC Leadbetter uses her police radio to update DCI Carter about Jenny's exam, her brows are drawn together as she talks quietly.

I'm still holding on to Jenny's hand as she starts to sit up, her head shakes from side to side and her arms wrap around her body in a reassuring, defensive move.

'No!' Jenny sobs. 'No!' She rocks from side to side and her eyes close, as tears gush out of her red puffy eyelids, like a waterfall down her face.

I take her in my arms and hold her tightly, giving her all the strength within me. The world that we had, our world of hopes and dreams, it's suddenly become so small, so tiny. So hopeless.

The doctor's voice breaks in. 'I'm going to take some blood. Do some tests to find out what you've been given. Then I'm going to give you something to help you to sleep for a little while.'

After the tests are completed and the sedative has been given, I stroke Jenny's hair until she starts to dose. I hope it's a strong one, she needs respite from her nightmare.

'I'm sorry,' she whispers before her eyes finally close.

She's sorry. She's fucking sorry. Not half as sorry as I am, for not protecting her from that bastard. When she's finally asleep, I quietly leave the room. Rose and Henry are sitting in the waiting room as I walk towards the exit.

'Stuart!' Rose stands.

'How is she?' Henry asks, following me.

God. I need some fresh air.

'Hey guys. Just give me a minute, will you? I'll be back in five.' I rush past them, into the busy foyer of the hospital and through the automatic doors which lead me into the cold October early evening. It's dusk, not too dark. There are people coming and going, ambulances, taxis and a constant stream of cars entering and leaving the car parks.

I have a sudden overwhelming need to throw up. Searching quickly, I see a litter bin a few feet to my right and, just about make it there, before everything that I've eaten and drunk today finds its way into the bin.

The taste and smell of vomit hits me, as people stare my way, on this late October day, it's a day that will be imprinted on mine and Jen's memories forever. With a feeling of absolute misery, I turn around and head back into the hospital, find the bathroom, rinse my mouth and wash my face.

When I reach the waiting room, I collect Rose and Henry from their metal seats and apologise.

'Sorry about that. Needed some air. Let's find somewhere quiet to talk,' I say, motioning for them to follow me to a quiet corner booth in one of the hospital coffee shops, where I leave them briefly to order and pay for three cappuccinos. Several minutes later we sit with hot drinks in front of us.

Rose and Henry look worried.

'She's asleep,' I say. 'They've given her a sedative. The police probably won't interview her until tomorrow morning now.'

Rose looks at Henry and I pick up the vibes that they want or need more information from me.

'Can I see her?' Rose asks quietly, tucking her straight light brown shoulder-length hair behind her ear.

'Yes. When she wakes up. But there's something you both need to know.' I hesitate for a moment.

Henry looks at me and says wearily, 'just tell us straight, Stuart.'

'Felix,' I swallow the lump in my throat and stare at the table. I don't want to hurt these good people, once I tell them I can't take it back. I lift my head and look hard at Rose and Henry as they sit before me in their unbuttoned coats. I know I'm about to break their hearts.

'Felix. He bloody raped her,' I say bitterly. There's a flatness to my tone that sums up my mood.

Rose puts her hand to her mouth, holding in an anguished gasp. Her eyes brighten with tears. Henry just stares at me. I look at him with the same defeated look, berating ourselves because we should have protected her. Breaking into our thoughts, we hear Rose softly sobbing.

'Oh my God. How could he? Not our Jenny,' she says the words and question that we want to say aloud.

'He was her bloody uncle,' Henry sneers, rubbing his hand over his face.

'We can be upset about this later,' I say briskly. 'But for now, we need to focus on Jenny and helping her to get through this. We also need to find Felix or help the police to find him. The way I feel, I would happily take him into the woods, castrate him and put a bullet through his head. I would bury him deep in the woods.

'Son,' Henry puts a hand on my arm. 'I'm there with you. I'll kill the bastard the minute I see him, I don't care if I do time.'

'Henry! This is not going to help Jenny. Both of you boys need to calm down and let the police do their job. Jenny needs us, we're the only family she has.'

'Mrs Dean's right,' a familiar voice cuts in, sitting down next to me in the booth, DCI Brian Carter.

'Any sign of the bastard?' I ask.

'He took out money from a cashpoint in the centre of Bristol at 11pm last night,' Carter says. 'We found his car abandoned near Chippenham railway station and CCTV cameras at Bristol

Temple Meads show him arriving at the station at 15.38pm. I've alerted Bristol police and they're monitoring all CCTV cameras in the centre of the city and surrounding areas. Is there anywhere that you can think of that he may go? Anyone he would go to if he needed help or to lay low?'

'His personal assistant at the Gloverman Corporation?' suggests Rose, tightening and flexing her fingers as her hands rest on the table. Her gold wedding ring catches the light briefly, taking my mind briefly away from my dark thoughts.

'There was a friend he had mentioned, someone from his university days. I think his name is Andy,' Henry looks at Carter. 'Can't remember his surname though. Lived on the outskirts of Bristol, I think. He was into property. God. What was it called? Naylor Property Services, or something like that?'

'Thanks. I'll get on to those leads. Meanwhile, try and keep out of trouble, both of you,' he stands up, and gives Henry and me a stern look, before moving away. He stops and turns back.

'Oh, and I'm going to interview Jenny tomorrow morning if the doctor says she's fit enough. See you in the morning.'

We sip the dregs of our coffees in silence, each of us in our own personal hell, worrying about Jenny and wanting Felix caught before he harms anyone else. The thing that bothers me most is that he was supposed to be her guardian, her protector. He took her against her will, he kept her against her will, and he abused her against her will. In my book, he is the lowest form of human being.

'Let's go and see how she is. If she's still asleep, I'm sure the nurse won't mind if we just sit with her,' I stand and lead the way to Jenny's room. Rose and Henry solemnly follow. She's not dead, I feel like saying. She's alive. That's what counts, that's what is important.

As we reach the nurses station, Staff Nurse Skinner steps out from a side room and starts to use the mouse to navigate through different windows on the flat screen on the desk. She looks up.

'Mr Greyson."

"Please call me Stuart.'

'Stuart. Jenny is still asleep. I suspect she might be out for most of the night.'

I gesture to Henry and Rose.

'This is Henry and Rose Dean, very close friends – the only family Jenny has,' I make a conscious effort not to mention dear Uncle Felix.

'Would we be able to sit with her for a few minutes? We'll be no trouble,' Rose begins, the look of a mother's love on her face. This woman has the emotional resilience of a lioness guarding her cub.

'That'll be fine. Please don't wake her. At the moment, it's best that she rests where she can. Tomorrow will be another big day.'

Slowly I open the door to Jenny's room. It's in darkness apart from the overbed wall light that filters through enough light to check vitals on the patient. Jenny looks so small in the bed. The nurse has pulled the blanket up to her neck and she lies in peaceful repose.

I quietly move a chair to one side of the bed and motion Rose to sit, while Henry takes the seat on the opposite side. Rose lightly strokes the back of Jenny's hand. I put my arm on Rose's arm to comfort her.

'It will be alright,' I whisper. 'She will be alright. She's strong. Stronger than you think.' Rose pats my hand.

'Let's hope so,' she replies sadly.

After about thirty minutes I suggest that Rose and Henry go home to get some rest. I'm going to stay. I told her I wouldn't leave her, and I won't. I'll sleep in the chair next to Jenny's bed. If I'm lucky I might be able to loan a blanket from the store cupboard. Rose is bringing a bag of nightwear, toiletries and daywear clothes tomorrow. She says that they'll be in around 9am.

Once they're gone, I head to the hospital restaurant to grab a bit to eat and another hot drink. On the way, I see one of the nurses and explain that I am staying with Jenny tonight. She's going to put a couple of blankets and a pillow on the chair for me. My mind and anger has settled a little now, we're getting over the first hurdle and we need to focus on what needs to be done next. It's about prioritising and utilising what you have, to make it work for you.

So, I'm sitting here contemplating what might or might not happen tomorrow. Questions keep popping into my mind. Where is Felix? Will he come back? Does he want to finish what he started with Jenny? Is she in danger? Did he use a condom? Is she pregnant?

A shadow moves over my personal space and Dr Tracker looms over my shoulder holding a takeaway coffee.

'Hey, Mr Greyson. You OK if I sit down?'

'It's Stuart and yes, please do.'

I look at her and study her face, my first impressions thought her brisk and emotionless but now I see the mask has fallen a little and she seems quite pained by Jenny's situation.

'Is she OK?' I ask.

'Yes. Still asleep. I gave her enough sedation to see her through most of the night.'

We take a sip of our drinks and I begin to open my packet of sandwiches.

'Stuart, there is something I need to tell you. I didn't tell Jenny earlier because I thought she'd had enough to worry about for one day.'

Oh no. This doesn't sound good. I put down my half-opened packet and look at her. Can this day really get any worse?

'Just tell me,' I say in a low voice.

'He didn't use a condom. He finished in her, wiped her down and re-dressed her.'

'Fuck.' I look down at the table, absorbing the words. You won't believe this, but I don't usually swear. However, today I feel all I've done is to say the word fuck.

'The bastard. How could he do that to her? She is his niece for Christ's sake!'

'I know. What he did to her is despicable. It shows the worst part of human nature. I'll tell her tomorrow. Offer her emergency contraception.

This is a living hell. What do you do when your girlfriend is drugged, kidnapped and raped? How do you help her? The rage is building within me again, it's burning into my bones, creeping through the very heart of me. I don't think I will ever rid myself of it. How can we move forward when we're stuck in the present? Wait, drugs?

'He must have drugged her.' I murmur, 'there's no other way. It's the only explanation for why she didn't know what he'd done to her.'

'Not, unless – she was conscious but had blocked it out,' the doctor looks at me directly.

I shake my head, ‘I can’t see Jenny doing that.’

‘We’re testing the water bottle. I suspect he was keeping her mildly sedated but decided to increase the dose to knock her out. That would give him plenty of time and leverage to do what he wanted to her.’

Her phone bleeps, interrupting our thoughts. Sorry, she mouths as she takes the call.

‘Yes, alright. Thanks for that,’ she disconnects the call and looks at me.

‘The water contained a high dosage of Flunitrazepam, known commonly as Rohypnol. She’s lucky she didn’t go into a coma.’

‘So, now we know,’ I look at her and shake my head mournfully. I think of Felix, trying to get out of the country, wondering if he’ll try to come back to Gateshead before he goes. I need to punch something. Hard. But my punchbag is at home, hanging from the garage ceiling.

That man had better hope he never finds himself alone in a room with me. Let’s see how he copes with someone who is able to fight back.

The doctor pats my hand.

‘Try to get some rest. You’ve both got a big day tomorrow,’ she stands, picks up her drink and disappears down a corridor.

I sit for a moment, staring at the uneaten sandwiches. Jenny won’t wake for a few hours yet and it’s still only 7pm. On a whim I decide to book a taxi to take me home. At least I’ll be able to pick up my car, charger and laptop and anything else that springs to mind. I stuff the uneaten sandwich into my jacket pocket and forty minutes later I’m in my room at my parent’s house, collecting my laptop and charger and packing a change of clothes for the next few days.

I'm about to leave when I remember that it'll be Jenny's birthday tomorrow. A couple of weeks ago, I'd ordered a pair of silver lighthouse earrings online for her. One of Jenny's passions was visiting old and unusual lighthouses. I don't know why; she was simply captivated by them. I pick up the small brown box from my bedside table and push it into my jeans pocket. It may not be the right time, after what she's been through, but I feel like we should at least acknowledge her birthday tomorrow. I had planned to take her away somewhere nice for the weekend, but that needed to be put on hold.

My parents aren't very involved with my life, so it's no surprise when they don't make a comment as I pass through the lounge with the TV blaring, on my way back to Gateshead to pick up my car. The taxi is still waiting outside. Thankfully, I'm back at the hospital by 8.45pm and ready to settle in for the night.

What a day! I settle down in the chair next to Jenny's bed. A couple of pillows and a couple of blankets have been placed on top of the nearby cabinet. I get my laptop out and try to find out some information on where Felix might be. It's not long before I'm on the Gloverman Corporation website, checking out the director's page and am staring at the face of the man who had drugged, kidnapped and raped my girlfriend. Bastard. I also search Naylor Property Services.

I jot down a few notes and snap photos of anything that might be helpful. I take out the cheese and pickle sandwich from my jacket pocket and force it down me. I need to eat something. It won't help Jenny if I become ill. Finally, my head and limbs grow heavy as exhaustion claims me. I quickly put my phone on charge, pack away my laptop and grab the pillows and blankets.

Better get some rest Greyson. Tomorrow will be a big day.

I must have gone out like a light because the next thing I know is peace.

‘Stu,’ a quiet voice tries to wake me. ‘Stu?’

Somewhere at the back of my mind I can hear Jenny’s voice. My eyes fly open and I sit up straight. Remembering where I am, I find her leaning towards me, hand outstretched.

‘Sorry, I must have dozed off,’ my voice sounds sluggish, sleepy.

‘You stayed,’ her eyes are bright.

‘I did,’ I smile.

I look at my watch. It’s 4.00am. ‘How do you feel? I ask her, leaning forward.

‘Better. Rested. Thirsty,’ her voice sounds a little less disorientated.

I stand and pour her some water from the jug that sits on her overbed table. She takes it gratefully and sips. Her blue eyes hold my gaze.

‘I love you,’ I say simply, sitting down and stroking her arm. I’m not sure where that came from. I hadn’t planned to say it, in this context, I was waiting for the right time, but when something like this happens, it makes you want to grab every moment while you can.

She studies my face. The pain and fear from earlier are gone. She’s coming back to me.

‘You’re not just saying that because of what happened, are you?’ She leans forward to study my face.

‘Nope. Well, yes. I’m saying it because it happened. Because I never want to let you go. Because when I thought you’d left me, then realised that you’d been kidnapped - it felt like a huge piece of me was missing. I’m saying it because I need to tell you. I need you to know.’

She puts the cup down, lifts her face to me and begins to smile. Amid everything that has happened to her and the consequences of her uncle's actions, she is smiling. That smile breathes life back into me. Between us, we will make this work. She's the strongest person I know.

In that moment I lean in to kiss her, gently but firmly. A kiss to build our new hope, our new lives and our new dreams. Our world just got a little bigger.

Jenny breaks away, her eyes hold mine.

'I love you too,' she whispers.

Part 3

Jenny: Two days earlier

Peace, warmth and stillness surrounded me as I snuggled into the cocoon of a warm duvet. Peace. Warmth. Stillness and darkness. I felt a rush of air flow through my lungs and in that moment my eyes flew open. Everything was black. Panic took hold of me, overshadowing everything that might have helped me to make sense of where I was. Panicking at the blackness surrounding me, I bolt upright and bang my head on something hard. I am not in my bedroom. There is no duvet offering a cocoon of safety. No comfy mattress and pillow on which my body can rest.

'Jesus!' I mutter and tentatively use both hands and arms to feel around me. I'm encased in something hard and cold. A wooden box maybe. I'm not sure.

I reach out to touch, to feel the space between myself and the box. I need to find something to pull, grab or kick. My fingers find a square area covered in what feels like wired mesh.

I realise that I'm still wearing my red long-sleeved top and purple pyjama bottoms. My feet are completely bare. Oh my God. What has happened? How? Was I drugged? This is the only logical explanation for me to be oblivious to the fact that I have been taken from my bed to this box of horror. I take a short, sharp breath as a mewling sound comes from my throat. A sound as though someone is having an asthma attack and trying to drag air into their lungs.

Pulling forth memories of the last things I'd been doing before waking up in the darkness, I think of the last person I'd seen, or the last meal I'd eaten or drank. I try to compartmentalise my panicking thoughts. Stuart, my boyfriend of six months and I had had pizza, delivered as a Friday night treat in the Den, at home. Gateshead. We had shared a bottle of red wine, enjoyed an action film on Netflix. After Stuart had left, Uncle Felix had caught me in the Great Hall and invited me to the Blue Room for a brandy nightcap. I couldn't get out of it. If Uncle Felix asked you to do something, you usually did it.

I had meekly followed him to the Blue room and reluctantly sipped the nearly full brandy glass. I remember suddenly feeling extremely tired and deciding to go to my bedroom. From there, things become hazy. I vaguely remember changing into my nightwear and dropping onto the bed. That's the last thing I remember.

Keep calm Jenny, think, I tell myself. What would Stuart do? My fingers continue to move along the sides of the box, searching for any information to say what I am being held in, and why I am here. My hands come upon another shape, a small plastic bottle with liquid that swished as I rolled it. It was placed near my hip. Water? I quickly grabbed the bottle and held it to the light near the square mesh. The bottle was unmarked, and the liquid was clear. Water? I carefully put the bottle on to my chest while my hands reached above me to assess the height of the box. I touched the top of the box and guessed that I probably had about two feet before I would hit my head and do some damage.

I can't stop the panic bubbling up inside me any longer. I can feel my heart racing. Keep calm, keep calm I tell myself, do something, call for help.

'Help! Help! Help!' I shout, banging on the box lid and kicking the base board with my feet until they began to ache.

'Let me the hell out of here!' I scream at the top of my voice.

A distorted voice vibrates through the mesh area near my head.

'Keep quiet. You have water.'

My mind stores the fact that there is someone, somewhere who knows that I'm here. For now.

'Forget the bloody water, just get me the hell out of here.'

'Keep quiet,' the voice repeats.

'I'm sorry, I'm sorry. Please let me out,' I beg amid quiet sobs to the voice.

Nothing.

Shit.

Now what?

I stared into the darkness. I didn't know what to do, I felt helpless. There was nobody coming to help me. At that moment, the only thing I knew for sure, was that I was going to die.

I thought of my mother and father who had died five years earlier while on a business trip to France. Their private plane, which was also carrying my paternal grandparents, had suffered engine failure after a strike of birds flew into the rotors. They had gone down somewhere over the English Channel, lost to those dark, murky unrelenting ice-cold waters. My whole family had gone, and I couldn't even bury them properly.

Rose, Henry and I had struggled at their memorial service in an Oxford cemetery, wondering how life would carry on when everyone keeping this place and the company together, was dead. I wasn't as close to them as I'd like to have been. My mum had beautiful short light brown curly hair, she was pretty and petite. My dad, taller in stature, mid-brown short hair, handsome. My parents were devoted to the family business, they wanted to leave a worthwhile legacy. And, they did, of sorts. Jesus, just thinking about them makes me feel lonely and despondent and I can't stop the tears rolling down my cheeks.

It won't be long now, you guys. I can be with you again. Soon. Maybe, in the next life we will be a proper family? Be a family that spends time together. Mum, Dad, I don't know why I'm in here, but if I can't get out and Stuart doesn't find me, then this will be my last few hours here on this earth. We will be together again.

Wiping my eyes, my thoughts turn to Uncle Felix, my dad's brother. He came to live with us at Gateshead the family estate in South Oxfordshire, after my parents and grandparents had died. In a sad twist of fate my maternal grandparents had died in a car accident, before I was born, and I think this may have impacted on why my mother didn't want to give all of herself to me. Perhaps, she was protecting herself from more pain. Thankfully, I've always had Henry and Rose with me, they've been like surrogate parents for as long as I can remember.

Henry was the Estate Manager and Rose, the Housekeeper. Well, that was their unofficial titles, together they ran the place for my parents who needed the reassurance that the house and estate were looked after well, and that I had people who cared for me, to rely on.

Uncle Felix had taken me under his wing and had become my guardian. I didn't like him. I knew he was only staying with us for the lifestyle and the guardianship allowance. As the next of kin, he had access to the Gloverman finances, lived liked a lord at Gateshead and commanded a certain respect that came with wealth and successful business.

According to my dad's will I am due to inherit millions of pounds from the company, alongside eighty per cent equity, when I turned twenty-one. Which just happens to be in three days. Correction. Now two days. What an absolute nightmare.

I can't feel my legs. I try to move them, but they've gone numb. I've got dead legs. Bloody hell, that's all I need. You know what? Whoever this bastard is, I am not going to give him the satisfaction. I plan to stay strong and hope that someone finds me.

The heavy weight of the bottle on my chest jolts me to take a sip of water, to keep myself hydrated. Slowly, I take the bottle and twist the lid, tilting it to my nose first, in a sideways motion I attempted to sniff the liquid to determine any unusual smell. There is nothing. Which is a good sign. I tilt the bottle up slightly to allow the liquid to hit my tongue and slide down my dry throat. It tastes like water. I'll take that for now.

I offer a silent prayer to whoever is listening and allow my brain to methodically work through the questions that desperately need answering.

Question number one: who is doing this to me? And, number two: why is he or she doing this to me? To answer these questions, I need to look back.

I'd better start at the beginning.

I was born Jennifer Marie Gloverman, twenty years ago to Kelvin and Millicent Gloverman at Gateshead. By all accounts I was a good baby, I didn't cry much, I had a cheerful disposition, and I smiled whenever anyone spoke to me.

By the time I was five years old, I could recite the alphabet backwards and my favourite pastime was gymnastics. In their own way my parents adored me, they gave me everything they could and more. The one thing they struggled with giving me was their time.

My dad's family came from money, the family business which could be described loosely as a dynasty was founded by my great, great paternal grandfather, Richard Fairfax Gloverman.

Ah, yes. The business that kept me in the best clothes, schools, the top university for my chosen degree and the luxurious family estate. The business that ensured that my life was shaped by Rose and Henry Dean, and a succession of inefficient nannies.

Dear Rose and Henry. They have looked after me and supported me throughout the years. It was Henry who took me to the dentist aged eight when I'd chipped a tooth on a triangle of fridge cold Toblerone. Rose stepped up when my parents died, always checking in with me, encouraging me to spend time in the kitchen with her and its aroma of freshly baked cakes and bread. They had both stepped up. I don't know what I would have done without them. I imagine they're worried sick about me now.

I know you're dying to know what business could bring this all about and take over the lives of generations of Gloverman men and women folk. If you're thinking the family business is oil, you'd be wrong. Nothing quite so spectacular as that. The sex industry? I hear you ask. Nope, nothing as seedy as that. I would venture to say that the family business when said out loud, sounds largely mundane.

Drum roll, it's coming. The Gloverman family business is focused on the making of fine wine, well champagne to be exact. We also dabble in high quality red wine, but that is on a smaller scale. The vineyards we own in Provence and Bordeaux, produce grapes and like a well-oiled machine, the business is structured in such a way that everyone knows their roles and responsibilities and each area of expertise is utilised for maximum production and profit.

Of course, over the years the business has become more lucrative, a fact I found out when going through the books recently, part of my grooming to take over the Gloverman Corporation at the tender age of twenty-one.

My degree at Bournemouth University in Business and Management will be completed in seven months. That's where I first met Stuart Greyson. He'd transferred from another university to finish his final year in Business and Management at Bournemouth.

He'd walked into the refectory at University one lunchtime and our eyes had settled on each other instantly. How did that work? Instant attraction? Who knows? I'd been eating lunch with my friend Charlotte Peckham, who I affectionately call Lottie, and Stuart had come to our table to join us. It was as simple as that.

My friend, Lottie is the best. She's kind, loving, protective, pretty and has stunning red hair that falls in curls down her back. A true friend. We needn't have worried about Stuart, he was courteous, easy to talk to and soon fitted into our dynamics. Stuart asked me out on a date a couple of weeks later, that was six months ago, and we've being together ever since. Lottie enjoys hanging around with us too, but I know that deep down, she wants to find her Mr Right too.

Unfortunately, the family business is now managed, by Uncle Felix. He's about six feet tall, a little on the portly side with short black curly hair and a moustache that sits snugly above his upper lip.

The way he watches me when I walk into the room, his eagle eyes following my every move, it's bloody creepy. The worst thing of all though, is that he finds any excuse to touch me. His slimy hands touching my arm, stroking my arm, patting my hand. It makes me feel dirty.

Eventually, I plucked up the courage to tell Stuart about it one day, about a month ago. He went absolutely crazy and wanted to challenge Felix about his behaviour towards me, to warn him to keep his distance. Like a panicked fool, I'd begged Stuart to leave it be.

In my mind, I could deal with it. In fact, I'd told Stuart that I'd begun to make plans for Uncle Felix to be removed from the main house and made to live in the Summer House on the estate. I needed my own space, without having Felix following me or leering at me. My plans were to upgrade the Summer House so that the plumbing, wiring and wireless networks were all working well. The house was plenty big enough for him, with its attractive outside pale green woodwork, white wooden veranda encasing the property and matching white front door.

There was a fitted kitchen, lounge, cloakroom, dining room and master bedroom with en-suite bathroom on the ground floor. On the first floor there were another three bedrooms and a shared upstairs bathroom. I think that one of the upstairs bedrooms had been converted into an office.

The renovations are due to start in two weeks, I'd booked the builders, plumbers, electricians and decorators. If only I had made the booking for a couple of weeks earlier.

Cramp shoots down my right leg. Holy Mother of God. I really need to move. I wriggle my whole body and try pushing the roof to see if it moves at all. There is a little movement but nothing that gives me hope for an escape.

My body is supple, I practice yoga regularly, was an accomplished gymnast until I left school and I'm a runner. I am tall at five foot eight, with long straight blonde hair that reaches my shoulders. Stuart had said that my hair had been the first thing he'd noticed about me when we'd met seven months ago at University. Stuart Greyson, the same height as me, good-looking with an easy manner and rakish humour. Stuart with his handsome face, sleek swimmer's body and short, mousy hair.

A sudden feeling of anger and desperation overwhelms me. Tears slip down the side of my cheeks. The bleakness makes me begin to sob. At the same time, I'm angrily drying the tears on my cheeks. Oh Stuart, where are you when I need you? Please find me Stuart, I really need you to find me. I don't want to die in this godforsaken box.

***

How long have I been in here? I can't tell. I bang my hands on the lid and turn towards the mesh.

'Hey! I need to pee,' I shout.

Silence.

'Hey! I need to pee!' I stamp the hard wood beneath my feet until they hurt.

Silence.

I lie still, holding my breath and listening for a sound.

After what seems like an age, I hear a noise. It sounds like a door being unbolted. Feet shuffle, then walk across the floor followed by the sound of a key being used to undo a padlock. I'm still holding my breath as movement closes in on me and the lid to the box begins to move. I count to ten, my heart is beating so fast I think it's going to burst from my chest.

The lid opens slowly, and my eyes try to focus, but as I look up, there's nothing but sea of darkness. There is a brief rustle of movement before my upper arm is grabbed roughly.

'Please don't hurt me,' I wince as I'm hauled out of the box, my stiff limbs struggling to negotiate the manoeuvres to step up and over the wood. Stupidly, I feel thankful that my capturer is holding me so tightly that whoever it is, seems to be guiding me out of the box. Otherwise, I believe I would have fallen.

Looking around, I search for something familiar to help me work out where I am. There is a small desk lamp sitting on the floor in the far corner of the room, which adds a strip of light, so that the room isn't in total darkness. I try to make out my kidnapper's face, but my brain is playing tricks on me because all I can see is a dark outline.

Thick fingers pinch my shoulder with an agonising grip as I'm pushed across the room. My feet are bare and the first thing I notice is that there is no carpet on the floor and that I must be walking on hardwood or lino, which means I must be being held somewhere inside. I stub my toe on something hard and can't help the tears that spring to my eyes, or the silent curse as a sharp pain ricochets through my foot.

All the time, I can hear the sound of low useless sobs, sobs that were beginning to hurt my ears, until I realise with dismay that the sound is coming from my own throat. I wished at that moment, that I was brave, like Scarlett O'Hara from Gone with the Wind.

Suddenly we stop, the hand leaves my shoulder, and a bag, made of rough material is forced over my head. I shake my head in panic:

'Bloody hell. I can't breathe,' I mutter, my breathing becomes heavy, as I desperately try to get it under control before I pass out.

No sound. Would I recognise the voice? Is that why he or she silent?

I take several deep breaths to calm myself. A door opens, and the fingers pinching my arm push me forward and then to the side. I move silently with the person behind me. I realise three things:

I can see through the hood. Not too clearly, but clearly enough to see where I am going.

I can see that there is a light on and that I am in the upstairs hallway of the Summer House at the bottom of the east garden by the lake. Jesus. I've been kidnapped but am still on the site of my own property.

I can see that my captor is indeed a man, wearing dark jogging bottoms, a dark sweat top and a balaclava covering his head.

Thinking on my feet, I know instantly that I need to pretend to fumble when moving and not appear to be too sure of where I am going. I try to figure out what room I'm being held in but feel a little disorientated, which is impeding my decision-making.

I am being led to the bathroom at the back of the house, on the upper floor. Storing the information at the back of my mind with numbers one to three, I wait for instructions on where to go next. My captor stills for a moment and I panic, asking questions. Trying to provoke him to speak.

'Where am I going? I need to pee.'

A door in front of me is opened and I am pushed inside the generous sized bathroom which houses a toilet, sink basin, a large mirror and a vanity unit. The door is kept ajar by the kidnapper's leg as I begin to feel around for the toilet basin, making sure that the lid is up. He's made sure that the door is still wide enough for him to watch me.

I slowly pull down my pyjama bottoms and seat myself carefully onto the toilet. The need to pee is far stronger than the thought of being watched. It is imperative that my captor has no idea that I can see through the hood.

'Thank you,' I say sincerely.

I relieve myself, making sure to keep both my hands on the toilet seat to maintain balance. I keep my head facing down; I don't want him to think that I'm watching him. I sigh with relief as my bladder empties, slightly raising my head. Before I know what is happening, the kidnapper begins to lift his balaclava mask. No please don't do that, I plead silently. Don't take it off. I don't want to see your face.

And then my world falls apart as the face of the person who has probably drugged me, imprisoned me and who is now watching me attend to my own personal needs, is none other than my Uncle Felix.

As the hood comes off, I lower my head quickly and try to mask my horror of finding that Uncle Felix is my captor. I bite my lip to stop myself from screaming. Shit. Calm down. My head is buzzing, my fate has been sealed. I'm going to die.

I desperately need to keep my head, to keep calm. He must never know that I know who he is. If he finds out that I know it's him, my chance of survival will drop significantly.

Unfortunately, I am not quick enough to miss the smile on his face as he watches me wipe myself with toilet paper and push myself to a standing position. And, I am certainly not quick enough to stop him as he moves forward and very slowly drags my pyjama bottoms up, stroking my skin as he does so.

Shit. Shit. I think I'm going to vomit.

'Hey! Don't touch me! Don't you dare touch me!' I scream at him with shaking shoulders. Felix steps back at once, as though shocked by his actions. I make sure my bottoms are secure around my waist and begin to feel around for the sink, turning the tap on and splashing my hands under the water. I pat them dry on the front of my pyjama bottoms and turn back to Felix. This time, he's pulled his balaclava back over his head and the role play begins again. He grabs me roughly by both arms, pins them behind my back which pushes my chest out, and starts to move me forward.

As I'm pushed down the hallway my mind wanders to Stuart. I wonder what he's doing. Is he looking for me? Does he know I'm missing? I must have stopped walking because there's a sharp punch to my lower back and a vice-like grip takes hold of my neck and pushes my head forward. I move with him, tears falling down my cheeks. I won't give him the satisfaction of knowing how upset I am. Felix you bastard. You coward. Face me like a man.

When we reach the darkness of the room with the box, he grabs my hood and yanks it off my head. I can't see a thing, and I can only feel his grip on my arm as he manoeuvres me to the edge of the box. He taps my leg to climb in.

My feet are so cold they feel numb. I fumble my way into the small space and lie down. He stoops down towards me and I'm afraid he's going to kiss me or worse. Instead, I feel him reach for something next to my hip. I hear a swishing sound. Shit. He's not taking the bottle of water, is he?

Before closing the lid, I hear a sound of rustling before several small objects hit me on the chest. Jesus! What was that? Finally, I hear the lid snap shut and wait for the padlock. Nothing. So, I'm no longer padlocked. Interesting.

I feel around my body for the things he'd thrown at me. Feeling them carefully, there are some small bumps, like muesli bars. I lay them side by side on the far side of me, away from the mesh. I think they may be cereal bars. I'll hold out as long as I can, before eating them. I'm not hungry. I'm too worried about my situation. I think about what it means to find that Felix is my kidnapper.

I'm going to be twenty-one in two days. Then the estate, money, control of the business, basically everything comes to me. Felix has been my guardian and acting Chief Executive Officer or CEO of the Gloverman Corporation for the past five years. I have been asking questions lately, making a bit of a nuisance of myself, trying to get to know the business more. Perhaps I've overstepped?

My thoughts turn dark as I wonder if he has been embezzling the company funds. What has he been up to? What has made him stoop to such despicable acts? Why would he want to hurt me?

I think of my birthday and push the fact that I will probably be spending my twenty-first birthday locked in this box to the back of my mind. This has got to be connected, to my birthday, my coming of age to take my inheritance and place within the company. The timing surely isn't coincidental. I'll bet my life on it.

He can't be working alone, can he? Maybe he doesn't plan to release me. Maybe he hasn't decided what to do with me. I don't even know if he wants a ransom. Deep down, the not knowing is almost as bad as being held prisoner.

I look up into the blackness directly above me. What time is it? How long have I been in here? I'm losing my sense of time.

It's strange to think that the last time I slept in the Summer House was about ten years ago, when I'd had a birthday sleepover here with friends. My parents had allowed me to have ten girlfriends for a sleep over. We had shared sleeping space over the three upstairs bedrooms, whilst my parents had taken the ground floor bedroom suite. This was one of the few good memories I had of my parents. One of the rare times when my parents were home. Now those memories will be forever tainted with this nightmare.

I am developing the ramblings of a deranged mind. I find myself smirking. I don't know why. Being held hostage in a box without water is no laughing matter. My hands search for the water bottle. Nothing. My feet feel for the bottle. Nothing. Yep. The bastard took my water.

If I ever get out of here, I'm never taking anything for granted again. Because life is so fragile, and everything could be gone in a heartbeat. I understand that now.

Stuart, do you know how much I like you? If I'm honest I would venture to say I'm in love with you. I think of you and I see the other half of me. You see me, not my privilege or money, but the real me behind all of that. You see the person I am on the inside as well as the outside. I'm trying to imagine that you're here with your arms around me keeping me warm, keeping me safe. I guess I'm hoping for a miracle, please God, please let Stuart find me.

Tears fall down my cheeks and there's a wetness under my nose as it starts to dribble. I use my sleeve to wipe my face dry. There's something very liberating about silent crying, no one can tell you're crying unless they're watching you. It's as though you're in a bubble of pain and despair, where you can grieve personally, and no one can see you.

A bubble, yes. That's me. In here, in the box, in a bubble. I chastise myself and tell myself to 'Pull my socks up' which sends me into a half-hysterical laugh because I have no socks on and my feet are freezing.

I open one of the bars and begin to nibble. It's not easy eating when you're lying down. I'm paranoid I'm going to choke. In between nibbles, hysteria sets in as I begin to talk to myself:

'I spy with my little eye. Something the colour of blue. Blue sky, blue sea, navy blue, light blue, aquamarine, dark blue.

'I spy with my little eye. Something that's warm. The sun, a radiator, a warm bath, now that's tricky. Come on Jen, pick an easy one.

'No, let's try this. The quick brown fox jumps over the lazy dog. Peter Piper picked a piece of pickled pepper.'

I decide to try my hand at singing:

'I believe I can fly. I believe I can eat a pie. I don't know any more words to this, and it sounds like it could be shit. I believe I can fly, I believe I can touch the sky, if I could get myself out of this box, my feet could do with a pair of socks.'

Give it a rest Jenny, I whisper to myself. You're going to give yourself a headache!

I finish the bar and try rolling a little from one side to the other. I move my feet, trying to get some feeling back into them. God, I'm so bored. If I don't die of lack of water or malnutrition – I'm going to die of boredom.

My brain begins to meander into nonsensical musings again:

'Hello, is it me you're looking for?' Bloody hell, not Lionel – anything but Lionel.

'I want to break free, because I need a pee, I want to break free from this box it's so narrow and dark, I can't see. I just want to break free.'

'Running with the.' You've got to be kidding me, I didn't even know I knew so many Lionel Ritchie songs.

Finally, having exhausted myself with what can only be described as useless ramblings, I close my eyes and try to block out everything. I must have dozed off because when I wake, I'm struggling to breathe. It's as though my subconscious has remembered where I am. I take a deep breath and count to ten, repeating this several times until I'm breathing regularly again.

How long has it been since I've been to the toilet? How long since I've had no water. God my mouth is so dry. I feel filthy and the coldness is seeping into my bones. I'm so stiff, even my bottom has gone numb.

I think of my dissertation. I'm about a third of the way through. Will I get to finish it? I hope so. I hope I get to finish my degree after all the hard work I've put into it. I would love to put something of what I've learned into practice in the business.

I want to live. I don't want to die like this. Like an animal in a cage, left to die. I haven't achieved anything yet.

I wonder what time it is. I feel like it might be morning, but that's just a guess. Maybe it's still evening, and I haven't slept very long? There's a noise. I can hear the door opening and the sound of feet moving across the floor.

The lid to the box unclips and the lid is slowly opened. The room is still in darkness and I think Felix is wearing his balaclava. A part of me wants to shout at him that I know it's him and that he's a cowardly bastard, holding me against my will like this. My gut tells me to hold my tongue though, to watch and listen until he makes a mistake.

He leans in, grabs me by both arms and yanks me out of the box. When I'm standing in front of him, he holds me at arms-length for a minute until I'm no longer unsteady on my feet. Out of his pocket he produces a bottle and hands it to me. Quickly I unscrew the top and drink half of the cool liquid. It tastes a little different, but I tell myself that it's probably my dry mouth. I keep drinking until I hear the plastic scrunching, and the bottle is empty. Swiftly he takes it from me and throws it into the box.

'Thank you.'

With one hand firmly on my arm Felix pushes me across the cold hard floor to the door. He stops me briefly, and I fear that the hood is coming next.

‘Please don’t,’ I plead.

The hood comes over my head as he opens the door and pushes me into the hallway. There’s a heaviness building in my limbs and my mind starts to shut down one tiny piece at a time.

I let him direct me along the corridor, even though it seems as if he’s half pulling, half carrying me. My brain is fuzzy, all worries and panics are forgotten as Felix manhandles my unwilling body, to God knows where. I don’t care anymore. Just let me lie down. I feel so sleepy, so tired I need to lie down. Please, just leave me alone. Sluggishness overwhelms me. Then everything goes dark.

***

Peace, warmth and stillness surround me as I snuggle into the cocoon of a warm duvet. Peace. Warmth. A sudden gasp and I’m jerked awake. I thought I’d been having a nightmare, but this is no nightmare, this is my reality.

I think I must have fainted. Dear God, how long have I been in this damn box? I’m so cold and my head is throbbing. There’s an uncomfortable, full feeling in my bladder. I need the toilet. I feel around for a water bottle, but only find the empty scrunched up one that Felix threw into the box earlier. I look towards the mesh square and note that the light that was previously there is now gone, and I somehow know that Felix has gone.

‘Hey’ I shout. ‘Hey.’

‘Hey prick, I need to pee.’

No answer. Just silence.

‘Hey. I need to pee, and I need water!’

Silence. That’s not good. Where is he?

I move around a little. My body feels cold and my limbs are sore. I wriggle and try to move onto my side to ease the cramp in my aching joints.

What day is it? I can’t remember. I don’t know how long I’ve been in the box. I know I’m supposed to have an early lunch with Lottie on Saturday, but I think I’ve missed it. If I have, I’m sure she’ll check-up on me. Please let her check-up on me.

Stuart and I are also taking Rose and Henry out to dinner on Saturday evening to celebrate their twenty-fifth wedding anniversary. Of course, they’d both stated that they’d be happy with fish and chips from the local fish and chip shop, but Stuart and I want to mark their twenty-five years together with something a little special. I’ve even ordered them a cake and Stu will collect it from the cake shop in Oxford on Saturday lunchtime. I’ve booked a table at one of my favourite restaurants which caters for a variety of food tastes. I’m sure they will love it.

My head aches and I close my eyes, rubbing my temples to try to relieve the pain. I’m never getting out of here, am I? I don’t think I’ve ever felt so desolate in my life. I can’t hold it in anymore, as a warm wetness soaks my pyjamas.

Why Felix? Why would you do this?

I allow myself to float away, until all I feel is nothingness.

Part 4

Stuart: One day earlier

It's 8.30am on Saturday morning. I'm up bright and early and in the white painted garage of my parents' home in Dorchester on Thames. They've allowed me to set up some gym equipment at the far end and I've added a hanging brown punchbag. My workout routine consists of fifty leg presses, fifty shoulder pulls, fifty sit-ups and fifteen minutes on the punchbag. I love this routine, need it. It helps to clear my mind. Helps me to focus. Later I'll head out for a five-mile run and pick up Rose and Henry's twenty-fifth wedding anniversary cake before picking them and Jenny up to go to the restaurant.

Usually, I work at my local Tesco in Abingdon at the weekend and get up early to do my morning workout, before I go. I've taken this weekend off to help organise the anniversary celebrations.

I have a ring in my jacket pocket. It's a white gold band with a blue square sapphire. It's been burning a hole in my pocket for the past two weeks. I'm going to give it to Jenny tonight, when we get back to Gateshead.

I'm pounding the bag, imagining it was Felix's head when mum pops her head around the garage door. She's wearing her nightdress and covers it with her thick pink quilted dressing gown.

'Hey Stu, this was just pushed through the door for you. It hasn't got a stamp on it.'

Mum looks old for her age, her short dark hair has long since turned grey and she has the hunched walking gait of a woman much older than fifty-four. She's holding a sealed envelope which has my name type-printed on the front.

'Thanks,' I say taking it. I'm about to ask if she saw who delivered it, but when I look up, she's gone. I don't know why I'm surprised, she doesn't like the garage, it's cold and bleak.

I stare at it. I've no idea what this is. Opening it carefully, I'm intrigued to find a short letter printed on a piece A4 white printer paper. My eyes scan the words.

'Dear Stuart,

I am going away for a while.

It's over. Please don't hate me.

Jenny.'

My first thoughts are that this is a joke. I mean, I know it's not April Fool's Day, but a prank can be played at any time, right? Everything about the note rings alarm bells. Forget the fact that if Jenny wanted to break off our relationship, she's the sort of person who would just say so.

I fumble in the pocket of my workout trousers to reach for my phone to call Jenny. The phone rings, then goes to voicemail. I leave a message hoping that she will see it and get back in touch with me.

'Hey Jen, it's Stu. I need to speak to you. Give me a call when you can.'

I carefully fold the note back into its envelope and head out of the garage and upstairs to shower and change. After my shower I rush to my room and throw open my brown wardrobe doors and pick the first thing that I see, a black T-shirt which has 'Flying with Style' written across the front in dark green letters. I yank my favourite dark blue knit button top jumper from its hanger before turning to the matching brown drawer unit. I pull open the top drawer and take out a pair of plain black boxers and matching socks.

Without pushing it back in fully, I pull out the drawer below and find a pair of dark grey jeans. A chill stops me in my tracks, making the hairs on the back of my neck stand up. A cold wisp of air passes through my body, like a ghost stepping through a corpse. Bloody hell. Something doesn't feel right.

Why hasn't she called back? God, I need to talk to her. I don't know what's going on, but something is not right. I can feel it. She's typed a short note that isn't in character with the woman I know. It certainly doesn't make sense and why isn't she answering her phone?

When I'm dressed, I drive my dark green Toyota into Oxford to pick up Henry and Rose's anniversary cake. The note sits heavily in my jacket pocket. It's as light as a feather, but the typed words, the fact that it's here in my possession at all, leaves me with a terrible feeling of foreboding.

I hope the cake is ready, Jenny will go mad if it's not. By this time, I've convinced myself that the note was just a stupid prank. Of course, I'm burying my head in the sand. I know it rarely works, pretending there's nothing wrong, when clearly there is.

I call Rose at Gateshead. She answers the landline on the second call.

'Gateshead, Rose speaking. How can I help you?'

'Rose. It's Stuart. Is Jenny there?' I silently cross my fingers, hoping she'll say yes and put Jenny on the phone.

'Hi Stuart. No. I was just saying to Henry that she didn't come down for breakfast. I'd assumed that she'd spent the night with you.'

'No, she didn't,' I tell her, making a mental note not to alarm her too much. 'Look, I'm on my way to you. I'll be there in around thirty minutes. Oh, and Rose?'

'Yes?' She answers.

'Try not to worry.'

I'm back in my car. The cake is carefully ensconced in the boot, wedged in between coats and carrier bags. It's 12.30pm and there's still nothing from Jenny.

I call again but get the same repeated voicemail as before. Again, I leave a message.

'Hey Jen. Please call me. I'm worried about you.'

I'm just about to turn on the engine when my phone rings. My heart races as I grab it, checking the caller. It's Lottie, Jen's best friend. My hopes fall.

'Hey Lottie. How are you?' I try not to sound too deflated.

'Hi Stuart,' her familiar, usually relaxed tone sounds breathless and anxious. 'Have you seen Jen? I'm supposed to meet her for lunch today in Abingdon.'

'No. What time was she supposed to meet you?'

'Noon. It's not like her, not to turn up. She would usually send me a text if she was late or not coming.'

'Have you tried her phone?' I asked her, wondering what the hell was going on.

'Yes. It went to voicemail. I left a message,' her voice is slightly raised in panic.

'Me too, she's not answering. I got this strange typed note posted through my door this morning.

'I'm worried,' she says flatly.

'Lottie, can you meet me at Gateshead?' I ask, the more people looking for her, the better chance of finding her. 'I've got a bad feeling about this.'

"Sure. I can be there in about a quarter of an hour."

"Thanks. See you then.'

I sit for a moment, thinking. Jenny is my priority. I need to find her. It'll take me about twenty minutes to get to Gateshead if I hit no traffic, and I pray that there have been no road traffic accidents on my route this Saturday lunchtime as I pop the clutch into first gear and set off towards Stadhampton.

Lottie's blue Focus is already parked outside the main house when I arrive. I take the swerved circular driveway and park my Toyota next to hers and leave the cake in the car. The gravel crunches as I rush to ring the bell to the front door.

The door is pulled open immediately. I see a glimpse of worry in Henry's eyes, the strain on his face. I'm relieved that I'm not the only one becoming paranoid about Jenny's disappearance. Something is seriously wrong here.

'Hey Henry,' I pat him on the shoulder as I walk past him and through the Great Hall.

'We're in the kitchen,' he says in answer to my raised eyebrows.

I find Rose and Lottie who are sitting around the large farmhouse-style kitchen table, with a pot of tea and biscuits. Lottie's vivid red hair sits in long loose curls on her shoulders, almost down to her back. She has a pretty heart shaped face, with a few freckles dotted on her cheeks. She likes to wear bright colours, and today is no different. Her summer dress is white with a rainbow assortment of large spots painted on to it.

'Any news?' I ask, as I pour stewed tea into a mug and sit down.

'Nothing. There's no sign of her,' Rose takes a sip of her tea.

'Something's wrong,' I look at their worried faces. 'I got a note this morning. Typed, hand-delivered – supposedly from Jenny, telling me that she was going away for a while and not to hate her. That is so unlike Jenny. I thought it was a prank.'

'Have you got it on you?' Henry asks.

'Yes, here,' I take the folded note from my jacket pocket and give it to him.

'Jesus. What's going on here?' Henry says studying the piece of paper. 'It doesn't give any indication where she is or where she's gone. You're right. It isn't in character with her, she would never say those things in that way.'

I tip the mug up and let the last of the hot tea seep down my throat. Pushing my chair back, I look at the small group of people in front of me, with lost looks on their faces and announce, 'I'm going up to her room to see if anything is missing or out of place.'

'I'll come with you,' Lottie stands, and moves to my side.

'One more thing. Have you told Felix?' I ask, wondering why I haven't seen his sleazy face since I'd arrived.

Rose looks at Henry, who nods his head.

'No,' she replies. 'I saw him briefly this morning. He was in his study. He was a bit agitated, so I left him alone. He doesn't like answering questions at the best of times.'

I nod. Shaking my head. What's the bet that he's got something to do with this? I take the stairs, two at a time with Lottie following closely behind. When we reach Jenny's bedroom, the door is closed. I knock, then slowly open the heavy framed door. Sunlight gleams from the hallway, skimming across the room. The first thing I notice is that the curtains are still drawn. I take in the untidy bedding and the light blue top, that lay on the floor beside her bed, next to white cotton underwear. This in itself is strange. Jen is a stickler for folding clothes or putting them into the laundry basket.

'Don't touch anything,' I tell her. This could be a crime scene.

'Where is she, Stu?' Lottie asks softly.

'I don't know,' I say quietly. 'The only things I know for sure is that she didn't type that note, she's not answering her phone, she didn't turn up for your lunch date and that no one has seen her today.'

Taking a small pencil from my pocket, I turn to the light switch near the doorframe and prod it to bring light to the room. Now I can see where we are, I move to the white wooden bedside table and find her phone, still on charge next to the white metal-framed double bed. It springs to life as I tap the phone face with my pencil. The screen comes to life, showing several missed calls on the screen, before it darkens again. Shit. That's not good. Now, I'm beginning to get seriously worried. What the hell is going on here?

Lottie moves to the dressing table. 'Look!' she says pointing to the brown square handbag sitting on the hardwood. 'Jenny's bag's still here.'

'Now. Who goes away without taking their phone or bag?' I muse, moving to the ornate French white wooden wardrobe. I prise the pencil through the handles and carefully open its doors.

All of her clothes are here. There are no gaps, no spare hangers. Everything is as it should be, as if she was still here. The hairs on my arm prickle as I look around the bedroom. Jesus. What the hell happened here? The shrill of the landline phone in the Great Hall fills the silence. It rings a few times before Henry answers. I can't hear what's being said, I'll find out when I go downstairs.

I quickly check the bathroom, everything looks tidy, in order. Just how Jenny likes it. Where are you sweetheart? Give me a clue. Anything that will help me find you.

I'm just about to leave the room when a sudden thought hits me, building on my suspicion I retrace my steps to the bed, use the pencil to lift the two pale blue paisley pillows to see if Jenny's nightwear is usually where she keeps it. With bated breath I check. Nothing. Shit. Where is her nightwear? I check her laundry basket in the bathroom.

I manoeuvre Lottie out of the room. There is something seriously wrong here. We need to call the police. A chill suddenly sweeps through me, as though someone has walked over my grave. I head back to the kitchen table, with its never-ending supply of hot tea.

'Who was that on the phone?' I ask Henry.

'It was Felix. He'd forgotten to say he's away on business for two nights.'

'Did he say where he was staying?' I ask, boiling the kettle. I need a coffee.

'The Marriott Royal, Bristol.'

'All right. Well, that's another coincidence, isn't it? And where's Jenny's car?' I ask, pouring boiled water onto the coffee granules, adding milk and stirring with a metal teaspoon.

'I don't know,' Rose says, with tears in her eyes. 'Something has happened to her, hasn't it?'

‘Yes. I believe so. We need to call the police. If she’s been kidnapped there will almost certainly be a ransom call, sooner rather than later. Her phone and handbag are still upstairs, and her clothes are strewn on the floor beside the bed. Her nightwear is missing.’

‘Oh my God!’ Rose puts her hands to her face in distress. Henry walks over to her and pats her shoulder.

‘We’ll find her Rose. We’ll find her.’

I look at my watch. It’s 2.45pm. Jesus. We need to call this in. I walk to the phone on the console table in the Great Hall and dial 999.

‘999. Emergency. What service do you require?’ A woman’s curt voice says in my ear.

‘Police,’ I answer, hoping that I’m not sending them on a wild goose chase.

‘I’ll put you through,’ the woman’s voice states.

‘Emergency. Police,’ a deep male voice answers, ‘how can we help you?’

‘I think my girlfriend has been kidnapped.’

‘Kidnapped Sir, what leads you to that conclusion?’

‘She’s not been seen since last night. Her phone and handbag are here, her clothes are here. There is a typed note.’

‘Note Sir?’

‘Yes. Saying that she was going away,’ it sounds plausible as I say the words.

‘Could she have gone away?’ the deep voice asks.

‘What with no money, no clothes, no phone, no personal possessions? She wouldn’t get very far.’

‘What about her car, does she have one?’

‘Yes. It’s missing,’ Jesus! Even saying that makes me feel like I’m in a Patricia Cornwell novel.

‘Could she have taken it?’ The questions continue.

‘I don’t know. I haven’t looked through her handbag to see if the car keys are there.’

‘Sir. Is this in her character, has she done this before?’ The police officer asks.

‘Never. Please send someone quickly. My girlfriend’s name is Jenny Gloverman. She is the heiress to the Gloverman Corporation. In two days-time she will turn twenty-one and inherit her parent’s legacy. She will be worth ten billion pounds.’

‘I see. That puts a different light on the situation. Let me have your address and I’ll get someone out to you straightway.’

‘Thanks,’ I say, reciting the Gateshead address details to him. I am genuinely thankful for his help as I lay the phone back in its base, and I also feel a huge sense of relief that the police are now involved

I don’t know where you are Jenny, but I will find you. You just need to hold on until I do. Find the strength to hold on. Don’t play the hero. Just do as they say, do whatever is needed to keep you alive. There are so many things I should have said to you, sweetheart. So many things that should have been said. I love you. I have always loved you. I always thought we had time.

People always think they have time to do those planned things, such as build a future, get married, have babies, that nothing will happen to change this. I always thought we’d have time to do these things, but it appears that time is not on our side right now.

I feel an arm on my shoulder, I turn to see Lottie standing next to me.

'We'll find her, Stuart. We have to,' her voice holds a note of desperation.

'I hope so. I can't lose her. Not now I've found her,' the sound of my voice is flat, my shoulders slump as though there is a heavy weight pushing down on them. And, as I walk slowly alongside Lottie to the kitchen, it seems to take forever. For such a short distance, it never felt so long.

'The police are on their way,' I announce, sitting down. 'I don't know how long they'll be.'

Henry stands, stares at the table, 'I need to have a quick word with Graham, the gardener about fixing a fence on the third field.' He stands with his hands in his pockets. 'Call me when they arrive, and I'll come back,' he looks at Rose and waits for her to nod. She understands that he needs to keep busy. He'll drive himself mad with worry if he doesn't keep himself busy.

'Are you staying here tonight Stuart?' Rose asks. 'I can make up a bed.'

'Yes,' I answer, patting her shoulder. 'If that's all right. But I don't want to make any more work for you, you've got enough to do.'

'It won't be a problem. It'll be good to have you here. I feel a little on edge.' She looks across the room, and her eyes rest on Lottie. 'Charlotte, are you staying too?'

'No, Mrs D. I need to get back to my Mum. She recently had a fall and I need to check she's OK. I'll be back tomorrow morning though.'

'No problem dear. Can you give me a hand with putting fresh sheets on the bed?' Rose walks out of the room, with Lottie in tow.

‘Yes, of course,’ I hear Lottie’s distant reply from along the hallway.

I’m sitting in the Den when I hear the crunch of tyres on the gravel and the metallic tapping of the iron door knocker. I get up and move through the house, past priceless vases and treading on Persian carpets. It means nothing. It’s just a different way of living. Without Jenny, life is meaningless.

The door knocker bangs again, and I open the front door to the rugged, good-looking face of a tall man wearing brown cord trousers, a black raincoat, blue shirt and brown tie.

‘Hi. I’m Detective Chief Inspector Brian Carter, Cowley Police,’ he opens his warrant card and shows it to me. He gestures to the police officer standing beside him. She’s pretty, probably about twenty, short brown hair.

‘This is PC Leadbetter.’

‘Thanks for coming. I’m Stuart Greyson. I made the 999 call. Please come through.’

I take them through the Great Hall and into the kitchen. Rose and Lottie are putting teacups into the dishwasher and the kettle is boiling away in the background.

‘Do come in, sit down,’ I motion to the kitchen table. ‘This is Rose Dean, she’s the Housekeeper at Gateshead. She’s known Jenny for most of her life. This is Jenny’s best friend, Charlotte Peckham – everyone calls her Lottie. Jenny was supposed to have lunch with her today, but she never turned up.’

The DCI addresses Rose and Lottie:

‘I’m DCI Carter and this is PC Leadbetter. We’re here following up the phone call from Mr Greyson.’

‘Call me Stuart,’ I say.

'It appears that Miss Gloverman has disappeared and that you suspect foul play.'

'I'll give Henry a quick call to tell him you're here,' I take my phone from my pocket. 'He's Rose's husband. It is their twenty-fifth wedding anniversary today and Jenny and I were taking them out for a meal tonight.'

'We just want our Jenny back. Safe and sound,' Rose says putting milk and sugar onto a tea tray and laying it on the kitchen table. She smiles weakly as the DCI pulls out a wooden chair and sits at the table, he motions to PC Leadbetter to do the same.

'Can I interest you in a cup of tea or coffee?' Rose asks as she picks up the kettle and pours the boiling contents into the teapot. DCI Carter looks at his colleague and gives an appreciative nod. I wonder if they often get offered tea or coffee when they're in someone's home, or if it is just a myth.

Keeping Rose busy is important, she seems to be functioning on automatic, keeping the house tidy and people visiting filled with hot tea or coffee. I see her face, there's a mask hiding her fear and panic, keeping it at bay. Her eyes, sad, watery, flittering around the room, to the doorway, give her away.

I search for Henry's name in my contacts, press call and when he answers tell him that the police officers have arrived. I sit at the table and take the mug of tea offered from Rose, before announcing, 'He's on his way.'

PC Leadbetter takes out a small note pad and pen and rests them on the table as Rose brings the hot drinks to the table. A dull silence takes over the room as we wait for Henry, even Rose sits and stares at the steaming mug of tea in front of her. Several minutes later we hear the front door open and the sound of footsteps heading our way. A panting Henry, red-faced from rushing on this cool October Saturday afternoon, enters the kitchen and holds his hand out to DCI Carter.

'Henry Dean,' he introduces himself to the police officers. 'Any news of Jenny yet?'

'DCI Brian Carter, and this is PC Julie Leadbetter,' he gestures briefly to the brown-haired PC. 'No news yet. Sir,' he addresses me, 'we're going to start by taking your statement.'

Henry sits next to me, elbows on the table, hands clasped together.

'So, let's start at the beginning,' Carter says bluntly. 'Who was the last person to see Jenny?'

'That would be me, I think,' I answer, there's nothing for it, but to implicate myself. Clearly, I'm the last person to have seen her, apart from her abductor. Blast, but what else can I do? I need to be honest and upfront, or we'll get nowhere.

'We spent the evening together yesterday. I arrived around 5pm, straight from work. We ordered pizza, which must have been around 6pm and then watched a Netflix film. We shared a bottle of red wine and I left around 11pm.'

'I saw them saying goodbye to each other around that time,' Henry confirms. 'I was heading upstairs, to bed. I was tired and Rose had already gone to bed.'

I was relieved that Henry had backed up my story. The truth can sometimes leave you vulnerable and I'd hoped to move on from what I'd been doing with Jenny as we said goodbye. Particularly the kissing part.

'I'm sure I heard Felix's voice not long after the front door closed,' Henry said as he stared at his folded hands. I'm not sure if he was talking to us, or to himself.

'Felix?' asks DCI Carter.

'Yes. Felix Gloverman. Jenny's paternal uncle. He lives here,' Henry says before explaining the family dynamics to the DCI. 'Felix took over as CEO of the Gloverman Corporation five years ago when Jenny's parents died. He moved in here and became Jenny's guardian at the same time. I think he invited her to the Blue Room for a nightcap.'

'Tell me about Felix? Where is he at this moment in time?' DCI Carter asks.

'He's about six feet tall with a bit of a belly on him,' Rose volunteers the information. 'He's got curly brown hair and a moustache, and no one has seen him since yesterday. He called this morning on the landline to say that he was staying at the Marriott Royal Hotel in Bristol for a few days on business.'

Carter looks at Leadbetter.

'This morning I also received a hand-delivered printed note to my home address,' I shuffle slightly so that I can reach the folded paper and envelope from my jacket pocket.

'Here,' I hand it to Carter. 'I thought it was a prank. She would never do that. Type a short note like that. Totally out of character.'

Carter studies the A4 paper.

'Can I keep this?' He asks me, and waits patiently for my nod, before searching his coat pocket, finding an evidence bag, putting the folded paper inside and returning it to his coat pocket. It's of no use to me. He looks my way, his intense gaze holding mine, 'is it possible that she has vanished for a couple of days? Taken a quick break?'

'No,' I tell him firmly, I look at a photo of a smiling Jenny, on my phone screensaver. 'She'll be twenty-one on Monday. She'll take over the reins of the corporation and become the major shareholder of the Gloverman Corporation. Worth ten Billion pounds. She was looking forward to carrying on her parent's legacy. She only has seven months left on her business degree. It was her plan.'

My thoughts wander as my hands keep warm on the hot mug. I begin to doubt myself. It was what she wanted, wasn't it? No one was pushing her. We supported her in whatever she wanted to do. Rose, Henry, Lottie and me. We supported her.

We would have known if she'd changed her mind. Surely? We would have known it if it was all too much for her. Wouldn't we?

Lottie looks at the DCI, arms folded across her chest and her eyes fiery and determined.

'She would have said if she was unhappy. Nothing about her behaviour has changed. Nothing. One minute she was here and the next, she's gone. I was due to meet her for lunch at 12 noon today. When I called to check on her at about 12.15pm, her phone went straight to voicemail. Her phone is still charging in her room, along with her handbag.'

'You've been in her room?' Carter eyebrows rise in query. His face is grim. I don't think he's happy with the news that we've been in Jenny's room.

'Yes,' I tell him, with a slight edge to my voice. I won't apologise for trying to find out where my girlfriend is. 'Lottie and I went into her room a couple of hours ago. We didn't touch anything.'

'Good, we need to restrict activity in the room until it's been processed,' Carter says. I will also need to take fingerprint samples from everyone here, to eliminate you from our enquiry.'

'Fine,' I say looking at the others. Let's just get the ball rolling and start looking for her.

‘I’d like to see her room now, please,’ Carter says, rising from his chair. He has an air of assurance, of perceptiveness and intuition about him, which gives me hope.

‘Sure. I’ll take you up there,’ I say, as Carter and Leadbetter follow me up the stairs to Jenny’s room. I stop when I reach the door, my hand sits on the round brass door handle. ‘Look, there is something you should know,’ I turn to them. ‘I think it has something to do with Felix Gloverman.’

They look at me, eyes questioning. PC Leadbetter gives her boss a quick look, but DCI Carter steadfastly stares my way.

‘Yes?’ He asks. ‘Why do say that?’

My eyes hold his. As equals. Neither of us blinking. ‘He isn’t a nice man. He’s perverted. Jenny revealed a month ago that he had begun touching her without her permission and making inappropriate comments to her.’

‘This Felix chap is definitely a person of interest. Let’s look in Jenny’s room and go from there. Then we’ll go through Mr Gloverman’s rooms here, with a view to bringing him in.’ He turns to address me, ‘would you mind staying downstairs, Stuart? That would be helpful. Thanks.’

I nod and slowly retrace my steps to the kitchen. I sit down at the table and put my head in my hands. God almighty, how can this be happening? I’ve got an anniversary cake in the boot of my car, for crying out loud. The absurdity of it all.

We sit in silence. Lottie, Henry, Rose and myself. I can’t sit here waiting, but I don’t know where else to go. I need to wait and see what Carter plans to do.

There is movement on the stairs as Carter and Leadbetter finish checking Jenny’s room and head back to the kitchen. They are talking quietly. Then I hear Carter on the phone:

'Mike. Get SOCO here, will you? Something's not right. Her clothes, handbag and phone are all here but there's no sign of her. Her car and keys are gone. I'm going to check out his bedroom and study but get SOCO to go through it with a fine-tooth comb. Find his tablet, laptop, phone etc. I need you to find Felix Gloverman.'

There's a pause, before he continues. 'Yes. Go to the Gloverman Corporation HQ and check out what he does exactly, his personal assistant, fellow board members. Find out what type of man is he. Julie has checked the Royal Marriott Bristol and there's no sign of him. So where was he phoning from this morning? Thanks Mike. I'll catch up with you this afternoon at the office.'

'Stuart?' He calls from the Great Hall.

I stand immediately and walk over to the police officers.

'Where's Felix's study?' He fidgets around his coat pockets until he finds what he's looking for. A pair of vinyl gloves dangle from one hand.

I take him down a corridor to the right and point him to the second door on the left.

'Here,' I open the door and step aside to allow them to walk through.

'Thanks.'

'Stuart?' The low husky female voice shocks me. It's the first time PC Leadbetter has spoken.

'Yes?'

'Can you get me a recent photo of Jenny? Also, what car does Jenny drive?' She asks.

'Yes, to the photo. There are a quite a few dotted around the house. The car is a dark red Volkswagon Tiguan.'

‘And Felix?’ Carter asks.

‘I think he’s got a blue Audi A4 Saloon. Henry or Rose might know for sure. I don’t know the registration numbers, I’m afraid.’

‘Thanks,’ replies Leadbetter. ‘I’ll get those checked out, see if we can locate them.’

‘I’ll find that photo of Jenny. Lottie needs to go home soon. Is that all right with you?’

‘Yes,’ says Carter, already walking into Felix’s study. ‘Can you get her to write down her contact details in case we need to speak to her?’

‘Will do. Detective Chief Inspector?’ I can’t hold my fears for Jenny back any longer. ‘I’ve got a really bad feeling that something bad has happened to her. To Jenny. Please find her.’

‘I’ll do my best Stuart.’

‘I appreciate that,’ I tell him, looking at my watch. Jesus! It’s 6pm. I need to cancel the table for tonight, I tell myself absently, as I scroll through the photos of Jenny on my phone. I select a nice one of her sitting in the Barley Mow pub garden in August of this year, after an early evening meal. Her blonde hair flowed down to her shoulders and rested on her pale blue linen top. She was poking her tongue out at me.

‘Found one?’ The DCI asks, and waits for me to nod, before taking my phone and forwarding the photo to himself. ‘My number is in here now, in case you need it,’ he mutters, handing the phone back to me.

Where are you Jenny? Please find a way to come back to me. I need you. Rose, Henry and Lottie need you. We all need you. I didn’t realise how lonely I was until I met you, with your radiant smile, your vitality. You are my heart. You ground me and make me feel like I belong. That I matter. I am going to find you, Jenny.

Even, if I need to crawl on my hands and knees over shards of glass, until my skin becomes bloody and raw. I will find you.

Part 5

Jenny

There's a weight bearing down on my right side. I shuffle, open an eye. A man's form lays on his side, his leg and arm are wrapped around me. Stuart. I remember now, he had climbed onto the bed in the early hours of the morning, to hold me close. We must have fallen asleep. My cannula catches on the bedclothes. 'Ouch,' I mutter, rubbing the back of my hand carefully.

Staff Nurse Skinner walks briskly into the room. 'Good morning!' She says as she moves to the window and draws back the curtains. 'How are you today?' She asks her lips forming into a warm smile.

I lift my head to face her. 'Feeling better,' I say trying to muster a smile, 'I think Stuart's worn out though.'

'I can imagine he is,' she states picking up the water jug and refilling my plastic glass. 'He didn't stop yesterday. From the moment he brought you to the hospital to liaising with the police and Dr Tracker, in addition to looking after Mr and Mrs Dean when they came to see you.'

'Rose and Henry were here?' I query, my thoughts are a mixture of anxiety and sorrow of the worry I've put them through over the past few days.

'Yes. You were out of it. You needed the rest.'

'I know. I'm feeling quite hungry now.'

'I'll arrange for someone to bring you both a cup of tea and some toast.'

Stu begins to stir from his sleep, he opens his eyes and looks at me as though he can't believe I'm really here with him. His hand reaches up to stroke my face.

'Sorry, I went out like a light,' his warm hand caresses my cheek, as he offers a sheepish smile.

'Don't be sorry. I'm glad you were here,' I smile back at him. He stretches his long limbs and moves to a sitting position, trying not to knock me off the bed. He checks his watch.

'It's 7.30am.'

'I'm going to bring you both tea and toast, that should put some colour into your cheeks,' Nurse Skinner smiles. 'Dr Tracker will be in to see you around 9.30am. I think we can take the cannula and drip off today.' She checks my medical chart, returns it to the bottom of the bed and disappears through the door.

When we're on our own, Stuart puts both of his hands on my face and kisses me gently on the lips. I close my eyes, taking comfort in his touch.

'I've been wanting to do that since I found you yesterday,' he whispers.

'Stu.'

'Somewhere between losing you and finding you, my heart stopped beating and I couldn't breathe. It was as though someone was sitting on my chest restricting my airway, and no matter what I did, I couldn't push that damn weight off my chest. Not until I found you again.'

'Stu' I try again. I need to address the elephant in the room.

'Yes.'

'About yesterday,' I wish this conversation was over already, but I have to make him understand.

'Yes?' He asks, swallowing a lump in his throat.

'I was raped,' the words seem detached, as though they're not expressively linked to me.

'I know babe,' he takes my hands.

'I don't remember anything,' I mutter, in a low voice.

'Perhaps that's a good thing.'

'Bastard,' I mutter the curse before I can stop myself. Damn Felix Gloverman.

'Precisely,' he said solemnly. 'If you'd heard me yesterday, all I said was the word fuck.'

'Stu!' I can't help but smile.

'I don't care. You're still you. Whatever he did or tried to do. Don't let his actions define you.'

I let his words sink in, it's going to be hard not to – let his actions define me, I mean; when the whole reason I'm lying in this damn hospital bed is because of what he did to me. Felix. Where was he? He'd better keep away from me, I don't think I will be responsible for my actions if I see him again.

'Jen?' Stuart queries, his voice sounds worried.

I look up into his eyes, which remind me of a clear blue ocean surrounding a tropical island. I hold those eyes without wavering, and mime. *I love you.*

There's the rattling of wheels, a quick knock and the door is opened by a young plump man dressed in pale green trousers and a matching pale tunic, with short dark hair and a friendly face, pushing a catering trolley laden with tea and toast. The name on his badge says Kenny.

'Tea?' He asks jovially, as the cups rattle on the trolley.

'Please,' I say gratefully, looking at Stuart and waiting for his silent nod. 'Two cups, both with milk and sugar.' I watch silently as the young man, grips the handle of the large white teapot and tips its contents into two small white cups. He places the cups onto small saucers and puts them on to the portable overbed table. He reaches to the metal boxed unit that sits on top of the trolley and takes out teaspoons, plastic milk pots and sugar sachets before placing them on top of the bed table.

'There you go,' he says, his voice almost singing with a sense of achievement. 'Would you like some toast?' He points to the lower shelf on the tray with large plates laden with white and brown toast. There's also butter and jam,' he says with pride.

'Thanks. Brown toast please, butter and jam,' I say, 'I'm starving.'

'And you, Sir?' The young man looks at Stuart.

'Brown, please. Just butter,' he nods, watching the tunic stretch as the man bends down to retrieve our toast. As he puts the toast on to small plates, he starts to chat. 'Are you that woman who was kidnapped?'

I look across at Stuart, how does he know about me? Was it on the news? I look quickly at Kenny, feeling my face redden with shame and panic. Stuart's voice cuts in:

'Yes,' he says quietly, 'she is. How do you know about her?'

Kenny's face scrunches in an apologetic smile as he shrugs his shoulders. 'It was on the TV in the staff room. It's hard to miss it. You're Jenny Gloverman, heiress to the Gloverman Corporation. They keep telling everyone that you haven't been found.'

'Oh God!' I rub my hand over my face. I don't want people to know what happened to me. Not until they've arrested Felix. Stuart leans over and pats my arm.

'It's all right, Jen,' he mutters. 'Everything will be fine.'

'Sorry,' Kenny says, his face reddening 'I didn't mean to upset you.'

'Did the TV news people say anything else?' I ask him.

'Yes, they're looking for your uncle, Felix Gloverman. His face is all over the news,' he states, stroking his cheek.

'Good, the sooner they catch the bastard, the better,' there's no mistaking the anger in Stuart's voice or the fire in his eyes. A frown falls across his face and I have an overwhelming feeling of guilt in the pit of my stomach, because I know he feels this way because of me. My shoulders slump, adding to my morose mood, as I stare fixedly at the cups of tea and toast on the table beside me.

'I'll leave you to it,' Kenny says, walking into the corridor to move onto the next patient.

Stuart walks to the trolley and places his hands either side of the top of the trolley. 'Would you do me a favour?'

Kenny looks up. 'Sure, what's that?' He asks Stuart.

'Ask the staff not to mention that Jenny has been found. I'll get DCI Carter to clarify what information needs to be released about Jenny. But for now, her safety is paramount.'

'Of course, I'll tell them,' Kenny looks embarrassed. 'Enjoy your tea and toast,' he quipped, before hastily pushing the clinking trolley along the corridor.

For a few moments there is a weary silence. Our eyes meet and Stuart's frown slowly transforms into a warm smile, lifting my spirits.

'Poor Kenny,' he gives me a wink, 'I bet he spends his day dispensing tea and toast and putting his proverbial foot into everything.' I can't help but picture Kenny doing just that. Stuart spreads butter and jam onto the cooling brown toast and hands me a slice. I take a mouthful. Bliss. Toast is the one staple that you never really tire of.

'Mm. This is delicious. Just what I needed,' I mutter in between bites. I finish the toast and pick up another half slice.

'Whatever happens Stu,' I say in between bites. 'I won't let it beat me. What he did, he should be held accountable for. As long, as he is punished, I'm OK with that.'

'That's my girl,' he says, as we sit in companionable silence finishing our hospital breakfast. He touches me often, a gentle stroke on the arm here or a soft pat on the hand there, as though reassuring himself that I'm here and alright. Is it possible to love this man more each day? When your whole world spins on its axis and you need someone in your corner, you can't help but feel blessed that you are cared for and loved.

This will give me the strength and courage to move on.

Staff Nurse Skinner pops her head in the room. 'Feeling better?' She smiles. 'Do you feel up to a shower?'

I sit up straight. God yes.

"Oh yes please. Can you detach this thing?" I point to the drip.

"Sure. Stuart and I will walk you to the shower room, it's nearby."

The drip is detached, and we slowly walk to the door. As we reach the corridor, I notice a police officer standing with her back to the wall, next to the door. Is this really necessary? Surely, I'm no longer in danger?

'Am I in danger?' I look at Stu.

'They're just being cautious,' he assures me with a grim smile.

Cautious or not, having a police officer guarding my hospital room doesn't install a feeling of confidence. If only I was back at Gateshead, in familiar surroundings, resting in my own bed.

I close my eyes and let the hot water roll off me and soothe my thoughts. Just having clean hair and a new gown lifts my spirits, as each small step helps me to feel more human, more like myself. Staff Nurse Skinner enters the room, points to the fluid drip and quickly puts the line back onto my cannula and offers me a kind smile before leaving us alone again.

Rose and Henry arrive at 9am. Rose has put together a small case stuffed with spare clothes, nightwear and toiletries. She's a godsend. Each of them has tears in their eyes as they stand either side of my bed and reach over in unison to hold me tightly.

'I can't tell you what a relief it is to see you up and about,' Rose smiles as a solitary tear makes its way down her cheek.

'I'm alright,' I reassure them. 'Or I will be. I just need to get the next few days over with and then I can start getting on with my life.'

There's a knock at the closed door, and just as I'm about to shout, 'Come in', an emotional Lottie pushes it open and throws herself into my arms. 'Jen! I'm so glad you're all right,' she sighs and tightens her grip around me, so that I wince. 'You really had us worried there for a minute.'

'Lottie. Sorry I missed our lunch date,' I know it's not my fault, but I want her to know that I know I let her down.

'I should have known something was wrong. You never miss an opportunity to eat out!' She laughs, as I take a pretend swipe at her hand.

'And, there she is!' I laugh, 'the woman with the cheek. Thought I'd lost her for a moment!'

These people are my anchor, my lifeline, what would I do without them? I'm pondering this thought when Doctor Tracker enters.

'Hello doctor.' I say, offering her a little smile.

'You're looking better this morning,' she smiles. There's something lurking in her eyes, something that she wants to tell me, but is reluctant to divulge. That's not a good sign, is it?

'Would it be possible for your friends and family to go the day room for a little while?' Dr Tracker asks, tucking a piece of blonde hair behind her ear. 'I need to examine you and talk over a few things.'

Everyone nods and Stuart stands, ready to go with them.

I reach out to him, take his hand. 'Stay?'

'Of course,' his fingers thread through my hands. He looks unsettled as though he knows what's coming.

Once the room is clear, well apart from Stuart who sits beside me still holding my hand, the doctor pulls up a chair to sit on the other side of me.

'Jenny. The swabs are back. The DNA is confirmed as belonging to Felix Gloverman.'

'OK,' I say slowly, unsure about what she is trying to tell me.

'There's no easy way to say this,' she begins. 'So, I'm going to just come out and say it. Felix drugged you. We found Flunitrazepam, which is also known as Rohypnol in your system. A lot of it.'

‘Rohypnol! Jesus, I didn’t stand a chance, did I?’

‘No,’ Dr Tracker shakes her head sadly.

‘He then raped you. What I haven’t told you is that he didn’t use a condom.’

‘He didn’t what?’ I’m beginning to shake, with fear and with anger. How could he? How the hell could he?

‘He raped you and then he wiped you down. That’s how we were able to get his DNA.’

‘You mean, I could get, could be?’

‘Pregnant,’ she finishes for me.

‘Shit,’ I look at Stuart, ‘did you know about this?’

‘Yes,’ he sighs heavily, he’s still wearing yesterday’s blue jumper. ‘The doctor told me last night. I’m so sorry Jen.’

I take my hand away from Stuart’s. I feel so alone. So isolated.

‘I’m sorry Jenny, but you’re going to need to take emergency contraception.’

‘There’s no need,’ I say, ‘I’m on the pill.’ I glance at Stuart, and his weary face nods at me.

‘Oh. Thank goodness. I’m going to give you the emergency tablets anyway as you won’t have been taking the pill for the last couple of days. I will feel better knowing that there is absolutely no chance that you will conceive as a result of this harrowing ordeal.’

‘All right,’ I put my head down. I can’t get over the fact that he didn’t use a condom. The realisation that Felix meant for me to die in that box infuriates me. Bastard.

'I'm sorry Jen,' Stuart takes my hand again. 'I wanted you to rest before you tackled the repercussions of what that bastard did to you.'

'I know. I get it. Just give me a little while to process everything,' I try to smile as I look at our connected hands, but I just can't find the energy.

'I'll bring you the emergency medication, you'll need to take the first dose straight away.'

'Thank you,' I say quietly to Dr Tracker. I watch her sad smile as she quietly leaves the room. Jesus.

I find myself staring at the window. What have I done to deserve this? Did I upset Felix? Lead him on? Give him mixed signals so that he thought I was flirting? I'm wracking my brain and wondering why he would do this to me?

'Don't!' A sharp voice pulls me out of my reverie.

'Don't? Don't what?' I ask.

'Don't blame yourself,' Stuart's voice is deep with emotion. 'Felix did this,' he says, with an edge to his voice, and then he stares at our entwined hands, a softness spreads across his facial features. 'He got the drugs, he put them in your drink, including your water. He imprisoned you.'

I put my hands to my ears to block out his words. They were true, but they damn well hurt. 'He planned your kidnap with meticulous calculation,' Stuart continued, 'to make sure he could keep you prisoner for as long as he needed. Felix raped you. I suspect he wanted you out of the picture so that you were unable to claim your inheritance. This was all on him.'

'I keep telling myself that,' my voice is shaky, 'but the doubts creep in.'

'I know. But what could you have done differently? You weren't to know that he had put Rohypnol in your brandy. By the time you'd ingested it, it was a done deal, he had all his cards carefully lined up. All he had to do was let you go to bed, wait and then transport you to the Summer House in your car. He had everything set up. Tell me Jen, what could you have done?'

I look at him, and sigh, 'nothing.'

'That's right. Nothing. Because he had you where he wanted you. The bastard. I could kill him for simply laying a finger on you. You can well imagine what I would do to him if I found him?'

He holds his clenched fists together, determined to keep his temper under control despite his anger and frustration.

'Stuart. I wish I could turn the clock back.'

'Me too sweetheart. But we can't. What's done is done,' he walks to the side of my bed and strokes my cheek. 'You are the strongest person I know. We'll find a way through this. Once he's been arrested and imprisoned you will have some peace of mind.'

I burst into tears. I cry for the person I was before this happened. For the couple we were, for the life I had, and we shared, that no longer feels like mine or ours. I cry for Rose and Henry who are also living through this ordeal, worrying about me and feeling guilty for not keeping me safe. For Stuart who didn't give up, who found me. Well, the shell of the person that I now am. I cry for Lottie, who kept her vigil while I was imprisoned and never gave up hope.

And all the time, Stu holds me firmly almost crushing me. I didn't need gentle. I needed his strength and he gave it to me, every last ounce. I wept until there were no more tears left. Then I looked up into his eyes and knew that it was time to fight back, to find my new self, to find us again.

'God. I needed that,' I said after my sobbing had subsided. 'I just needed to let it all out.'

'I know,' he said and slowly pulled out a small box from his trouser pocket.

'I know you probably don't feel like it, but today is your birthday Jen. Happy twenty-first baby. I love you so much.'

The box holds a pair of silver earrings each in the shape of a lighthouse. I've been crazy about lighthouses since I was little. We've visited many different ones in the past six months.

'Thank you. They're beautiful,' I smile, admiring their exquisite shape and detail.

Staff Nurse Skinner steps into the room. She moves to the jug of water and tops up my glass, quietly pushing the moveable overbed table towards me.

'Here. Take this.' She lays a small white capsule on the table next to the glass of water. 'You'll need to take another one in twelve hours.'

'Can you look after these for me?' I ask him, handing him the earrings. 'I don't want to lose them.' He nods and reaches out until our fingers touch, the frisson causing our eyes to meet as he takes the small box back and pushes it deep into his trouser pocket.

I pick up the capsule and glass of water, slip the capsule onto my tongue, take a gulp of water and swallow. It's a bitter pill, never mind the pun. To know that you're preventing something that should be a natural experience for most women. The morality is not lost on me. Do I do nothing and live with the consequence of Felix's rape, or do I manage the situation? I need to feel in control again, need to be able to make my own decisions. I decide to manage the situation.

Staff Nurse Skinner looks at the saline drip. It's empty.

'I'm going to detach your drip. I'll leave the cannula in for a short while, just in case we need it,' she snaps on some gloves and detaches the line that's connected to the cannula. 'There. That's better. You're free to move now.'

'Thanks. I think I might put my own nightclothes on. Rose dropped off a bag of stuff for me earlier.'

'Good idea,' she says. 'Do you need a hand?'

'No. I'll be fine. Stuart's here if I get stuck.'

Stuart picks up my bag and unzips it. He starts looking around for my nightwear and underwear inside the bag and pulls out a few things.

'Here you go.'

I turn around so that he can untie my gown. My heart starts to beat rapidly as he touches my skin, pushing the material off my shoulders. I flinch, I can't help it. Damn. I don't want to push Stu away, but I suddenly find it hard to breathe. I think I'm having a panic attack. Take a deep breath Jen. Calm yourself. It's Stu. One, two, three. That's better.

'You alright?' He asks.

'Yeah. Sorry. I'm finding it hard to be touched.'

'That's understandable. Here. Put your arms up,' I follow his directions as he slips my nightgown over my head.

'Arms out,' his husky voice directs me. I do as he asks and find myself suddenly encased in my soft white towelling robe from home. Stu ties the belt gently around my waist and the robe begins to close, until it's sitting snugly near my neck.

'Underwear?' His voice is low, his eyebrows raised.

'I can do that. Can you, can you turn around please?' I ask feeling a little awkward.

'Sure. Whatever you need.'

Thankfully, he doesn't seem offended by my request, so I grab my underwear, quickly step into them, pull them swiftly up and over my bottom. It's the fastest underwear dressing I've ever done.

I sit down on the bed and look at him. He's looking out of the window, hands in the pockets of his faded blue jeans. His shoulders are slightly slumped, as if in defeat. He wants to help me but we both know that it needs to be on my terms. For the moment at least.

'You can turn around now,' I say, sitting on my hands.

Slowly he turns to me. His face is serious. His blue eyes display a calmness I know he doesn't feel. They also mirror mine. A look that says we're lost, and we can't find our way home.

'I want to kill him,' his voice is harsh, flat.

'I know. Me too.' I soothe.

He steps forward and reaches to take my hands, gently but firmly and says solemnly, 'Whatever you need. Whatever it takes. We'll get through this.'

A single teardrop escapes and slips down my cheek. Quickly, he raises his hand so that the pad of his thumb gently wipes away the wet track of my misery. He leans down and holds his forehead against mine.

'Whatever it takes babe,' his deep voice repeats.

We stay like that for what seems like an eternity. A knock at the door shakes us out of our peaceful reverie.

'Is it safe to come in?' Rose cautiously pops her head in the door.

‘Yes,’ I say, shuffling back onto the bed as Stuart moves to the window and leans his hips against the frame.

‘How were things with the doctor?’ Henry asks, standing against the wall so that Lottie can take the chair opposite Rose.

‘It’s possible I might be pregnant after what Felix did to me.’ I can’t seem to say the word rape. Especially to them.

‘He raped you?’ Lottie blurted out. ‘He bloody raped you?’

‘Yeah. But he drugged me first,’ I mutter in a casual tone, ‘so I don’t know anything about it. Thank God.’

‘Bastard,’ Henry chirps up, sitting on my bed and rubbing his hand across his chin.

‘Henry!’ Rose admonishes him.

‘Well, he bloody well is.’

‘Any news on his whereabouts yet?’ Lottie asks.

‘Nothing yet,’ Stuart admits. ‘DCI Carter will be here soon with PC Leadbetter. I’m sure they’ll let us know if there are any updates.’

‘I’ve got my shotgun ready. If he turns up, there won’t be much left of him by the time I’ve finished with him,’ Henry cuts in.

‘Henry! This is not helping,’ Rose tells him crossly.

‘It may not be helping but it makes me feel a damn sight better,’ he can’t help but retort.

‘Is there anything I can do? Anything you need?’ Lottie asks, holding my hand.

‘I can’t think of anything.’

Staff Nurse Skinner opens the door and pops her head into the room. ‘The police are here. Are you up to seeing them?’

I give Stuart a quick look before answering. 'Yes. I suppose so. Might as well get it over and done with.'

Everyone stands.

'We'll come and visit you after dinner tonight if that's alright with you?' Rose says.

'I'll be back in the morning,' Lottie promises me quietly. 'Get Stuart to call if you need anything.'

I find myself receiving careful, gentle hugs from Rose and Lottie and a pat on the hand from Henry. They don't know how to treat me. They're already treating me differently. I don't want to be different. I just want to be me.

'Stuart,' I say quietly.

'Want me to stay?'

'Please.'

He smiles, that semi-confident, that's my girl, kind of smile.

DCI Carter and PC Leadbetter walk into the room. They look like the FBI in their dark coats.

'Hey Jenny. How are you feeling today?' Carter asks me, as he takes off his black raincoat and holds it casually looped over one arm.

I remember PC Leadbetter vaguely from yesterday. She seemed nice. I look at the DCI to answer his question as my fingers start to tap on the bedframe. It's the only physical sign that I'm feeling nervous. 'Better, thanks. I would like Stuart to stay, if that's all right?'

'Sure,' says DCI Carter as he takes one of the seats opposite me and drops his coat to the floor beside him. PC Leadbetter folds her coat on the back of the chair and sits by my bed, before finding her notebook and pen.

Stuart leans against the windowsill again, arms and legs casually crossed.

'Before we start, I just want to let you know that there's been a leak and that news of your disappearance is now being announced on national TV. They've said we're also looking for Felix.'

Stuart scrunches his forehead, as though remembering something, he looks at Carter, 'One of the hospital staff, Kenny, asked Jenny if she was the person they were looking for on the news. Can you have a word with the doctors and hospital staff to make sure they don't say anything about Jenny being found and that she's here at the JR?'

'Already done. I've told Dr Tracker and the staff that there will be serious consequences for the hospital if news of Jenny's presence here gets out.' Carter faces Stuart and nods. There seems to be a developing respect forming between these two men. 'Right, back to your statement, Jenny,' Carter looks her way. 'What is the last thing you remember before waking up in the box?' he asks.

'I remember saying goodnight to Stuart. Then Felix came into the Great Hall asking if I'd like a brandy nightcap in the Blue Room. I didn't want to cause a scene, so I followed him to the Blue Room and left as soon as I'd finished my brandy.'

'We didn't find the glasses. We think he put them both into the dishwasher, there were several clean glasses in there,' PC Leadbetter fills in the missing gaps.

'Do you remember getting ready for bed?' asks the DCI, leaning forward, clasping his hands casually together.

I look at him and take a deep breath. 'Very vaguely. I remember using the bathroom and putting on my long-sleeved top and pyjama bottoms. Laying down on my bed. Then there was nothing.'

'What happened next?' PC Leadbetter asks.

‘I woke up.’

‘You woke up, where?’ DCI Carter pushes.

‘In the box,’ I tell him, closing my eyes to rid myself of the vision. It didn’t help. ‘It was dark and cold. I could hardly move. He’d cut a square shape into the side of the box and covered it in mesh wire. I could see a little light.’

‘Was there anything else in the box? A blanket?’ The DCI asks. ‘Food? Blanket?’

‘No,’ I shake my head. ‘No food or blanket. But there was a small bottle of water. Which I drank from.’

Frustration was building up inside of me. How on earth could they know what it was like, to be cooped up in a coffin? Waiting to die. ‘You have to understand. I was panicking, kicking, punching, screaming,’ my voice rises as the words fly out of my mouth, ‘trying to attract someone’s attention, desperately panicking because I was stuck in that hellhole. I was shaking, my feet were cold and sore from the kicking and so were my hands and knuckles.’

I look across at Stuart. His face was pale and expressionless. He was trying to keep calm. Trying to mask his feelings. I could see the tightening of his folded arms, the stiffness in his shoulders.

‘Then what happened?’ the DCI is trying to mask his feelings too, but there’s a deep frown building between his eyebrows.

‘Then I started shouting again. Shouting that I needed to pee,’ I tell them. ‘How degrading is that? To have to shout for help because you need to use the bathroom. What am I, three years old?’

‘What happened next?’ PC Leadbetter’s voice interrupts my thoughts.

This was the hard part. The part I was dreading having to retell, because it was when I found out where I was and who had kidnapped me. That bastard. 'A distorted voice spoke. A bit like one of those voice changer contraptions. Then he came into the room, it was dark, apart from a small lamp on the floor in the corner. He unlocked the padlock, opened the box and hauled me out. I was stumbling because my legs were cramped, sore and cold. He pushed me across the floor towards the door.'

My voice sounded so normal, as if I was talking about a daily event, such as going to the shops, meeting friends for dinner. Not reliving the nightmare that had shattered my life into a thousand pieces. I carried on recounting what had happened to me at the Summer House:

'He wore a balaclava over his head to disguise his face. Then he threw a hessian hood or cloth over my face. I thought I would suffocate. What he didn't know was that I could see through my hood. I realised that I was on the first floor of the Summer House.'

'Did he say anything else to you?' the DCI pushes forward with his questioning. I want him to stop. I don't want to tell them. Please don't make me tell them.

I looked at each of them in turn and said in a flat voice, 'No, he just pushed me along the hallway to the bathroom.' God, this is going to be hard. I took a deep breath, rubbed my hands and closed my eyes. Thankfully, they didn't push me.

After composing myself I felt the need to finish what I'd started, 'I found the toilet, sat down and relieved myself, while he stood watching. Then he decided to take off his mask. And, I almost fainted. I was horrified to see that it was Felix. I was desperate for him to not know that I knew it was him, so I carried on fumbling around, pretending that I couldn't see.'

‘I think pretending that you didn’t know it was Felix, and that you were unable to see through the hood, may just have saved your life,’ DCI Carter states. His eyes brighten, with emotion.

Now, I came to the part of my capture that I’d been dreading to recount. ‘One more thing. Felix was smiling when I was urinating. He was watching me.’ My shoulders began to shake as the image rolled in front of my eyes like a scene from a film. ‘It was as though he was getting turned on.’ I catch Julie Leadbetter’s eyes, the brief look of shock on her face before she dips her head and lightly skims words across her pad.

I pause momentarily, to rub the top of my arms. They feel so cold. And then, before I can change my mind, I say the shameful words that haunt my dreams. I wipe unshed tears with the sleeve of my dressing gown. ‘When I had finished my business on the toilet, Felix leaned forward to pull up my pyjama bottoms and then he began to stroke my thighs. I pushed him away and told him in no uncertain terms to keep his hands to himself.’

‘Jesus!’ Stuart said, his face distorted with anger. The emotion was so strong, I could almost feel it radiating from his body.

‘I’m sorry,’ I mutter, feeling helpless. ‘I should have tried harder to get away from him.’

‘No,’ says Stu simply.

‘No?’ I look at him, could see the frown sitting between his brow. And in that moment, I felt like I’d let him down badly. I held my breath, waiting for him to speak.

‘No, you shouldn’t. You did the right thing. You survived. The best way you could,’ Stu says flatly, looking at his hands.

Slowly, I allow myself to exhale and take a lung full of air. Thank God. He doesn’t blame me.

'After you've visited the bathroom, what happened?' PC Leadbetter asks, looking quickly at DCI Carter.

'Then, he put his mask back over his head, grabbed my arms and pushed me back to the room with the box. The room was in darkness still. He pushed me into the box, threw some cereal bars at me, pulled my hood off my head and took away my water bottle.'

I take a deep breath and carry on, telling them my worst fears. 'When he leant into the box to get the bottle of water, I was worried he was going to kiss me.'

There's a sharp intake of breath, it comes from the window. I close my eyes momentarily, trying to block out the memory.

'He closed the lid but didn't put the padlock back on, he just clicked the lid into place, and it seemed to self-shut. I pushed it but it wouldn't open.'

The memory was almost too much to bear. I sat there, staring at my pale hands as they twisted into the bed sheets. I couldn't seem to raise my head.

'Are you alright to carry on or would you like a break?' PC Leadbetter asks. There's a slightly strained look on her face. She's trying to remain composed, but it's hard not to be affected when you're listening to someone's experience of imprisonment and abuse. It's more akin to a Stephen King novel, than an easy to listen to audio romance.

I rub my forehead and look at Stu, his face is pensive and fraught as he stares my way, lost in thought. I feel as though I have lost him at some point during my statement, that he's drifted in another direction. Away from me. Maybe I should have sent him to get a coffee, to do anything but listen to my ordeal at the hands of Felix. The pain at the front of my head pounds relentlessly, pulling my thoughts deeper into the darkness.

My mind takes me back to the Summer House, back to Felix and what he did to me. I'm back there in the confines of the box, that cold, hard, dark place. Where I prayed fervently to find the strength to stay alive until someone rescued me.

I'm afraid to look at Stu, to acknowledge him. *Please don't shut me out. Don't look at me with pity in your eyes or disgust. I never wanted this, never wanted any of it.*

'Yes. Can I take five minutes please?' I tell PC Leadbetter in a despondent tone, and reach for my white buzzer, to press the green button and summon the nurse.

'Of course,' PC Leadbetter replies putting away her pen and notepad and drawing herself to a standing position. 'Would you like me to get you a cup of tea? Stuart?' Stuart doesn't answer. He is so quiet, still in his trance-like state. It's killing me. I keep my eyes away from him.

'Yes please. White one sugar,' I tell the PC, who smiles at me.

'You're doing really well Jenny. Really well.' She pats me on the shoulder and leaves the room.

'I'll go for a quick wander for ten minutes, see if I can catch up with Dr Tracker,' DCI Carter stands and follows his police constable.

That leaves just Stuart and me. And silence. Like two strangers, two people who used to know each other, but lost contact for many years. My head is throbbing as the door opens and a nurse I haven't seen before pops her head in.

'You buzzed?' She asks with a bright smile and tuneful voice.

'Yes. I've got a headache. Can you get me some painkillers please?'

'Of course. I'll see what I can do,' she's too chirpy for her own good.

'I need some fresh air,' Stuart says abruptly, and without looking at me, he walks to the door and yanks it open. It feels as though he can't bear to be in the same room as me, that he can't cope with what's happened to me. His withdrawal is not helpful in any way. And, just like an Agatha Christie novel, I realise that there is only me left in the room. Me. On my own. As my world crashes to the ground.

Alone with my thoughts. A feeling of deep sadness overwhelms me. It's better he leaves me now, rather than later. If he can't handle what's happened to me, I should know about it. I can't make him see me differently. I can't undo what's happened. He said we'd be OK, he told me he loved me. Sometimes love just isn't enough.

The nurse brings my painkillers and I take them quickly, hoping that they'll make the pain in my head go away. But there is nothing I can do for the pain in my heart. I feel bereft. I think of the song by R.E.M 'Everybody Hurts.' Damn right, they do.

The door opens suddenly, interrupting the lyrics that are running through my head. Stuart is back. More confident, more like himself. More like the person I know.

He strides with purpose straight to the bed. Takes my hands firmly in his and threads his fingers through mine.

'I'm sorry Jen. So sorry,' he says looking into my eyes. His voice is gravelly, emotional, 'it's hard to hear what that bastard did to you.'

'I know' I start, desperately trying to make things easier for him. 'If it helps, you can stay outside while I finish the statement.'

'What? To save my feelings?' His voice is tense and there's a slight tick to his left eye. A sign of tiredness, of stress.

'Yes. If it's too much for you. You can't take it back once you know. I'm giving you a 'get-out' clause.'

'Fuck my feelings,' he says harshly. 'You don't get to play the martyr in this. You don't get to make it easier for me. I will stay, listen to every bloody word of your statement until it's finished. So, what if I'm hurting, angry, feeling guilty? That's on me. I don't want a 'get-out' clause. We're in this together. If I look like I'm going off on one again, you have my permission to slap me across the face. Hard!'

His anxious face transforms into a beautiful smile and a warm fuzzy feeling of hope works its way through my sore, tired body and starts to heal my heart.

The door opens and PC Leadbetter asks:

'Are you ready to carry on Jenny or do you need more time?'

'Yes. I'm fine to carry on,' I say feeling slightly brighter, 'thanks for the break.'

Stu studies my face, 'you sure?'

'Yes. I need to do this,' I'm not really, but I know it needs to be done, so I offer him a weak smile.

PC Leadbetter enters the room and resumes her previous position at the side of my bed and following her carefully carrying two cups of tea is DCI Carter. He puts them down on to the overbed table and takes the empty seat.

'Both have milk and one sugar,' he states before sitting opposite the PC.

Stuart leans into me, kisses my forehead and picks up one of the cups, murmuring 'thanks' as he moves to the windowsill and crosses his legs holding the scalding cup.

DCI Carter speaks first.

'Jenny. Let's pick up from where we left off. You're now back in the box, you still can't get out. What happens next?'

I mentally take myself back to the time when I was pulled out of the box for the second time.

'I was alone for a while. I ate a cereal bar but panicked that I was going to choke because I was lying down. I didn't have any water. I had nothing to help me if it got stuck in my throat.' I pause, 'then, after a while I heard a noise and he came back into the room, unclipped the box, hauled me out and gave me a bottle of water from his pocket. I was so thirsty that I drank it all. He took the bottle from me and threw it into the box.'

'Did he say anything? Anything at all?' asks DCI Carter.

'Nothing. As we got to the door, he put the hood on me again. I started to feel woozy, heavy headed, my legs wouldn't move, and I was finding it hard to walk. He was part walking, part carrying me down the corridor. Then everything went black.'

I looked at Stu. This time he held my gaze, turned to the check the windowsill, placed his cup on it, and nodded to me. Within seconds he'd taken two strides to reach the bed, sat himself down and taken both of my hands in his.

'You. Are. Doing. Really. Well.' he speaks the words slowly, emphasizing each word. His dark brown eyes never leaving mine.

'I am so proud of you,' he smiles. A strong, almost forced smile. A smile of encouragement, of love and of hope. He strokes the side of my cheek and I lean into his touch. He sits there, holding my hand. Keeping me safe.

I lift my head to stare at the ceiling, looking for marks or cobwebs to focus on, before continuing with my statement. 'When I woke up, I found myself back in the box. I was so cold. I had a headache and my limbs were sore. I called out to him but there was no response. Felix never came back. I talked to myself, sang, cried, panicked, you name it – I did it.

I must have fallen asleep and woke only when I heard Stuart calling my name. I kept banging on the sides and lid of the box, trying to let him know where I was. I thought he wouldn't find me. I thought I was going to be left there to die.'

Tears are rolling down my cheeks. I'm there in the box again, cold and alone. The trembling starts in my hands, trickles to my upper arms and seeps its way slowly into my shoulders and neck. My chest tightens and it's getting harder to breathe. In my panic, I think I'm having a heart-attack. In reality, it's simply the shock of telling them my story, it's just too much. The trauma of re-living the hell of my kidnapping starts to envelop every part of me. I'm having a panic-attack.

I feel pressure on my hands, someone is rubbing them gently, forcing warmth back into them. I feel like I'm having an out of body experience. That I'm hovering near the ceiling and looking down at myself. I shake my head, trying to bring myself back to reality. There's a pressing feeling, and a pair of strong arms take hold of me and pull me close. Into something hard. Stuart's chest.

'I've got you Jen. I've got you, you're safe,' he whispers in my ear.

Slowly, I twist into him, needing his warmth to keep me sane. My arms wrap around his slim frame and I slip my hands under his jumper and rest them on his soft T-Shirt. His scent comforts me. His presence calms me. And all the time, Stuart keeps repeating the same mantra, 'I've got you. I've got you.'

My trembling subsides as I cling to him. Holding him tight, never wanting him to let me go.

He rests his forehead against mine, eyes locked on to mine and he whispers, 'always.'

Relief and peace. There's a sense of relief that I've done it, given my statement and relived my ordeal. A sense of peace settles over me.

'Always,' I repeat.

A cough interrupts the peace.

'I think that will do for today,' DCI Carter states. 'We'll leave you to get some rest. Thank you, Jenny. Giving us your statement can't have been easy.'

He takes out a card and hands it to me. 'If you need me or think of anything else. Let me know. PC Leadbetter will check in on you twice a day until you are released and there will a police guard at the hospital and at Gateshead until Felix Gloverman is found and arrested. I'll be in touch.'

'Thank you, DCI Carter. I appreciate that,' I say, as a huge sigh of relief escapes me.

And with that, they were gone.

Time to start moving forward.

Part 6

Gino

The rich dulcet tones of Andrea Bocelli and Sarah Brightman sing the words to, 'Time to say goodbye' on the loudest volume setting of the Alexa speaker. The office is filled with a glorious orchestral accompaniment as their powerful voices reach a crescendo. I close my eyes, lean back in my dark brown leather chair, strum my steepled fingers to the beat of the rhythm and hum quietly to the music.

My huge mahogany desk is directly in front of me, minimal in its decoration, just the way I like it. My blue fountain pen with the black nib is placed to the right, my large white scribble pad sits in the middle of the table and there should be a space to the left, where the silver letter opener usually lies. A large leather notebook has been left open, and sits on top of the scribble pad, which is full of neat black important scribes of information, figures and names.

At the far end of the desk I have a silver beaded skull that was my treat to myself after my first killing. It set me back three-grand. The song finishes and I enjoy the silence for a moment before I allow my eyes to open. Time to face the world. I push myself from the leather chair and walk to the middle of the room and the expensive brown Italian leaf patterned rug.

I look down at the sad sap kneeling before me with his head drooping onto his chest. His blue sweatshirt, black jeans and black hair are covered in blood. He's going to make a right mess of my rug.

'What the fuck did you think would happen when I found out that you were using the girls for yourself and giving them too much heroin?'

Silence. What? The greedy shit can't be bothered to look me in the eyes and answer my question. I watch the two scruffy dark-skinned enforcers, Carlos and Antonio as they stand behind the kneeling bastard, uncertainty on their faces. I shake my head with mild irritation as they begin to shuffle backwards. They know what's coming.

I didn't want to dirty my brown hand-made Italian shoes, but fuck this man was greedy, couldn't follow orders and needed to be taught a lesson. I walk closer to him. I don't want to get blood on my pinstripe blue Italian suit either, it was a bugger to get out of it. So, the drycleaner says.

I use my left hand to grab his grubby shoulder length black hair. I want him to see me. To see my anger, so I yank his head back, so that he is looking up at me. That's when I understand why he isn't answering. His bloody nose is broken and there is bruising and some cuts to his jaw and cheeks. Most of his front teeth are missing and they've sliced off a small piece of his tongue.

With my right hand, I take the silver letter opener from my breast pocket, swing it high and with the full force of my anger, I ram it into the sap's neck. His eyes look up in shock as the object sits neatly embedded deep into his skin. I pull the silver opener from his neck, stare at the dark red liquid oozing from his neck and listening to the sap gurgle and choke on his own blood.

Frightened eyes stare up at me, bulging, pleading for clemency, as blood trickles from his mouth. I raise the opener again and thrust it straight between his eyes. Digging it in and leaving it there for a moment. It looks like piece of art. Like Jesus on the cross. That was the moment, the sap knew death was his friend.

There was a gagging noise behind the sap from one of my men. I tut at the gagging, shake my head and pull the opener out of the sap's face, before throwing it on the grey marble tiled floor.

'Feed this fucker to the pigs,' I growl at the men. 'Burn everything else. Get Lenny to take his place looking after the girls. Put that, I nod to the blood covered letter opener, 'in the fucking dishwasher and then back on my desk.'

'Yes, Sir,' they say in unison as they begin dragging the dead man out of the room.

'Smarten yourselves up a bit, you look like you've been living rough,' the men look at each other and nod. 'And find that fat fuck, Felix Gloverman,' I shout at them, 'his face is all over the news. I want him found, before the police get to him. He won't last two minutes in custody before he starts bleating like a fucking lamb about everything he's involved with. And that will lead the police to me.'

Shit. I look at my bloody hands and the explosion of dark red splatters that cover my jacket. I brush my hands down my trousers, drying them and wiping the sap's wet blood off me.

Fuck. The drycleaner is going to be livid.

Part 7

Felix

'Andy? Good to hear your voice,' I say with confidence when my call is answered. There are the usual comments that accompany the renewing of communication with an old acquaintance after several years. I listen patiently for one minute, then take the lead:

'Yes, long-time, no hear. Look. I need a favour,' I say trying to inflect some authority into my tone.

Andy Naylor's incessant nasally West Country chatter, waffles on without a break, squeaking through the speaker of my phone. Apparently, he'd thought of me often over the years, even admitted to missing me, which I thought was odd, as I haven't spoken to him or seen him in ten years.

My new old acquaintance asked what I was doing now, wondered if I'd married. I had to chuckle at that. I'm a free spirit, use them and lose them, is my motto. Well, apart from Jenny. Naylor hadn't married either, it seems, not found anyone to put up with his quirks. He always was easy to manipulate.

I'm in a bit of a bind. I can't tell him what's really going on. He's the only one I can think of who can help me to lay low for a few days. He manages property for wealthy clients you see. Clients who holiday frequently and don't reside in their properties full-time. I just need somewhere to stay for a couple of days, until I can clear my head and work out what to do next. I tilt my wrist to look at my gold Rolex. Bloody hell, it's 10am already.

'Andy. Sorry to interrupt,' I tell him, trying not to sound too harsh, I really do need his help.

I stare at myself in the wooden rectangular mirror, that sits on the desk. I don't recognise the person I've become. Was this really, always me? If it was, the change has come on slowly over the years. Bloody hell, I look old. I run my hands through my greasy dark, curly hair. It's thinning at the top, making me wonder how long it'll be before it becomes a problem. There's a ruthlessness about my eyes, I didn't know I had. I'm wearing a light blue cotton shirt, open at the neck and it must have shrunk in the wash, because I swear it used to be looser than this. My trousers are black.

'But I'm in Bristol and I need a place to stay. I've had to take some time off work, had a bit of a breakdown. Have you still got your property business?'

Andy's voice booms down the phone so loud, that I hold my phone away from my ear to make listening to him more bearable. I forgot how loud he talked.

'Of course, old chap,' his booming voice states, 'anything I can do to help. Yes, the old property business is doing very well. Do you want something in Bristol itself or somewhere on the outskirts?'

'In Bristol if possible,' I tell him, hoping that he'll be able to find me something.

'Give me half an hour and I'll call you back, old chap,' he booms back.

'Much appreciated,' I disconnect the call, relieved to be away from his annoying voice and pleased that he is willing to help me.

I pick up the bottle of red Merlot and pour some into the small china cup. It's not as good as the wine we make, but beggars can't be choosers. And, although I'm not a beggar. Yet. I'm in no position to be too particular about what I drink and where I live.

Bugger. I've got myself into a real mess here. I arrived in Bristol late on Sunday evening after leaving my car and catching a train from Chippenham station. I'd taken one of Jenny's credit cards from her purse and her car keys on Friday evening before I took her to the Summer House. I didn't realise how hard it was to carry a body any distance. She was bloody heavy. They always make it look easy in the films.

I gloried in the memory of pushing her into the back seat of her VW Tiguan and driving the short distance to the Summer House. After I'd laid her in the box and padlocked her in, I'd driven her car to a deserted lane I'd googled days before, about five miles away. I had driven my car there earlier in the day, remembering to wipe my prints off the steering wheel and door handle, I simply abandoned it. I was rather pleased with myself regarding the kidnapping and organisation. I should have been a master criminal.

I'd driven back to Gateshead, picked up my overnight bag which carried the important balaclava and hood, and a dark set of clothes I had purchased especially for this adventure. Everything else had been left hidden at the Summer House.

The main problem had been, travelling to and from the Summerhouse without being seen. In the end, I'd decided to simply stay there. That way I could keep an eye on Jenny and tend to her needs. And mine.

I drove my Audi to the rarely used entrance on the east side of the estate, parked it behind some bushes and left it there. I just needed to keep out of sight from Saturday to Sunday evening before I began the next stage of my plan.

I had booked myself into the nearest available low budget hotel, believing that no one would think to look for me there. Luckily, there was a cashpoint nearby and I'd located a well-known supermarket for supplies. You wouldn't believe how cheap their goods were. I had used Jenny's credit card to pay for the supplies. Simply tapped it onto the card machine and let the plastic do the talking. It's amazing how much stuff you can get for under thirty pounds!

And that sums up why I am sipping Merlot from a white china cup and slumming it in this low budget hotel in the centre of Bristol. Laying low and trying to find somewhere off the radar is my top priority, at this moment in time. I had thought of Andy late last night and decided to give him a call this morning.

By 10.30am, there is still no phone call from Naylor, and I'm going stir crazy. I wonder if they've found Jenny. When I left the Summer House I panicked, I only had Jenny's credit card, my wallet which had little cash and credit cards that I'm too afraid to use, and whatever was in my car. Which equated to some screen wash, a black winter coat and a woolly blanket.

I pat myself on the back, pleased with how clever I've been. Clever of me to call Gateshead on Saturday to tell them that I'm away on business for a few days. And, it was definitely clever of me to use the Summer House, right under Henry and Rose's noses. The voice changer device I'd purchased from Amazon a few days before, was sheer inspiration! Jenny would never recognise my voice, not in a million years.

I take a deep breath. I can't believe I went through with the kidnapping. It's been brewing in my mind for quite some time now. With Jenny's birthday looming, I knew that as soon as she took the reins at the Gloverman Corporation that she would know there's something wrong with the finances.

***

I've been besotted with Jenny since she was fifteen years old. If I'm honest, I've been in awe of her since the day I moved into Gateshead to become her guardian and look after the business. The sudden acquisition of serious wealth went to my head, I went from being comfortably well off in a four bedroomed detached new build, to living in this huge mansion, where there are 'staff' to do things for you, a pool for your own personal use and a few cattle. Suffice to say, that the world opens up significantly when you have money and an open bank account. People look at you differently.

I already knew a little about the business from my youth, but as the youngest son, I was not in line to inherit, that was Kelvin. He used to say that it was, 'both a blessing and a curse,' to have total responsibility for the Gloverman Corporation, it's employees and the company's future viability, resting on his shoulders. He worked himself to the bone, that man. As brothers, we weren't close. Sometimes that just happens, sometimes you find yourself seen as the underdog and that's the hand that you're dealt with.

It wasn't a problem, because I could get on with my life, indulge in my passion of buying and selling antiques, which enabled me to have the freedom to come and go as I pleased. I'd rented a small shop in Thame and it was becoming very popular with people in the surrounding villages. People with money. It went well with the monthly allowance from the corporation which allowed me to live a very comfortable lifestyle.

The strange thing is, I had assumed that I would inherit the business if Kelvin died. I was wrong. Apparently, father had thoughtfully put a clause into his will to give Kelvin the final word on who inherited the Gloverman Corporation.

If there was no will or stipulation from Kelvin, I would inherit. Following the plane crash that resulted in my brother, his wife and my parents' sudden death, it transpired that in his will, Kelvin had named Jenny as his sole beneficiary. Can you bloody believe it? The irony of it all was that I was asked by Kelvin, via the will to become Jenny's guardian and to become the acting CEO of the company until her twenty-first birthday. This company that I'd been bypassed for, for my whole life.

Five years ago, I found myself thrown into the family business and subsequently giving up my freedom and lifestyle to help manage and become the CEO of the Gloverman corporation. The money was in the champagne we made and I'm not ashamed to admit that I liked having the power to make decisions, and for those decisions to be respected. I gave up my home to live at Gateshead, which was no real hardship and I gave up my heart when I became Jenny's guardian.

I started to watch Jenny and began to have romantic thoughts that she would see me as her saviour, the person who took care of everything. I convinced myself that she would fall in love with me and that we could run the corporation together. She's so pretty, so physically fit and dynamic. She appeals to me on every level.

About four years ago, I told Henry and Rose that I'd found some dry rot in my bedroom and needed to get someone in to sort it out. That was when I'd had the safe fitted, low in the wall so it could be hidden behind a set of drawers. I kept a special scrapbook in there, a scrapbook which held many photos of Jenny throughout the years. God, she was gorgeous, the way her body changed from a girl into a young woman with womanly curves. Jenny was tall, she loved running, yoga and used to be excellent at gymnastics when she'd been younger. When did I start thinking about her in the past tense?

The sketching of her in various poses began purely by accident not long after I'd joined the household. I'd been watching porn on my laptop in my bedroom and in a moment of excitement, decided to sketch some of the positions. It was always Jenny's face and her long blonde hair on the bodies I saw, though. It was only ever Jenny.

Six months later, I subscribed to a website that specifically catered for men who were interested in sex with young girls. It gave me something to focus on while I waited for Jenny to realise that I was the man for her. Grooming, it's called. Of course, I was soon addicted. I couldn't help myself.

Two years later I attended my first gala evening in support of Oxfordshire and Berkshire New Business Entrepreneurs. It was there I first met Gino Camprinelli, the young good looking, dark haired Italian, with his tailored suits, crisp white shirts and a swagger that turned the heads of many of the opposite sex, and some of the same sex. He was an up and coming businessman who dabbled in a wide variety of business ventures, including property management and alcohol distribution.

Camprinelli had already begun to make a name for himself. Some say he was the brains behind the stolen batch of military M4 air rifles stored at a Military Supply Depot based just outside of London. Some say he was into people smuggling and under-age prostitution. I chose to believe that the benefit of having him as an influential ally, far outweighed the knowledge that he was a bit of a gangster.

If only I hadn't been so caught up in myself and my feelings for Jenny, I might have realised that our alliance would only last as long as I served a purpose to him. He wanted the glamour and power of being associated with a large corporate company like Gloverman. I wanted access to some of the darker websites he had connections to. You never put your hand into the mouth of a rottweiler without expecting it to be chewed off horribly and painfully. So, why would you sell your soul to the devil just to keep your dick happy?

The rape. I'm not sure when I made the decision to violate Jenny, but I think it was around the time I started to put my kidnap plan together. I was visiting a friend in Stow on the Wold about eight weeks ago. We'd had a nice lunch at a lobster restaurant and had later wandered through the town, browsing its glorious antique shops. From the moment I saw the mahogany chest with the polished flat lid I could picture Jenny sprawled across the top. I remember stroking the cool, gleaming wood, my eyes closed, as I imagined Jenny teasing me, straddled across it. Lust almost overwhelmed me. I had to shuffle my trousers a couple of times.

I bought the chest. I think everything escalated from there. A touch of research here and there, to make sure she didn't suffocate in the box, and notes on how to keep her sedated. Then, hey presto! The plan had some cohesion. By the time I'd ordered the Rohypnol and mesh online and cut a small square shape out of the side of the box I was excited beyond belief.

Fucking her on Sunday morning was everything I thought it would be, and more. Of course, I had envisaged her being awake when we finally did the business, but I'll take what I can when I can. I can't put into words how that made me feel, it was like she was really mine, at last.

Being able to take her at my leisure, it fulfilled my wildest dreams. I'd even had the forethought to take a few photos of her to remember the experience. I wanted so much for her to be pregnant, to bring my baby into the world, that's why I didn't pull out at the end. When I had finished, I took out my phone and took several photos of her to remind me of this special occasion. I'd felt so powerful in that moment. Her life and body in my hands.

I cleaned her up and re-dressed her in her nightwear, before laying her back in her box carefully. A pang of guilt hits me; my poor Jenny, lying cold and frightened in the box. Perhaps I should go back for her.

I'm getting hard, just thinking about her and the possibility of a repeat performance with her. My brain quickly calculates if I've got enough drugs left for another go at her. No, I used the last dregs on the water bottle.

Maybe I could tie her up and gag her. God. That would be thrilling. I could just leave her naked on my bed, hands and feet spread and tied – waiting for me. I grab my trousers and shuffle my groin area, my trousers are beginning to feel very uncomfortable.

The phone rings, I reach down and see Andy's number.

'Hey, Felix. It's Andy. Sorry, it took so long,' his droning voice booms down the line, as I accept the call.

'That's all right. Did you manage to find me somewhere?' I ask.

'Yes. There's a place that's been empty and for sale for three months,' he explains. 'The owner has moved to Marbella, never visits and won't budge on the price. I manage the property for him. It's a two-bed duplex/penthouse apartment, not far from the Hippodrome. You should be fine there for a couple of weeks.'

This is good news. It sounds ideal and will give me time to work out where to go from here. I tell him, 'that sounds wonderful, Andy. I appreciate your help.' I exhale, I didn't realise how tense I was, until my shoulders relax and the ache across the top of my back begins to disappear.

'Are you free for a drink tonight? I'll give you details of the apartment and bring the keys with me,' he asks cheerfully.

‘Yes, sure,’ I force myself to sound positive. I’m not too fussed about meeting him, but I need to show willing. It’s just a means to an end, I remind myself.

‘I’ll meet you at The Old Duke, 7pm? I’ll text you the directions,’ he says, and I feel my stomach plummet.

‘Sounds good,’ I tell him, knowing my words don’t hold the sincerity, that they should. ‘Thanks Andy. I’ll look out for your text and see you tonight.’

Thank God, that’s sorted. I concentrate on the next thing on my to do list. I need to return to Gateshead over the next few days to get my stuff out of the safe and a few personal things. I probably need to do this at night so that no-one will see me.

On the spur of the moment I decide to call the estate. I listen to the ringing tone and wait for Rose or Henry to answer.

‘Gateshead. Henry speaking. How can I help you?’ my mouth dries up, my hands become clammy and I can’t speak.

‘Gateshead?’ Henry’s voice has an edge to it, he sounds annoyed.

I was frozen, unable to make a sound. My mind was trying to calculate if he knew about Jenny or not. Once I’d spoken to him there was no going back. So, I say nothing. Just disconnect the call, take another sip of wine, and grab my phone, so that I can look at the glorious photos of Jenny again. I walk to the bathroom to relieve some of this tension.

Part 8

Henry

When Rose and I first saw Jenny, we knew she was special. We thought of her as our own. Her parents loved her, but they were always busy with the family business. That's not to say that they didn't give her everything she wanted, materially I mean. Rose and I were Jenny's secure base, the one continuous factor for a child who had lived with a succession of nannies. People who had wanted easy work, but found she was too bright and inquisitive for them, so left at their earliest convenience. We were the only people who would drop everything for her and move heaven and earth to help her.

By the time she was five years old her beautiful mousey blonde hair had reached her shoulders and consisted of bouncy, soft curls that gave her an almost fragile look. Often, she would ask to have it tied back because it got in the way. Even then, she was a no-nonsense type of child. What you saw is what you got. She had no airs, graces or precociousness that sometimes comes with children born into money.

When Jenny was six years old, she begged me and Rose to teach her how to swim. Gateshead had its own heated indoor pool in the Pool House, which had been built at the back of the main house fifteen years ago, along with a gym room, jacuzzi and steam room. Kelvin had orchestrated the building of the leisure facilities. He had loved swimming. It was a well-known fact that he would do sixty lengths every morning before breakfast.

Jenny was an extraordinary child even then. She loved gymnastics and her parents had booked weekly lessons. She was active, healthy and physically fit therefore, when Rose and I took Jenny to the pool, we knew that she would take to it like a duck to water.

'Come on Henry,' she'd called to me, after only the third visit to the pool, 'keep up with me!'

Her graceful arms had glided through the water in a breaststroke motion. Jenny was born to swim; it was as though she'd been introduced to the pool just after birth. She'd instinctively known to dip her chin in the water to push the stroke forward. For the longest time, I allowed her to believe that she was could beat me in the pool. I never told her that I was a proficient swimmer, self-taught, but very capable, and favoured the front crawl.

When Jenny went to Bournemouth University, I thought I was going to burst with pride. Rose and I had driven her there from Oxfordshire, dismissing Felix's offer to take her. We had sorted her registration, wi-fi, bus pass and student identification before settling her into student accommodation on the Oxford Road. Leaving her in her room, making her bed and adding personal touches, such as her alarm clock, laptop and phone chargers and sticking photos of her parents and myself and Rose to the pinboard, was one of the hardest things we've had to do. We didn't know then that the girl in the next room would go on to become Jenny's best friend, Lottie.

Rose had stood beside me by the car, her beige raincoat open and flapping in the wind. A dark blue scarf printed with tiny pink flamingoes was loosely tied around her neck and struggling to stay in place. I know she was afraid to get in the car, wanted to go back to the building to collect Jenny and take her back to Gateshead with us. Tears were running down her face.

‘What if she needs us?’ Rose had asked me, desperation evident in her question, with a red blotchy face. ‘What if she’s unhappy or forgotten something?’ she’d persisted in tormenting herself, as short manicured nails had grasped the sleeve of my brown suede jacket.

I hated seeing her like this. My heart was heavy, and I took a breath, trying to reassure her. ‘Then she’ll call. She’s got her mobile. We need to let her go, Rose,’ I told her patting her hand. I dreaded saying the words, but they were true, we couldn’t keep Jenny with us forever. She had a life of her own to live and experience.

‘But I don’t want to,’ Rose mumbled, flatly.

‘I know. Neither do I. I held her close and gently tucked a windswept mousey grey wisp of hair, from her eyes, behind her ear. ‘She’ll be fine,’ I kept repeating as though, I was trying to convince myself of the fact. ‘We’ll see her in a few weeks.’

We got through those first few heart-breaking weeks, determined to stop from calling her too many times. To try and give her space to make friends and to get used to her new environment. Though the feeling of emptiness never went away.

Experts tell you all the things you need to do to keep your children safe. Advice is readily available. Ensure babies sleep on their backs, don’t overheat or use cot bumpers. Then, as they get older, you’re told how long to allow your children to use their phones etc, not to talk to strangers, use a reputable taxi firm, exercise and eat healthily.

What they don’t tell you, in their infinite wisdom, is that you never stop worrying about your child even when she becomes an adult. Of course, she isn’t our biological daughter, but we’ve nurtured and raised her as our own. And, those so-called experts, never tell you to be wary of unsavoury relatives, such as uncles who might one day drug, kidnap and rape your daughter. Millicent and Kelvin must be turning in their graves.

No. People never tell you about that.

So, that's how I find myself sitting at the kitchen table with a steaming hot cup of tea in my hand, staring at the pale blue Smeg fridge freezer at the far end of the room. Rose opens the dark blue covered metal ironing board and sets the board to her preferred height. She reaches for the plug to the steam iron and pushes it into the socket. As the iron warms, Rose leans into the laundry basket and takes out an armful of white shirts, blue trousers and several skirts and dresses.

The police are upstairs in Felix's room, with crime scene investigators, who know how to find the tiniest piece of evidence. Hopefully, something that will give a clue to his whereabouts and what he plans to do next.

DCI Carter had tried to put a media blanket on the news. He didn't want anyone to know that Jenny had been found, apart from us, himself, his team and Stuart and Lottie. Someone has leaked the information that Jenny and her uncle are missing. Jenny's face, the Gloverman Corporation and Felix Gloverman's face are all over the news. Still, Carter insists that we don't advertise the fact that she's been found, and where she's currently staying.

There's a loud bang. Rose stops, stands the iron upright on the board, and looks at me, her eyebrows raised in question. I shrug my shoulders. Who knows what they've found up there? I expect someone will tell us soon enough.

The sudden shrill of the phone in the Great Hall breaks through my thoughts. DCI Carter puts his head over the banister and looks down at me.

‘If that’s Felix,’ his deep voice carries down the stairs, as he fires instructions, ‘Don’t let him know we’ve found her. Keep calm. We need to know where he is.’

I nod and answer the phone.

‘Gateshead. Henry speaking. How can I help?’

There’s a silence, as though someone wants to say something but can’t find the words.

‘Gateshead,’ I repeat, trying to keep the annoyance from my voice as I watch Carter descend the staircase.

The line suddenly disconnects, and the dialling tone replaces it. Jesus. It could’ve been Felix, but who knows? I put the receiver back in its cradle and wait for Carter to reach me.

‘Is that a good idea? Letting him think that we don’t know?’ I question him as his hands slide deep into his pockets, ‘What if he’s watching the place and sees the police cars? Or, if the people you’ve contacted have told him that you’re looking for him?’ I can hear my voice rising, until I’m almost shouting at him.

‘We need to let him think he’s safe,’ he counters, “He’ll know we’re looking for her and hopefully, drop his guard and head this way. We’ve got a bug on the phone to help us locate him. The quicker we find Felix the safer Jenny will be.’

‘I suppose so,’ I say begrudgingly.

‘Boss. I’ve found something,’ PC Leadbetter calls from the top of the stairs.

‘I’m on my way.’

I watch as he takes the staircase two steps at a time. I wish this nightmare would end.

‘Was that him? On the phone,’ Rose asks softly, as she stands by the kitchen doorway, a white shirt hanging from her fingers.

'I think so,' I tell her, I don't want to alarm her, but she needs to be prepared. 'I think he'll come back here. If he thinks she's not been found.'

'I think so too,' she agrees, her face begins to scrunch in anguish, 'I'm scared Henry. He's a man with nothing to lose now. Who knows what he'll do next?'

'Yes, and we'll be waiting for him,' I state, walking to her. *Waiting with a bloody shotgun.*

We hear the creak of the stairs as Carter and Leadbetter make their way to the kitchen. Carter's brooding face looks grim as he holds a handful of passports and a large blue scrapbook. He places them in the middle of the table. His voice holds a note of concern:

'We found these. They were in a safe hidden behind a chest of drawers in his bedroom.'

I look at Rose, hoping Felix had spoken to her and there was a simple explanation for the findings. 'A safe?' Her worried eyes, catch mine, and she shakes her head sadly. 'Passports?' I ask, raising my eyebrows. Why the hell would he need more than one passport? I wait for Carter to speak.

'I think you'd better sit down,' Carter's voice softens with compassion as his hand motions to the wooden chairs. I nod and gently touch my wife's back for her to sit. They wait for me to pull out a chair and join her. Patiently. There's a short silence when all we can hear is the harsh scrape of wooden chair legs, Carter and Leadbetter take their seats around the table.

With gloved hands, Carter picks up two passports and holds them out to us. 'There are a number of passports with Felix's photo on them, but in different names. That tells us that he had plans to leave the country. It also tells us that he was into something pretty seedy, to know how to get fake passports.'

'We didn't know him at all, did we?' Rose says sadly. 'We let him into this house, following Kelvin and Millicent's deaths. We let that man live here under this roof, not really knowing who he was.' She puts her hand to her mouth, to stifle a sob.

I put my hand on top of Rose's warm hand that rests on the white linen tablecloth and squeeze tight. Her eyes flicker my way. There's a fear in them. A fear of the unknown.

'We didn't have much choice, Rose,' I bow my head in shame.

'What really bothers us, is the scrapbook,' Leadbetter's fingers travel along the top of the blue scrapbook until they reach the edge of the book. The front page is peeled back, and she doesn't rest, until the book is fully opened. Beige and pink sugar paper reveals several cut out photos of Jenny aged about fifteen. She's leaning over her desk wearing a dark blue jumper and black jeans. She's in her bedroom, engrossed in her homework. Felix had interrupted her, there's the biggest pout on her face, and she doesn't look happy. 'It's full of photos of Jenny. There are also a few drawings. They are quite graphic.'

'Oh my God!' Rose's eyes move across the photos and stop abruptly. She puts her hand over her mouth and close her eyes. When she opens them, she stares at a drawing of a woman's unclothed body, which has been pulled to the end of a bed with her legs splayed open. Thick rope binds each upper thigh and are tied to heavy chairs each side of the bed, keeping the woman in place, accessible.

Long hair spread across the bed and there were familiar features where Felix had tried to capture Jenny's sharp nose and full lips. Rose is transfixed, unable to move. As the spell breaks, she puts her hand to her forehead and holds it there. Her head droops with despair, shock evident in every pore of her face.

'Look at this one here,' Carter says, turning a page and pointing to a drawing. It was sketched in such a way that shaded the wooden pattern of a large box, a chest of sorts. On top of the box he'd placed a naked body, face down, legs open again. Long hair had been added to the shape of the head.

'When you find him, give me just five minutes with him,' I mutter, my voice thick with emotion. If I got hold of Felix, I'd hurt him so badly, I'd probably go to prison.

'I can't do that Henry,' Carter replies, but something about his dark eyes makes me think that this man would quite happily take my place and give Felix a beating on my behalf.

'Stuart will go mad when he hears about this,' I rub my forehead, feel the added wrinkles that this sordid business is giving me.

'Henry, do not give Stuart another excuse to go after Felix!' Carter looks at me sternly. Of course, I wouldn't put that on Stuart. He needs to be there for Jenny, not spend the rest of his days in some awful prison. I give Carter a brief nod.

'The sooner you put him away, the better,' Rose mutters. I am staring at one of the photos in the book. It's one of Jenny smiling and happy on her sixteen birthday and wearing a red swimsuit. We had surprised her with a pool party with some friends at the house. I feel like Felix has sullied that happy memory. It makes my blood boil.

Rose takes my hand and strokes my knuckles to calm me down.

'The scrapbook clearly shows Felix's fixation with Jenny. The drawings are sexually explicit. We need to find this man. Now,' Carter states, pushing back his chair and standing.

Carter takes out his phone and apologises while dialling, 'excuse me for a moment.' He walks into the Great Hall and talks fast to his colleague. His voice carries through to the kitchen, and it's hard not to listen.

'Mike. Can you get SOCO back to Gateshead? We've found a safe behind a set of drawers in Felix Gloverman's bedroom. Yes. ASAP. Any news from Jenny at the hospital? Good.' He's a busy man, with a sharp mind. 'Is Stuart Greyson still with her?' He stops for a moment and looks my way.

'I need you to put in a request for a warrant to check the finances and office of Felix Gloverman and the Gloverman Corporation. I want to find out what he was up to. Find out who he talked to and who, if anyone, he trusted. I'll be back in the office at 8.30am tomorrow morning. Get the team ready for a debrief.'

Carter disconnects the call and returns to us, addressing myself and Rose.

'You've got two officers covering the house, one each at the front and back,' he looks at Leadbetter. 'Julie. Can you head back to the hospital before going home? Check in with Jenny. See if she remembers anything else. Get an update from the doctor.'

'Sir,' Leadbetter stands, acknowledging his direction and looks at Rose and myself. 'Thanks for the tea,' she smiles warmly. 'If you hear anything, please let me or DCI Carter know. Here's our direct numbers,' she leaves a card on the table.

Rose and I stand, to walk them to the door. Carter looks at us. A tired but determined look on his face. PC Leadbetter moves to his side.

'We will find him. He will face the consequences of his actions,' he reassures us as he moves towards the Great Hall, Leadbetter hot on his heels. 'We'll let ourselves out.'

I stare at Rose. Her face is the same kind, caring face I fell in love with, but there are more wrinkles. I know she's worried sick about Jenny and what's she's been through, and I feel helpless that I can't comfort her the way I want to. I am so mad. Mad at everyone. I let my arm fall around her shoulders, 'she'll be all right, love. She's strong, we'll help her get through it,' I try to reassure her.

She pats my hand and sways slightly into my side. For a moment, the closeness gives me comfort, makes me forget what is happening here. Slowly, I remove my arm and let her go.

'I need to catch up on some paperwork, I'll be in my office,' I tell her, before making my way to the Great Hall and along the corridors that lead to the back of the house.

There are some things that you are better not knowing, that are better left unsaid. Unspeakable, evil things that make you see another person and the whole world in a different light. Like knowing that the young woman you helped to raise was kidnapped, drugged and violated. There's no going back from that.

I'm sixty years old. I joined the Gloverman household twenty-six years ago, when I was thirty-four. Came straight from one of her majesty's forces where I'd been a sergeant in the Royal Marine Commandos and fought for my country in the far east, until I'd eventually been given a medical discharge following an injury to my arm during a mission in Iraq.

Rose came to work here as the housekeeper six months later, we connected straight away, and a year later we were married. It was love at first sight. For both of us, it seemed. I never spoke to Rose about my life in the Royal Navy. Well, technically speaking, I was in the Royal Navy, I just wasn't a sailor. I'm not sure why. I think it was because it was a chapter of my life that was finished, and I was happy to move on. Despite this, I did occasionally meet up with old marine mates from my former units. Those links you forge, where you are responsible for another's life, where a mistake can lead to the death of your whole unit.

So many memories, good and bad. I lost a few close friends. Memories of missions, and of strong ties formed with those you trust with your life. Lifelong friendships, nights of drinking, laughing, visiting exotic destinations, keeping the peace with the local people and among the unit, when things got out of hand.

But my dreams were haunted by the memories of blood and death, and the sound of explosions and gunfire. I'd formed a close bond with, one of my former captains, Captain Mickey Shakespeare. He's one of the good guys. We're way overdue for a pint. I take my phone from the pocket of my black and brown checked work jacket and bring up my contacts. I find Mickey's details and press the call button. The ringing tone continues for several seconds before there's a click and a crackle, a heavy sigh and the deep familiar drawl of a Geordie accent speaks.

'Hello?'

'Mickey? Mickey Shakespeare?' I ask, surprised and relieved that he had answered so promptly.

'Yes, who's this?' the voice asks.

'It's Henry Dean, Mickey,' I say, a half-smile on my lips, as I prop myself on my office chair and lift my legs to rest crossed at the ankles on my desk.

'Deaner?' Mickey's voice breaks into a laugh, 'Good to hear from you, old friend.'

'You too, Mickey,' I reply. It was good to hear his voice. I feel like I'm not on my own now, keeping it together for Rose and having no control over what was happening. 'Don't suppose you fancy a pint? Got a problem here and could do with a bit of help.' I tell him.

There's a moment of silence and I hold my breath, waiting for his answer. He comes back on the line and his words are firm. 'Of course, Deaner. Anything you need. Tell me where and when.'

I disconnect the call and move to a wooden trinket box which sits next to a Winston Churchill biography, situated on an upper shelf of the floor to ceiling, fitted mahogany shelving unit. The box is full of drawing pins. I carefully take off the lid and fumble around until my hand finds the small key that opens the large silver metal case that is hidden underneath paperwork in the bottom drawer of my desk. When I've located the key, I bend down to open the desk drawer, pushing papers aside as I bring out the metal case.

I look at the shiny surface of the case as it sits on the top of my desk. It's been a long time since I opened this case, a lot of stuff has happened, and many years have passed. I put the key in the lock and turn it, hearing the distinct click as the lever keeping it in place is released. I slowly raise the cool metal lid, until it sits comfortably open, and in place.

Thank God, it's still here.

I look at the black compact Beretta 92, sitting on the bed of an old red pillowcase. Fitted snugly beside it, are two black full bullet cartridge holders.

I take the gun out of the case and hold it carefully in my hands. It's not big, but it feels heavy, heavier than I remembered, and yet, the feeling as I run my fingers over it, the familiarity of years gone by, gives me a sense of control, of calm. I know, above all people, that this is a deadly weapon and needs to be carefully primed and cleaned. I'll need to find somewhere quiet to get a little practice in, because there's a single bullet that has Felix Gloverman's name written on it.

Time to get organised.

Part 9

Jenny

'Get your hands off me! Don't touch me!' I thrash into my bed sheets, turning this way and that. I must have dozed off, started dreaming.

'It's OK. You're safe,' a strange, deep, male voice, someone with a slight Scottish twang, breaks into my consciousness. There is a note of concern to the voice. I don't think I need to feel afraid. I open my eyes.

Sitting on a green cushioned chair next to the bed, a man wearing a white coat leans towards me. His hands are clasped together and are resting on his knees. He's got that Liam Neeson, medium-brown, wispy hair and slight stubble look about him.

'Hello Jenny. I'm Dr Daniel Scott. I'm the resident psychiatrist here. I've been asked by Dr Tracker to come and see you following your ordeal. She thought it might help to talk to someone.'

I don't understand. I don't feel like I need to talk to someone. Do they think I'm going mad?

'Where's Stu?' I ask bluntly. I want him here, with me.

"He went to get a bite to eat from the café. He said he won't be long.'

He looks across at me, his eyes assessing me, waiting for my response.

'What you've been through must have been a terribly frightening ordeal,' he continues, studying my face as he talks to me.

I sit staring at the top of his head. I'm not going to talk to him. I've decided. If I need to talk to someone, I'll talk to Stuart. I rest my hands over each other on my blanket-covered thighs and sit quietly.

'What were you dreaming about just now?' His voice cuts into my thoughts.

'Something bad,' I say flatly and roll my eyes to the ceiling. So much, for keeping my mouth shut. I think he's either very good at his job or I really am losing the plot.

'Did it have something to do with your uncle?' Dr Scott asks.

'Yes!' I look at him. Angry with myself for answering yet another question.

'What was he doing?' he asks. Nothing good, my mind whispers.

'He was pulling up my pyjama bottoms.' Damn. He's good.

'Is this when you were held prisoner?' He makes it sound so sordid, so real.

'Yes,' I mutter, twisting the bed sheet and blanket, 'I'd finished using the toilet. He was watching me. Smiling.'

'He wasn't wearing anything to cover his identity?'

'No. He'd taken the damn balaclava off. That's when I realised it was Felix.'

I was looking at my hand, at the cannula – which I think is being taken out later today. At the sheets that my fingers are playing with. Trying to keep busy.

'That must have been quite a shock. Finding out that it was Felix.'

I stopped focusing on my hands, raised my head and looked straight at him.

'What do you think?' I asked flatly.

Silence. He didn't say anything. Before I can stop myself, I start babbling.

'It made me so mad when I realised it was him. So mad and frightened at the same time. I mean, he was my uncle for God's sake,' my voice rises and becomes harsher.

"I get it,' he says, 'you were right to be angry and frightened.'

'When he took his mask off, I nearly gave myself away with the shock. Do you know something? He was smiling as he watched me relieving myself.'

'What a knob!' he answers.

'I'm sorry?' Did he just call Felix a knob? I waited for him to repeat his comment and looked at him for the first time. Really looked at him. Took in his hazel eyes with a hint of green. He wasn't the enemy. Felix was the enemy.

'I said,' he mutters, in a flat tone, 'what a knob.'

For the first time since we'd started talking, I found myself stifling a smile.

'He is a knob,' I agree, and my mouth lifts in amusement.

Dr Scott pushes himself to his feet, and walks to the windowsill, his open, white coat swishing as he moves. The same place that Stuart had stood when I gave my statement. He stares at the grey sky through the blinds for a short while, before he turns to me.

'Do you think he'd intended for you to die in that box?'

I'd thought long and hard about this question, when I'd woken up during the night. Deep down in my bones there was an ache that knew the truth, that I was never meant to be found. I look at the doctor, glimpse a crisp, white shirt and black chinos under his medical coat, and watch as he casually resumes his seat beside me.

'Yes, I think that was his plan. To let me die in there,' I speak, deep in thought. 'I remember watching him as he slowly pulled up my pyjama bottoms, the feeling of his hands as they stroked my thighs.' I shiver. I can almost feel the touch of his fingers. 'I pushed him off and told him to leave me alone.

'You didn't know you'd been raped?' his eyes hold mine for a second as he leans forward in his chair.

'No. I felt woozy, then everything went black,' I close my eyes, trying to erase the memory of my uncle's face. Of the sheer panic and fear. 'When you lose sense of time and your movements are restricted, you're not eating or drinking properly, everything becomes disorientating, frightening, unsettling. I just thought I'd passed out.'

'When you woke, did you feel sore?' he asks casually, and my eyes fly open. His hands are clasped together on his knees, as if we're talking about the weather.

'A little, and my head was throbbing,' I admitted, and felt my hand lift subconsciously to rub my head, even though it no longer throbbed. 'I felt cold and cramped. I thought it was because I'd been stuck in the box for so long.'

'It's probably good that you didn't remember any of it,' he shuffled in his chair and crossed his legs.

'That's what Stu said.'

'If you do start to remember Jenny, if you begin to have flashbacks, you need to contact me, and I'll talk you through it. Promise me you'll do that?' Hazel eyes focus intently on my face, until I raise my head again and meet his gaze.

Swallowing back a sob, I suddenly realise how lucky I am to have supportive and caring people around me. In a low voice, I say, 'I promise.'

'How do you feel right now?" the doctor's face is serious, and his brows are drawn together.

'A bit up and down. Angry, very angry. With Felix,' I mutter sullenly.

'That's normal. Just keep talking it through with Stuart or call me. I'll see you again before you are discharged and then make some follow-up appointments for you to come and see me. Don't bottle it up. There is one thing that you need to remember though, Jenny.'

'And what's that?' I ask.

'That none of this is your fault,' his smile lit up his face, offering support and reassurance.

'I will. Thanks Dr Scott.'

'Daniel. Just call me Daniel.'

'Thanks, Daniel.'

Someone knocks on the door and it opens. Stuart comes in carrying two paper cups.

'Hey,' he says with a grin. He studies Daniel and then my face.

'Hey,' I smile at him.

He smiles back, nodding to the doctor, 'Dr Scott,'

Daniel shrugs, putting his hands in his pockets, 'just call me Daniel.'

Daniel steps closer to the bed, looks at me like a father would look at his daughter.

‘You’re doing well Jenny. As I said, I’ll pop in to see you again before you go home. If you need me before that, just tell one of the nurses and they’ll let me know.’

‘Thanks Daniel. Sorry if I was a bit off with you at first,’ I apologise.

He smiles, his hand on the door ready to leave.

‘Don’t worry. I’ve had worse, I’m pretty thick-skinned. Oh, and happy birthday,’ he says casually as he walks through the door, leaving it slightly ajar.

I smile in acknowledgement.

‘Have you been flirting with Dr Neeson?’ Stu smirks, putting the paper cups on the overbed tray. Ah, so he’s noticed the resemblance to the famous Irish actor too. I push the table along slightly so that I can get out of bed, slip my feet into my slippers and don my dressing gown.

I move to the window. God, why is everything so hard? I stare through the vertical blinds, catch a glimpse of the car park below. Where people are probably carrying on with their everyday life, waiting in a queue, searching for a car parking space, rushing into a hospital building. In its own mundane way, it reminds me, that despite everything, life goes on.

‘Only a little,’ I tease, turning to face him. My heart begins to flutter at the sight of his handsome face, from the angular shape of his chin, to the way his mousy fringe flops on to his forehead.

His dark brown eyes hold mine, as he stands by the bed, offering a smile, ‘anyone who manages to make you smile is OK in my book.’

Can it be possible to love this man too much? He’s so at ease with himself, so caring and confident. Like I used to be. ‘He was surprisingly easy to talk to,' I tell Stuart, as I walk to him and drop onto the bed with a sigh.

'Good,' he tilts his head down, and I watch entranced, as his face becomes serious. He lifts a hand and gently strokes my cheek, 'because you need to talk about it, Jen. It will help to process what's happened to you.' I close my eyes and savour the sound of his deep voice.

When I open my eyes again, I put my hand over his, feel the warmth of his skin. 'You sound just like Daniel.'

He lifts a brow, accompanied by an easy smile, before sitting on the bed. He's not the jealous sort, and I'm relieved to enjoy some easy banter for a change. Stu's phone pings, and he takes it out of his pocket to look at the text.

'It's Henry. He says that Felix called the Gateshead landline, but wouldn't talk.'

'Do you think he knows I've been found?' I turn to face him. I can't believe that my life has changed so much over the past week.

'I don't know. I hope not. DCI Carter wants to keep it quiet in the hope that he will return to Gateshead,' he explains. 'His car was found abandoned at Chippenham Railway Station. We think he's in Bristol. I've been trying to piece together what happened once I'd left your place on Friday night. This is what I know so far.

'I think you had a nightcap of sorts with Felix who'd drugged the brandy he'd given you. I think you probably passed out in your room. Where he undressed you, putting your dirty clothes into the laundry bin in your bathroom and dressed you in the nightwear you usually keep under your pillow.

'He then, took your car keys, carried you to your car and drove you to the Summer House where he put you in that godforsaken box.'

My hands fly to my mouth. To hear Stu says the words out loud, it makes Felix sound calculating. I didn't see it coming. None of us saw it coming. Bloody hell.

'On Saturday morning,' Stu takes hold of my right hand, the one without the cannula, threads his strong fingers through mine. 'A typed note, supposedly from you, was hand-delivered to my parent's house, telling me that you were going away and that we were finished.'

'Wait! What did you say?' I interrupt him, pulling my hand from his as anger built like a tornado inside me.

'I had a note telling me that we were over,' the storm of feelings, turned his brown eyes to black. I could see, by the slight twitch in his right eye, that he was angry too and trying to hold on to his feelings.

'Stu. You know I would never do that. Would never type something so callous,' I hear the pleading, almost whining sounds to my words.

He turned to me and placed his hands on my shoulders, 'Jen, sweetheart, it's all right. I know you wouldn't do that, type a letter to end things.'

I shuffle on the bed, so I'm looking directly at him. The poor man. He must have been so scared, so angry. I feel the tears threatening my eyes, so I reach out to stroke the skin of his neck, before lowering my hand and resting it on his heart. I leave it there for a moment, while he continues his story.

'Don't worry about it. At first, I thought it was a stupid prank, but then I called you and there was no answer, just got your voicemail. I left a message, then went to pick up Rose and Henry's anniversary cake in Oxford.'

'Oh my God. I forgot about the cake!' I put my hand to my mouth, 'poor things, we missed their anniversary.'

'Again, don't worry. They had other things on their minds. Namely, you. Anyway, back to the story. I called Rose and Henry at Gateshead to see if they'd seen you. Of course, they hadn't. Then, I got a call from Lottie asking if I had seen or heard from you as you hadn't turned up for your lunch date.'

My mind was whirling, as I sat there, processing this information. I kept quiet though, and let Stu tell the rest of the story.

'By this time, I was really beginning to panic. I suggested to Lottie that we meet at Gateshead where we could catch up with Rose and Henry and check out your room.'

'God! I've caused quite a fuss, haven't I?' I tell him, beginning to feel a little guilty about causing so much trouble.

'Jenny,' he looks at me sternly. He must be serious he hardly ever calls me Jenny.

'That wasn't your fault. None of this is, or was, your fault. I need you to believe that. It's nothing compared to what you went through.'

'But!' I try to interject, to say I'm sorry. My head drops with frustration, he just won't let me.

'No buts,' he takes my hands, his thumbs stroking my skin, 'This. Is. Not. Your. Fault.' he says softly, his eyes holding mine. 'I will keep saying it until you believe it. It is not your fault.'

I hold his hands firmly in mine, taking strength from their warmth and comfort. I know it sounds corny, like something out of a cheesy romance novel, but Stu has become my rock, my reason for living.

Somehow, I always knew he had emotional strength, because his parents had let him down miserably when he was young. Due to a family tragedy, they had emotionally withdrawn from him, and left him to fend for himself without the emotional support or connection. He'd had to become an adult when he'd been nothing more than a child.

The situation that Stu and I were in was unique. Similar to a freak accident not everyone could come back from it, and if they did, they may not be the same person they were. It was going to be an awful long process for me, Stu and my small family unit to begin to recuperate from the horror of me being kidnapped, drugged and raped.

Consequences, such as the pain of reliving my ordeal during my interview, the memory of Stu's horrified face, will stay with me for a long time. I know that people will look at me differently now. See me as that poor girl who was kidnapped.

There's a knock at the door, which stands slightly ajar, and PC Leadbetter's voice flows into the room. I turn and smile. 'Are you feeling up to visitors?' She asks, her bright smile is warm and friendly. She's wearing a dark blue top, black trousers, and a black jacket. There's a black crossover bag hanging over one shoulder.

I look at Stuart and gesture with my fingers for her to enter the room. 'Sure, come in.'

'Thanks,' she says, helping herself to a chair beside the bed and gives Stuart a quick smile. She looks around the room, her eyes eventually settle on our clasped hands on the bed. 'how are you feeling?'

'Much better thanks,' I'm grateful for her concern. I know it's her job but there's a feeling of trust and sincerity coming from her. 'I feel more like myself today.'

'Good,' she smiles, 'just take each day as it comes, small steps and all that.'

I move off the bed and sit down on the chair opposite her so that I can look at her while we're talking. 'Is there any more news on

Felix?' I ask, wondering if they were ever going to catch him. I'd feel much happier if he was no longer walking the streets.

'Please call me Julie,' she smiles warmly. 'Not really. We think he's in Bristol and we're checking out known contacts, but that's all we know for now. We haven't got him in custody yet.'

I shiver. The thought of Felix being free to come and go as he pleases, to do whatever he wants to whomever he wants, it's beyond terrifying. I mean, what happens if he tries to drug or kidnap another young woman? Or even worse. The scenarios work their way through my stress addled mind. I can't think about it. It's too much.

'There is something I need to update you with,' her voice changes its tone, it's as if she's got something to say, but is unsure how to say it.

'Just tell me, Julie,' I say flatly, my shoulders slump with the feeling of yet more bad news. My hands clasp tightly together.

Julie looks quickly at Stu, waiting for his reaction. He gives me a quick look before nodding at her.

'I was checking out Felix's bedroom again early this afternoon. Something didn't sit right with me, I felt like I was missing a vital piece of evidence, so I looked behind his set of drawers and found a safe that had been built into the wall.'

'A safe?' Stu asks, looking my way. His face is blank. He seems as surprised as I am.

I shake my head. 'I had no idea.'

'Yes. It had a six-figure rolling lock on it. After several attempts, I tried using Jenny's date of birth and it opened,' Julie explains.

Stu jumps off the bed, steps to my chair and takes my hands, careful not to knock the cannula or the top of my left hand. I'm pulled to a standing position and, before I know it, I'm sitting on his lap on the chair. I'm not sure, but I think he's doing this because he thinks there is bad news heading our way.

'Go on,' my voice is quiet, and has a huskiness to it.

Julie clears her throat. 'Inside the safe, DCI Carter and I found some fake passports relating to Felix and a scrap book. The scrap book worries us more than the passports.'

'Why?' I ask, warily. 'What's in it?'

'It had numerous photos of you from the age of fifteen and quite a few drawings. Which I'm almost sure were done by Felix. The drawings were not nice.'

Stu's whole-body tenses and his grip tightens on my waist, 'What do you mean, not nice?'

'They are graphic drawings, Stuart. Very graphic. Of Jenny in various sexual positions, one of which showed her splayed over a large box, similar to the one she was held in at the Summer House. SOCO are going through it with a fine-tooth comb as we speak.'

'Oh my God!' I scrunch my eyes closed tightly, tears that never seem too far away, threaten to spill from my eyes. This cannot be happening. Will it never end?

'Jen?' I turn to Stu, can't hide the sadness and despair on my face, shining in my eyes. I just want this to stop. Is that too much to ask? Stu's thumb softly caresses my cheek.

'Was it me? Did I do something to make him like this?' I say, feeling totally helpless.

'No!' both Stu and Julie say at the same time.

'It's not your fault, Jen,' he puts his forehead to mine, forces me to look into his eyes, 'he's ill, twisted in the head. It's not you.'

'But,' I argue, 'I must have done something to make him this way.'

'Not. Your. Fault.' he repeats slowly, our skin still touching. I know deep down that he's right, but feelings of guilt still grate, fill me with shame, making me question if I did something to encourage Felix to be this way. To make him do these terrible things to me.

'On another note, we've found your car Jenny. It was abandoned in a derelict lane a few miles away. It was untouched. We found your uncle's car at Chippenham Railway Station.'

'Chippenham? Where was he going?' I ask in disbelief.

She looks at me carefully, before replying, 'Bristol.'

'What on earth would he be doing in Bristol?' my voice is slightly louder; I'm getting frustrated with the whole situation. What the hell is he doing in Bristol?

'We're checking the Gloverman finances to see if Felix has been up to anything,' Julie leans forward, rests her arms on her legs. 'Do you know of anyone he might be close to, that he might blackmail, engage in criminal activities with or ask for help?'

'Not really,' I say, 'his personal assistant, might be the one to talk to. Her name is Amy Wilder, she's tall, slim with long blonde hair, a little like me.' I stop, suddenly realising what that means. My heart beats so hard in my chest, I think it's going to explode. This is so unreal. I have to ask the question, even though I already know the answer.

'Do you think he hired her because she looked like me?' I ask Julie. My eyes plead with her not to say yes.

'Very possibly,' she answers, 'I'm sorry, Jenny.'

'Oh God!' Stuart loosens his grip on me briefly, leans back and closes his eyes. 'I'm finding it really hard to keep my temper when I think of that man,' he says quietly.

'I know,' Julie sympathises, 'I wish I could have a few minutes with him myself.'

'Wait a minute!' I stand, and walk to the bed, my face never leaving Julie's, 'about four years ago Felix announced to Rose, Henry and me one morning during breakfast in the kitchen that he'd found some dry rot in his bedroom and needed some building work done to sort it out. That may have been the time he put the safe in.'

'The timeline fits. I'll let DCI Carter know. I don't suppose you remember the name of the company?'

'No. Sorry. Has he really been having these sordid thoughts about me since I was fifteen?' I shiver. Thinking of Felix makes my skin crawl. I stop pounding the floor and look at them both in turn.

Julie's brown eyed gaze holds my attention.

'If I'm honest, I would say yes. It would have been slowly building from the moment he came to Gateshead, a year later he decided to have the safe put in. He needed somewhere that was completely secure to keep his most precious possessions away from prying eyes.'

Stuart sits forwards, his hands clenched and nods his head in agreement.

'Jen,' he studies me, 'I think Julie's right. Felix came to live with you when you were fifteen years old, just after your parents died. Something warped his mind as you grew older, I suspect he became delusional about you and your relationship with each other, probably not long after he moved into Gateshead.'

His lips form a hard line, 'it's possible he never really saw you as his niece, but more as a family friend, which then gave him carte blanche to extend his sick fantasies of you.'

'Sadly Stuart, I think you're right,' Julie stands, turns to the door, 'I'm going to head off home now, but I'll see you tomorrow. You may get discharged tomorrow or at some point on Thursday. We need to see how you go through the night, though.'

She stops abruptly, reaches into her bag and drops a business card on the bed 'You have my work number. Call me if you remember anything or need to talk.'

'Thanks,' I tell her suddenly feeling tired. 'See you tomorrow,' I pull the covers back from the bed and slide down into the comfort of the firm mattress, crisp white sheets and thick beige coloured blankets.

'I feel a little tired,' I tell Stu. 'Are you OK if I close my eyes for a moment?' As my head touches the pillow, I begin to feel an overwhelming tiredness. This Felix business is exhausting.

'No problem,' he says, getting up from his chair, 'I'll go to the café and pick up a drink and snack. Do you need anything?'

I don't reply. I don't see his brave smile or feel the gentle kiss he puts on my forehead. My mind shuts down and I allow myself to fall into a blissful sleep.

Voices. I hear voices. They're quiet, I can't hear what they're saying. More mumblings and then the words become clearer.

'Hush, you'll wake her,' a familiar, deep voice says. Stuart.

'Too late,' I mutter, my eyes open, and I struggle to focus through my sleep-filled brain, 'I'm awake.'

Someone leans over me. Silky, soft hair trickles across my nose as Rose kisses my cheek. She smells of oranges.

'Jenny dear, sorry if we woke you,' her warm, dear voice sounds very motherly, as she strokes my forehead.

'That's fine. Sorry I missed your anniversary,' I say quietly, looking at Rose and Henry in turn. Rose in long ivory jumper and navy jeans, and Henry with his white shirt and blue trousers. I can see the strain of the last few days on their faces, a few extra wrinkles, dark marks under their eyes.

They shake their heads, and both smile at me.

Henry's voice becomes rough with emotion, 'we don't care about that. Just having you back with us is all that matters.' He walks to me, the father-figure who has always been there for me, to pick up the pieces.

Unassuming Henry who says very little, but what he does say is to the point and worth listening to. Henry who never rations his time or hugs for me. He puts his hand on my shoulder and leans into me, 'it doesn't matter. Don't go worrying yourself over something you had no control over.'

Stu leans against the windowsill. His arms and legs are crossed. He looks relaxed. He's watching the familiar tableau of Rose, Henry and myself and a smile begins to form on his lips.

'Stuart dear, can you pass me that carrier bag from the side of the bed please?' Rose asks.

Rose seems pleased with herself and I think I know why. I watch as Stu hands her the bag and Rose carefully reaches into it and brings out a small chocolate birthday cake. 'It's not the one I had made for your birthday party, but it will do,' she smiles, taking two candles from her pocket and sticking them firm into the cake. 'We can't have you turning twenty-one without marking the occasion.'

I smile and catch Stu's slight apologetic smile.

'Thanks,' I smile with love at my little family, 'I appreciate the thought. I think cake is just what the doctor ordered!'

I give myself permission to enjoy the moment. To forget about Felix, the scrapbook, the rape and all the bad things that have happened to me from the moment Felix first drugged me. Small steps.

Part 10

DCI Brian Carter

Let me tell you something. If there is one type of crime that I really can't stand, from all my fourteen years in the police force. One thing that gets me riled more than any other crimes I've experienced and been witness to. It is crimes against women and children. Particularly sex crimes. In my mind, sexual assault against women and children is in a completely different category to other violent crimes. Of course, that's only my personal opinion.

I look at my team. It's 8.30am and we're all here, apart from Julie Leadbetter. Mike Jones, my Detective Sergeant sits at his desk, typing on the keyboard. Wisps of dark hair fall across the collar of his white shirt, as he studies something on the computer screen. He's got a bright future ahead of him. Focused, determined and ambitious. I can see him going all the way to the top. He's a good-looking guy, with a fashionable face stubble, and has an easy confidence about him. Reminds me of the actor, Richard Armitage. I hear on the grapevine that those piercing blue eyes of his have a smouldering effect on the ladies. Don't tell his girlfriend I said that, though. I don't think she'd be very happy about that.

My IT specialist is Detective Constable Laura Sheppington, affectionately known as Shep to those who know her well. Her confident stride, shoulder length red hair and pierced nose stud, brings much needed colour to the unit. I like that she's not afraid to say what's on her mind. What she doesn't know about cracking passwords, finding information on mobile phones and electronic devices isn't worth knowing. She's an integral part of the team.

Finally, there is Police Constable Julie Leadbetter, who is covering maternity leave for DC Josie Lampton. Julie is studying for her Detective Constable exam, and I've decided, I'm keeping her on the team. She doesn't know that yet, that she'll be a permanent member of the team, when she completes her DC training. I like Julie, she's like a sniffer dog, if something doesn't feel right, she'll keep chipping at it until she discovers what it is.

Julie is calm, considered and totally professional. She's the quiet one of the team. With her short brown bob, cute freckles and heart-shaped face, she's very easy on the eye. I'm attracted to her, but at this point in time, I would never admit that to another living soul. Of course, I would never act upon my feelings because we need to maintain a professional cohesive working team. That's what I constantly tell myself.

I walk to the incident board, with my open case file, and wait for the others to follow me. There are photos of Jenny and Felix Gloverman, Stuart Greyson, and Henry and Rose Dean, which I put up first thing when I got in at 8am. It's always strange seeing your own writing on the board, summaries, names, history. Mike has added several photos of the Summer House and the box Jenny was held hostage in. Shep has put Stuart's typed note and a photo of the hidden safe and its contents, under Mike's paperwork. Together, we are building a picture of what happened to Jenny Gloverman, and where or how we might find her uncle.

Shep follows my lead and pushes her wheeled desk chair closer to the board. Julie walks into the room with her phone in one hand, and a dark blue jacket in the other, she strides purposefully to her desk, throws the coat over a black padded chair, and dips her head to take off her trademark black crossover bag. Picking up a notepad and pen, she pushes her desk chair across the floor to

Shep. She looks cool, calm and collected in the black and white colours of her police uniform, low heels and captivating ocean-blue eyes.

'Sorry, that was the hospital about Jenny. Nothing to worry about. I'll update everyone in a minute,' she says to the team.

She looks my way, and I can't help but nod my head and offer a brief smile to let her know, without words, that it's all right. For a moment, I imagine I see the ghost of a smile on her face, a brightness in her eyes when I'd smiled at her.

'Ready?' I say, looking over at Mike, who's still engrossed with his computer screen. The whirring sound of the printer coming to life, and I clear my throat, to alert him that we're ready.

'Sorry,' he says, standing up out of his chair, he reaches across his desk to take a sheet of paper from the printer and moves towards our small group. He stops at Shep's wooden desk, places the paper on the desk and leans his bottom casually against the edge. His arms and feet are crossed and he's deep in thought.

I quickly outline what we think we know happened to Jenny Gloverman.

'Late last Friday evening, Jenny was invited for a nightcap in the Blue Room at Gateshead, the family estate in Stadhampton, Oxfordshire by her paternal uncle, Felix Gloverman.

'According to his bank details, Gloverman had recently ordered the drug, Rohypnol from a company he found online, last month. We think he added the drug to a glass of brandy he served to Jenny.'

'Possibly the clean glasses that were found in the dishwasher,' Julie adds.

Shep looked up from her notes. 'The drug was found in her bloodstream?'

Julie nods and scribbles a few comments onto her pad.

'Yes,' I answer, checking the board, and a sadness sweeps over me when I see the photo of Jenny's face. 'And, we have the bottle which was left at the Summer House. It's being analysed as we speak.'

'The next bit is hazy,' I look to Mike, who nods briefly. 'We think he followed her to her room and waited for her to pass out. Jenny admits to feeling suddenly very tired as she undressed herself and put on her nightwear.'

Mike pushes off the table and walks to the board. He points to a photo of Jenny's bedroom, 'Stuart Greyson, Jenny's boyfriend, confirms that this was Jenny's usual bedtime routine, consisted of putting her worn clothes in the laundry basket in her bathroom.'

'Good. At some point Felix took Jenny's car keys and carried her to her car where he drove the short distance to the Summer House,' I say, following the thread of the story.

The long dark piece of storage furniture that Jenny had been kept in, stares at me from the incident board. It gave me the creeps just thinking about being locked in there with the lid closed. It must have been horrific.

'Once he had her where he wanted her,' Mike's voice is flat, disconnected from the subject matter he's talking about, 'he put Jenny in a large wooden mahogany chest. Or, as Jenny calls it, the box.'

I pointed to the two photos of the box. The photo on the right was the inside of the box, showing where Gloverman had cut out a small eight-centimetre squared area to talk to Jenny through. Bloody hell, it looked so crude, as though he'd used an implement with a serrated edge to do the job.

'Felix had fashioned a mesh section into the side of the box, and it looks like he used this to communicate with her,' I told them.

'He'd also added a padlock to secure the box. When Jenny woke, she found a water bottle which Felix had left for her. She had no idea that he had tampered with it and added Rohypnol to the liquid.'

'Poor woman. She must have been terrified,' Shep's brows pull together in a frown. She's angry, and I don't blame her. I wouldn't mind taking a pop at him myself when we finally catch up with him.

'We know he took her to the bathroom and put a hood over her head that, unknown to him, she could see through. At that point, she realised it was her uncle and where she was being held.'

The group listens quietly. They know most of it, but the point of the debrief is that we all have the same information and assess where we are, so that we can work out our next steps.

I look at the team, 'we also know, from Jenny that, when she was returned to the box, Gloverman took the water bottle away. He did this in a calculated move to ensure that when he returned the water bottle with a stronger dose of Rohypnol that she would be desperately thirsty and would drink the whole bottle.'

Serious faces glance at each other, the air in the room becomes heavy. Depressive. I know what they're thinking. How the hell could someone do that to another person, let alone to their niece? Julie closes her eyes, shaking her head in disbelief.

Walking to the opposite side of the board, I begin to feel a tightness in my shoulder blades, as anger builds up inside me. Anger for what has happened to this young woman. No person should have to go through that. And, no person has the right to do what Felix Gloverman did to his niece.

I rub my hand over my forehead and through my hairline. The team sit quietly, waiting.

'He kept her lightly drugged and she remembered him stroking her inappropriately when he took her to the bathroom. Later, he gave her a couple of muesli bars, but no water.'

My limbs feel heavy. The emotional stress, the dead weight that comes with every case that involves torture, kidnap, rape and murder, settles deep within me, and I tell them, 'the second and final time that Felix came for her, he gave her the drugged water bottle. Within a short period of time she had passed out. We think that it is around this time that he raped her.'

The silence in the room said it all. The feeling of anger was palpable, I wanted to punch something hard, just to release the emotion pushing down on my chest.

'Bastard.' Shep folds her arms in a defensive gesture, and stares at the photos on the board. 'What sicko gets off raping someone who isn't even conscious?'

I shuffle my dark brown shoes, focus my eyes on the intricate patterns in the leather, so that I don't say anything too unprofessional. 'He's a sick person, that's for sure.'

'Mike. Do you want to pick up from when Stuart Greyson calls 999?' I walk to the desk he's leaning against and watch as he nods and takes over.

Mike walks to the board and points to Stuart Greyson's photo.

'Stuart Greyson, 22, lives with his parents. He studies Business and Management at Bournemouth University. Like Jenny, he's only got seven months to go before he completes his degree. He's been seeing Jenny for about six months. On the night of the kidnap he and Jenny had spent the evening at Gateshead. They'd had a takeout pizza. He left around 11pm.

Shep raises her hand, 'can we confirm that he left at 11?'

'Yes,' Julie flicked through her notes, 'Henry Dean confirmed he'd seen Stuart saying goodnight to Jenny, at that time.'

I nod and wait for Mike to continue, 'at 2.45pm, on Saturday 18th October, the emergency services received a call from Stuart Greyson asking for police assistance regarding the disappearance of Jenny. Greyson was calling from Gateshead, the family estate.

I raise my hand to butt in, 'and, here's where it gets interesting. Jenny Greyson turned twenty-one yesterday. On this milestone her net worth increased to ten billion pounds.' I hear an intake of breath, and Julie shakes her head, whilst Shep whistles. 'Jenny is now legally able to step into the helm of running the Gloverman Corporation. So, now we've got motive. The loss of income, jealousy.'

Mike looks my way and I dip my head, for him to continue. 'There were no clothes missing, apart from Jenny's pyjamas which are usually under her pillow, and her car keys. Her phone, handbag and purse were left at the house. Her bed had not been slept in. It was as if she'd disappeared like a ghost in the night.'

I study the photo of the uncle on the board, the face of the monster makes my stomach turn. With his short black curly hair, matching moustache, a pot belly that sits on a six-foot tall frame, he has that entitled smirk and arrogance about him. What I wouldn't give to be able to smash that face into a very hard object. Repeatedly.

There's a niggle I can't quite put my finger on, is he really working on his own? Who's helping him? I share this with the team, 'Something doesn't add up. I think someone's helping him, but I don't who.'

Mike walks with confidence to me, he leans over the desk and picks up the paper he'd taken from the printer earlier, and a pin. He pins the paper on the board. 'Andy Naylor from Naylor

Property Services,' he states, pointing to the photo of a thin faced man with short blonde hair, sporting a long nose and triangular chin, 'his former university buddy isn't answering his phone. I've got an address, so I plan on taking a trip to Bristol today.'

'Good idea,' I tell him, 'I'll speak to a friend of mine at Bristol nick, see if they've got any interest in Naylor.' I make a mental note to do this when I've finished the debrief.

I turn to Julie and smile, 'Julie, what updates have you got on Jenny?'

Julie clears her throat. 'On the whole Jenny is doing well, all things considered. Dr Tracker reports that she's now had the second and final dose of the emergency contraception medication, so that should put paid to any unwanted pregnancies. In addition, she's had antibiotics and undergone several tests to ensure there's no infection.'

'Tosser,' Shep cuts in quietly, crossing her legs to shift position. Julie turns to her and gives her a nod.

'Yes, he is,' Julie agrees. 'Jenny has also seen the resident psychiatrist and will see him again before she's discharged. The hospital will book her several sessions following discharge. The psychiatrist reports she's doing well, although she's exhibiting strong feelings of guilt, that she's somehow precipitated what her uncle did to her. He says that this is not uncommon.'

Mike looks at the board, studying Jenny's injured feet and hands. 'We need to find this guy and nail him to the ground,' he growls, trying to control his anger.

'Finding him is our top priority, Mike,' I reassure him as I sift through the toxicology report in my file.

'Anything else, Julie?' I ask, deliberately not catching her eyes. This was work.

'Yes. Just one last thing, Doctor Tracker said that they took Jenny's cannula out last night, she's eating and drinking well. They're aiming to discharge her tomorrow or Thursday.'

'I think we need to make sure that we have someone guarding the Summer House, as well as the main house,' I say, thinking out loud. My eyes catch Mike's, 'can you sort that out before you head to Bristol?'

Mike nods, finds a pen and writes a reminder on his hand.

'Shep,' I look her way, 'where are we on the note, laptop, emails, company finances, phone history etc?'

'Well, I'm working through it slowly. I've spoken to the Gloverman Corporation lawyer and he's being very cagey.'

'Julie and I will visit the Corporation this morning. I want to chat to Amy Wilder, Gloverman's PA, see what she knows. Has the warrant come through to check the Gloverman finances, Gloverman's finances and the man's office yet? Who's next in charge and where is the company based?'

'Nothing yet,' Shep says, looking at the dark grey fax machine, standing on a wooden table next to my office, and as if the machine had heard her words, the machine comes to life and begins printing.

Shep turns to Julie with a small smile, 'spooky.'

I walk over to the fax machine, grab the paper, scan it quickly, before folding it and pushing it into my trouser pocket. 'Shep, I want you to concentrate on any patterns between the company and Gloverman. I want to know if he's been taking money.'

'Yes, Boss. The company are based at Ditton Park near Slough,' Shep continues, 'the deputy CEO is David Dueller. I'll forward you their details.'

‘Thanks. Can you give the PA a call to say that we’ll be visiting them this morning?’ I close my file and look at Shep, ‘anything on the typed note given to Stuart Greyson yet?’

‘Nothing yet,’ she replies. ‘I’ve passed it onto the lab to check for fingerprints. I’ll give them a call first thing tomorrow. His laptop is very interesting. He has huge amounts of deleted history over the past month, which I’m working my way through. He’s got a lot; I mean a lot of deleted porn in his history. The porn is quite specific to girls as young as fourteen years.’

‘Shit,’ Mike stands up and looks at me.

‘Looks like we’ve got a would-be paedophile on our hands,’ I shake my head. I can’t believe we haven’t heard of Felix Gloverman before now. How did we not have him on our radar?

‘He had his phone with him, but I think he dumped it,’ Shep explains, ‘he’s probably got a burner phone by now, so we can’t trace it. I found several interesting emails. The first was from about eight weeks ago. It’s from an antique shop in Stow on the Wold which piqued my interest. It’s related to the delivery of a large mahogany chest.’

‘Bingo! Give them a call and see if they can provide a description of the buyer and a copy of the receipt,’ I tell her.

‘There were four email receipts from different suppliers for 2mg of Flunitrazepan, otherwise known as Rohypnol,’ Shep announces steadily, trying to keep the anger out of her voice. It makes you realise how vulnerable you can be when accepting drinks from strangers, and people you know.

‘Right,’ I say, my voice is hard, commanding, ‘we know Felix is in Bristol. And we know he’s got access to money. Let’s find this guy. Was he close to anyone at work? My gut tells me that he’s reached out to Naylor, so it’ll be interesting to see what he’s got to say for himself, when you catch up with him Mike.’

‘The thing that keeps coming back to me,’ I muse aloud, to no one in particular, ‘is the feeling that he will return to Gateshead. I’m not sure if he’s aware that we’ve found Jenny. I’m pretty sure that he doesn’t know we’ve found the safe and its contents. My gut tells me that he’ll come back for the contents, or for Jenny. He will need his fix of her photos and his drawings to keep his fantasies alive.’

‘Let’s meet back here at, say,’ I look at my watch, ‘4.30pm to see where we are and to sum up the day. It’ll give SOCO enough time to see if they’ve got anything from the safe, the scrapbook, passports and the rest of the room. His fingerprints aren’t on file, but we have his DNA.’

A shuffling of chairs and murmurings follow as the group disperses to begin their tasks. Mike makes a call and I half catch the words ‘additional protection’ and ‘Jenny Gloverman’ as I walk to my office. My mind is whirling in ever increasing circles as I mentally tick off information to chase and check.

Back in my office, I haul my black computer chair forward so I can rest my arms on the desk. Taking my phone from my pocket I search my contacts for Edward Creakston and type his number into my office landline, I quickly press the speaker mode button. The dialling tone rings for a while before a voice I haven’t heard for nearly a decade, eight years ago to be precise, answers. The voice is loud, brusque and very familiar.

‘Bristol CID. DCI Creakston.’

I can’t help but smile, fond memories of working with Eddie spring to mind. We’d shared a case for six weeks and took to each other straight away. ‘Eddie. It’s Brian. Brian Carter from Oxford.’ I hope he remembers me! I pick up the receiver and turn off speaker and balance the receiver between my shoulder and my cheek.

'Brian? Brian Carter from Oxford?' he says jovially, 'Well, isn't that a way to brighten my day? That's a name I haven't heard in a while.' I can almost hear his questioning smile filtering its way down the phone line.

Despite his rough exterior, he's as soft as brush when it comes to affairs of the heart such as loyalty and friendship. If you're a friend of his, you're one for life. His moral compass mirrors my own, I think that's why we got on so well. He's the one you'd want to have your last pint with, if the world was about to end.

Eddie's short dark mop of hair must be thinning by now. He was physically fit, slightly short in stature, but made up for it with his purposeful long strides and air of confidence.

'The one and only, mate. How are things in Bristol?' I ask him. It's good to hear his voice.

'Things are fine here,' Eddie's rough voice softens. 'The nice folk of Bristol are keeping me busy. How are you?'

'I'm good, thanks,' I can picture us sitting in his local pub, sipping our pints after work. Good memories.

'Look,' I tell him, 'I've got my DS coming to Bristol this morning. He's visiting a chap called Andy Naylor of Naylor Property Services. I wanted to let you know that he's asking a few questions in your area. I also wanted to ask if you've got Andy Naylor on your radar at all?'

There's a quiet knock on my door and I swivel my chair to see who it is. Julie. I curl my fingers forward to motion for her to enter. She does so, with her black crossover shoulder bag accentuating her petite frame. Her jacket falls from her hand and she rests against my desk, near to the phone. She looks at me intently, her dark blue eyes piercing mine, as she watches me speak.

For a minute I forget what I'm doing, as I wonder what it would be like to lay her down on the desk, kiss her thoroughly and give her an early birthday present. A pink blush travels up her neck, slowly filling her cheeks and she folds her arms over her chest, as if she can read my mind.

'What has this Andy Naylor done to deserve your attention?' Eddie's deep voice booms through the receiver which I've managed to wedge under my chin, and instantly blocks my rampant thoughts. Jesus, Carter. Get a grip.

'I'm chasing a man by the name of Felix Gloverman, an old friend of Naylor's, who drugged, kidnapped and raped his niece a few days ago. I alerted the BTM Transport Police yesterday and they've passed the message on to stations in the area. We think he's now holed out in Bristol.'

There's a sharp inhale before he speaks. 'Great! That's all I need. Another bloody pervert. What makes you think he's on my patch?'

I take a deep breath, look at Julie and slowly exhale, before speaking into the phone again. 'He abandoned his car at Chippenham Railway station yesterday. CCTV has Gloverman arriving at Bristol Temple Meads railway station at 15.38pm yesterday. He came in from Chippenham. That's as much as we know. My DS, Mike Jones is visiting Naylor Property Services this morning. No answer from Naylor's phone as yet.'

I can hear the tapping of keys as Eddie checks his database for information on Naylor. 'I'm checking, but nothing's turned up on him,' he says, as he continues his search. 'The man is clean. He's never even had a parking ticket. Can you fax me a photo of Felix Gloverman and I'll get CID to keep a look out for him? Do you think Naylor is hiding him in one of his properties?'

‘Yeah. That’s our thinking. I’d appreciate that.’ I say, pushing up out of my chair, grabbing my mobile and pushing it into my trouser pocket.

‘Get your DS to give us a call when he’s near to Naylor’s place and if someone is free, I’ll send them to him as back-up,’ he tells me. This, right here, is why this man is a good police officer. He cares.

‘Cheers mate,’ I say sincerely, ‘I appreciate that.’

‘Mine’s a large whisky, next time we meet Bri.’

‘You’re on.’ I smile and disconnect him.

‘Right, I suppose I shouldn’t procrastinate any longer. Ditton Park it is,’ I tell Julie as I grab my coat from the hook and head out of the office. I need to speak to Mike before I go. He’s at his desk with his phone sitting against his ear, he’s sorting out the police guard for the Summer House. Good man.

‘Mike?’ I say as I walk over to Shep. ‘Can you call Bristol force when you get near Naylor’s place? Shep will give you their number. Ask for DCI Edward Creakston. They’ll try to come and give you a hand. A bit of gentle persuasion.’

‘Will do, Boss. Thanks.’

‘Shep,’

She’s furiously making notes on a pad, from information on her computer screen. Her neat writing looks slightly odd next to her flourishing doodles scrawled randomly around the page.

‘Shep?’

She looks up, ‘sorry, Boss. Thought I’d found something.’

‘It’s fine. Can you fax a photo of Felix Gloverman to DCI Edward Creakston at Bristol Police Station? Put it for his attention or it might get side-tracked. Thanks. Right. Julie and I are off to Ditton Park. Call if anything comes up.'

'You know, you don't have to wear your uniform while you're working in this unit, Julie. You can wear civvies, the choice is yours,' I mutter as we take the stairs to the car park.

'Boss,' she acknowledges quietly, her face facing forward as though she doesn't want to look at me, 'I'll think about it.'

'Up to you. Thought you might feel more comfortable.'

'Thanks. I'll still think about it though. I'm used to wearing this uniform, it feels natural. Wearing civvies to work might not feel so normal.'

That's the most she's said to me that wasn't work related. Ever. I'm taken by surprise, which to my frustration, sends a warm feeling to my stomach. I'm supposed to be her boss, I need to keep our relationship professional, but I can't help but feel that I'm going to miss out on something quite unique if I don't take a leap of faith.

'You all right to drive?' I ask her, taking the car keys from my pocket and holding them out to her. As our fingers touch, a tingle sears through my hand, and I can't help but look into her eyes, to see if she felt it too. and a rose blush catches her.

'Sure,' she nods as we walk to the pool car we've been allocated. It's a black 2018 Vauxhall Insignia and a nice drive, I should know I've got one myself. I open the passenger side rear door and throw in my black raincoat. I notice that her blush makes the freckles on her face seem more pronounced against her clear skin She is a beautiful woman and I can't help a smile as I watch her bend her head slightly to take off her shoulder bag and throw that and her coat on to the backseat of the car.

I find the Ditton Park postcode, that Shep sent me, on my mobile and put the postcode into the car navigation system. I'm quiet for a while, pondering the Felix Gloverman situation. Wondering what we will find when we get there. Lawyers, the CEO, his PA, possibly someone who was close to the man. I'm hoping for a bit of luck today.

My phone rings as we make our way along the A40, towards the M40 at Milton Common. I check my watch. It's 10am already, I don't know where the time goes.

'Carter,' I answer.

'We've got fingerprints confirmed on the scrapbook and passports and they match fingerprints found on a deodorant can and aftershave bottle in Gloverman's bathroom,' Shep's voice booms through my ear. 'Oh, and I've faxed his photo to your friend at Bristol.'

'Thanks, Shep.' I press the disconnect button.

Suddenly, there's tension in the air as an expensive-looking Audi begins to tailgate us. Jesus. What is the matter with these people? Don't they know that they're one step away from causing a serious, if not fatal accident.

We're in the fast lane, Julie is already doing 50mph, which is the speed limit on this road. I turn around to try to take a photo of the registration number, but the car is too damn close. We can't move into the slower lane because it's too busy. I press a button on my phone to call the Emergency Response Team, to give details of the black Audi that's trying to drive us off the road.

'You all right?' I ask her. 'Slow down slightly.'

'Yes. Whoever it is, they're being a jerk,' she says, making me smile.

There's a gap in the slow lane and the Audi driver decides to undertake us, but not before pulling up to the side of us, winding down the side window and shouting obscenities.

I took the opportunity to snap a photo of his registration number as he almost collides with the car in front of him because he's trying to get in front of us. Car horns beep as drivers alert each other that there's a maniac on the road. I can see clearly now, it's a man. With a beard, messy shoulder-length black hair pushed behind his tunnel pierced ears and wild eyes, he looks high as a kite.

The car swerves and the driver manoeuvres the car so that it's in front of us. Shit, what a nightmare. The traffic is building up on both lanes and there's literally no place to go.

'He's playing silly buggers Julie, be careful,' I warn her. I can feel the anxiety pouring off her, as she rubs her forehead with one hand. She's doing well,

The car in front, suddenly brakes – causing Julie to do the same. I'm jolted forward, my hands bracing against the dashboard. 'Sorry,' she glances my way.

'Not your fault,' I tell her, checking the speedometer to see that we're now crawling at 30mph.

'Where the bloody hell are traffic?' I curse.

'Boss, everyone is crawling to a stop,' Julie keeps her eyes on the road, 'there must be an accident ahead.'

As we come to a standstill, Julie puts the car in neutral and applies the handbrake. The impatient Audi driver decides to try and push its way out of the lane. I'm not sure why. It's not as though he's got anywhere to go. Cars peep their horns, telling him to be careful. I faintly hear sirens, look in the wing mirror and see the blue lights of the Emergency Response drivers. Thank God.

Bump. A heavy force jolts us forward and the car immediately screeches backwards against the handbrake. Shit. Can you believe this idiot? The driver behind us panics and presses his horn several times. By sheer bloody luck we managed not to hit him. Thank God, he'd left a safe distance, between us and him.

'Jesus, did he just hit us?' Julie asks, shaking her head.

'Yeah, hold on,' I say, putting my arm across her body to protect her and bracing for impact. Audi man reverses into us again and we hear the scraping sound of metal on metal as he tries to push the car back again. This time we move back and stay back. There's a scratching sound as we grind the bumper of the car behind.

The stupid prick in the Audi has seen the blue lights and is desperately trying to get out of the traffic jam. It won't make any difference; clearly, he can't get into the slow lane and there's no space available for him to drive into.

'Bloody maniac!' I scowl, as I feel Julie's arm wrap around mine as she grabs on to my hand. Through my wing mirror I can see cars moving onto the safety barriers to allow the police car to get through. Another minute and the car will be with us.

'Thank God!' Julie says, and I give a disappointed sigh because I have to let go of her, to leave the car. I slowly unpeel her arm from mine, just as the familiar blue and white police traffic car pulls up beside us, its siren still blaring.

'Are you all right?' I ask her. She's not, her eyes are wide with shock, but she bravely nods. I open the car door and look back at her pale face. 'I'll be back in a minute,' I reassure her. I want this guy. High or not. I don't care. I take out my warrant card and walk towards the two officers.

'DCI Carter,' I announce, showing my card.

The tall, slim officer with a mop of short black hair and a slightly crooked nose introduces himself.

'Sergeant Jacobs,' he says holding out his hand. I take it and offer a firm shake. 'You called it in, Sir?' he asks.

I nod, 'yes, he tailgated us, shouted obscenities, drove in front of our car, all the time driving without due care. Then he started reversing into us, ramming us.'

I watch as the officers approach the black Audi. Let's see how big you feel when you're faced with the law. The officers haul the man out of the driver's seat, turn him around and cuff his wrists together. They read him his rights.

'I didn't do anything!' he shouts, slurring his words, 'Get your hands off me! It was this idiot, trying to wind me up. I'm going to sue you lot for police brutality, if you don't get your fucking hands off me!'

The police officers turn the man around to face me.

I lean into him, my face almost touching his. His dilated pupils show fear for a brief second. I am seething, fisting my hands at my side so that I don't grab him. Because if I do, I'll pummel him to kingdom come. 'What the hell is the matter with you? You could have killed someone!'

We stare each other down for a short while. Then I remember that Julie is still in the car and that this man is just not worth it.

'You. You little shit. Are nicked!' I growl at him, before thrusting my hands in my brown trouser pockets and strolling back to the car to inspect the damage on the front bumper. 'Cretin,' I mutter, as I look at the large dents and scratches. What an absolute arse.

'Sir,' Sergeant Jacobs walks over to me, 'can you get your car onto the hard shoulder? I'll drive the Audi, put it next to yours. We'll get recovery to pick them up.'

'Sure, no problem,' I reply, taking out my phone to order a replacement car, 'we'll wait here until our replacement arrives.'

'Great,' he says, 'I'll adjust the lanes so that you can get through.'

'Thanks for your assistance today Sergeant Jacobs. I appreciate it,' I give him a quick nod, open the door to Julie and lean in.

'Sorry about that,' I turn to Julie, as I get into the car. She looks pale, I don't blame her. I'm sure she must be shaken. I'm shaken too, 'I needed to look that prick in the eye before he was carted off to Oxford.'

'No problem,' her voice is quiet, but she's brave, this woman. So, I'm not surprised when she continues talking, 'I've called it in.'

'Great. Good job. Sergeant Jacobs is making space for us to drive onto the hard shoulder while we wait for the recovery truck and replacement car. Whichever arrives first.'

I look at her face and hold her gaze. I curl my hand into a fist to stop myself from reaching out and tracing my fingers along the soft skin of her cheek. 'You did good, Julie. Kept calm and handled the situation well. Do you want me to take over driving?'

Of course, she wouldn't want me to think she's anything but fine. 'No. I'm fine boss. Thanks,' her soft voice replies.

Sergeant Jacobs knocks on the windscreen and indicates that he's cleared space for us to drive onto the hard shoulder. Slowly, Julie switches on the ignition, puts the car into gear, takes off the handbrake and manoeuvres the car diagonally to the cleared space allocated to us on the hard shoulder. The car rattles and creaks as it moves. Apparently, the front bumper has taken more of a beating that I'd originally thought.

I'd said earlier, I was hoping for a bit of luck today. Well, this isn't what I'd envisaged when I'd said that. However, being cooped up in a car, in very close proximity to someone with whom I've developed a bit of an infatuation, can be almost construed as the glass half full rather than half empty scenario.

The engine is switched off.

I disconnect my seat belt and indicate to Julie to do the same. 'We need to collect our stuff and stand by the car.'

She nods her head and 'How long do you think they'll be?' she asks, opening her car door. I mimic her actions, and we both reach into the back seat from our respective sides and collect our coats and she dips her head to drape her bag over her shoulder. I gently take her arm and lead her to the bushes on the far side of the car, away from the now fast-moving traffic.

'I don't know. Hopefully, not too long,' I quickly scan the scene and note that the police officers are distracted. 'Here, give me your hands, I bet they're freezing,' I say, holding my hands out. Without hesitation she slips her cold hands into mine and I cannot help but watch her, as she stares down at our joined hands.

I begin to rub warmth into her cold soft skin.

'As soon as we can, we'll stop somewhere for a coffee. We could both do with one,' I announce, still rubbing her hands. Her eyes close momentarily, and I'm relieved to feel the warmth start to return.

'Boss?' she queries, her freckles catching the sunlight.

'Call me Brian, when we're alone. This situation is awkward enough without having a needless hierarchy.'

Her face tilts upwards and her eyes catch mine. Long eyelashes that frame her beautiful sapphire coloured eyes, that mesmerise me, make it impossible to look away.

'Boss,' her soft voice holds a questioning tone.

'Brian,' I remind her.

She smiles shyly, 'Brian. Do you think this is wise?'

‘Wise? What do you mean?’ I realise that I’m still holding her hands.

‘I mean, the changing of our relationship. The touching, the first names,’ she says quietly, with some hesitation.

‘I hear what you’re saying,’ I tell her, ‘it won’t change our professional relationship. I’ll make sure of it. But there’s something here, between us. I’d like to explore it at some point. Maybe not now, or tomorrow but at some point. The ball is in your court Julie, if you want to explore further, then tell me. If not, nothing between us will change. I’m not that kind of guy.’

She takes her hands back and holds them on her pink cheeks. She looks flushed. Taking a deep breath, she looks steadily at me as if seeing me for the first time. ‘I didn’t know,’ she says softly, ‘that you felt this way, I mean. I know I’ll probably talk myself out of this by tomorrow morning but before I do, I need to tell you that I feel that something too. And, I think I’d like to explore it. It’s a big change though, can you give me a little time to think about it?’

‘Of course, there’s no pressure,’ I reassure her, secretly pleased that she feels the same. I can’t stop the grin that begins to form on my face. The sound of someone clearing their throat brings me back to the reason why we’re standing on the side of the road. Julie’s eyes dart over my shoulder, and I turn to find Sergeant Jacobs waiting patiently to talk to me.

‘Is the car here?’ I ask him.

‘Yes Sir. We’ll park it next to you,’ he reaches to his shoulder and speaks into his radio.

‘Great. Thanks Sergeant,’ I say and look across at Julie, ‘time to go.’

We walk to the almost identical car, another black Insignia which is moving slowly to a halt beside us. A slim, good-looking uniformed police officer with short black hair, steps from the car.

'Hey Pete,' Julie's voice calls from behind me, 'how are you?' I can hear the warmth in her voice as she walks past me and puts her hand on Pete's shoulder.

'Julie,' Pete smiles, and his large hand rests briefly on top of her hand. On his shoulder. A big, warm smile brightens her face, making it obvious that something special has been shared between them in the past. Julie turns to me, her arms out, gesturing to make an introduction.

'Pete. This is my boss. DCI Brian Carter,' Julie explains, her breathing is quick, and I can hear the quiver in her voice as though she's embarrassed to be seen with me. Shit.

I nod. Try to smile, but I'm annoyed. A bit jealous, if I'm honest.

Pete puts his hand out, 'PC Uxton, Sir. I brought your car.'

I bite back a snide reply, and take his hand in a brief, firm handshake.

'Thanks,' I mutter. What is the matter with me today? It's not Pete's fault I'm annoyed with him.

'How is your wife? And the kids?' asks Julie. The breath I hadn't realised I was holding, suddenly caught up with me, as I let out a huge sigh of relief.

'They're good, Julie. All good. Anyway,' he looks at me, 'I'd better get going. I'm grabbing a lift back with one of Sergeant Jacob's team. It's all yours, Sir.' Pete hands me the car keys.

'Cheers, Pete,' I say, taking the keys. I begrudgingly like him.

Sergeant Jacobs heads our way, still talking into the radio. 'Sir, the sweeper has just finished clearing the debris. You're free to go.'

'Thanks, Sergeant. If you're ever in my neck of the woods, pop in. I owe you a pint.'

'That's very kind of you, Sir,' he smiles, before turning away to instruct his officers to let our car through.

Thankfully, the car is clean, and the petrol tank is full. 'I'll drive,' I tell Julie after we've dropped our coats and her bag into the car. Julie nods, offering no argument. I guess she's not bothered about driving for the moment.

I check my phone for a motorway service station before we get to Slough and put the postcode into the car navigation system.

'Right, we'll stop for a quick coffee at Beaconsfield Services,' I say, pulling the car away from the incident site.

'Sounds good,' Julie answers, 'I could do with a stiff drink really,' and I chuckle at her joke.

My mind focuses on work and what we need to do when we reach Ditton, 'So, when we get to the Gloverman place we're looking for the Deputy CEO, David Dueller and Gloverman's PA, Amy Wilder. I'm assuming they will have their lawyers on standby to cover their back. That's how these places usually work.'

'Want me to talk to Wilder? While you start on Dueller?' she offers.

'Yes. We'll divide and conquer,' I grin. My mind still wonders about Pete and his relationship with Julie. It's completely none of my business, but I can't get it out of my thoughts. My curiosity gets the better of me.

'Pete. Were you and he?' I ask.

'A couple?' she finishes, her eyes flicking my way, 'Yes, a long time ago. When we were both doing our initial police training.'

'Was it serious?' I ask, my heart thudding. Stupid heart.

'At the time, yes. But we were both young and ambitious. Then he met Beth, and we sort of grew apart.'

'He left you for another woman?' I queried, a bolt of anger shoots through my chest. He hurt her.

'Yes. But it was all right. I think we both knew we were fizzling out, but we didn't want to upset each other. We were too frightened to say the words.'

I think about what she's saying. It's hard putting yourself out there. Not wanting to hurt someone or make them feel uneasy. I feel a bit guilty for making Julie step outside our professional relationship today. Not guilty enough to want to take it back, though.

After a quick coffee break, we finally arrive at Ditton Park. We stop at the security kiosk where a thick set, ageing security guard wearing a beige shirt and large black glasses, pops his head out of his open window and asks for our credentials. I show him my warrant card and wait patiently for him to make a phone call, hand over two red visitor lanyards and direct us to the visitor car park.

Grabbing our coats and Julie's bag from the back of the car, I lock it up, put the keys in my trouser pocket. We briskly walk across the immaculate landscaped gardens towards the circular fountain that leads directly to the entrance of the building. The concrete walkway lies proudly over the water filled moat that surrounds the front of the building. With its wildlife, including a set of five ducklings swimming behind their mother following the slight current of the water, I can't help but be impressed by the enormous glass and steel building before us. What a place to work.

As the floor to ceiling automatic glass doors open, we are greeted by another security guard. Tall and brooding with short cropped hair. His shirt is tight and the buttons strain against his chest and upper torso as though he's outgrown it.

'DCI Carter?' he asks, with a Polish accent.

'Yes,' I reply, absently twisting my lanyard as I look around the entrance hall, 'and this is PC Leadbetter.'

'Wow,' I say looking at the red and black sleek Formula Three racing car, displayed in the centre of the room, 'nice car,' my eye catches Julie and I watch with interest as she raises one eyebrow.

'It is, Sir,' he answers bluntly. 'Please follow me,' he gestures towards an unmanned glossy white desk with several tablets raised by a swivel arm, 'can you please sign into our visitor database? You'll find Mr Dueller and Miss Wilder on the second floor.'

I sign us in, we look around the huge glass and white painted open space for the stairs or a lift. At that moment a pretty, rather thin woman, with long blonde hair and a heart-shaped face, walks towards us. She looks to be in her early twenties and is dressed in a just above the knee, dark blue linen dress, a grey cardigan and dark blue low-heeled shoes. I can't help but notice there's a roundness to her tummy. I look across at Julie, catch her eyes as they flicker across the front of her dress, she looks my way and nods in agreement. I'm no expert but she looks around five months pregnant.

The woman smiles, a warm sincere smile that makes me think of innocence and cruelty in equal measure. She leans forward to face me, and for the first time I notice that her eyes are a little red, as though she's been crying. She holds out her hand, 'DCI Carter?'

I don't know why but I'm surprised that her voice is so soft and mellow. I take her warm outstretched hand and give it a brisk shake. 'Miss Wilder?' I query.

'Yes,' she smiles, 'please call me Amy.'

I don't know why but I feel like she's trying to work something out, trying to assess me. 'This is PC Julie Leadbetter. Thank you for seeing us this morning,' I look at my watch and shake my head, it's now 11.50am. Bloody hell, where did the time go this morning?

Amy Wilder's lips tilt into a warm smile as she offers her hand to Julie, 'lovely to meet you. I'll take you to my office, please follow me,' letting go of Julie's hand. 'I know it's only two floors, but it's a habit that's hard to break,' she says apologetically pressing the button to summon the lift.

The lift is quite small, it's mostly steel and glass and there's not a lot of privacy. As the lift jolts to move upwards, Amy Wilder puts a protective hand to her tummy.

'Sorry, the movement always wakes up baby.'

'How far along are you?' asks Julie, a smile forming on her face that lifts her freckles.

'Five and a half months.'

'Over the morning sickness yet?' Julie asks. How did she know that? There are so many things I would like to know about her, if only she will give us a chance.

'Yes, thank goodness,' Amy says with a sigh, 'just need to get through the next few months, before the hard work really begins.'

The lift comes to a discreet halt and we let Amy lead the way as we walk through an open white painted space which is enhanced by floor to ceiling glass windows. A corridor appears to the right of us and we follow Amy to a set of glass doors which open automatically as we approach, and we find ourselves in a large white painted office.

The desk is beechwood in colour and looks expensive. On it sits an open silver laptop, a scribble pad, and a full pen pot. There is also a white switchboard phone system and a grey and wooden name slate that reads 'Miss Amy Wilder, PA'. A black leather swivel chair sits snugly behind the desk.

There is a long matching beechwood storage unit in front of the large window. On it sits an espresso machine, a thriving lily plant with stunning dark purple leaves and a white desk-top printer. As I look around the office, I wonder how well the Gloverman Corporation pays their employees, in relation to the grand opulence of this building.

I scan the room and see the wooden beech door that makes part of the back wall. A brass plaque is embossed with black letters that reads, Felix Gloverman, CEO. The inner sanctum of a suspected paedophile and kidnapper. Snapping out of my reverie, I remember why we came here.

'I need to talk to David Dueller,' I look out of the window at the landscaped gardens and the pathways that lead over meadows and across bridges.

'Of course,' Amy looks pensive, her smile seems almost forced as she moves to the white switchboard phone, picks up the receiver and presses a button, 'I'll give him a call, tell him you're here.'

'I'd appreciate that,' I say, moving across the room to Julie while Amy is on the phone. 'Can you check out Felix's office, see if anything looks out of place or odd,' I say quietly, 'find out from Amy Wilder what sort of boss he is, what it's like to work here. Find out if he has any close contacts.'

'Yes, Sir. Sorry Sir. I'll bring them to you,' Amy sounds apologetic and her voice wavers as she speaks to the deputy CEO of the company. Her shoulders slump as she places the phone back onto its base. For a moment she looks down at the floor. I may not be Sherlock Holmes, but it doesn't take much effort to realise that David Dueller may turn out to be a nasty bully.

'I'll take you to Mr Dueller,' she says, her brow is furrowed as if being near David Dueller is her least favourite thing to do.

'Thanks. I don't want to get you in anymore trouble, just point me in the right direction and I'll find my own way,' I say as I follow her, 'PC Leadbetter will stay here to look around Mr Gloverman's office and ask a few more questions.'

Amy's shoulders sag with relief. 'Thanks,' she says after we step through the automatic doors, 'if you follow the corridor back to the lift area and turn right, you'll find the adjacent corridor with another set of automatic doors. They'll lead you to his PA, Samantha and she'll take you in to him.'

'It's like visiting the Prime Minister,' I mutter.

'Oh yes,' she says, with a grim smile on her face, 'since Felix, I mean Mr Gloverman missed a couple of important meetings at the weekend and didn't turn up to work today, Mr Dueller as the Deputy stood in, to take his place. He's doing this with erm, great enthusiasm.'

'Thanks for the heads up, no need to come any further. I'll be fine,' I reassure the young pregnant woman, before I turn to walk down the corridor. God, it doesn't feel like a good place to work. Clearly, there are power struggles going on here, people ready and waiting to take over the large corporation.

I make my way to the adjacent corridor and through the automatic doors, I'm greeted by a short white-haired woman in her early sixties, wearing a pale blue button up cardigan and matching skirt. Her office is almost identical to Amy Wilder's, with its beech desk and unit under the window. Devoid of personal possessions, this room looks very clinical.

'DCI Carter,' she says in a soft deep voice as she peeks at me over her dark blue glasses, 'Mr Dueller is waiting for you. Please go straight through.' Her hand rises to knock on the heavy wooden door belonging to David Dueller, Deputy CEO.

I murmur my thanks and push the brass handle on the door to enter. I don't know what I expected David Dueller to look like, but his appearance took me by surprise. He had unkempt brown hair that hung in wisps about his chubby red face, a face which was currently being dabbed with a white handkerchief to catch the sweat that dripped from his temple.

His suit was brown, with thick-set shapes around his shoulders suggesting that they were well padded, possibly to give him height. It's been a long time since I've seen a man wearing shoulder-pads. Dueller's eyes were so small that it was hard to see their colour and even harder to read behind his words and mannerisms.

David Dueller moves from his standing position behind his black desk, 'DCI Carter, I presume,' in a high-pitched voice that seems to bounce off the walls. He holds out his hand to shake mine, and I look at it, wondering if I really want to shake that sweaty, wet, white handkerchief he was still holding.

He looks at my face, and I see the nervous tick that settleds high on his cheekbone before my gaze moves to his hands. He shoves the white cloth into his brown jacket pocket. 'Sorry about that,' he screeches. Shit. What a strange sound. I feel the urge to burst into laughter. Without thinking, I quickly shake his hand and discreetly wipe my hand on my trouser clad bottom to sweep off the stickiness.

‘Thank you for seeing me, Mr Dueller,’ I say calmly. I don’t want to upset him, not with his tick and that high voice. ‘I want to talk to you about Felix Gloverman,’ I look at the blue cushioned wooden chair by the desk and stride to it, ‘do you mind if I sit?’

‘Of course,’ he says, attempting to smile. ‘Please do,’ he moves to his dark red leather chair and I wince when it creaks, as he slumps into it, ‘what can I tell you about Felix? Have you still not found him?’

‘I’m afraid we haven’t found him yet,’ I fold my hands and look at David Dueller. He takes his handkerchief from his pocket, and nervously pats it across his cheeks and forehead. ‘Do you have any idea where he might be?’

‘No,’ he shakes his head vigorously. ‘I’ve no idea, he left me to pick up the pieces when he didn’t turn up for work today. He had two meetings booked with new clients over the weekend and one of them left a message to say that Felix never arrived, the other turned up at 9am this morning, demanding to see him. It was very unpleasant,’ he says looking distressed.

I take the search warrant out of my pocket and unfold it, ‘here’s a search warrant to look around his office and to check the finances of the company.’

‘I’m sorry, but you’ll have to go through our lawyers for that,’ Dueller’s voice becomes considerably louder and squeakier.

‘Sorry, but the warrant says otherwise,’ I say, standing up. A loud banging breaks the stand-off. It sounds like furniture being thrown. The hairs on my arm suddenly stand up when I hear male and female voices shouting at each other. There’s a loud scream and I’m heading out of his office. A chill runs down my spine when I hear Julie’s clear voice, shouting.

‘Stop right there! Thames Valley Police!’ There’s a short silence and then, she shouts, ‘Hey!’ I hear her call my name, ‘Brian!’

'What's that noise?' Duellers distant voice calls, as I run past Samantha to the adjacent office. I call out to her to get security to Amy Wilder's office asap. Jesus! My heart is racing as I pick up the pace, I don't know what's going on here, but it doesn't sound good. I think the women are in trouble. As I reach the lift area and turn to run down the corridor that leads to Amy's office, I'm faced with two men in dark almost black suits, heading my way.

'Hey!' I shout, half-running towards them. 'Stop! Thames Valley Police. You two are under arrest!' The men, in their late twenties with tied-back black hair, just look at each other and then at me.

'We don't think so,' the slightly taller one says, with an Italian accent as he continues walking my way. I watch in anger as 'tall guy' takes a knife from inside his jacket, 'out of our way!'

Oh, it's like that is it? Today has been bugger of a day, I've been car rammed by a bloody Audi driver, high on whatever drug he could get hold of. I've had to wait for another pool car and we're now behind schedule. Meanwhile that paedophile Felix Gloverman, is enjoying his last few days of freedom somewhere in Bristol. I am pissed as hell.

'Really?' I growl, 'Is that all you've fucking got?' I note that he's lowered the knife to his side and that the sharp end is pointing to the floor, so I raise my foot to kick his knee backwards and enjoy hearing a sharp crack, as I watch his leg buckle beneath him. I may not be into martial arts, but I know how to look after myself.

'Shit man!' the man mutters, leaning against the wall and rubbing his knee, 'That fucking hurt!'

His friend moves my way. 'Do you know who we are?' he leans in menacingly, 'you mess with us and.' But I didn't give a flying fuck who they were. I tighten my shoulders and force my head back, just far enough to get momentum, then I give it all I have and butt him, in the top part of his face, deliberately catching his nose and forehead. He didn't finish his sentence. It hurt like a bitch, but it was worth every second of pain.

'Boss!' someone shouts. The urgency in Julie's voice, makes me realise that I have to leave them there in the corridor and hope they are still there when I get back. There's a sharp sting in my back, just below my ribcage, shit, the knife. I turn to see 'leg man' just behind me, his hand still on the knife. 'Tosser', I hear myself mutter.

Strangely, the first thing that comes to my mind is that the team at work will never let me live it down if they hear about this. I've been literally stabbed in the back. I don't think he pushed it too far in as the pain wasn't that bad, so I reach around, knocking his hand away in the process and shuffling my pained shoulders, until I find the hilt of the small knife. I yank the bugger out.

Tutting at 'leg man' I shake my head and see the look of shock on his face when I haven't gone down. I punch him square in the face before stashing the knife in my pocket and making my way to Julie and Amy.

My back is hurting like a bitch and I have shooting pains all over my shoulders whenever I move, but all I can think of is making sure that the women are all right. When I reach Amy's office, the first thing I notice is that the desk has been knocked over, the chair is on its side on the floor and Felix's door has been kicked in. The second thing I notice is that Amy is sitting on a chair holding on to her tummy. Julie is kneeling beside her.

'You OK?' I ask Julie, trying to keep the worry from my tone. She nods, patting Amy's arm gently.

'I've called for an ambulance,' she says quietly, looking to the ground. I follow her line of vision to the black blue granite floor and see the blood pooling beneath Amy's chair. Shit. I hear heavy footsteps as two security guards run in to the room, and stop in front of us, slightly out of breath.

'Are the two men still in the corridor?' I ask the tall, short-haired guard, we'd spoken to on our way in.

'No. There's no one there now,' he replies as he places his hands either side of his hips and takes in the upturned furniture and the pregnant woman sitting on the chair.

'Shit,' I mutter aloud in between quick breaths. My back feels like it's on fire.

There's a call on the guard's walkie talkie, 'the ambulance is here. They're on their way up.' He tells Amy, 'I'm so sorry, Miss Wilder. I don't know how they got in.'

The security at Ditton Park is something that needs to be addressed sooner rather than later. I watch as Amy is attended to by the paramedics and taken to the ambulance. As tempted as I am to seek medical assistance, my stupid pride has got in the way. Besides, I'd rather be in a car with Julie than in an ambulance with strangers.

Julie and I walk to the car.

'One interesting thing I found out,' Julie says, bending her head slightly to cross the strap of her bag over her shoulder.

'And that is?' I respond, my legs are starting to feel heavy.

'Apparently Felix Gloverman is the father of Amy Wilder's baby. She says they've been going out for six months.'

'Shit, really? I wouldn't have seen that coming,' I mutter. I'm beginning to feel a bit weak now.

'Any chance you can drive back,' I ask, reaching into my trouser pocket to give her the car keys.

‘Sure, no problem. Are you all right, Brian? You’re looking a little pale.’

‘Think we need to make a quick stop at A&E,’ I mutter. And the world goes black.

Part 11

Gino

The Armed Man by Karl Jenkins blares on my car radio. I love driving my dark blue BMW with the music pounding from the speaker system at top volume. The music stops, I'm doing eighty on the motorway, I press the brake slightly and slow down to seventy-five. I scan the console screen and see I've got an incoming call. Shit. The ringing tone shrills throughout the car, it feels like it's bouncing off the walls, almost hurting my ears. Bugger, I need to turn the volume down.

'Yes?' I say, checking my rear view and wing mirror, before I move into the slow left-hand lane. I turn the volume down.

'Gino Camprinelli?' a loud male voice booms through the speaker.

I wince. 'Yes. Who wants to know?'

'This is an associate of Felix Gloverman's.'

Interesting, I muse. Let's see who's come out of the woodwork for dear Felix. What's up with his voice? It sounds as though his nose is broken.

'An associate? Not a friend?' I query.

'No,' he says, his voice sounds smug, 'I heard from a friend of a friend that you are looking for him.'

'Which friend of a friend?' I ask, trying to keep my temper in check. I crawl to fifty miles an hour, but now I'm wedged between two lorries. Shit. I check my mirror, but there's no space for me to move out. Christ, where did all this traffic come from?

'I can't say, Mr Camprinelli, I need to protect my source.'

'I appreciate that, Mr?'

'Naylor, Andy Naylor. I know he's in some sort of trouble and I need to distance myself from him.'

'Good man,' I smile. I'm having a bit of luck at last. 'Tell me where he is, Naylor.'

'I'll text you his address.'

Gloverman. Your days are numbered.

Part 12

Felix

Give me strength! There's a constant babble of people chatting, moving and talking on their phones, all around me. I pull my blue cap down lower onto my face and readjust the brown framed glasses. My nerves are frazzled, my throat is dry, and I could murder a drink. The house fell through with Andy Naylor. There was just something odd about him when I met him for drinks last night.

When I say odd, I mean more than usual. He was too eager to please me, to give me the keys to the penthouse and I had a feeling in my gut that something wasn't quite right. So, I took the keys, and the £100 of crumpled notes he'd shoved into my hand, went back to the hotel and packed my bag.

I couldn't sleep, with my bag dumped on the floor next to my bed, worrying about what to do next. I'd stared into the darkness, and the only thing that made sense was to go back to Gateshead. At least there, I could empty the safe in my room and collect Jenny from the Summer House. This morning I'd pulled on yesterdays crumpled clothes of a blue shirt, black trousers and shoes, and watched the BBC breakfast news.

The news report stated that they were looking for Jenny Gloverman, heiress of the Gloverman Corporation, who hadn't been seen since Friday night and it went on to say that they were worried about her disappearance. Bugger. They're looking for me too. I'd made a point of keeping my face to the floor as I'd made my way to a nearby coffee shop for breakfast. After a couple of pastries and a cappuccino, I decided to collect a few things from Poundland, and a shaver from Argos to change my appearance before heading briefly back to the hotel.

It's Tuesday, howling with rain and I'm on a train. I paid £24.20 cash for my 2.30pm train ticket from Bristol Temple Meads to Oxford and I get the joy of changing trains at Didcot Parkway. It's bloody inconvenient, sitting here in standard class with its incessant hustle and bustle and kids playing their stupid games on full volume and the never-ending chatter of families. God, it's hard trying to ignore them when all I want to do is drag them by their hair from their seats and punch their stupid faces until they shut up.

I need to get to the Summer House, to get Jenny. She's the only one I want. I think of the heavy brown parcel tape sitting at the bottom of my bag, I'm going to need that to bind her mouth, hands and feet. I'll have to be careful not to catch that glorious blonde hair of hers in the sticky tape. Jenny understands that sometimes I need to hurt her, it's just a developing part of our relationship.

My mind shifts to a time four years ago when I'd met a young woman, with my favourite shade of blonde hair colour, who'd reminded me so much of my niece that I'd felt the strongest urge to connect with her. I'd been showcasing some of my best pieces of furniture and decorative accessories, at an exclusive antiques fair in London, when she'd strolled past my table.

'Mmm. Love this,' she'd smiled at me, her fingers stroking an exquisite jewellery box.

I walked her way, my eyes mesmerised as her long pale fingers stroked the wood. 'It's a Palais Royale Musical Jewellery box,' I'd told her.

‘It’s beautiful,’ she’d paused, absently stroking straight blonde hair that reached below her shoulder blades, resting on her tight, just above the knee short-sleeved black dress, ‘is it mahogany?’

I’d taken a deep breath, hoping that my voice sounded casual. ‘No,’ I’d explained, ‘it’s mulberry wood, sarcophagus-shaped, and the small ornate handle on the top is cast bronze.’

‘May I open it?’ she’d asked.

‘Be my guest.’

Her slender fingers carefully opened the lid and one of the three tunes began to play automatically.

‘It’s lined with cream silk.’

‘Oh my,’ she whispered, ‘it’s stunning,’ her fingers slowly traced the inside of the box and I felt my dick stiffen. I picked up my clipboard that held the list of itemised pieces and their information that I’d brought with me today and placed it low on my stomach covering myself. ‘I’ll take it,’ she announced in a clear, warm voice.

‘Would you like to know the price first?’ I asked, surprised that she didn’t ask or wasn’t prepared to barter with the price of the piece she was buying.

‘No.’

‘It’s £750, but I will knock a hundred off, if you’ll let me buy you coffee,’ I’d said.

‘It’s a deal,’ she’d smiled, shaking my hand.

Her name turned out to be Sherry. Short for Sheridan, which I thought was lovely as it was. Our ‘coffee’ had turned into several dates, before I decided to push for sex. It was then, when she began to refuse me, that I realised she was nothing but a prick tease. The last time I saw her, I’d dropped her off after our date at her house and pushed her up against her front door. I was determined to get a reward for my good behaviour, so I'd shoved a knee between her legs forcing them open and ripped her grey silk blouse in two, so that I could fondle her breasts. She was crying and saying 'no', but in my mind, she was really saying 'yes,' so I'd bit her neck, pinched her nipples, and walked away. Shit.

What was the matter with these women? They were so shallow, so beguiling with their svelte figures, smart clothes and beautiful faces. With eyes that smouldered in a 'come and get me' invitation and soft voices to bring you to your knees. Jesus. They were all talk and no play, no excitement or adventure. They probably just wanted your ring on their finger and a good home.

My thoughts move to that stupid whining bitch Amy, my PA from work. She was always trying to please me, batting her eyelids and smiling. Alright, so she was good at her job, efficient at following my directions and she certainly knew her way around a laptop and the logistics of the company. It's one of the reasons I kept her around, she's quite bright. The main reason though, is that she looks a little like Jenny, which calms and excites me. I know how strange that sounds.

We've been on a couple of dates over the past few months, but nothing serious. She fills a temporary need. A physical need that keeps me sane in my private hell, as I watch Jenny and that upstart Greyson, smiling and touching each other, becoming closer each day. The problem is that Amy has convinced herself that we're in a relationship. No. We. Are. Not. We're not serious. We're not a couple. We're not anything. We just fuck.

If only things were that easy and life wasn't so complicated. Of course, the woman had to go and get herself pregnant. How did that happen? When she should have been on the pill! She told me she'd got it covered. Why would she do this to me? I don't want to be bloody trapped like this. It's not in my plans. At the back of my mind, I even convinced myself that the baby wasn't mine and she was already up the duff before we went out.

I kept seeing my face plastered over the BBC bloody breakfast news this morning, in connection with Jenny's disappearance! They were asking for anyone who might have seen me or her, or know anything about her disappearance, to get in touch. In addition to the photos of myself and Jenny, there was a photo of a police officer called DCI Brian Carter who had been put in charge of the case.

Of course, I'd had to change my appearance. I had one last look at the old me in the mirror in the hotel bathroom, before giving myself a drastic makeover. Firstly, I shaved off my moustache, then I started on my hair, shaved the whole lot off until I was completely bald.

The feeling is not unlike walking through a town wearing no clothes. There's a nakedness to me, even with my cap drawn down over my head. My senses heightened as the cold breeze brushed across my bare skin, causing a tingling sensation as I walked to the train station. What was left of my dark, curly hair was sitting in a white plastic waste bin next to the sink in the hotel bathroom. Naylor's penthouse keys were left in the hotel room when I checked out.

Now, I've decided to go back to Gateshead, to Jenny, it's imperative that I get there as quickly as possible. I don't want Jenny to suffer too much, I need her alive. In addition, I have to prepare myself that I may come face to face with the Dean's. They'll have questions.

***

Someone kicks the back of my seat. Hard. I close my eyes and take a deep breath. I really don't want to bring attention to myself. The kick thuds again. It's becoming bloody annoying, and before I can stop myself, I twist my head around, pull my cap over my eyes and say in a cold voice. 'Hey, you need to stop that.'

The person behind me is not a child, but a young adult woman, who has long blue and black striped dreadlocks, wears a silver nose ring, dirty black clothes and, by the look of her face, a ton of attitude.

The girl-woman glares at me, her eyes, framed with thick black eyeliner, trys to intimidate me as she thrusts two fingers my way, in a V sign. Bloody kids! I stand up, step to the seat behind mine, hold onto the blue headrest in front of me and face her.

'You little slut,' I hiss in her face, with venom in my voice, 'I've seen better manners on a dead pig.' I push a finger into her shoulder, 'you kick the back of my chair again, and I'll fucking show you how good my manners are.'

A glimpse of fear falls across her eyes, her mouth opens as if she's about to say something, then it closes as if she decides it's not worth it. Her head lowers as she studies the floor, and I nod, satisfied that she will behave from now on. I try to hold back my smile as I return to my seat and let out a sigh. I just want a little peace, is that too much to ask? My phone vibrates in my pocket, I lean my head back, close my eyes and take my phone out. Oh God, the number looks familiar, it's that idiot Naylor.

'Hello,' I say, 'Andy?'

'Yeah, hey Felix. How're you doing?' he asks.

'Fine. You?' I'm not giving him any information. I don't trust the guy. After our drink last night, I realised that there's something very odd about him. Don't know what it is, but he's giving off some weird vibes.

'You at the house yet?'

He's obviously fishing for information, so I lie, 'Yes, just got here. Can't tell you how I appreciate you finding this place for me.'

'Happy to help, old chap,' he says, 'look, I'll call you back later. I've got a call waiting. Just wanted to check in with you.'

'No problem,' I close my eyes and end the call. Prat.

The train conductor's voice breaks through my thoughts to announce that we're approaching Didcot Parkway. One more train, a taxi from Oxford and then I'll be at Gateshead. One step closer to home. One step closer to Jenny. Hang on baby girl, Uncle Felix is on his way.

Part 13

Stuart

Jenny's head rests heavily on the passenger window of my car as I pull the Toyota to a stop next to the police car, on the gravelled drive. It's 4.30pm, and I don't know where the day has gone.

I set the handbrake and make sure the gear stick is in neutral before turning to her. She looks like Jenny, smells like Jenny even, but she's not the Jenny I knew a week ago. A quieter, changed person sits with hunched shoulders in front of me, enveloped in a long thick grey jumper which threatens to swallow her whole. It screams, leave me alone, I'm hiding from the outside world.

She turns to look at me and I'm floored. My determination to be strong, leaves me momentarily and I sigh and shake my head. I feel so weary. So bloody weary. I can't shift the helplessness that engulfs me, trying to rip my insides apart. I take a deep breath, silently telling myself to be strong for Jenny, because I know that there will be many months, if not years, before we are able to come to terms with what happened to her.

I gently lay my hand over hers, as it rests on her black jean-clad leg and study her face. There is no disguising the sadness in her eyes, sometimes I catch a hint of the first Jenny, underneath, when her eyes light up, and then it falls, just like that, replaced by a sadness, fear and doubt. Her face is paler, her profile, more serious. She stares at the empty police car, another reminder of the ordeal she's been through. She glances at the tall, female police officer with jet-black hair, who is standing by the front door, before her focus moves to my hand, sitting on top of hers.

'You ready?' I ask in a low voice.

Jenny nods, a tight smile spreading across her face. Her brows are furrowed, giving her a deep frown as she begins to unbuckle her seatbelt. I open the door and walk round to help her out of the car, but she's already got the door open and has one black boot on the gravel.

'Let me help you,' I say, pulling the door wider and holding out my hand. Our eyes meet, and she doesn't hesitate when taking my outstretched hand. This is a good sign. It's a huge step for Jenny, to touch me first, to respond to me. I try not to make too much of it, as our hands curl around each other. We're not linking fingers yet, but I'm happy with whatever makes her feel comfortable. Everything that we do, from now on, needs to be on Jenny's terms.

The large brown wooden door to the house is thrown open. Rose, wearing a yellow dress with a pale blue apron dotted with white rabbits wrapped around her shapely frame, moves quickly down the two stone steps and walks our way.

'It's good to have you back, Jenny,' she says, taking Jenny by the arm. I hear the sharp intake of breath and see a small wince shadow across her face at the physical connection. I don't think Rose realises how vulnerable Jenny feels with physical contact at the moment. I make a mental note to ask Rose to be careful in future. Collecting two carrier bags and a brown holdall from the rear of the car, I follow the women into the house.

'Where's Henry?' I ask, dumping the bags against the walnut cased, square grandfather clock in the Great Hall.

Rose turns briefly, as she walks Jenny through to the kitchen, 'he's in his office.'

'I'll head that way,' I say, 'I need to have a quick word with him.'

Jenny stops, unravels Rose's arm from her own and turns to me.

'You be all right for a short while?' I ask.

A shadow of doubt flits across Jen's face, before she swallows a lump back. 'I'll be fine,' she says with a smile that doesn't reach her eyes.

It takes two strides for me to reach her. I gently cup her soft cheek and search her face. She closes her eyes with a sigh at my touch and leans into me. It comforts her.

'I won't be long,' I say quietly.

I smile at Jenny's slow nod and go in search of Henry. She's being so brave. Walking past several doors in the corridor, eventually I reach his office. The door is partly open, and I can hear voices. I'm about to go in, but for some reason I'm rooted to the spot. I step back a little, and peer through the narrow open-door frame. Henry's back is facing me, his customary white shirt is creased as he bends over his desk, grabs a pen and walks over to a small white-framed window. Still holding the pen and notepad in one hand, he holds his phone to his ear and stares out at the green lawn.

'Are you sure it's him, Mickey?' Henry asks, his voice carrying across the room. It's raised slightly as if he's heard unwelcome news.

Who is he talking to? Who is he talking about? I stay still, holding my breath. A feeling of dread fills me. Something feels wrong. Something has happened.

'Bloody hell!' Henry curses, 'Bald head, glasses, no moustache? How on earth did you recognise him?' Henry's voice graduates to a louder, harsher tone, before stopping abruptly as he waits for an answer.

'Why the hell was he still wearing the Rolex?' Henry asks, leaning forward, and I step to the side of the open door so that I can see what he is doing, he places the pen and pad on the deep windowsill and slowly wipes his finger along its frame, as though looking for dust.

'Yes, well I guess his voice and mannerisms are quite distinctive,' Henry says with a harshness to his voice, 'we're lucky that he caused that scene with the young woman. Send me a photo, will you?'

I step quickly behind the door to make sure that I'm fully hidden. What the hell is Henry up to? This sounds like serious shit. I hear a low buzz and crane my neck to the edge of the door frame. The sound comes from Henry's phone, the photo must have come through.

'What time is his train due to arrive in Oxford?' he twists his wrist and looks at his watch, 'Bugger! He could be here within the next hour or so. He may not come straight to Gateshead; he might wait until it's dark. Tell your man to keep his eyes on him. He's not to make contact though. I'll let DCI Carter know he's heading our way.'

Then it suddenly dawns on me, and the short hairs on my forearms begin to rise. This is the 'something wrong.' They're talking about Felix. My heart starts to hammer in my chest. He's on his way here. The shock realisation that Felix Gloverman is heading our way, is quickly replaced by an anger so strong, I can almost taste it. One thing is for sure, I need to get Jenny out of here. Get her somewhere safe. Where he can't get his hands on her. My mind starts racing. What on earth am I going to say to Jenny? How do I tell her? I need to keep her safe.

'Do you still keep up with your rifle practice?' Henry asks, casually.

Hold on, one moment. Rifle practice? Who the hell is Henry talking to? And how does that someone 'keep up with rifle practice', unless they are a spy, in the forces or a gangster? It appears that there is quite a lot I don't know about Henry Dean. I know he manages the Gateshead estate. I know he and Rose are married. And I know that they have looked after Jenny since she was a baby. I know that Henry and Rose are her parents in every way, but biologically. But, this cloak and dagger stuff, this is not the Henry I know.

'Good. Are you sure?' Henry's voice breaks into my thoughts, 'I'd appreciate you being here. Yes, bring anything that you think you'll need. Jenny must be protected at all costs.'

Holy shit! Who is this man? An hour ago, he was just plain old Henry, with his checked jackets, plain white shirts and short, grey hair, going about his daily business of keeping this place running. He was Henry Dean, the Gateshead Estate Manager. Now, he's some sort of secret agent or something.

Can this week get any weirder? There's been a kidnapping, a rape, a missing perverted bastard of an uncle and now an ageing estate manager slash father figure who is involved in some very shady dealings. I feel like I'm in the plot of a Tess Gerritsen novel.

'Text me when you arrive,' he finishes before ending the call.

I step to the wall next to the door, turn around and lean my long frame against its cold, hard surface. I take a deep breath, before retracing my steps along the corridor. After five or six strides, I about turn, clear my throat and start walking back to Henry's office.

'Henry?' I call, 'you there?'

'In here!' he shouts from his office.

I reach the office door and push it open. He is standing in the middle of the room facing me, with a grim smile on his face.

'How is she?' he asks, his brow furrowed with concern, and in that moment, he looks just like the Henry I thought I knew.

'All right, I think,' I answer, 'she's with Rose.'

'Good,' he rubs a hand across his face and his shoulders slump. For a moment, he looks old, his face reminding me of an old pair of leather boots, you know, the ones that have been lovingly worn until their shade and texture have roughened and faded slightly. He isn't old, not in the grand scheme of things, but I would venture to say that he had stepped out of his prime now he was in his early sixties and was heading slowly towards retirement. 'Sit down, Stuart. I need to tell you something, and it's not good.'

Ah, here goes, a simple explanation is all I need. I'm relieved that he's going to explain what's going on to me, as I sit in the medium oak chair with the dark red padded seat by his desk.

'I've just had a call from an old friend of mine,' he starts to talk.

'An old friend? Someone I know?' I ask casually, I'm determined to hide the fact that I overheard his phone conversation.

'No,' he shook his head, 'someone I knew a long time ago,' his eyes don't leave the emerald green carpet. Bugger, I can't see if he's telling me the truth or not.

'He's just an old friend,' Henry repeats, more forcefully this time, 'and he says that he's found Felix.'

'Shit! Where?' I try to sound surprised, lowering my head to mask my reaction.

'He's travelling by train and making his way to Gateshead,' Henry says in a flat voice.

'He's coming back for her,' I mutter, 'for Jenny. He thinks she's still in the Summer House in that damn awful box.'

'Yes,' he leans back, settles his rear on the edge of the desk, 'but we'll be waiting for him this time.'

'When is he due in?' I ask.

'I don't know, but he was due to change at Didcot Parkway to get the train to Oxford Station.'

'It's imminent, then,' I say flatly, folding my hands on the desk. My heart is hammering in my chest.

'Yes. He's shaved his head, is wearing glasses and has shaved off his moustache, but he's still wearing his Rolex watch,' Henry takes out his phone, presses a couple of buttons and brings up the photo.

'Bloody hell.' I say, feeling frustrated, as I stare into the changed face of Felix Gloverman, on the phone in front of me. I am also annoyed because I can't tell him that I'd overheard most his earlier conversation. 'Can you send me that?' I ask.

He nods and forwards me the photo.

A moment later, my phone acknowledges receipt of the updated photo of Felix.

'I need to get Jenny out of the house,' I say with a sharpness to my voice I can't help, 'who knows what might happen when he realises that she's not in the Summer House.' I notice there's no mention of Mickey by name, no talk of rifle practice, or of the person who was following Felix. It's hard to trust a person when said person is keeping things from you.

'I agree,' Henry says quietly, 'but our first course of action is to tell DCI Carter. When I've done that, I'll call my friend to see where the bastard is.'

'This is a bloody mess, Henry,' I can't help raking my fingers through my hair, 'we need to get him into custody before it's too late, he's still a threat to Jenny. I'll call DCI Carter,' I stand and begin to walk, 'we need to get back to Jenny and Rose.'

I find Carter in my contacts and call him. We need back up as soon as possible. The phone is ringing but there's no answer. I disconnect the call and try again. Shit. Where is he? Why won't he answer?

I feel in my jeans pocket for the business card with Julie Leadbetter's contact details that I'd taken from Jenny's hospital bed. The white typed information looks smart, set against the blue background, as I press the numbers of her work mobile into my phone, and touch the green call sign.

I hold my breath as we walk to the kitchen to Jenny and Rose, then I stop. I don't want Jenny to hear the latest news about Felix while I'm telling someone else on the phone. The dialling tone connects the call, and a short-clipped voice comes through the earpiece. Julie.

'PC Leadbetter?' I ask, exhaling slowly and staring at Henry, 'It's Stuart Greyson. We've got some news.'

I tell her how Felix has changed his physical appearance and is making his way, via train to Gateshead. 'We're going to need more of you guys here, watching the Summer House, waiting for him. I can't get in touch with DCI Carter.'

There's a silence on the phone and I wonder if Julie is still listening. Then she begins to talk.

'I'm afraid DCI Carter is in hospital. He's been stabbed. DS Mike Jones is going to run the investigation for a day or so, until DCI Carter is back on site. I'm just waiting for him to come back from Bristol.'

'Jesus!' I say, standing still to let the words sink in. Stabbed, with a knife? Surely not by Felix? A cold chill runs slowly through me and makes its way down the centre of my back. I shiver, shaking my shoulders before asking her, 'Is he all right?' Henry is standing beside me, his hands in his pockets, he's watching me intently, and I move my head from side to side in disbelief.

'Yes, I think so,' she continues, 'he just needs to rest for a couple of days.'

'Do you know who did it?' I ask, wondering if Felix had resorted to hiring henchmen to do his dirty work.

'It wasn't Felix Gloverman,' she responds, as if reading my thoughts down the line, 'two men came to Ditton Park looking for him, while DCI Carter and myself were there. Italian, or Spanish, smartly dressed.'

'Jesus!' I mutter, 'I wonder how they're connected to Felix?'

'We're not sure yet, but we're going through mugshots to find them and who they work for. DCI Carter was talking to Mr Dueller at the time, and I was with Gloverman's PA, Amy Wilder. They wanted information on Gloverman and his whereabouts. Miss Wilder got in the way.'

'Is she all right?'

'She's in hospital. She went into early labour. She was five and a half months pregnant.'

Bloody hell! The poor woman. I've never met her, what an ordeal.

'How is she?' I ask again, almost dreading what she is about to say. There's a pause on the line.

'She lost the baby,' Julie's voice echoes in a quiet, sad tone.

Oh no. What do you say to that? How can there be any words that will make sense of what has happened to Amy Wilder? When I was four years old, my mum had lost a baby she was carrying. At such a young age, I hadn't understood what was happening when dad had rushed mum to hospital for a scan because she'd felt no baby movement two weeks before her due date.

We had no living relatives and I was left in the care of the nice young couple who lived next door, for a couple of days. Sadly, the baby, my little sister had died in the womb. Her name was Rosalie and she lies under a shiny white headstone with an angel carved into it, in the local cemetery. She would have been eighteen now. I don't think my mum and dad ever fully recovered from her death. Of course, they moved on with their lives, living in a sort of daze and with an air of sadness surrounding them. That was when they began to detach themselves from me.

'Stuart? Are you still there?' Julie's voice brings me back to reality and I push those old memories to the back of my mind.

'Yes,' I say quietly, 'still here.' I rub my head, 'that's so sad, about the baby I mean.' I can feel an anger bubbling inside me, trying to break through, 'it's Felix's fault. Again. Indirectly – or not, but it has Felix written all over it.'

'I agree,' Julie says, 'but our main priority now, is to keep Jenny safe. I'll radio the officers guarding the main doors to your house to update them and DS Jones and I will be with you soon. We'll keep DCI Carter in the loop.'

'I'll forward Felix's updated photo to you,' I tell her, before I disconnect the line. I look at Henry.

'Sounds like trouble,' he says.

'Yes,' I say, walking towards the kitchen. I update Henry on the stabbing of DCI Carter and the assault on Amy Wilder.

‘Bloody hell,’ is all Henry can say when I’ve finished talking, ‘that means that someone else is looking for Gloverman too. Shit! This situation is getting seriously out of hand!’ He stops walking and takes my arm.

‘You think?’ I shake my head and thrust my hands deep into the pockets of my jeans, ‘Why are those men looking for Felix? What’s he done now?’

‘I have no idea, I bet he’s got himself involved in something shady,’ he answers.

‘Bugger,’ Henry mutters again, ‘we’d better get back to the women, they’ll be fretting.’ I nod and we don’t talk again until we reach the kitchen. My mind is racing. So many questions remain unanswered. Does Henry know these men? Are they connected to the man on the phone?

Jenny is sitting at the kitchen table with a mug of tea in front of her. She looks tired, her face is serious, and her brow is drawn. Rose has her back to us, she’s frying mince, onions and carrots in a black frying pan and there’s a large silver saucepan bubbling away on the six-ring gas stove.

‘You’ve been a while,’ Jenny says, with a note of reproach in her voice.

‘Sorry,’ I say, pulling out a chair and sitting next to her, ‘we lost track of time. Also,’ I wait and look at Henry until he gives me a brief nod, ‘there are things that we need to tell you both. Rose, can you come and sit down for a moment please.’

Rose turns around and wipes her forehead with the back of her hand. Worry is written all over her face. As if remembering the food, she returns to the stove and turns the gas off. When Rose and Henry are seated, I wait for Henry to start talking.

‘There’s no easy way of saying this, so I’ll come right out with it,’ he stalls for a moment, trying to find the right words. I’m not sure what he'll tell them, probably the same as he told me. 'I've had someone looking for him. Felix, I mean,' his voice sounds husky, full of emotion. 'He's been found,' he says, looking at Jenny.

Her fingers are threaded together, and her hands rest on the table. My gaze drops, to the whitening knuckles as her whole body becomes taut with anxiety. Jenny looks at me, and her hands reach for mine for comfort and reassurance. I stroke her knuckles with my thumb.

'Where is he?' Jenny asks quietly.

'He's changed his appearance,' I say, ignoring her question. Once I've told her, I can't take it back. 'He's shaved his head and his moustache, he's wearing glasses.'

Henry takes his phone from his pocket and brings up the photo, 'here, this is what he looks like at the moment.' The phone is handed around the table.

'He looks so different,' Jenny whispers, as she stares at the photo on the phone in front of her.

'Where is he?' Jenny repeats, her voice stronger.

We stare at Henry, and I can't help but notice his Adam's apple move as he swallows, 'he's on his way here. He's coming back to the Summer House. He's coming back for you, Jenny.'

Jenny's eyes lift to mine, her pupils are dilated, and she looks terrified. She's silently begging for me to say it's not true. I wish it weren't, I wish the bastard wasn't coming this way, but he is. So, I nod. I put pressure on her hands.

'No!' she shouts, dragging her hands from mine and scraping her chair back. She stands and slams her hands on the table, 'that's not fair, he can't come back here!'

'He is Jenny. And we need to be ready,' I say, standing next to her, 'we have a police officer at the front and back of the house. I've told PC Leadbetter. She's on her way over with DS Jones, I think they plan to trap him at the Summer House.'

Jenny puts her arms around her shoulders and starts to pace, 'he'll get me again. I know he will.'

We watch helplessly as she begins to sob.

'No, he won't!' I say sternly, pushing out of my chair and taking her by the shoulders to stop her from pacing. 'I won't let that happen.'

'We won't let that happen,' Henry reiterates.

'But for now, there are a few things I want to show you and Rose,' I gesture for Rose to come to me.

'I'm going to show you several simple ways to protect yourself, against anyone who means to do you harm, including Felix,' I tell them. I point to my throat, 'there are many weak spots on the male body, from the throat, to the eyes and nose.' I point to my face, 'use your fingers, push hard into the eyes to incapacitate and allow yourself time to get away.'

I walk to Jenny and take her hand gently before turning it over and pushing it towards my nose, 'the palm of your hand pushed hard into someone's nose, will put them off kilt. As does getting your fingers into nostrils and yanking them up.' Letting her hand go, I continue talking. In my life, I never anticipated ever telling Rose and Jenny these self-defence tips, but they may help them if they were ever in such a situation.

'Use your hands, fingers, even your head as a weapon to butt against your target. Into his or her nose or head.' I say. Jenny and Rose simply stare at me as if I've gone mad.

'Look,' I say quietly, nodding to them, 'I'm not trying to frighten you. I'm trying to make you realise that you can use whatever weapon is at hand, your knee into a groin, your foot into the back of a knee. A nearby object to attack with.'

Ten minutes later and Henry taps me on the shoulder. It's time to get organised.

'I want both of you to stay in the kitchen, lock that door and draw the bolts,' Henry looks at the women, 'I need to have a word with the police officers, check that they've been updated that Felix will arrive imminently. Stuart?' He turns to me, 'can you check all the windows and doors are locked.'

'Of course,' I reply, moving to the heavy door, turning the key and drawing the top and bottom bolt. My eyes move to the kettle. 'Rose, can you make another pot of tea? I'll be back before you know it.'

Rose nods and wipes her hands down her apron, all the time, her eyes follow Jenny. I know she's worried about her.

Jenny rushes to me and grabs my shoulders with both hands, 'don't go,' she pleads, 'please don't leave us.' There are tears in her eyes and it's breaking my heart, but I need to check the doors and windows, make sure that the house is secure.

'Jen,' I gently take her hand off my arm and reach up to touch her cheek. 'You'll be fine, sweetheart,' I say softly, 'I wouldn't leave you if I thought you were in danger. I need you to be strong. I won't be long. Help Rose with the tea.'

Leaning into her ear, I whisper, 'I love you,' before walking to the door, and making my exit. There is no time to waste, Felix could be here at any moment, I look at my watch. It's already 5.10pm, I need to secure the house.

Bloody hell. As I stride with purpose through the corridors, my head starts to spin, as my brain goes through several scenarios of what Felix might or might not do. He'll go to the Summer House first. I was quietly confident of that. Will he venture to the main house? He shouldn't get that far if a police officer is waiting for him in the Summer House. I walk along the off-white painted corridor walls, to my first stop – the utility, come boot room.

As far as I know, this is the second access point to the back of the house, alongside the kitchen door. I focus on the lower floor windows next. In the utility room, I turn the key to the brown wooden door to ensure it's locked. There is a bolt at the bottom of the door. I slide the cold metal across the bar and into place and put my hands on the hard surface to push and bang the door. It doesn't move. It's solid. Looking around the room, I search for any weakness that will enable entry to the house. There is no window and no visible small spaces, thank goodness.

I move on to the third part of the house that has direct access to the outside world. The opulent dining room, with its rich and blue hues, mahogany furniture and French doors which lead directly to the rear garden. The doors are locked, so I take this opportunity to unhook the heavy blue velvet tie backs, before drawing the curtains together. The room is in darkness. At least he can't see inside the house.

Rushing to the Great Hall, I take the carpeted steps two at a time, to secure the bedroom windows. Fifteen minutes later and I walk into the last of the eight bedrooms, the Garden Room. It's the one I've been using over the past few days. Everything seems in its place, the window is locked, and I find myself looking out into the darkening early evening light.

My eyes catch a movement in the garden, and a sudden chill flashes across the skin of my arms. There's a shadow walking on the pathway leading to the Summer House. Felix. I rush to the top of the stairs.

Felix.

I rush to the hallway, and almost throw myself down the stairs. As I move, I call out:

'Jenny, Rose, Henry, make sure the front door is locked. Now!'

There's a flurry of movement as I reach the lower floor. Several things happen at once. Loud shouting can be heard outside.

'Hey, Police Officer. Stop!' clearly from the officer standing by the front door.

A crunching on the gravel suggests that someone is running. Away or towards the door, I'm not sure.

Henry reaches the front door ahead of the women and quickly slides two heavy brass bolts across the latch and slams them into place. Rose stands in the Great Hall with a tea-towel in her hand, she looks as if she's about to faint. Jenny rushes over to me, worry etched on her face.

'I saw something when I looked out of the window. It was a dark shape, like a figure. It was moving to the Summer House. I think it's Felix.'

'Bloody hell!' Henry curses, there is genuine worry etched across his face.

'What about the police officer?' Rose asks, her eyes glancing to the front door.

'Forget the police officer, for now,' I told her. 'Let's get to a safe place.' I lead them to Henry's office and usher them inside, kicking the door shut. As I turn to them, to reassure them that we're safe I'm stopped in my stride by a huge bang, like a firecracker. Jesus, what was that? An explosion of some sort?

A high-pitched ringing tone fills my ears, and I watch helplessly as a crystal glass vase filled with vivid orange sunflowers, judders forward and falls, with a thud, onto the blue carpeted floor. Luckily, it doesn't break.

In my panic, I put my hands over my head and crouch, believing that the roof will come crashing down at any point. When the moment passes, and I realise that we are safe, I rush to Jenny and draw her into the warmth of my body. Henry puts his arm around Rose in a protective gesture.

'What the hell was that?' Henry asks in a sharp voice.

'I don't know,' I look at Henry, his brows are furrowed with worry. What the hell is happening here?

'You all right? Sweetheart?' I ask Jenny, looking into her fear-filled blue eyes and taking hold of her shaking shoulders. She doesn't speak, just nods her head. My heart goes out to her, she's supposed to be resting, but she's had little chance of that since she came home. The silence is broken by harsh shouting, followed by a flurry of heavy footsteps. they sound closer as if they're in the house.

Letting go of Jenny, I rush to the red padded mahogany chair, perched in front of the desk, and drag it effortlessly across the room, before securing it under the door handle. Henry walks to the bookshelf and silently takes the lid off a small red hexagonal shaped box. His fingers deftly search inside until he finds what he's looking for. Holding aloft a small silver key, he strides to his desk, drops to his knees and begins to pull out a drawer.

There's a clatter as something is taken from a drawer and Henry rises to his feet holding a shiny silver metal case, and places it onto the hard wood of the desk. We watch, in silence as he uses the key to open the tin.

The lid creaks as Henry takes out a black object. Shit. It's a gun. He's got a bloody gun. Watching him hold it, I can't help but think how comfortable he looks holding the deadly weapon. It's as though he's held a gun in his hand many times before. I watch as he takes another object from the case, it's rectangular in shape, and he pushes it securely into the lower part of the handle of the gun.

'Henry!' Rose says, her face is pale with shock.

'Holy shit!' Jenny mutters.

'Jesus, Henry!' I raise my voice, closing the distance between us, 'You've got a gun? Who the bloody hell are you? To have a gun. A spy?'

'Close, but not quite,' Henry says, giving the gun a quick check before tucking it into the waistband of his trousers.

'Henry?' Rose's voice sounds strained, her eyes flicker from Jen to me and then concentrate on Henry. 'Henry? Why do you have a gun?' I watch the scene unfold in front of me, watch Rose look at her husband, and his head bows in shame. She steps purposely further away from him, 'I don't know who you are any more, Henry Dean.'

'Rose,' Henry pleads, moving closer to his wife, 'it's a long story, and this isn't the time, to tell it.'

Suddenly kicking and banging sounds filter into the room. It's difficult to say where the noise is coming from, but it sounds like it's near the front door. An almighty crash ricochets through the house, followed by the sound of something smashing into the wall.

'Bloody hell!' Henry mutters, as heavy footsteps can be heard running along the hallway and through the house.

'What was that?' Jenny's voice is quiet, there is panic in her eyes, her fingers squeeze tightly on to my lower arm.

'It's the front door, I think,' I say, 'it's been forced open.'

'He's in the house!' Jenny cries, throwing herself at me, 'Please don't let him take me again. Please Stu.'

I hold her as tightly as I dare. 'Shh...shh, sweetheart,' my hand strokes her hair, to calm her, 'no one is taking you or anyone anywhere.' My hand takes her chin, tilting it gently, 'not as long as Henry and I are here. We will protect you both.'

'Rose and Jenny,' Henry rushes to stand on one side of the door and growls, 'get behind the desk, now!' I push Jenny away, mouthing 'go,' grab a brass letter opener that sits on top of an unopened pile of post and stand on the opposite side of the door.

'Everyone,' Henry says in a low voice, taking the gun out of his trousers, 'keep quiet.' I watch as he holds his gun carefully in both hands and aims it at the door.

The room is so quiet, I can hear myself breathing. Looking across at Jenny and Rose holding each other tightly near Henry's desk, I see the worry etched across their faces.

Bang! Bang! Bang! There are several almighty thuds. I watch as the door moves forward an inch and the top of the chair squeaks, thankfully it stays in place, jarring the door handle.

'Police! Open up!' a male voice shouts.

I look at Henry, shrugging my shoulders. I don't recognise the voice.

'Mr Dean, Mr Greyson are you in there? It's DS Mike Jones.'

We remain still. It isn't that I don't believe the man, but we are hiding in a room with God knows what happening on the other side of the door, and I am in no mood to take any chances.

'Stuart, it's PC Julie Leadbetter,' a familiar female voice shouts from the other side of the door, and I exhale a sigh of relief. I look across to Jenny and catch her eyes.

'Julie', she whispers pressing her fingers to her temple.

'Hold on,' I shout to Julie and her DS, as I reach over to move the back of the chair that jammed the door handle. 'For God's sake Henry, put that bloody gun away,' I mutter, glancing quickly at the man who I'd looked up to, and respected from the moment Jenny brought me into her home.

My hand stays firmly rooted to the chair, while I wait for Henry to respond to my words. I see the slight dip of his head, a nod of acceptance, perhaps even a reluctant thank you, before his eyes sweep to the box on the desk, he unclips the cartridge from the gun, carries both to the box and drops them inside. I heave a sigh of relief as I watch Henry lock the case and place it firmly into the desk drawer.

I unhook the chair properly from the door handle and set it down next to me. The handle moves slowly in a downwards motion until it releases.

Jenny reaches out to Rose and pats her arm, 'don't worry, Rose. Please don't worry.'

Rose smiles, a hint of sadness to her eyes, 'it's not you, I'm worried about, it's him,' her eyes stray to the back of Henry's head. 'I can't believe he has a gun and didn't tell me,' her hand reaches out to reassure Jenny, 'I'm fine, really I am.'

She doesn't look fine. Neither does Jenny. They both look pale and shaken.

The door is thrust open and a tall dark-haired man, wearing a black jacket, dark trousers and a white shirt strides into the room. His eyes quickly taking in the scene as he nods to each of us in turn. I'm assuming that this is DS Mike Jones. PC Julie Leadbetter, walks quietly behind her sergeant. There's an undeniable look of worry etched on her face. She's wearing a navy, lightly padded jacket, black trousers and flat boots. There's a small, black crossover bag covering her front. She looks different out of uniform. Less formal.

'DS Mike Jones,' the DS announces with an air of authority. He's a good-looking man, with designer stubble, which women seem to like these days. He looks around the room, and his gaze rests, finally on me, 'you must be Stuart Greyson?'

'Yes,' I nod, offering my hand and watching in silence as his firm, cold hand takes mine in a brief acknowledgment. 'What happened outside?' I ask him. He looks at me, his lips in a grim line, and casually lifts his hand and brushes it absently through his hair. It's a defensive, agitated gesture, I've seen it before. My dad used it a lot when I was younger, when he knew that he and my mum, should have been taking better care of me.

DS Jones ignores my question. I'm not sure why. Studying his face, I watch him turn his attention to Henry and Rose.

'Mr and Mrs Dean?' he asks, addressing each one in turn. They're not standing together. Rose stands next to Jenny, Henry stands broodingly, behind his desk. Rose and Henry look warily at him. And nod. Henry's voice is deep, flat, 'Stuart asked you a question, DS Jones.'

'And you must be Jenny,' DS Jones ignores Henry's comment, and walks to Jenny, 'how are you?' He sounds genuine but Jenny doesn't know the man, so I'm not surprised when she doesn't answer him. Julie Leadbetter shadows her DS's steps, walking across the room and protectively putting her hand on Jenny's jumper clad arm.

'Are you all right?' she asks Jenny in a low voice.

Jenny's voice is almost a whisper, 'yes.'

'Look, we've secured the premises,' DS Jones says, 'let's get out of here. The kitchen might be a better place to talk. I think everyone could do with a cuppa, and I'll explain what just happened.' He gives me a look, indicating for me to lead the way down the hall.

Julie Leadbetter glances to Rose and Jenny. 'Please be careful as you walk, there is a lot of mess.'

Warily, I step into the hall. The first thing I see is a framed print lying on the floor, a large splinter had formed across the middle of the frame and small shards of glass had broken from the corner and shattered across the carpet. I keep on walking.

What the hell happened here? Just before we reach the Great Hall, there's a distinct smell of smoke and petrol, I turn around to look at DS Jones, who shrugs, another one of those 'I'll tell you in a while' shrugs. In the distance, I can hear fire engine sirens which get louder as they move nearer to the house.

As I enter the Great Hall, I sidestep the up-ended antique walnut umbrella stand and step around several umbrellas and Rose's tea towel, that lay strewn across the floor. The fumes of smoke are much stronger here. 'Put your hands over your mouth,' I tell the others.

The front door is open, and a fire engine crunches onto the gravel driveway. Crackling flames and acrid smoke billow from the police car that is parked on the driveway. In a bizarre twist of fate, my car remains untouched. The police officer we saw on arrival now stands, with furrowed brows in the Great Hall by the door architrave, talking quietly into her radio.

'Don't worry about the door,' the DS says dismissively as he follows me, 'I've got someone coming out to secure it tonight.'

Exhaustion drags its weary cloak over me, my head feels heavy and my limbs move slowly, screaming for rest and peace. Catching the darkening day outside, it lends a gloominess to the evening. It gives you that feeling that it's later in the day than it really is.

Gateshead, with its gravelled driveway, grey stone walls and sharp angled Tudor facade, lending a gracefulness to the house. Gateshead, which had always stood so proud and unapologetic, with its red and white solid brick walls. Once impenetrable, against the outside world and protecting those who seek haven within its walls, now simply feels fractured. Vulnerable.

When we reach the kitchen, everyone but Julie Leadbetter and Rose takes a chair from under the large kitchen table. A melancholy feeling hangs over us. Rose uses the silence to fill the kettle, before joining us at the table.

Julie Leadbetter stands with her back leaning against the sink. DS Jones leans his forearms on wooden tabletop.

'As you might have guessed, Felix came to the house,' he begins, talking in a slow manner as if he thought we all had learning difficulties.

'I saw a figure moving outside, heading towards the Summer House. I thought it was Felix and rushed downstairs to alert the others.'

'We're pretty sure it was him,' DS Jones states.

'Pretty sure?' Henry's voice rises, as the electric kettle reaches its crescendo, 'what the hell does that mean?' He gets up, patting Rose's shoulder gently, 'I'll make some coffee.'

'It means, it was dark and PC Jeffries,' DS Jones clarifies. 'who was guarding the front door, couldn't make Felix out clearly. She thinks Felix realised that Jenny was no longer at the Summer House, and took his chances, by making his way to the main house.'

The room is silent, as we listen to DS Jones. In the background, Henry bustles about making a pot of coffee, adding sugar, milk, spoons and mugs to a wooden tray. Another police officer a tall gangly young man, with charcoal streaks across his face, around twenty years of age, rushes into the room, he holds the gardener, Graham Foster, in front of him.

The red-haired man wears his usual blue jeans and green sweatshirt and has his long hair pulled back from his acne marked face. His eyes hold a coldness, that baffles me. Why would he be this way with us? He's always had a smile on his face, whenever I've passed him on the grounds, he shuffles uncomfortably, and I realise why his arms are behind his back, because his hands are cuffed. The officer yanks his hands and Graham winces.

'Graham?' Henry's eyebrows meet on his forehead, 'what's going on?' He looks at both men, his eyes finally resting on the charcoal streaked officer, 'why have you got Graham in handcuffs?'

'Sir, I was guarding the back door, when I heard something and found this man running along the side of the house with a petrol can and box of matches in his hand,' the young officer's Scottish accent booms through the room, as he addresses DS Jones.

'Graham?' Roses soft voice asks, her face waiting patiently for Graham to give a plausible explanation for his actions.

'I'm saying nothing,' Graham's deep voice cuts across Rose.

'Well, that's your right,' DS Jones addresses the gardener, 'but it's one thing helping out a friend, and quite another to take the entire blame for Felix Gloverman's actions.'

DS Jones looks at me. I'm astounded, I cannot believe that this man, a man who Jenny had told me, had worked at Gateshead for a number of years, would mean them harm. I'm angry, just give me five minutes in a room with Graham, I'll soon find out when he became Felix's lackey, it won't take more than five minutes to knock some sense into his thick skull and shed some light on what happened here this evening. I hope that DS Jones and his team have some luck when they interview Graham later.

'Lovatt,' the DS looks at the young officer, 'read him his rights, and get someone from Cowley to come pick him up.' The officer nods and is about to move when he turns slightly to look at his superior.

'One more thing, Sir,' the officer's eyes focus on DS Jones' face.

'Yes, Constable,' DS Jones asks, and I can see his Adam's apple move as he swallows.

'The door at the rear of the property has been kicked in. The intruder may have been in the house.'

'Why the hell didn't you tell me that in the first place?' DS Jones' voice is harsh and raised. 'You said the house was secure!' He curses in a low voice, before he turns to Julie Leadbetter. He rises from his chair, strides to the sink and speaks to Julie, 'Radio PC Salcombe from the Summer House, both of you check out the rest of the house. I want every room searched, focus on Jenny's and Felix's bedrooms and his study. I'll stay here with the family, until we get the all clear.'

'Sorry Sir,' PC Lovatt apologises, his face staring at the floor.

We watch as Julie nods and quietly leaves the room.

'He was in the house!' Rose's face reddens, in fury. I've never seen her so mad. Her voice is harsh, and there's an edge to it. I watch her hands slam against the table, as she pushes her chair back, the sound of the wood screeching against the grey slate floor, makes me wince slightly. She stands upright, holds her back straight and looks directly at Graham, we can hear the accusatory tone in her voice, 'we trusted you!'

Graham stares at Rose and shrugs his shoulders.

There's a resigned feeling in the room, an atmosphere of loss and betrayal covers every quartz surface and wooden shelf. Loyalty and trust, it feels as though no one understands the meaning of the words.

Jenny's quiet voice breaks the heavy silence, 'what did we ever do to you, Graham?'

Graham lips form into a snarl, his face is pale. Nothing. The bloody man says nothing, and by omission, he's admitting his part in this sorry tale. He's in league with the devil, let him suffer the consequences of his actions. Graham lowers his head onto his chest, before he's taken out of the room to the waiting car.

'I don't believe what I've just seen,' Jenny looks down at her trembling fingers, which are threaded into a fist shape, as they rest on the table, and says solemnly, 'Felix and Graham, they are people we've known for years. People we trusted.'

'Yes,' I whisper, stroking her knuckles with my thumb.

Heavy footsteps come through the Great Hall, a tall, older looking firefighter, with short blonde hair, and stubble, dressed in black, holding a helmet and a walkie talkie, stands in the kitchen doorway, 'DS Jones, the police car is safe to be collected now and we've done a full check of the grounds and given them the all clear. We're going to head off.'

'Thanks, Sergeant. Appreciate that,' the DS responds with a nod, watching him leave. Immediately, he walks to the kitchen door and reassures himself that it's locked, before he closes the only other door in the room.

He turns to look at Jenny, there's no disguising the tiredness of his drawn face, the shadows creeping under his eyes. His eyes hold Jenny's, and with sadness reflected in his voice, he mutters, 'unfortunately, we see this all too often in this type of work. Particularly within family situations. Gaining someone's trust to take advantage, it's a common theme.'

Henry mumbles something rude under his breath, and Rose gives him a stern look. She is still angry with him over the gun. I don't blame her, I would be too if I'd been in her shoes, and I had found out that Jenny had kept something significant from me.

DS Jones picks up a teaspoon, adds two heaped spoons of brown sugar and milk to his coffee, before stirring it several times, 'we have Felix walking up the drive from the Summer House, and Graham setting fire to the police car as a diversion. Now, one might ask what Felix is up to. Does he plan to escape with Jenny?

For the first time since we came out of Henry's office, I see Rose reach out to Henry. She uses both of her hands to take his and fold them against her chest. He looks surprised, perhaps he hadn't expected her to forgive him as quickly. His eyebrows lift in a question, as they look at each other, and I watch her nod, lips trembling as though she's about to burst into tears.

'Sir, the house is clear,' Julie rushes into the room and stands next to the Detective Sergeant. 'But we found something in Jenny's bedroom!' she pulls out her phone and finds her photo app, before giving him the phone, 'it was on her bed.'

'Shit!' the Detective Sergeant has given up trying to curse in a lower tone.

'What is it?' I ask.

'Tell us,' Jenny says flatly.

DS Jones shows us the photo. It takes a moment for us to realise what it is, but then it hits me, what I'm seeing. It's Jenny's blue striped pillowcase and is has something small and black on top of it. It's a pair of Jenny's pants. On top of the underwear is a white piece of paper folded into a triangular shape, long scrawling letters cover the note.

DS Jones enlarges the photo and Jenny reads the familiar letters, written in the black ball point pen that Felix uses, *'I'm coming for you. F.'*

'Noooooo!' Jenny's face pales in distress, her eyes find mine, panicking, worrying. I curse the day, that Felix Gloverman was born, the moment he took his first breathe and began to take his first steps, because somewhere along the way, he lost the ability to know the difference between right and wrong.

A seed of evil, that was planted long ago, began to grow and flourish and take over his heart and soul. I watch Jenny, she'd only just come back home from her kidnapping ordeal, she was supposed to be safe now. What a joke. Jenny's hand covers her mouth, and heavy tears are falling down her face. 'Not again!'

I pull her to me, take her in my arms and rock her slowly. I feel so useless. 'Bastard!' I say, more to myself than to the others, 'He just can't help himself. Bloody bastard. He really thinks that I'm going to let you go again. Not a fucking chance.'

'We won't let that happen!' the DS says curtly.

'I can't stay here, Stuart,' Jenny mumbles into my shoulder, 'I just can't. I don't feel safe.'

'You don't have to sweetheart, we'll find somewhere else,' I reassure her, before looking at Henry, 'maybe, we should all leave for a few days. Let things settle.'

'Do you want me to find you a safehouse?' DS Jones interrupts, 'It wouldn't be what you're used to, but I would at least, be able to sleep knowing that no one knows where you are.'

'No,' I cut in, 'no thank you. I think we'll be fine as long as you can spare a couple of people to watch the house and accompany us to the hotel.'

Henry nods, 'A hotel seems a good idea. What do you think Rosie?' He looks at his wife, his hand stroking her arm and waits patiently for her to nod in agreement.

'I need the bathroom,' Rose stands and straightens her dress, she pats Jenny on the shoulder, 'I'll be back shortly.' Jenny gives a brief smile and touches her hand.

'I'll follow you,' Julie gives the older woman a small smile. 'Just in case. We haven't found Felix yet.'

Rose murmurs her thanks and she pulls open the kitchen door that leads to the Great Hall. Julie is about to follow her when her phone pings, and with an air of frustration she swipes her finger across the screen, bringing it to life. A big smile spreads across her face, as processes the information that stares back at her.

'Got it! That's them,' she says aloud, excitement in her voice. She shows DS Jones her phone again.

'Bloody hell! I know those two,' he says, staring at the screen, 'they work for Gino Camprinelli! He owns half of South Oxfordshire, from nightclubs, to taxi firms.' He tuts in disgust, 'I should have known he was involved in this somehow. Now, how the hell did Felix Gloverman get involved with Camprinelli?'

'Shall I call Shep and update her?' Julie asks him.

'Yeah, tell her to pull his file and book us in to see him first thing tomorrow,' he rubs his hands together and watches as she moves to a quiet corner of the kitchen to make the call. 'Also,' he checks his phone, 'ah yes, ask her to chase the bloody locksmith for the door. I want this house secured as soon as possible.'

PC Jeffries' tall frame walks into the room, her eyes settle on DS Jones, 'Sir, there's someone to see Mr Dean, says he's a friend.' Behind him stands a tall, thin gentleman, about Henry's age. He has a neat moustache and short-cropped greying brown hair and is dressed in chinos and a navy sweater.

'PC Jeffries?' Julie asks, pulling her phone from her ear, where she'd been talking quietly. 'Can you please go and check on Mrs Dean, she went to use the bathroom a few minutes ago?'

PC Jeffries nods as her colleague and leaves the room. I can't believe the amount of footfall and goings on we have here at Gateshead at the moment.

Henry's face lights up, 'Mickey!' he shouts to the stranger, with a genuinely warm smile, and scrapes his chair backwards and pushes up from the dining table.

'Mickey!' he holds out his hand, and then changes his mind to grasp him by the shoulders in a firm hug, 'Thanks for coming mate.'

'No problem Deaner. Henry. Good to see you, old chap.' Mickey returns the hug.

Henry pulls away reluctantly, before looking at us and raising his arms in gesture, 'This, everyone, is an old friend of mine. From my marine days. Captain Mickey Shakespeare.'

I look at Mickey and hold out my hand, 'good to meet you Mickey. I'm Stuart Greyson. I'm Jenny's boyfriend.'

Mickey's hand has a firm grip, 'Henry was my sergeant in the Royal Marines.'

I concentrate on stroking the top of Jenny's hand, lightly with my fingers. I wonder how we're going to get through the next few days, even the next few hours. So many things have happened over the last five days, from losing Jenny to that pervert Felix, to finding her in that damn box and learning about what she'd been through at the hands of that monster. She has been so brave, braver than I think I would have been in her situation.

Even with support and counselling to help her come to terms with what she's been through, I know it may take many months, possibly years, for Jenny to begin the healing process and start living her life again. I have to accept that Jenny may never be the person she was before the kidnapping. I know for sure, that I am not the same man I was before this business with Felix.

I take the opportunity to google hotels for the night on my phone. I quickly scan the selection in front of me, and settle on one I'd been to for a friend's 18th birthday celebration, at Sandford-on-Thames, not far from Oxford, and press the call button to speak to them about their room availability.

Several moments later, I disconnect the call and am just about to set the phone on the table, when there are several piercing screams accompanied by a bout of whimpering.

'Hey, stop!' a female voice ricochets through the house. It belongs to PC Jeffries. 'Do not move!'

DS Jones, Julie and I, quickly exchange glances when heavy sounds of crashing and banging filter into the room, and finally we hear a door slam shut. We're by the open doorway when we hear heavy footsteps coming from the Great Hall. PC Jeffries runs into the kitchen, her nose is bloody, her cheek red and she's breathing heavily as she comes to a stop in front of DS Jones.

'She's gone! Mrs Dean has gone!' her voice is low and strained, and she looks agitated, 'It was Felix Gloverman. He must have come back to the house and bumped into Mrs Dean.'

'What do you mean, she's gone?' Henry's concerned voice. Mickey's hand grabs his shoulder to offer support. 'Where the hell is my wife?'

'What happened?' DS Jones runs his hands through his hair. The man looks annoyed, and I don't blame him. I'd be scowling if I were in his shoes.

'I came across them by the bathroom,' PC Jeffries admitted, 'he had his arm around Mrs Dean's neck, as I approached him, he suddenly dropped Mrs Dean to the floor, stepped forward and punched me in the face. I was stunned for a moment and he took off, half-carrying the woman. He took a car, didn't see the make or registration, but it was silver.'

'Bugger,' says Julie Leadbetter in a low voice, looking at her DS.

'I'm sorry,' the PC is upset with herself, but no one was listening, because everyone apart from the officer and Jenny, has left in the room. We race through the house, to the lower floor bathroom, past the overturned mahogany table, and the shattered glass trinket box. We bolt out of the open utility door, over the grass, past the Pool House and follow the concrete path that leads to the driveway at the side of the house. And all the time, Henry's anguished calls for his wife were met with silence.

There was no sign of them. She had gone.

'We need to find them!' Henry's voice is urgent, as he looks at the senior police officer.

'We will,' the DS answers, reaching into his trouser pocket for his mobile, and orders an alert for a silver car in the area. It's a long shot and he knows it. The world is full of silver cars.

We walk back to the kitchen in silence. Henry is shaking his head in disbelief and Julie's face is pale. DS Jones simply shakes his head. Mickey Shakespeare follows behind.

'I'm sorry Jenny, but she's gone,' I tell her, 'Felix has taken her.' I watch helplessly as the colour leaves her face. Her body seems to fold in on itself and before I can catch her, she crashes to the floor

.

Part 14

Felix

The grey-haired woman snores softly on the back seat of Graham's silver Volvo. Her eyes are closed. There's a large red bruise forming on her right cheek and her eye is red and puffy, where I punched her, to stop her from screaming. It was pure luck that I ran into her as she came out of the cloakroom. I'd been hiding in the disused small cupboard under the stairs.

And, in that split second, I made the decision to take her with me, as we stood facing each other, her eyes petrified and wide. I'd slapped her face hard, watched her arms reach out to protect herself and, in turn knock a glass box, that sat on a nearby table, to the carpeted floor.

Murmuring Jenny's name, I could see that she was about to cry out to alert the others, and pulled back my fist, like a cowboy in a spaghetti western. I swung fast and with determination, until my fist connected with her upper cheek bone and eye socket. Her eyes rolled back, but no sound came from her mouth. I managed to catch her, just before she hit the ground. Unfortunately, in the process, I'd caught the table leg with my foot, and it had toppled over. What a bloody nightmare.

That's when the female police officer found me. I looked guilty as hell, standing there with my arm around Rose's neck. She'd shouted at me to stop and told me not to move, but I'd got nothing left to lose, now I'd come this far. Giving myself up wasn't an option, so I let go of Rose, stepped into the police officer's personal space and for the second time in my life, I punched a woman. My knuckles were already sore from hurting Rose, but I needed to hit her hard enough to give me time to pick up Rose and escape.

Taking advantage of the female offer being discombobulated, I quickly unbolted and unlocked the utility door, swung it open and hauled Rose through it, dragging her heavy body over the grass, past the Pool House, across the concrete path that led to the driveway where Graham had left me his silver Volvo. Didn't think I'd had it in me to punch a woman, but then I never thought I'd be able to kidnap and rape my own niece. I'm not going to win the Uncle of the Year award, anytime soon. One thing is for sure, I am not the person I was a week ago.

Rose's hands are tied together at the front with an old pair of nylon tights I'd found in Jenny's room, from Jenny's underwear drawer, along with a pair of pants, on which I'd left Jenny a little note. Thankfully, Rose's hands are hidden by the red and black, plastic backed picnic blanket I found in the boot of the car. I'd thrown it over her to stop her dying of hypothermia. A dead body is no good to me. As an afterthought, I reached for my phone to take a couple of photos of her. At some point, I may need to prove that I actually have her with me.

I think of last night, and how mad I'd felt when I'd walked behind the giant conifers leading to the Summer House and spied a police officer standing by the front door. I had no bloody idea that she'd been found! There'd been nothing on the news about her, that's why I returned to Gateshead in the first place. Jesus! Never trust the bloody press. I couldn't believe it when I'd bumped into Graham as I hid at the side of the Summer House, we'd chatted a few times over the years, and become friends, of a sort.

He'd told me he'd seen Jenny arrive at the house with Stuart earlier that evening and that there were police officers guarding the front and back of the house. He'd said there were a ton of things being whispered about me at the big house, that I'd kidnapped Jenny and wanted to hurt her. Luckily for me, he'd just shook his head and told me that he didn't believe any of them.

Graham had been happy to set up a distraction for me to get into the house. I'd sure thought he was playing the part of Howling Mad Murdoch from The A Team, as he set fire to the police car. The female police officer had seen me, then the car exploded, and all hell broke loose as she ran to the car and saw Graham running away. He'd even given me a hammer to gain entry to the front door, if my key didn't work.

The hammer did the trick when I realised that the door had been bolted. I'd kicked and chopped at the hinge and eventually the door gave way. I'd rushed to my bedroom, only to find that my bloody safe had been opened and everything taken. Without thinking, I'd ran upstairs to Jenny's room, found the tights and her pants, and left them on her bed, with the note. That would teach her.

I was grateful when he'd offered me his car to use for transport. That was, until I'd seen the inside of it. Christ. it's a bloody mess, full of empty wrappers, single gloves, and a variety of bags. There's an awful stench of stale pizza, which I assume is connected to the pizza box left on the shelf in the back of the car.

It's early Wednesday morning and I'm parked in the car park at Wittenham Clumps. Dark shadows of trees and hedgerows, sway gently in the breeze against the grey drizzle, giving it a hauntingly atmospheric feeling. In the semi-darkness I creak my neck from side to side, trying to alleviate the stiffness and ache, that is seeping through my muscles.

Not sure what I'm going to do with the old bat yet, but she will be useful in helping me get Jenny back. I reach into my trouser pocket to get out the pay as you go phone to text Henry. I'm hoping I've remembered his number right. He'll probably be awake, worrying about his wife.

'I am willing to give you back Rose, in exchange for Jenny.' I type, setting the phone on the passenger seat and pulling my jacket around me to wait for his reply.

I need to switch the ignition on, to get some heat into this damn car, but I keep putting it off. I don't want Rose to wake up yet. The light flickers across the screen and the phone begins to vibrate. I grab it clumsily and look at the screen, my fingers are beginning to feel like shards of ice.

'No. I want them both.' Henry replies.

Shit. This is no time for him to be playing the bloody hero. I need to get rid of Rose as soon as possible, before she becomes a liability. She's too old to be freezing on the back seat of a car for another night. Knowing my luck, she'll probably fall into a coma and die.

'Not going to happen,' I type the letters into my phone.

'You'd better not hurt her,' comes the reply.

'Wittenham Clumps Car Park. Long Wittenham. 8pm. Tonight. Bring Jenny. Come alone,' I tell him.

If he's got any sense he'll be here, and we can sort out this business. I just want Jenny. It's only ever been Jenny. Is that too much to ask? I hold my breath while I wait for his reply.

'I want to see her. Send me proof she's OK,' the following text read. I've got no choice. I find my photos and send him one of the photos I took of her earlier. It seems like forever, before he sends a reply.

'If you've hurt her, I will hunt you down and kill you.'

'See you at 8pm,' I send him a final text.

'I'll be there,' he finishes.

I stare at the words, and slowly exhale. Thank God. There's movement in the back of the car and I turn my head to look at Rose. Her eyes are open, well the good one is.

'Felix?' her voice is croaky. She doesn't move, not even her head, instead, she just stares at me in horror as though I'm the devil himself.

'Rose,' my voice is stern, 'keep quiet.'

'Thirsty,' she whispers, and I can see tears forming in her eyes. Her hands begin to move under the plastic picnic blanket. 'Agh,' she winces, 'cramp. In my wrists.'

'Shut up, woman!' I say sharply, over her moans, 'Or I'll give you something to moan about.'

She goes quiet, and I watch through the rear-view mirror as she lies motionless. The only things moving are the fat tears that roll down her cheeks. Bloody women!

A white carrier bag sitting in the footwell of the passenger seat, next to an empty McDonalds happy meal paper bag, piques my interest. I lean over, pick it up and search through its contents. A huge packet of popcorn, a half-empty children's fruit drink, a bottle of vodka, a packet of baby wipes, a tin of dog food and a folded over, stapled paper bag. An eclectic mix, if ever I saw one.

I study the bag, it intrigues me. Now, what do we have here? It's addressed to Graham. My heart rate picks up as I rip open the bag, the tearing sound seems harsh against the silence of the morning. I tip the contents on to my lap. There are two boxes, one is a Ventolin inhaler used for relief in asthmatics and the other is an unopened prescribed box of 20 mg Temazepam tablets, called Restoril. Prescribed to Graham. Bloody hell, how lucky am I to have those thrown into my lap? Those tablets could certainly come in useful with Rose. Very useful indeed.

Keeping Rose quiet and immobile will make the day more bearable, as we’re stuck together in this dirty car.

Maybe, I’ll flick through the photos of Jenny, on my phone. That will pass some of the time.

Part 15

Jenny

'Are you sure you're all right? I can come over to you,' Lottie's concerned voice asks over the phone line, after we'd had breakfast the following morning. It's 9.45am. I feel cold, chilled to the bone. I can't seem to get warm, despite being fully clothed in my black jeans, boots, white T-shirt and thick, green cardigan. I play with a button on Rose's oversized green cardigan and absently look around the hotel room. I was too tired to take much interest when we arrived yesterday. Tired and a little disorientated, following my fainting fit.

As I study the modern, clean bedroom with its white walls and matching bed linen, my eyes settle on the splashes of colour around the room. I take in the comfortable-looking, pale blue leather chair near the window and the abstract pale blue and yellow painting on the wall. A duck egg blue throw lies draped across the bed. Teak wood furniture completes the look.

'No, don't worry,' I try to reassure her, 'I'm fine.'

I'm sitting on a blue padded chair, next to the teak dressing table. My arm rests on the table and I can hear the faint tapping of my buttons clashing, as I twiddle them with my right hand.

My mind keeps coming back to Rose and Felix. Henry texted Stuart at 7am this morning, to say that Felix had been in touch, it was almost a relief.

Last night was surreal. I'd geared myself up to coming home. I needed to rest and recuperate. I simply wanted to spend a few quiet moments with Henry, Rose and Stuart, and then all hell had broken loose. Explosions, deception, panic and finally, Rose had been taken.

I hadn't realised how fragile I was, until Stuart had returned to the kitchen and confirmed that Rose had been taken. The shock of hearing this news, literally took the wind out of me, I'd dropped like a lead balloon to the floor. I came to, in Stuart's arms a little while later.

Shortly after this, Henry and Stuart had quickly packed overnight bags, from whatever rooms DS Jones had said weren't off limits and we'd set off, with Henry's friend Mickey, for the hotel. We left Julie and her DS behind, we needed to get out of there. We simply couldn't stay. It didn't feel like home anymore, and I didn't feel safe. We'd finally got here to the hotel, around 7pm. Stuart had taken one look at my face, seen the exhaustion and worry, etched on it, before he'd taken me to our room, sat me down on the edge of the bed, sunk to his knees and pulled off my boots.

'I'm worried about Rose,' I'd told him, putting my hand in front of my mouth to stifle a yawn.

'He won't hurt her,' he'd assured me in a deep voice, putting his hands either side of me on the bed, 'she's his leverage to get to you.'

'I know,' I'd met his gaze, I was too tired to feel depressed. I just wanted to close my heavy eyes and sleep for a long time.

Then, without saying a word, he'd taken my hand, drawn back the heavy bedcovers and helped me into the bed.

'Get some sleep, sweetheart,' he'd said, pulling the covers over me. My body was weary, and my mind had closed in on itself, taking me to a faraway place, with a sandy beach, where the sun kept me warm, and the only sounds I could hear were the distant breaking of the ocean waves. Bliss.

At 3am I'd been woken by a nightmare. Everything was dark, and I'd sat up with a start. I felt as though I couldn't breathe, as if I was suffocating. Once again, I was enclosed in that dark, hard wooden box, where I couldn't move. A heavy weight of pressure seemed to be sucking the air out of my lungs. I'd pushed Stuart's heavy arm off my stomach and bolted upright.

I was frightened because I couldn't catch my breath. Couldn't settle it enough to regulate my breathing. Stuart had woken and calmed me while stroking my back.

'It's all right Jen, it's all right,' he'd repeated in a low voice, 'you've had a nightmare, or flashback. Daniel said this might happen.'

The soothing strokes on my back had brought me back to reality, and I could feel my chest taking in air and settling, as my breathing returned to normal. Thank God! I'd thought I was going to die.

'I thought I was back there, in that room. In the box. I couldn't breathe,' my voice was quiet in the darkness.

'I'm here now, sweetheart,' he'd soothed, rubbing my shoulders, 'and I will never let him hurt you again.'

I'd turned into his shoulder and cried, my face wet with tears. In a place where I knew I was s afe; I'd let the tears fall. I'd wept for myself, for the pain and anguish Felix's actions had caused. And finally, when there were no tears left, I'd let Stuart gently lean me back onto the soft pillows and tuck me under his shoulder. Wrapped in the warm comfort of his arms, exhausted beyond belief, I'd sunk into oblivion.

In the bright, sunlight of a chilly October morning, I'd woken with a heavy arm resting on my stomach. Stuart was protecting me, even in his sleep. A new day, a new start. Small steps.

***

'No, it's OK,' I repeat to Lottie, as I jolt back to the present, 'Stu's next door with Henry. Mickey, an old friend of Henry's, is also with them, he arrived last night. Apparently, they used to work together in something very cloak and dagger like. They're figuring out what to do next. Felix wants to meet Henry at Wittenham Clumps car park at 8pm tonight.'

'Don't tell me Henry is going? Can't the police go?'

'I suspect they'll be hiding behind a bush somewhere,' I say absently, using my index finger to swipe a speck of dust from the table.

My eyes daze for a moment, fixated on the wood and I feel unable to tear them away from the spot where my finger sits.

'Felix has offered to swap Rose for me. I'm going to try and talk sense into my Uncle,' my voice is quiet, defeated. My shoulders slump and I suddenly feel so very tired again.

'Jesus Jenny!' her voice cuts in sharply, 'Don't you bloody dare!'

'Lottie,' I begin, but she stops me immediately.

'No, Jen. I'm being serious, don't you dare give yourself back to that man, not after what he did to you!'

I hear her panic as her voice gets higher and more strained. I try my best to calm her.

'Lottie, it's all right. I won't do anything stupid.'

‘Thank God, Jen. We need to get Rose back, though. It’s all such a bloody mess,’ her voice sounds relieved and frustrated at the same time.

‘I know,’ I exhale slowly, ‘I’ve told Henry, I’ll go with him tonight. There’s no way I’m letting Felix keep Rose. We’ll find a way. I’m hoping the police will have a plan.’ I couldn’t bear the thought of being near Felix again, let alone being touched by him. I close my eyes and silently count to five.

‘I can’t imagine what he’s going through,’ Lottie says.

‘Me neither. Felix is a very disturbed person. I’m worried for Rose. I can’t even bring myself to think about the things Felix did to me, let alone what he might do to Rose,’ I shuffle my feet. I can’t believe I said that out loud, I hope Lottie doesn’t pick up on it. It’s the first time I’ve admitted that I’m finding it hard to come to terms with what happened to me.

‘Disturbed is an understatement,’ Lottie adds, and I’m thankful that she was showing no indication that she’d understood what I was really saying. ‘I hate him,’ her voice drops to a brittle, lower tone, ‘I hate him for everything he did to you. For not getting arrested and for walking free. I hate him for things that he’s done and may do in the future.’

She was so right, about the hating part. There was a coil of anger, wound so tight in my chest that it hurt. I wanted to tell Stuart, about my feelings, about the frustration that coursed through my veins because I’d allowed myself to be kidnapped, and put in that damn box, in a place well-known to me, but I felt Stuart was already hurting too much.

I am angry with myself. I’m angry that I’ve allowed Felix to hurt me in so many different ways. How did I not know that the brandy was drugged? Why did I not take extra precautions for my own safety, when I had my suspicions about Felix? I completely ignored the small voices inside my head, that were shouting at me, *Stop! Stop being so bloody hard on yourself! How were you to know about the brandy? Could you read his mind? How could you know what he had planned?*

The rape, I'm just thankful that I didn't remember any of it. In my darkest moments, when I felt weary and unsure of myself, I found it increasingly hard to stop my mind from imagining a hundred different ways in which Felix violated me.

'I feel so guilty. This is my fault. It's me he wants,' I say, feeling despondent, 'I would be prepared to give myself to Felix, if it meant that he'd let Rose go.'

'No!' Lottie's voice rises, 'Don't say that! None of this is your fault!'

Yes! It was! My inner voice screams. I should have somehow stopped it. Fought back. Not allowed that monster to do those things to me. I should have tried harder to get the lid off the box, to get out. I move my head from side to side, trying to clear my thoughts and put what happened to me in perspective. Deep down, I knew it wasn't my fault. I knew that I did what I could to stay alive in the hope that someone would save me. And that someone did. Stuart.

'I know,' I say, after what seems like an age, 'deep down, I bloody know that.' And then I realise that I've spoken my frustrated, angry words aloud. Shit.

'Jen?' her question is quiet. It's low and questioning. The line crackles and then clears.

'Yeah?' I answer, pushing the side of the button hard into my hand.

'Let me in. Scream and shout. Anything, but don't give in to those dark thoughts.'

I blink back the threatening tears. ‘I’ll try. It’s just hard, you know,’ I tell her in a voice that doesn’t quite seem my own. I wipe away a tear that trickles down my cheek.

‘I won’t pretend to know what you’re going through,’ Lottie’s words sound strained, ‘but I know what it’s like to have control taken away from you, to be put in an impossible position, where the only thing that matters is that you survive.’

My heart plummets to the ground, a shiver makes it way up my back and to my shoulders, they begin to shudder. Not Lottie, please not Lottie, I silently scream. I can’t bear it if she tells me she’s been violated, abused.

‘Lottie?’ I whisper, ‘What happened to you?’

‘Not now, Jen,’ she says, and an overwhelming sadness seems to float down the phone line, connecting us, ‘it was a long time ago.’

‘But Lottie,’ I persist, ‘if you’ve been hurt, I want to know. Want to help you.’

‘No,’ she says flatly, ‘it was a long time ago. Maybe one day, I’ll tell you.’

‘I’m here for you,’ I say, my head is still reeling from Lottie’s admission, ‘anytime.’

‘I know, sweetie,’ she sounds a little brighter, ‘for now, we need to look after you.’

The squeak and motion sound of a door handle turning, panics me momentarily, as the heavy hotel room door opens, and I watch with relief as Stuart comes into the room. He’s wearing a maroon sweatshirt over a black T-shirt, and grey jeans. His hair is mussed a little. My heart flutters at the sight of him, taking me back to when we first met, last year. It seems such a long time ago now. Where did the time go? I wish I’d met him sooner, wish things were different. Wish I was the original Jenny, the Jenny before

Felix. The Jenny who hadn't been raped. You know what they say, if wishes were horses.

***

Cheese and ham paninis are my favourite lunch time staples. I closed my eyes and savoured the tangy mouthful as I sat in the university refectory. My friend Lottie, sat next to me, rocking her wooden chair backwards, precariously balancing it on its back legs. Every so often, she took a mouthful from her chicken sandwich.

'You're going to break your neck doing that, one day,' I muttered, in between bites.

'Stop worrying. It won't happen, and if it does, you'll be there to catch me,' she grinned. Our eyes wandered to the main entrance, where a tall, lean brown-haired man, wearing a brown jacket over a navy top and dark grey jeans, had walked forward and stood scouring the room, as if assessing where everything was, and what everyone was doing.

He was handsome in the classical sense, with a straight nose, oval face and good cheekbones. For someone who'd had virtually no interest in boys over the years, I'd found this man stunning. He'd simply taken my breath away. I couldn't take my eyes off him, as his focus had rested briefly on the catering counters, displaying an enticing selection of food, before moving on to a group of students who were eating their lunch in the dining area.

And then his eyes reached mine, locked on to me, making my heart race as though I'd just run a quick sprint. A warm feeling had worked its way up my body, and my cheeks had started to burn. I'd tried to turn away but couldn't. I was rooted to the spot. After what seemed like an age, I'd given in first, and lowered my eyes. The disconnection had made me feel uncomfortable. Melancholy.

‘God! He’s a bit of all right,’ Lottie had broken into my thoughts. He certainly was, a bit of all right I mean. Thankfully, I hadn’t spoken the words out loud.

‘Lottie!’ I’d chastised, ignoring the butterflies that were fluttering in my tummy.

‘He’s looking this way, quick, smile back at him!’ she’d said, a little too loudly.

I’d dropped my gaze and taken another bite of my panini. It felt familiar and comforting.

‘Jen!’ I’d kept my head down, deliberately trying to downplay my unfamiliar feelings.

‘Nope, if he’s interested, he’ll come over,’ I’d said nonchalantly, picking up my phone and checking the emails.

I’d felt him before I saw him, when a frisson of excitement had begun tingling its way along my shoulders and spiralling into my neck.

‘Hi,’ a deep voice had said.

I’d slowly turned my head, and croaked out, ‘hi,’ as I’d looked up into brown eyes so dark, that they looked almost black. Eyes that held intrigue, confidence and hope.

He’d put out his hand, ‘I’m Stuart.’

I’d stared at his hand, unable to move, locked in place. Slowly I’d put my hand into his, curling my fingers to his grip. Warm. Soft. Strong. And then there was a short jolt, like an electric shock pumping through our veins. I’d gone to pull away, but he’d held me firm. I thought he’d felt it too, because his eyes had darted to our joined hands and a puzzled expression had come over his face. It was in those first few moments of meeting him, that I'd realised that I'd liked his hand, holding mine. I'd liked his touch. Very much.

'Jenny,' I'd said, in a slightly husky voice.

'Hi Jenny, I'm new here. Any chance I can sit with you guys?' his eyes had darted between us both, silently asking our permission.

'Of course,' Lottie had gulped down her food and bounced her chair to the floor, 'I'm Lottie, by the way.'

'Nice to meet you Lottie,' he'd said, giving her a warm smile, before turning his face back to me. When I'd looked down, I'd realised that we were still holding hands. Kismet.

***

I don't know how long I'd been daydreaming for, but when I come back to reality, I find myself still holding Stu's phone to my ear. Lottie's voice is still chattering away trying to make sense of the events that had taken place over the last week.

Despite suffering at the hands of a deviant uncle, I seem to be coping. Just about. There is a constant feeling of anticipation, as though I'm waiting for the earth to swallow me up, finish the job that he'd started. This is life, after Felix.

'Hey Lottie, I need to go. Stu's back,' I study Stuart's face as he walks towards me. There are dark circles under his eyes, and his skin is drawn. The stress of the last week is beginning to take its toll on him. I say goodbye to my friend and watch as Stuart comes to a standstill in front of me, offering a warm smile.

'Lottie?' he asks, reaching for my hands and drawing me to my feet.

'Yeah,' I murmur, reaching up to cup his cheek. I find it hard when other people touch me, but with Stu, it's different. I need his touch. Need to feel grounded by him. For the first time in what feels like forever, I lean forward and put my lips to his, gently encouraging a kiss.

I hear Stu's intake of breath, he's holding back. I can tell, there's a stiffness to his shoulders, as though he's scared to be himself with me. I push my tongue gently through his lips, teasing the tip of his, and, caught up in the moment, I can't help but offer a moan.

'Stu?' I whisper.

'Yes, sweetheart?' his hands hold my hips.

I pull back, hold his dear face in my hands, and force his eyes to meet mine, 'I love you.'

Stuart exhales sharply, and I watch in wonder at the brightness of his eyes, the upward tilt of his mouth.

'I love you too, Jen,' his voice is husky with emotion, 'so damn much.'

My hands fall lightly to his shoulders and gently rub the knotted muscles. He murmurs in appreciation as my fingers push a little harder, unlocking the tension he's been holding on to. I reach up to circle his neck and hold him to me. This man. He is everything to me. He's strong, kind, protective. He is beautiful inside and outside. Despite everything that has happened to me, he loves me, and wants to be with me.

Above all else, he understands me. Understands that we need to make new memories. I watch mesmerised as he slowly dips his head to reach mine and takes my mouth in a long, searching kiss. A kiss to mark our new beginning, and thankfully, a kiss that blots Felix Gloverman's face temporarily from my mind. God, I love this man.

When we pull apart, we are both smiling, despite everything that is happening around us, despite not knowing where Rose is, or that the house was broken into, and that Felix is still free to create havoc wherever he goes. We are still smiling.

‘I have a question,’ I say, walking to the bed and sitting close to the end.

He looks up, ‘yes?’

‘What do you know of Lottie’s past?’ I brush my hands down my jeans, ‘Do you know if she was abused as a child?’

‘To be honest, I don’t know much about her past, she’s never talked about it to me,’ he says, raking his hand through his hair, ‘what makes you think that she’s been abused?’

‘It was something she said, about having control taken from her, and doing anything to survive,’ I state flatly.

‘If she has been abused, we need to support her. Give her opportunities to tell us,’ he says, then adds, ‘but only if she wants to. We can’t force her.’

‘I know,’ I say sadly, ‘but I want to try and help her if I can.’ I sit quietly for a moment, clasping my fingers together, I need to talk to him about tonight, about what Felix wants to do at Wittenham Clumps. I know he’ll get mad, but I need to tell him what I plan to do.

‘Listen, Stu,’ I begin, slowly, ‘about tonight.’

‘No!’ his voice cuts in, reading my mind. ‘No matter what happens, I’m not letting you give yourself back to that monster.’ He puts his hands firmly on my shoulders. ‘No,’ he says, his deep voice becoming louder, ‘not for Rose, not for anyone, do you hear me?’

‘But!’ I argue.

'No!' he pulls away and starts pacing the dark grey carpet, I watch as he thrusts his hands deep into his trouser pockets. I can tell he's agitated and trying to keep himself calm, so that he doesn't upset me. A hand leaves his pocket and he rakes it through his short hair in frustration. *Talk to me Stu, tell me what's going through that head of yours.*

Two quick strides and he's by my side, his head tilting down as his eyes bore into mine. Although we're not touching, I can feel his warm breath on my face, caressing my skin. Stu's face comes closer, and I'm immobilized as we lock eyes.

'We'll think of something,' his voice is husky, 'we'll find a way.'

Part 16

Gino

Bloody paperwork. It's the bane of my life. I'm in my office, all is quiet, apart from the steady beat of the music from the black Alexa that sits on my desk. I place my pen on the desk and lean back in my chair. The movement sends a shooting pain across my lower back. God, that hurt. It gets like this every month now, sitting, standing, it doesn't matter what I do. What I really need is a massage. I'll get Dawn, my personal assistant, to book an appointment with Tina, who works in the sports shop I own in Headington. Tina's training to be a masseuse and I've had her quite a few times, over the past six months. When I say, I've had her, I mean not just lying on a table and having her hands massage me, but also in the biblical sense. I've had her.

Devoid of emotion, I look at my sore, bloody knuckles. Another shitty day at the office. Another reason to pack it all in and buy a villa on Lake Como. Charlotte Church begins the first few bars of, Andrew Lloyd Webber's, Pie Jesu and I close my eyes in contentment, letting the notes caress my throbbing body. Her voice is stunning. So pure and clear. I purse my lips, trying not to smile, the irony is not lost. It's something I'll never be. Pure and clear. I pick up my pen and study the deeds on the lease of an old warehouse I've just purchased, over in Watlington. As I stare at the sheet of paper, there's a small movement in front of me.

Shit. I forgot about them.

'Qui tollis peccata mundi,' Church sings, 'Dona eis requiem.'

I close my eyes and steeple my fingers together. I hear a thud and peer over my desk, as the second verse starts, 'Pie Jesu,' and the words flow over me like a caress. I'm calmer than I was an hour ago. Pushing my chair back, I move to the front of the desk and rest my arse on it, studying the two men.

Antonio and Carlos sit on my new Persian carpet, back to back. They're bound together with rope. A lot of rope. Their heads droop onto their upper chests. Bloody stupid bastards. What is the matter with them? They should know better. Blood drips from Antonio's nose and Carlos' right eye is bulging, bleeding and closed. I feel disconnected, as I look at my red raw knuckles. Disconnected and fed up with the lot of them, including Felix fucking Gloverman.

The need to find that bloody man has turned into nothing short of a farce, with that creep Naylor giving me false information on his whereabouts. Of course, the bastard wasn't at the address I'd been given. I'm still in two minds whether to send a couple of men over to Naylor to let him know how displeased I am with him.

I look at these two idiots in front of me, they couldn't even go to the Gloverman Head Office, to ask about Gloverman, without stirring up more trouble.

'What is the matter with you two?' I ask, 'All you had to do, was find out where Felix Gloverman is holed up. Is that so bloody hard?' I tut and shake my head. Imbeciles.

I push off from the desk, dig my hands into my dark grey trouser pockets, and walk around them slowly. I stop beside Antonio, staring at his blood splattered white shirt.

'The last thing I said to you was, to tread carefully, to ask his secretary if she knew where he might be,' I can hear my voice getting deeper, my words becoming angrier, 'and then I find that you've gone in, all guns blazing and dropped me right in it. What the fuck did you think you were doing by threatening a pregnant woman and stabbing a bloody copper!'

'Boss,' Antonio pleads, struggling to breathe through his bloody nose, as snuffling sounds accompany his words, 'we're sorry.'

'Shut the fuck up!' I hiss. 'Did I tell you to speak!' I continue walking slowly around the carpet. They're making a bloody mess on it. I'll be lucky if it comes up clean.

I stand in front of Carlos with my hands in my pockets, his head is still lowered. I know he's listening. 'Give me one reason why I shouldn't kill you both right this second.'

Carlos lifts his head slightly, shaking it. His eye looks as if it's about to explode. 'The girl,' he whispers.

'What girl?' I snap.

'The police officer,' his head stays low, his voice quiet.

'What about her?'

'I know where she lives.'

I pick up his chin and tilt it in my direction, 'and, how will that help us?'

'She'll lead us to Gloverman,' his eye focuses on me, watching closely, as I register what he is saying.

'Good, that's kept you both off my to-do list today,' I tell them, walking to the phone on my desk. I depress a single silver button and hold it down, to call my personal assistant.

'Dawn, book me an appointment with Tina,' I order, and as an afterthought, 'also, get Big Tommy in here to sort out these two idiots, and arrange for this bloody Persian carpet to be cleaned.'

I'm about to disconnect when Dawn clears her throat and tells me that there are two police officers here to see me. This shitty day has just got worse. Raking my hands through my hair, I walk myself through each stage. Find a quiet area, offer food or drink. Find an excuse for the knuckles.

'Take them into the small office. Offer them refreshments. I'll be there in a minute,' I shout, stabbing the disconnect button. Shit. That's all I need.

Part 17

DCI Brian Carter

The John Radcliffe is like any other university city hospital, it's busy, sterile and under pressure. There are several buildings on one main site, a number of car parks that don't sufficiently meet the need of those visiting and for all intents and purposes this teaching hospital is a leading centre of medical excellence.

The hospital was named after an 18th-century physician and Oxford university graduate, John Radcliffe. I know this because my grandmother, a former teacher at an Oxford secondary school, had spent much of my youth explaining that John Radcliffe had been a graduate at Lincoln College and, had several buildings named after him.

From the now closed Radcliffe Infirmary, to the Radcliffe Camera, Science Library and Observatory. All named after this man, who was in the right place, at the right time to become immortalised in Oxford history. Not for the likes of a working police officer like me.

Of course, I hadn't been a graduate at Lincoln or any Oxford college or any university. I was a boy from a small Oxfordshire village called East Hagbourne, who'd left school at sixteen with nothing but a few token GCSEs.

Mrs Smith, short blonde hair, with balding patches, amid fine wisps of hair that sprouted from bare skin on the top of her head, as though she had a medical condition. Mrs Smith, the kind natured woman, whose duties included being the school counsellor as well as the secretary, who had steered me to the nearest job centre at sixteen, based in a nearby commuter town, called Didcot. When I think of it, things could have turned out a lot differently for me if I hadn't seen the police recruitment advert in the job centre that day.

With no key qualifications, apart from a distance learning BA honours degree in Criminology and Psychology, I'd taken with the Open University, I slowly made my way up the Thames Valley Police promotion ladder.

During that time, I'd also had a couple of crossover cases with the Bristol and Basingstoke constabulary teams, learning from a variety of skill sets, taking in tips and meeting good people, like Eddie Creakston. I guess having a degree was nothing to sneeze about, but I was under no illusions that someone would name a building after me, let alone, one in Oxford. I mean, The Carter Playhouse or the Carter History Museum, doesn't have the same ring, does it?

Holy Mother of God that hurts. I wince as I shuffle my upper body into an upright position. It appears that hospital beds can be a nightmare when you're trying to sit upright in them. You start off propped up on a pillow and then gradually slither down the bed, until you're almost lying flat.

I look at my watch, 3pm. Where has the day gone? I can't get comfortable, so I push myself into the sitting position, swing my grey pyjama-clad legs over the side of the bed, and lower them until they rest on the floor. I sit like this for a while, listening to the muffled sounds coming from outside my room.

Suddenly there's a commotion in the corridor, a bleeping, clattering of metal on metal and rushing feet. A male voice shouts, 'Code Blue, Code Blue.' Shit. That can't be good. More running feet, mumbling and shouting. And then, everything goes quiet for a moment, until a female voice yells, 'No!' before bursting into heavy sobs. Jesus. I close my eyes, muttering a silent prayer for whoever has just lost their life.

After a few moments, I ease myself gently to a standing position, all the time holding onto the wooden unit at the side of the bed, to give me more support. My legs are fine, but it hurts like hell when I move the top part of my body. My chest and back have been tightly strapped with bandages to restrict my movement and support the injury.

Moving slowly, I cross the room until I reach the high-backed chair by the window. Reaching back to grab the arms of the chair for stability, I close my eyes and lower my sore body into the chair. That feels much better.

Day two in the hospital, fondly referred to as the JR, and, I'm stuck in here, in this damn place, dying of boredom, while Mike takes over the Jenny Gloverman case. It's not in my nature to be still, in fact I can count on one hand how many sick days I've had in my working life.

Now I'm here, with my mind racing at one hundred miles per hour, replaying that day, the one with Julie, with the crazy, wild-eyed Audi driver causing chaos on our way to Ditton Park. The day when I made a damn fool of myself by telling Julie about my feelings for her.

I'm kicking myself for bringing the subject up with her, and I'm annoyed with myself for putting Julie in such an awkward position. In my defence, it was a moment of pure adrenalin, that left me wanting to be honest with her. Well, it's out there now, I've told her how I feel and, now it's up to her to make the first move.

The doctor said I'd been lucky, because the knife hadn't gone in very deep. At the time, I didn't feel so lucky, though. The last thing I remembered was telling Julie that we needed the hospital. Then everything went blank.

Mike had visited when he'd got back from Bristol, he'd asked for my house keys so that he could collect a few toiletries and a set of clothes for me. He'd been quick about it, and within the hour he had returned with a rucksack full of stuff for me. I was bowled over, by his kindness.

I sense her before I can see her.

There's a quiet knock on the slightly open door.

'Come in Julie,' I say, my eyes are still closed.

'How are you?' she asks quietly, her footsteps moving closer to me. After a moment, I open my eyes and look at her. She's wearing black jeans, black ankle boots, a long-sleeved purple top that really suits her and lip gloss. Her small, black crossover bag sits at her waist and casually thrown over her arm is a black jacket. She is beautiful, and the strange thing is, I don't think she realises it.

She's got a brown hessian short-handled bag, dangling from one hand and I watch as she places it on the bed, with her jacket, before reaching into the bag to take out a long length of wire that looks like a phone charger. She scans the room, looking for plug sockets, finds the one nearest to the bed and picks up my dead mobile from the bed tray.

'There,' she says, putting the phone on charge, 'this should do the trick.' I can't help but feel pleased that she's fussing around me, as though she cares. This woman is fast becoming an important part of my life. Whether that's my imagination, wishful thinking, or reality, I'm not sure. But I do know that she brings out the best in me, makes me want to try for a new relationship.

'Thanks,' I say, lowering my face, to hide the smile.

‘At least we can contact you now. How are you feeling?’ she asks again, the heels of her boots click as she moves forward to stand in front of me. I watch as her long, slim fingers hook around the outside of her pockets.

‘I’m fine,’ I mutter.

‘Fine?’ she looks at me, ‘Brian, you were stabbed.’

I can see the storm in her dark blue eyes and her voice carries a note of worry, even anger.

‘Julie, I was hardly dying,’ I mutter, I don’t want her pity. ‘It was nothing more than a scratch.’

She takes a deep breath and puts her hand on my good shoulder. It feels good, like something I could get used to. I try to remember the last time I’d had a relationship, a proper dating, chatting, touching and physical relationship. It must have been a couple of years ago. God, how had it been that long? How had I let things slip? I curse under my breath. Annoyed with myself.

I know she’s heard my comment, I wish she hadn’t, but it was too late to take it back. She inhales sharply, as if she’s come to a decision and then, without warning she leans into me and cups my cheek with her free hand.

‘Brian,’ she whispers, so close that her breath sprinkles across my skin, and I can’t take my eyes from hers.

‘You were stabbed,’ her words are so soft, ‘and, I thought I’d lost you.’

‘Julie,’ my voice is husky with emotion.

‘Let me finish,’ her warm fingers stroke my chin. ‘I said I needed time to think, back in the car. Honestly though, I can’t get the picture of you falling to the ground in front of me out of my mind.’

I reach up and place my large hand over hers.

'I can't think of anything I would rather do than explore what we've both been trying to avoid,' she mutters thickly.

I remove my hand from her face, and push myself upright, ignoring the pain in my back, as I move.

'Come here,' I tell her, reaching up and placing my left hand on the soft skin at the nape of her neck. I close my eyes, inhaling her scent of jasmine and vanilla. And the world stops. I feel like I've come home. And, I haven't even kissed her.

Julie sways into me and lifts her chin, her lips parted. In this moment, as our lips touch tentatively, slowly and with nothing more than the briefest contact, I feel as though I've found my own private heaven. I didn't know how the hell I was going to coming back from this. Didn't know if I even wanted to come back from this.

We pull apart, and I study the long lashes that shutter her still closed eyes, and softly trace her warm cheek with the back of my knuckles.

'That,' she says, her eyes flutter open, 'was.'

'The start of something,' I finish for her, in a low growl, 'special.'

'Did you feel it too?' she asks.

I can't stop the smile forming on my lips, 'yes, and we hardly touched. I think that you, PC Leadbetter are bewitching me with your touch.'

'Casting you under my spell,' she laughs, her hands reaching for mine, taking them gently in her own, 'can't say as I've ever knowingly bewitched anyone before. I feel rather powerful.'

'Heaven help me,' I look up at the ceiling with mock seriousness, 'I'm going to need to save my strength.'

She lets go of my hands, her face alight with joy. I like seeing her happy, making her smile.

I sit down on the end of the bed and the mattress dips slightly when she sits beside me. After a few moments, I begin to think about Jenny Gloverman and our current case. Julie must have been thinking the same.

'I popped in to see Amy Wilder on my way here,' she says, 'they've got her in the Women's Centre.'

'Poor woman,' I rub the stubble on my chin, 'how is she?'

Julie picks at a piece of fluff on the white sheet, 'not good. Her brother was with her. He's in the Royal Marines, came in his gear. They don't have any family, just each other, she was telling me, so he's taken compassionate leave to look after her.'

'He sounds like a good lad. She'll need someone to take care of her,' I hoped this would be enough. Amy Wilder had been through a lot. Abused by a monster, carrying his child, assaulted by people looking for said monster, which culminated in losing her child. I wouldn't be surprised if she didn't need counselling for the rest of her life.

Warm fingers lightly stroke the back of my hand, and, I look at her. She understands, and that thought, makes life a little easier. The moment I stop caring, is the moment I give this damn job up.

'How is Henry Dean holding up?' I ask her, changing the subject.

'About as you'd expect,' she says, moving her hand, 'an old marine pal of his has turned up, a Mickey Shakespeare. They go way back. Turns out they used to be Royal Marine Commandos together.'

'No way! Aren't they like the SAS?' I ask and wait for her nod, before continuing, 'this case is bringing up more surprises than an Agatha Christie novel.'

'Tell me about it,' she shakes her head, 'Felix Gloverman wants to meet Henry tonight at 8pm at Wittenham Clumps, to exchange Rose for Jenny. Jenny wants to do it, but Stuart has put his foot down and categorically refuses to let her go.'

'Can't say I blame him,' I mutter, 'he's already lost her once.' Something is bugging me, not sure what it is, but Jenny's uncle is like a cat with nine lives, he has an ability to find his way out of every bad situation.

'Mike spoke to Andy Naylor,' Julie explains, 'he says he's not seen Felix Gloverman for years.' She feels around for her phone and takes it out of her back pocket. Holds it in both hands. 'The strange thing is, he's got a black eye and two of his fingers on his right hand are bandaged together. Looks like he's got himself involved in something shady.'

'Shady, as in Gino Camprinelli shady?' I ask.

'Possibly,' she muses and shrugs her shoulders.

'Let's check out Naylor's properties. See if he's rented out any places in the immediate Bristol area, in the last couple of days?' I tell her. She nods, I know she's got her hands full keeping an eye on Jenny Gloverman, and Rose's disappearance, but she can get Shep to do it.

'Gino Camprinelli,' I'm on a roll now, my head is clearing and, for the first time in twenty-four hours, I feel like the mist is finally lifting from my brain, 'I thought those thugs looked familiar. What's he got to say for himself?'

'He says he knows Gloverman,' she says in a flat tone that hints of disbelief, 'but only as a business acquaintance. They've met at Chamber of Commerce galas, business enterprise forums, that sort of thing. He stresses that they don't socialise on a personal basis.'

‘Of course, they don’t,’ I mutter, more to myself, ‘but my gut feeling tells me that there’s more to their relationship than meets the eye, especially with the level of adult only clubs Camprinelli is involved with. Not to mention the massage parlours, betting shops and sports shops, all of which seem to be fronts for his other business ventures.’

Julie looks at her watch.

‘I’d better get going. I need to get back to the hotel to check in with Jenny and the others, make sure they don’t do anything stupid.’

I turn to her, rest my hand on top of hers before she can move, ‘be careful, while Felix Gloverman is still out there, he’s desperate and there are people after him. Watch your back.’

She leans in and brushes her lips softly to my cheek. ‘I’ll be careful,’ she promises softly, as she pushes up off the bed, grabs her jacket and leaves the room.

I stand up, look at the empty doorway, watching the shadows of people walking in the corridor going about their business. The niggle, the one I had earlier about Felix Gloverman, suddenly hits me, like a slab of concrete. Shit. The silver car. The one Gloverman got away in. Does it belong to the gardener?

I reach for my phone and call Mike.

Part 18

Felix

The steaming hot cappuccino burns my lips as I take a slurp. God, I need this. Leaning forward in the metal and wood chair, I let my elbows rest on the wooden table, all the while my hands are wrapped around the hot, scalding mug.

I look around the café of the garden centre near Brightwell-cum-Sotwell, on the way to Wallingford, and note with relief, that most of the tables are empty. I tilt my wrist and check my Rolex, bloody hell, it's only 4pm. I've left Rose pumped up with Restoril and vodka on the back seat of the car. She's now snoring like a bloody pig. I needed a break from her.

What do you do, when you know that there's nowhere to go, and you can't go back? When you have moved so far away from the person you thought you were, and have done things that would even make your mother cry, if she were still alive? When you look in the mirror and you don't recognise yourself?

I try the cappuccino again. The burn isn't so bad after a while. I close my eyes and blank out the world. One thing is for certain, I need to get away from this place. From this area. From Oxfordshire. I would prefer to take Jenny with me, and I'm willing to bet my life that she will insist on offering herself to me, in order to save Rose.

Crumbs from the leftover fruit scone sit on the plate, calling for me to lick my finger and dab at them, before sliding them into my mouth. Absently, I do just that. The sign on the front door says that they close at 5pm on weekdays, so I can't stay too long. I'll have a quick look around and head back to the car. Who knows, maybe I could pick up some string or cable ties?

Ten minutes later and I'm in back in the car. The windows shake with the rumble of Rose's snoring. 'For goodness' sake,' I mutter under my breath as I turn on the ignition and put the car into gear before making my way back to Wittenham Clumps to wait for Henry and Jenny. I turn on the car radio and raise the volume.

As the daylight begins to fade, I make my way past the Clumps car park, past the Earth Trust site entrance, and settle in the small deserted car park of Neptune Wood. It didn't pay to be on site too early. The surface of the road was so bad, that I nearly veered off the road twice.

The music from the radio settles me for a while, as I ponder and deliberate how this was going to play out. How do I get Jenny to come with me, rid myself of Rose and lose the police officers that will be almost certainly following Henry and Jenny?

My mind is buzzing with scenarios, trying to work out the most efficient way of getting Jenny into the car. Do I drag Rose into a bush and make them collect her first? Do I push her out of the car, once I've got Jenny in the passenger seat? Shit, I need to get this right.

I turn the radio off, to allow me to think straight, draw my black jacket around me and concentrate.

With the constant buzzing of my brain, weighing up what could happen, working out best fit possibilities, I hadn't noticed that the car was quiet. Didn't hear the silence. And my first thought, was simply, thank God, Rose had stopped snoring. I turn on the torch light from my phone and shine the bright light over her body.

Yes, she is fine. Then the light rested on her face and something didn't look quite right. Holy shit. Her eyes were open, and she was staring, just staring at the back of the seat. No, this can't be bloody happening! My heart stops and an icy chill makes it's way down my shoulders. Pushing open the driver door, I step outside, wrap my hand around the cool metal handle of the passenger door and yank it open.

'Rose?' I shout, hearing the panic in my voice, 'Rose? For God-sake, answer me?'

I touch her cheek. It's cool. Jesus! My eyes look to the half-empty vodka bottle sitting in the footwell, next to her. How many temazepam had I given her? Six? Eight? I can't remember. I'd smashed them with the hard surface of the tinned dog food and put them in the spirit. The almost empty packet of tablets glints in the darkness, I reach over Rose's body to look at them. I'd given her six. I thought that would be OK.

Obviously, I was wrong.

My fingers move involuntarily to her wrist, feeling for a pulse. I close my eyes to concentrate. 'Come on,' I mutter, 'come on. You're doing this on bloody purpose!' Nothing.

As I lean over her, my eyes closed and my fingers pressed to her neck, willing her heart to start beating, a sense of doom came over me. There was no pulse. This is the beginning of the end, for me. I would be hated by everyone. God, if my parents were alive, they would be horrified at the person I've become. Henry is going to bloody kill me.

I take Rose's shoulders and roll her onto her back. With locked fingers, I push, palm down onto her upper chest. I've never done this before, and it feels clumsy as I repeat the action for what seems like a minute. There's no way I'm giving her mouth to mouth, so I continue with the compressions, pushing harder and faster.

There's the sound of a crack. Shit. I've broken a rib. Bloody, buggering hell. Shocked with myself for being so rough with her,

I lace my fingers together at the back of my head and start pacing in the dark.

'Think, Felix. Think,' I mutter. Should I check her pulse again? Should I leave her here and disappear? Forget the whole thing? If they don't know what car I'm using, I'll have a head start.

I lean into the car again and put my hand on the cold skin of her neck. Bugger.

She's dead.

Part 19

Jenny

It's dark outside. I gaze at the moving shadows and flickering lights as Henry and I head through the Oxfordshire countryside, on the way to the Clumps. The winding country lanes twist and turn, I can feel my chest getting tighter, the closer we draw to our destination. To Felix.

'You are not getting out of this car, Jenny,' Henry's gruff voice warns, quickly taking his eyes off the road, 'I promised Stuart, I wouldn't let you get out of the car. We get Rose and we let the police sort out Felix.'

Stuart, Julie and DS Jones are following, at a safe distance, behind us. Julie gave me her iPhone, which I've put in my jeans pocket. It's got a tracker on it. Just in case. I won't let Felix take Rose, no matter what Stuart and Henry say.

I can't let him hurt her, if it's me he wants, then that's the way it is. I would willingly give myself up to make Rose safe. I look up at the twinkle of stars in the clear night sky and offer a silent prayer. *Please God, don't let him take me again. Don't let him hurt me. I don't want Felix to hurt anyone else.*

It's that final thought that spurs me on. Pushes me to face Felix, face my demons. Julie's phone vibrates and I reach for it, keying in the access code that Julie gave me. It's a text, from Stuart:

> *'You OK?'*

OK? Of course, I'm not OK! I'm about to meet the person who kidnapped and raped me a few days ago. I know it's not Stuart's fault, and I shouldn't take it out on him, but I feel so frustrated sometimes. Thankfully, I'm careful with my reply:

'I'm fine. A bit jittery.'

'Wish I was there with you,' he responds.

My chest warms, defrosting some of the ice sitting in the pit of my stomach. I wish he was with me too.

'Me too,' I tell him, waiting to see what he writes next.

'Don't leave the car,' he warns.

'I won't,' I know it's a lie, but I type the words anyway, I need to reassure him.

'Love you,' he types back.

Tears spring to my eyes and I absently brush them away with the palm of my hands. This man is everything to me, he knows what I need, knows that I'm hurting. Telling me he loves me, though, that's the best and the worst thing he could say, right now. Because, I will probably betray him tonight, and that's not sitting well with me.

'Love you too,' I tap in the words, *'see you soon.'*

I put the phone back in my jeans pocket, lean my head back onto the headrest, close my eyes and listen to the hum of the Land Rover.

***

'Happy birthday to you, happy birthday to you, happy birthday dear Jenny, happy birthday to you,' Henry and Rose finish singing, and I watch Rose lower the cake carefully onto the kitchen table, trying not to disturb the flames on the candles. I look at the beautiful homemade pink and white iced cake. A dark pink ribbon sits around the middle and there are iced pink and purple flowers and butterflies on the top. It's impressive. I can't help but smile. I love celebrating my birthdays with Henry and Rose.

The only thing marring this birthday is that my parents and grandparents are not here. They were in France for a business meeting, and they should now be flying somewhere over the English Channel, on their way home. They said they'd try to be back before dinner, but it's 6pm now and there's still no sign of them.

Rose smiles at me, as I sit at the kitchen table. Her hand rests gently on my arm.

'Make a wish sweetie,' she says.

I look across the table at Henry and close my eyes tightly. A sudden thought flits through my mind. *I wish my parents were here. They would know what to do.*

I take a deep breath and begin to blow out the candles. It takes several attempts, as there are fifteen of them. The white gold bangle that Rose and Henry gave me, inscribed with '*to our beautiful Jenny, H&R x'*, jingles on my wrist.

The smoke from the candles hits my nostrils, and then filters into the air, bringing me back to reality. I pat Rose's hand. 'Thank you, Rose. Both of you,' I say quietly to them, 'it means a lot, that you're here to share this with me.'

I watch as their eyes glisten. They love me. I know they do. They treat me as though I belong to them, that I am their daughter. It makes the constant absence of my business-minded parents, bearable. And for that, I'll be eternally grateful.

The shrill of the phone breaks the silence, Henry clears his throat, pats my hand, and pushes out of his seat to answer it.

‘Gateshead? Henry Dean speaking.’ he says, picking up the phone and putting it to his ear.

‘What? I’m sorry, can you repeat that?’ he asks, giving me a quick look. His voice sounds strained, shocked. He listens for a few minutes. A hand reaches out to the wall, his head is down.

‘Are you sure?’ he asks in such a quiet voice that I can hardly hear him.

Rose and I look at each other. Something is wrong.

‘OK. Thank you for calling. I’ll see you in an hour.’

Henry places the phone back in its cradle, slips his hands deep into his brown trouser pockets and looks at me, his face is pale. I know it’s bad news. My shoulders start shaking. I can’t breathe.

Henry’s head is down, his shoulders slump, as he walks slowly back to the kitchen. He stops when he reaches me.

‘I’m sorry Jenny, so sorry,’ his voice is deep, his eyes hold mine.

‘What is it? What’s happened?’ I whisper. My head feels light, and stars float before my eyes. I feel like I’m under water, sound and vision distorts as Henry speaks:

‘It’s the plane, the one carrying your parents and grandparents. It’s gone down over the English Channel.’

‘No! Don’t say that!’ I say, my voice sounds strange to my ears, ‘No!’ With a strength I didn’t know I had, I push away from the table, knocking the birthday cake from its plate and watching, as it slithered in slow motion with a plop onto the table. My parents were dead.

***

'Jenny?'

I rouse from my daydreaming, stretch a little and open my eyes. I'm warm and cosy and I'm in a moving car. Oh yes, I remember where I am, on my way to get Rose.

'You awake?'

'Yes,' I look across at Henry. Worry is etched on his weather-beaten face. I can't blame him.

'We're almost there,' he says, looking at the dark road ahead.

'Where are we?' I ask.

'We've just gone past the Barley Mow pub, heading to Long Wittenham now. We'll be there in about five or ten minutes.'

'OK. Where is your friend, Mickey?' I ask.

'He's meeting up with another marine mate,' he answers quickly, as though it's rehearsed.

'Henry,' I begin. I shuffle my hands deep into the pockets of my black jacket, absently rubbing my right-hand index finger over the point of a small, brown pencil which I'd found in my car a few weeks ago. I'd meant to drop it into the 'everything' kitchen drawer, but never quite remembered to do it.

'If anything should happen to me,' I say quickly, continuing my conversation.

'No. Nothing is going to happen to you,' he butted in.

'But!'

'No buts,' he says gruffly, looking at me, the car swerved slightly with his anger, 'you're not leaving the car. I'm not choosing between you and Rose.'

'We need to get Rose,' I insist, 'it's our main priority.'

'And, we will. But you do not, under any circumstances, get into a car with him. Do you hear?'

'Henry.'

'Promise me, Jenny.'

With an immense sadness welling up within me, I look across at his profile, caught the glimpse of concentration on his face as he navigated his way closer to Rose. All hope seems to have died, as my tummy threatens to relieve me of the little food that I'd eaten today. This was between me and Felix now. He'd crossed a line, the moment he'd decided to take Rose. If he'd hurt her, I'll kill him. It wasn't a threat, no, I'd passed that stage. This was the final chapter. Between Felix and me.

'I can't do that, Henry.'

We sit in silence as Henry takes the winding country road to the clumps. Everything is black, not a soul about. Good choice, Felix. Don't think I'm going down without a fight though. I'm not the person I was before you took me, I'm different now. Stronger. Harder. Less forgiving.

Turning into the Clumps car park, a set of car headlights turn on, guiding us to Felix. We park at the opposite side of the area. I think I'm going to be sick. I take a deep breath and watch the familiar shape of Felix, get out of the car. Even without hair, and wearing a baseball cap, he has the same swagger of entitlement, the same air of arrogance.

A fleeting moment of terror envelops me, taking me back into that dark room, with the hood over my face, being pushed along the corridor. Clutching at my neck, my lungs are struggling to work, I can't breathe. I can hear Henry's concerned voice through a haze. I must be having a panic attack.

What was that Daniel had told me to do? Close my eyes, think of Stuart, of a happy memory, count to ten and regulate my breathing. Stuart's face replaces Felix, and the darkness. He's holding my hand, his thumb strokes my palm in a loving, reassuring way. We're at the cinema, watching a romance called Five Feet Apart. I feel a whisper of a kiss on my cheek, as Stuart tucks a tendril of hair from my eyes. A happy memory.

Slowly, I calm down. Enough to remember what an absolute, useless specimen of a man Felix really is. He didn't deserve to have his freedom, to make me feel this way. No one has the power to do that. And, if I let him, have that power, it means he's won after all. I am the victim.

My blood boils with anger. Who the fuck does he think he is?

'You all right?' Henry asks, his face looks worried.

'Yeah. I'm fine,' I tell him. Let's get this over with.

'Wait here,' Henry warns me, as he opens the car door and begins to walk to Felix. I unwind my window, so that I can hear their exchange.

'Henry,' the familiar voice of my father's brother, makes me shudder. I close my eyes, blanking out last week and what this man did to me.

'Where's my wife?' Henry says curtly.

'Over there, resting,' Felix points to the shadowy outline of a tree, at the far side of the car park. 'I gave her something to make her sleep. She should be fine.' His face is devoid of emotion as he points to the Land Rover, looking for me.

'I want Jenny. Get her out of the car,' he orders Henry.

'No. I want to see Rose first,' Henry counter orders.

Jesus! It's going to be a bloody stand-off. We need to get to Rose quickly. I take Julie's phone out, dial Stuart and place the rectangular device into my jacket pocket. I can't sit here and wait for them to reach an agreement. Time is of the essence. I open the car door and step into the darkness.

'There she is!' Felix's voice booms through the night air. He sounds pleased with himself. As though he's just won the lottery. I close the car door and stand still, assessing the situation. I need to keep safe.

'Get back in the car, Jenny,' Henry shouts, he's angry, and I don't blame him, 'I need to find Rose.' He walks across the car park, towards the tree.

'Rose? Rose?' he calls, but all I hear is the wind blowing in the trees, 'Where are you? We've come to get you. Hold on.'

I follow his movements intently, focusing on the direction he is heading. I dig my hands deep into my jacket pockets and wait. It seems to take forever, those simple movements of crossing the car park and walking to the other side. Like watching a movie in slow motion. Where the hell were Stuart and the police officers?

Suddenly, my arm is wrenched from my pocket. Felix. Damn. I should have been watching him. Shit. My stomach plummets to the floor.

'Get your hand off me!' I shout at him, 'Don't you dare touch me!'

'Jenny, you need to get in the car,' he orders, dragging me to his car.

'No!' I yell so hard my head hurts. I pull my arm back as hard as I can, but he is stronger than me. Much stronger. Felix's arm went around my waist, as he begins hauling me along the rough, uneven ground. There is no way I am getting into that car with him. Not one iota. If he wants me, he'll have to fight for me. I reach into the pocket of my jacket with my free hand, grab the pencil with the sharp point, turn and aim. Straight for his neck.

I stab him with everything I have, watching as his head moves to look at his neck, before I smash the palm of my hand hard into his nose.

'You little bitch,' he mutters, releasing me in shock, 'fucking little bitch!'

I run, into the darkness. Come across the gate that leads up to the two Clumps. I yank it, but it won't open, so I climb up the gate and jump. Landing in something slimy, either mud or cow muck, I run along the pathway and up to the top of the biggest Clump. My heart is beating so fast, a mixture of terror, panic and determination to get away from him keeps me going.

I don't look back. I hear police sirens, shouting, someone crying, but I don't stop. Not until I've put some distance between us. There is no way on this earth, that I am making it easy for my uncle to take me again. No way. My mind races as I make the climb, slipping and sliding on the grass pathway in the dark.

I can hear footsteps behind me and instinctively know that Felix is closing in. Shit. I've got nowhere to go. Where are DS Jones, Julie and Stuart? I thought they were close by. Something feels wrong, but I don't know what.

Breathing hard, heart pumping, I keep running and don't stop until I reach the top of the hill, with its cluster of trees. The darkness adds a surreal, almost Bronte-like feel to the scene, making me think of Heathcliffe roaming the moors looking for his beloved Cathy.

I used to come to the Clumps when I was younger, sometimes with my parents, more often with Henry and Rose. It feels so different, from running around the top, looking for the area sun dial, where you can spy local landmarks in the distance and collate them with the information on the dial. Day's Lock at Little

Wittenham, sits at the bottom of the Clumps, to the left, and the red brick of Dorchester Abbey can be seen in the distance.

Without looking behind me, I shuffle behind a group of bushes, not far from one of the seating benches. And wait.

A familiar voice, floats through the darkness, 'Jenny! For God's Sake, give it up!' Felix. I'm not sure if he can see me. If he can, I'm done for. 'Come out!' the anger in his voice is unmistakable. I remain still.

I push some branches apart and can see small sets of flickering lights, people running up the hill. Thank God. I just need to stay hidden until they reach us. Holding my breath, I stay as still as possible. I count silently in my head. 2,4,5,8,10.

This has got to be one of the most surreal moments of my life. The night is black and I'm standing at the top of the biggest Clump at Long Wittenham, hiding behind a bush. Alone. When did my life become this terrifying, relentless battle?

For a moment, I continue to stand still. Waiting. Watching. Then, a feeling begins to burn through my bones, a strong, unmistakable feeling. It starts at my feet and worms its way up my legs, my body, my arms and finally reaches my head. Rage. A red-hot blinding rage sears through me, wanting the answer to one question. Why me? Why did he choose me to abduct and rape? Felix, you are my uncle, for God's Sake. The rage makes me bold, and before I know what I am doing, I step out of the bushes and find myself directly facing Felix.

'I just want to know, Felix. Why?' I ask, almost spitting the words out, 'Why me?'

Even in the darkness, as I study his features, his bald head, shaved moustache. His red, bloody nose, the puncture wound from my pencil in his neck, the blood that trickles from the wound. In this moment, as he stares back at me, I knew the answer. He wants me. Not as a daughter, but as a lover.

He seems to ponder my question, his brows raised, trying to find the right words, his fake glasses glinting in the moonlight, and then, he shakes his head and smiles at me. The smile represents everything he is thinking, satisfaction, arrogance, superiority, memories of what he'd done to me. My stomach rolls, and I can taste bile. Fighting hard to gain control, I push it back down. I am not going to be sick in front of this smug bastard.

There is a shuffling noise behind him, people are getting closer. DS Jones calls out, 'Stop, Gloverman! It's the police.'

Felix shrugs and ignores the warning, 'if you don't know, Jenny. You're not as clever as I thought you were.' His words are condescending, as though he is talking to small child.

'I want you to tell me, tell me why, Felix?' I persist.

He put his hands on his chunky hips. 'For crying out loud woman! Why do you think?' he shouts in a harsh voice, 'I've wanted you since I first came back to Gateshead. When you were fifteen years old.'

'Don't say that,' I spit at him, leaning forward, 'don't bloody say that. I was just a child back then.' Hearing him say it, say those words, feels like a dagger to my wounded soul. How could he have had those feelings for me?

'I know you were,' he shouts, moving a step closer to me, 'but I was besotted with you. It was sweet torture, watching you growing into a beautiful young woman every day. Watching you, with your friends, with Stuart. God, I could fucking kill him, when he put his hands on you.'

I put my hands up. 'No!' I shout, to shut his disgusting words up, 'Enough! Stop right there. You don't get to say those things and pretend everything is all right.'

We are almost facing each other. I can see the frustration pushing him further into the darkness, as he closes his eyes and his brows draw together. To my surprise, he raises his hand and begins berating himself by pummelling his forehead. I still, waiting for him to stop. Finally, after what seems like an age, he looks at me. His eyes glistening.

'Jenny Gloverman,' he says hoarsely, 'I love you.'

The reality of the situation hit me hard. Felix declaring his love for me in this remote, dark place, leaves a terrible pounding in my head. Stars float in my vision and my mouth is dry.

Two things take my mind off his words. One, there is a funny little red dot sitting on his forehead, and I can't work out what it is. It just sits there, still and reminds me of a chicken pox spot. And two. At the same time, I hear a whizz, as something flies past my head, and careers at speed into Felix's forehead.

It was the strangest and most terrifying moment. He is dead from the moment the bullet hits him. There was no time for him to react. I stand there with my mouth open, unable to move or speak. I expect him to fall backwards from the impact, but instead, he falls forward and slumps to the ground, not far from my feet.

The wooden hilt of what looks like a kitchen knife protrudes from the middle of Felix's back. I stand frozen, unable to move.

Bloody hell. What just happened? I put my hands over my mouth and scream. I don't realise I am still screaming until a shape runs to me through the darkness and a pair of strong arms wrap around me. Stuart. Within seconds, I am safely tucked into his warm body.

'Jen, sweetheart. It's me,' he says softly, taking my face in his hands. I look up at him and our gazes catch. His thumbs softly wipe the tears that are falling down my cheeks. 'You all right?' he asks.

I nod, yes to answer. 'He's dead,' I say quietly, 'Felix is dead. Someone killed him.'

'I knew something was wrong when you began to scream,' his arms tighten around me. 'We got most of your conversation with him on my phone,' he says shaking his head, 'why the hell did you get out of the car? I'm so bloody mad at you right now.'

His face is hard, it unnerves me. 'Please don't be mad, Stu,' I plead, 'I did what I had to do.' I lift my hand and touch his neck, hoping to calm him. My eyes fill with tears again, and I curse myself because I can't seem to stop crying.

I've never cried much in my life, even as a child when a beloved pet died, I choked back tears and told myself to be strong. And, now here I am, a grown woman who can't even talk to her boyfriend without tears threatening to slip from her eyelashes.

'Please,' I beg, my voice breaking in a sob. His face softens, he lowers his gaze, takes a deep breath. As he exhales, a sea of emotions washes across his face, anger, frustration and finally forgiveness. With slumped shoulders, he grips the top of my arms.

'No more heroics,' he says huskily, 'my heart can't stand the pressure.'

DS Jones and Julie Leadbetter finally reach us, walk over to Felix's body, their necks craning to assess the level of danger. 'Jesus!' DS Jones mutters, running his hands through his hair, looking at the large knife protruding out of Felix's back.

'You OK?' DS Jones asks me. 'I'll be with you in a moment, just need to make a couple of calls,' he says, taking his phone from his coat pocket. I watch in a trance as he presses a button and puts the phone to his ear.

'Yeah. Just about,' I mutter, 'but he's not doing too good,' I look at the ground at my uncle's body. 'He's dead. It wasn't me. I don't know who it was.'

I scan the faces of the small group of people congregating around me, 'where's Henry?' I ask, 'Is he with Rose?'

'Jenny, there's something you need to know,' Stuart's loving face contorts in anguish, as he updates me on the situation, 'Felix did something to Rose. We're not sure what. But she's.'

'No!' I scream, pushing him away. I don't want to hear the rest of that sentence, 'No, you'd better not be saying what I think you're saying.'

'Jenny,' DS Jones, steps forward, sliding his phone into his pocket, 'I'm sorry Jenny, but Rose is dead.'

'No……' I grab Stuart's jacket, I can't take this, it's just too much. Too much to handle. 'Please tell me it's not true.'

'I'm so sorry, Jenny. So bloody sorry,' his words fade, as I withdraw into myself. Bloody hell, how did this happen? Why would Felix hurt Rose, if he really wanted me? I did everything I could, and still, it wasn't enough. It was all for nothing, all for bloody nothing.

My legs give way and I allow Julie and Stuart to help me down the hill. My mind has shut down. All I see is a grey fog.

Part 20

DCI Brian Carter

Eighty per cent of police work is gut feeling. That's a huge amount. When you get that feeling, you learn not to dismiss it. In the pit of my stomach I know something's not right, can't put my finger on it. It's just a hunch.

After Julie left, that worry intensified, particularly with regard to Julie, her safety and this 8pm hand-over at the Clumps. So, I waited until 6pm, grabbed my stuff, got dressed and discharged myself. Of course, I needed transport, so I called work and told Shep to come and get me. There was somewhere I needed to be.

We are riding in Shep's black Citroen. She's wearing long silver rectangular earrings that catch the light every so often, and occasionally catch the collar of her dark purple hooded jacket. We're following Julie in her red Mazda, and I'm pretty sure she's going to the hotel where Mike and the others are.

It seems that we aren't the only ones following her. Gino Camprinelli is following her too. In his dark blue BMW. Shit. What is he doing? My hunch is that he is also after Felix, and he is hoping that Julie will lead him to him. How the hell did he know where she lived? That's not good. Not good at all.

'Should we call her and tell her she's being followed?' asks Shep, who drives as though she's just passed her driving test. A bit slow, if I'm honest. I ponder her question. I don't want to put her in danger, but I need to know what Camprinelli is up to.

'Let's leave it for the minute. We've got her covered,' I tell her, shuffling in my seat, trying to get comfortable. I'm wearing this navy padded jacket that is a little tight for me. I've had it for years, don't wear it anymore, for that very reason. 'I want to know why he's following her. Pretty sure he's hoping she'll lead him to Felix.'

'I think you're right, I just wanted to put the question out there. How're you feeling?' she asks, doing her mirror, signal, manoeuvre routine. She's a rather cautious driver, but that's fine because we're behind Camprinelli and he's behind Julie, and I don't want him to realise we're following him. 'Fine,' I say, 'just a bit sore.'

'Are you all right to ferry me around tonight?' I ask her, 'I want to be at the Clumps at 8pm for this hand-over.'

'Of course,' she smiles, 'Julie is a good friend, I don't want to be sitting at home while you guys have all the excitement.'

'Thanks,' I close my eyes, letting the car engine take my mind off things, dull my senses.

'When I say good friends,' Shep looks across at me, wrinkling her nose, so that the silver stud moves slightly. I feel her gaze on me. My peace is shattered. Reluctantly, I open my eyes.

'Yes?' I ask. Clearly, she has something to say.

'She likes you, you know,' Julie's voice has that knowing manner to it. The sound that comes when someone knows a secret and is desperate to share it.

'Yeah?' I ask casually, I can feel my heartrate picking up. I'm curious to know what she's told Shep about me.

'If I'm speaking out of turn, tell me now,' she says.

'You're speaking out of turn,' I joke, then wince as pain shoots through my shoulder.

'Sorry, Sir,' she mutters, with both hands on the steering wheel at the advised ten and two position.

'I was joking Shep. Julie's nice, I like her,' I mutter, annoyed with my open admission.

'Only like her?' she muses.

'Look Shep. Leave it,' I tell her, watching the BMW in front. I've changed my mind, I don't want to go down this route with Shep. 'It's for me and Julie to sort out.'

'I knew it!' she puts one arm in the air to make a victory swoop, before putting it back on the steering wheel.

We sit in silence for a while. I advise Shep not to get too far behind Gino, in case we lose him. Julie leads us to the hotel at Sandford-on-Thames, where we hide ourselves away from the other cars, and watch as she enters the building. Gino's BMW is parked near the car park exit. We sit tight and play the waiting game.

I google Gino Camprinelli on my phone. We've come across each other a couple of times in recent years. I know he's thirty-eight years old and has no wife or children. Google tells me he was born in Italy and moved to England when he was young.

He is a businessman through and through. Owns properties, massage parlours, gyms, a sports shop. He's also into some shady stuff. Attached to a couple of the massage parlours are two explicit adult shops.

The photos don't do him justice, he's a good-looking guy, dresses in smart suits and looks the part of a successful business entrepreneur. Word on the street is that he's hard as nails, is ruthless when he needs to get the job done. And demands total loyalty.

At 7.40pm, Jenny and Henry come out of the hotel with Stuart, Mike and Julie. Julie hands a small object over to Jenny, I think it's her phone, and gives the young woman's arm an encouraging squeeze. Stuart holds Jenny close, kisses her and watches sadly as she steps into the front passenger seat of Henry's old black Land Rover.

Jenny Gloverman is one brave lady. After all she's been through, she still has a quiet dignity about her. As they drive through the exit barrier, Gino turns on the engine and slowly follows them. He's definitely looking for Felix.

Mike leads Julie to his black Peugeot 2008 and, as soon as Stuart slides into the back seat, they make their way to Wittenham Clumps, following Jenny and Henry. It's like a bloody convoy as Shep turns on the ignition and we follow the Peugeot.

The road is quiet, with very few cars about, as we make our way into the village of Long Wittenham and turn left at the fork towards Wittenham Clumps. We turn right at the crossroads when we reach the smaller village of Little Wittenham to make the climb to the Earth Trust Centre and the nearby Wittenham Clumps.

I think of Gino Camprinelli and wonder what his endgame is. Does he plan to kidnap Felix Gloverman? Or, is his plan more sinister? Whatever his objectives are, I need to focus on the case. For now, my main priority is to get Rose back, keep Jenny safe and arrest Felix Gloverman. I concentrate on the job ahead, and fifteen minutes after we leave the hotel, we find ourselves pulling into the car park at Wittenham Clumps.

We park in between Mike's Peugeot and Henry's Land Rover. On the other side of the car park is a Volvo Estate and I'm relieved that, Mike and Henry have left their car headlights on, so we've got some light in the area. I notice two things. Firstly, that there is a distinct lack of people, and secondly, there's no sign of Gino Camprinelli, or his car.

I convince myself that they can't have gone far, not without their cars, but where the hell are they? Shep looks at me, and I shrug my shoulders, just as a wailing sound, like a wounded animal drifts through the air. It's followed by a howling cry. A deep, masculine sound. Is that Henry?

'Henry?' I call, 'It's DCI Carter. Where are you?'

'Over here,' he shouts. Scouring the semi-dark car park, my eyes settle on the outline of a person, waving their arms at the far end of the car park, near the trees. Moving closer, we see that Henry has Rose in his arms, and that he's kneeling on the damp woodland ground, holding her tight. Rose's eyes are open. He's rocking her gently from side to side.

There's something about this scene that doesn't seem quite right. Rose doesn't look responsive. She's sort of lolling. Immediately, I take out my phone and call for backup and an ambulance.

'It's no use,' he says sadly, as we reach him. Tears glisten in his eyes. 'She's gone. He killed her. That bastard killed her.' He half groans, dips his head into her neck and carries on rocking her. Watching a person break down like this is one of the hardest things to do. Particularly in my job. You never get used to it.

I look at the distraught man kneeling before me, can't help the lump that comes to my throat. 'Shep, check for a pulse, will you?' I can't leave this place until I know for sure. Shep lowers herself to Rose and gently feels for a pulse in her neck and wrist. She closes her eyes, concentrating, while I wait patiently for her assessment.

Shep looks at me, before her gaze shifts to Henry's hunched shoulders, he doesn't move. 'No, nothing. I'm so sorry,' she says in a low, sad voice.

'Shit.' I mutter under my breath, 'That bastard just keeps taking.'

'You need to find Jenny,' Henry lifts his face from Rose's neck, and looks up at me as tears fall from his eyes.

'Where is she?' I ask, and then it occurs to me that Felix, Stuart, Jenny and my team aren't here, 'And where are my officers, and Stuart?' I start to panic. My first thought is for Julie. I hope to God that she is all right. I know Mike will have her back, but still, I wish I was the one with her right now.

'I don't know. I lost it when I realised that Rose was dead. I think Felix chased Jenny up one of the Clumps. DS Jones and PC Leadbetter arrived with Stuart and after a minute or two with me, I sent them up the hill to find her.'

'Bugger,' I mutter. I seem to be doing a lot of that tonight. Muttering under my breath.

I leave the others and walk to the gate, hoping to see someone on the Clumps, there's a speckle of light on the large hill, near the top, that must be them. I'm just about to turn my gaze back to Shep and Henry, when I glimpse a moving shadow heading down the hill. No torch or light. Just a shadow. Hardly visible. I think I know who it is, but I'm not one hundred per cent sure. I follow the figure again, still working its way to the road at the bottom of the hill.

'What is it?' Shep asks, pushing herself to a standing position and coming to my side.

'Not sure. Wait here,' I tell her, taking out my phone, switching on the torchlight and walking along the road towards Earth Trust Centre, to the point where I think the figure will come out. My bandaged, upper chest protests as I take each step and I'm already feeling breathless.

I continue regardless, nothing short of a bullet in the head will stop me tonight. I pause when I hear feet thudding and the crackle of moving branches and wait in silence. A dark figure sneaks out of the bushes, and steps onto the road. A familiar figure wearing a dark suit, and muddy designer dark shoes.

'Gino Camprinelli,' I point my torch at his upper body, trying to keep my voice low, 'strange place to be walking around, of an evening?' I glance at the black gloves he peels from his hands.

In the semi-darkness, Camprinelli looks momentarily confused, and I see the exact moment, when recognition hits him.

'DCI Brian Carter. Of all the people I thought I might meet tonight,' he says in his Italian-English accent, 'you were not one of them.'

'You found him, then? Felix Gloverman?' it wasn't really a question, but I had to ask. Gino is calm as he pushes the gloves into his trouser pocket. His good-looking features freeze for a moment, as though he's unsure of what to say next. I wait patiently for his answer.

'Yeah, I found him,' he says eventually, looking directly at me.

'And?' it was like trying to get blood out of a stone.

Camprinelli shrugs, before speaking, 'he was chasing the woman, Jenny. Threatening her. There was someone else there, I don't know who. Someone shot him in the head, just before I pushed the knife in his back. I left it in there.' His words were matter of fact. Almost bragging. You've got to admire a person who doesn't give a toss about his actions.

'Someone else? A shooter? Bloody hell.' I'm mostly talking to myself, as I process his words. I turn the torch to face the floor, so we're both completely shrouded in darkness. Felix Gloverman was not a nice person. He had enemies, and he was living on borrowed time. And now, from what Camprinelli was telling me, Gloverman's life had come to an abrupt end.

There's a brief silence, before I say, 'he was a piece of shit.'

'Yeah, he was,' Gino steps forward, it appears he has something he wants to say to me, 'my boys got a beating for stabbing you. Stupid mistake.'

Appreciating his comment, I nod my head, before replying, 'Good. Your goons need to be careful, though. That young woman they were roughing up to get information was almost six months pregnant. She lost her baby because of them. They were too rough with her.' Anger seeps out of my words, they could have hurt Julie too.

I'm stressing, and I can't help it. I'm too bloody annoyed to bother with the sudden, sharp pain in my shoulder.

Nevertheless, I can't help but imagine the men, down on their knees with Gino Camprinelli standing over them. He was known for being ruthless. I expect they will be in a much worse state than me or Amy. I shine my phone into his face to see if he is being genuine or simply responding to what he thinks I want to hear.

'I didn't know,' he shakes his head, and I see the stern, apologetic look on his face. His eyes close momentarily as he mutters, 'bloody idiots, they'll be dealt with.'

'Good,' I nod, 'at least we're both in agreement on that.'

'Listen,' I tell him, as an idea comes to mind. A swift decision of sorts. I was sick of this whole business. That bastard Gloverman, deserved to die, especially after killing Rose. Faces of the criminals I'd put away over the years flood my mind, of rapists, armed robbers, murderers and kidnappers who were held behind bars, most of them for the rest of their lives.

Then, I think of the criminals who got away due to a technicality, and my heart sinks. A desolate feeling of failure and regret curses through my veins. I can't rid myself of the feeling that I'd let the victims and their families down. It's something that stays with you. And at this moment in time, my moral compass has no problem in telling Gino Camprinelli what I'm about to tell him:

'I didn't see you tonight, Camprinelli. We never met.'

He studies me closely. 'Are you saying, what I think you're saying?' he asks, his proud chin tilting up.

I stand eye to eye with him, my gaze never wavering, before speaking. 'This never happened,' I begin briskly, 'but if anything comes from the knife, or someone sees you, then that's a different matter.'

He nods in acknowledgement of my words. A gentleman's agreement. Risky, I know, but sometimes in life, you have to take a step out of the neat and tidy, into the squalor of real life.

'Now, get the hell out of here,' I tell him. I wait a moment, before strolling back to the car park. Bloody hell, I can't believe I just did that! Inwardly, I argue that it was the only way I could sleep at night. Jenny needed someone to save her, my people weren't there on time, and even though there is another person out there, who probably killed Felix Gloverman before he was stabbed, the main thing is that Gloverman can't hurt another human being ever again.

If my actions make me a bad guy, then that's what I am. I'm a bad guy who can look myself in the mirror every morning and know I did what was necessary. That I did my best.

The distant sound of ambulance and police sirens make their way closer to us. Thank God, they're here at last. Finally, I reach Shep and Henry who are standing by the tree where Rose was found. I'm relieved that she's made sure Henry doesn't move Rose any more than he already has. He's taken his brown suede jacket off and laid it over Rose's head and part of her body. I need this crime scene kept as sterile as possible.

Shep steps forward, her eyes search my face. She looks worried. 'Everything all right?' she asks.

'Yes,' I concentrate on her lips when I speak, I cannot meet her eyes, 'just thought I saw something.'

'And?' she asks.

'Turned out to be nothing,' I tell her, as I watch the ambulance and a police car crunch into the concrete and earth car park. I heave a sigh of relief at the distraction. Two paramedics rush to attend to Rose, as Henry and Shep explain to them what's happened. I watch the scene unfold in silence, note the bleeping of Henry's phone, the way he quickly responds to the text, before shoving the phone back into the pocket of his trousers. Interesting.

I take out my phone and call Mike.

'Mike, what the hell is happening up there?' My voice sounds sharp, I'm angry, but not at him.

'You won't believe this,' Mike replies, the howling of the wind, catches the phone line, 'but Felix Gloverman is dead.'

'Bloody hell! Dead?' I feign surprise. 'How so, what happened?'

'Julie will update you when she reaches the bottom of the hill with Jenny and Stuart, suffice to say, someone made sure that Felix Gloverman was not going to survive this night.' Mike said, without emotion.

'I'll be down soon, just waiting until SOCO arrives. I've put out an all-units alert to find the person, or people who did this,' he says.

'All right, I'll sort things out in the car park here. See you in a short while,' I tell him disconnecting the phone and sliding it into my trouser pocket. I walk over to the gate and scan the area until my eyes see their torch lights, speckles in the distance, moving slowly down the uneven path. What's taking them so long?

'DCI Carter,' I pull out my warrant card and show the two attending officers, walking towards me. The taller of the two has short, cropped hair and a moustache and introduces himself as Sergeant Tom Harper. I update Harper about Rose and tell him that my officer is on her way down the hill with Jenny and Stuart. I ask him to send his colleague to meet them.

It seems to take an age before they reach the gate. Stuart and Julie are holding Jenny up as I fumble with the gate opening mechanism to let them through. Jenny seems overwhelmed, unsteady on her feet. What did that bastard do to her?

'Hey, glad you're all OK?' I say, looking at each one of them in turn.

Julie looks surprised, and a little angry that I'm here. 'What are you doing here? You're supposed to be in hospital.'

'It's a long story,' I begin.

Julie carefully withdraws her arm from Jenny, and nods to the top of the main clump, 'Mike's still up there, waiting with the body, and for SOCO.'

I nod and focus on Jenny. Her head is down and her shoulders slump as if she has given up, the sooner we get her checked out, the quicker we can let Stuart take her back to the hotel.

Thankfully, a small, slim paramedic with short black hair and a tattoo of a bird on his arm walks over to us and introduces himself to her.

'Jenny, is it? I'm Andrew, I'm a paramedic. Can you come to the ambulance?' Andrew gently takes her arm, 'let's get you checked over. Have you been injured in any way?'

Jenny's head stays down. That's not a good sign.

'Jenny?' I say, carefully touching her arm, 'Jenny, look at me.' We stand for a while, silently waiting for her to respond. She remains still, unmoving. I worry that her mind cannot cope with everything that she has endured, that the only way she can cope with what has happened to her, is to shut down.

I hope she's not having a psychotic break. Then her head slowly lifts, until she's looking at me. I let out a deep breath. Thank God. I don't want this woman to suffer any more than she already has.

'Yes?' her voice is little more than a whisper.

'Hold on in there,' I tell her, 'Stuart and Andrew need to take you to the ambulance to check you over. DS Jones, or I, will catch up with you tomorrow, to take your statement.'

Her sad eyes meet mine, and I can almost feel her inward struggle, to not drown in her own sorrow. She nods and Stuart pulls her to him, stroking her arm, 'It'll be all right sweetheart. We'll get through this.' Jenny's feet begin to move as she allows the men to steer her to the ambulance.

'Is she? Is Rose in the ambulance?' I hear her ask as they move towards the ambulance.

I look at Henry, Shep and Harper at the far side of the car park. They're standing vigil over Rose's body until the pathologist, SOCO forensics and coroner's van arrive. Watching over her in silence. Protecting her dignity.

'No,' I hear the paramedic reassure her, 'she will go in the coroner's van.'

'Poor Rose,' she whispers into the night, 'I can't believe she's gone.'

I have a hollow feeling in the pit of my stomach, as her words drift across the night sky. How did this simple hand-over situation between Rose and Felix, turn out so badly? Both dead and for different reasons, it didn't make any sense. As soon as Stuart and Jenny are out of earshot, I turn to Julie for answers.

'What the hell happened with Rose?' I start.

'We don't know for sure,' her voice is quiet, 'she was dead when we found her. Felix may have drugged her, but we won't know for sure until we've had the autopsy and done blood tests.'

'Yes, I'm thinking the same thing. And, what about Felix?' I ask, looking at her.

Her eyes glint in the dark, 'he chased Jenny up the hill and during an altercation at the top, Felix was shot in the front of the head, execution-style and stabbed in the back.'

'Bloody hell! I didn't see that coming!' I say rather loudly, trying to sound as though this news is a shock. Which, of course, it isn't. It was only a matter of time before Felix Gloverman got what he deserved, and in my mind, he got off likely, because he hadn't suffered. With that in mind, I am determined to stand by my decision to allow Gino Camprinelli to walk free from stabbing Felix Gloverman in the back.

Julie shudders and I'm unsure if it's the cool night air or the events of the past few hours that are finally catching up with her.

'You OK?' I ask quietly, touching her arm.

She closes her eyes and nods a silent yes, just as her hand reaches out to stroke my arm and trickles down, until soft warm fingers gently encase my own. I look down at our entwined hands and back to her face. A life is not worth living if you don't make the most of it while you can.

A former girlfriend once accused me of not fully opening-up to her, not giving her enough of my time and committing to her. She said I was married to the job. She wanted more from me, more than I was willing to give. At the time I told myself she wasn't 'the one', that it wasn't meant to be. The usual things that swirl around one's mind when it feels necessary to analyse a misdeed, a failed relationship or sour event.

Why I had suddenly thought of Emily, after five years, I had no idea. Possibly, a feeling of guilt, for not giving her what she needed, what was needed to keep us together. The one and only thing I knew for certain, as I look into Julie's beautiful, calm face, was that I'd do anything to make our relationship work.

I reluctantly release her fingers, before gently sweeping a stray strand of hair behind her ear. 'Thank you,' I whisper in her ear, 'for giving us a chance.'

Her face lights up, and she offers the biggest smile. 'you're welcome,' her soft voice says quietly, and amidst this mess of a situation I can't help but smile.

Crunching tyres bring me back to reality, and the headlights of the coroner's van creep along the road looking for the car park. Behind it, a couple of police cars park in the lane, blocking the car park entrance. The chattering of the rotor blades from the helicopter, hovering high above our heads, reminds me that there is still someone out there who has committed a serious crime against Felix Gloverman.

I absently watch Jenny, sitting with Stuart in the ambulance. The paramedic is quietly talking to her, as she gazes across the dark car park to Henry, who sobs in Shep's arms. I can just make out the shape of Rose lying at their feet.

There's a sadness hanging in the air, I feel like I'm inhaling it with every breath I take. Two people, as close as any parent and child could be, who have lived and loved each other for most of Jenny's life, standing apart in their own private grief, unable to acknowledge or comfort each other.

Suffering.

Part 21

Jenny

I'm listening to music on Stuart's phone. His white earphones sit haphazardly in my ears as a song I haven't heard for a while, 'Life Uncommon' by a woman called Jewel, starts to play. The lyrics to the song mean a lot, they focus on moving forward, making a difference, *'Fill your life with love and bravery and you shall lead a life uncommon.'* I close my eyes and block out the world.

We're sitting in the waiting room of a grand Victorian brownstone house, on the outskirts of Oxford, near Dr Daniel Scott's office. It's the first time I've been to this house, away from the hospital, and I don't mind admitting that it feels a little strange seeing him 'off base.' White walls, heavy oak doors, and wooden floors make for a plain, classic look. I have an appointment at 10am. I look at my watch. It says 9.57am.

The paramedic gave me the all clear and DCI Carter asked one of the police officers to give Stuart and I a lift to the hotel. Before leaving, Julie came over to see how I was. She's such a kind police officer, and I'd said a sincere 'thank you', as I took her phone from my pocket and returned it to her.

My head is still all over the place, but the fog is beginning to lift. Very slowly. My guess is that it will take a while for me to get back to where I was before the kidnapping.

I don't know where Henry is.

I open my eyes and stare at the small phone screen, the lyrics come on to the screen then disappear, I steel myself, so I don't look at the grey-bearded man, wearing a smart navy suit, sitting opposite us. He is busy on his phone. Next to him sits a young girl, around twelve, in a long yellow flowery dress, her legs swishing back and forth through the legs of her grey metal chair.

Stuart's hand moves to rest lightly on my jean-clad upper thigh. He squeezes gently, offering reassurance. Absently, I let my hand rest on top of his, allowing the warmth to seep through my skin. I've felt cold since I got back from the Clumps last night. There's a chill in my bones, an ice-cold sensation that numbs my feelings and holds my emotions in check.

A loud creak makes me turn my attention to the heavy door next to me. It opens, and Daniel Scott, steps forward, scans the waiting area and settles his gaze on me. The first thing I notice, is that he's not wearing a white coat, just an open necked white shirt and blue chinos.

'Jenny,' his Scottish dialect is almost rhythmic, as he smiles. 'Stuart,' he nods a quick greeting. 'Do come in, Jenny,' he waits for me.

I stand and offer Stuart's phone back to him. He smiles, and his fingers linger on mine. 'I'll be here when you come out,' he says, with a warm smile.

'Promise?' I ask, pulling my green cardigan around me. Of course, it's too big, it belongs to Rose. Bringing the arm to my nose, I inhale deeply. It smells of Rose.

'Promise,' he says solemnly.

I bite my bottom lip, tuck my long hair behind my ears, and follow Daniel's gesturing to enter the room. My chest feels heavy, with each step that I take, as though I'm off to see the executioner to lop off my head.

I'm surprised how light and airy the room feels. On plain cream walls hang two large photo prints, one is a picture of a red and white lighthouse, and the second photo is that of a sunset taken from a sunny beach. The colours are very clever, giving the room a serene, calm feel.

A wooden desk sits at the far end of the room, in front of a large bay window that is fully bare, apart from heavy pale blue curtains which are held open by fitted brass hooks. Two wooden lounge chairs, with deep pale blue patterned cushions sit in front of the desk. A large yucca plant stands to my left, in a white ceramic pot, near one of the chairs, adding a touch of colour to the room.

I turn to Daniel and follow his outstretched hand that points to one of the chairs. I veer to my right and sit in the chair, before placing my hands on the wooden armrests. The silence is only broken by the creak of the chair against the floor as Daniel sits on the remaining chair, by the yucca.

'How are you?' he asks, leaning over to the desk and taking a silver pen and a notepad.

'OK,' I reply without any enthusiasm, unable to meet his gaze.

'You had quite an ordeal last night, I hear?'

He comes straight to the point, and I'm not sure why this surprises me. He's been frank and astute from the moment we met. Why should he be any different now?

'You could say that,' I answer, bringing my hands together and linking them loosely on top of my knees.

'Do you want to talk about it?' he asks.

'Not really,' I say. I haven't spoken to Henry yet, and that makes me feel bad. I didn't see him last night and haven't seen him this morning. We need to talk about Rose, I need to say I'm sorry. Sorry for bringing this into the family.

I keep telling myself that I could have done more, something that could have prevented Rose being taken. Rose, with her kind heart and big hugs. Rose, who had held my hand when I'd felt alone, and who had gently stroked my cheek when I had a fever. I can't believe she's dead. My heart aches and I feel responsible. And that's a heavy burden to carry.

'He can't hurt you anymore,' Daniel states.

'I know, it doesn't make it any easier though,' I reply. My fingers are threaded so tightly into each other, that they're beginning to ache.

'Easier? In what sense?' he focuses on me. His fingers fold gracefully around a silver ball point pen and are steepled over his notepad. He's yet to write anything. I wonder when I'll say something of importance that will make his pen flow across the paper.

'Easier, as in it won't bring Rose back,' I mutter, folding my arms around myself and rubbing some warmth into them.

'Cold?' he asks.

I nod and watch as he places his pad and pen on the top of the wooden desk, pushes himself from his chair, and walks casually to the back of the desk, before stooping slightly. I hear a drawer being pulled open and as he straightens, my eyes fall to a dark blue chenille throw. In two strides he's next to me.

'Lean forward,' Daniel says, waiting patiently for me to comply, before he drapes the throw over my shoulders and allows it drop down my back. I pull the warm material around me, holding it together and close my eyes.

'Better?' he asks resuming his seat. He sits back in his chair and crosses his legs casually.

'Yes, thanks,' I try to smile.

He casually places his hands on his thighs, before speaking again. 'You're right, it won't bring Rose back. Nothing can do that,' he tells me in a steady voice, before continuing, 'a tragic chain of events unravelled with Felix that no one could have foreseen. Not even you. You did everything you could to make sure Rose was returned safely. You were prepared to offer your life for hers.'

'And yet, it wasn't enough. It made no difference. She died anyway,' I say, with a weariness I can't shake. I still can't believe she's dead. She and Henry were like parents to me. More so, since my parents had died. They were all I had.

Again, I feel an urgent need to see Henry. To see how he is, to tell him I'm sorry. In addition, I am tormenting myself with the thought of Rose's last moments with Felix. She must have been so frightened and probably in pain. It makes me feel sick.

'That's true, she died regardless of your efforts,' he sits forward, leaning his arms on his legs. His face is serious, as he studies me. 'It's important to remember though Jenny, that you did everything you could. You overcame your own fears to offer yourself as bait for Rose. You put yourself in harm's way, despite your horrific ordeal at the Summer House.'

Tears begin to fall down my face, as I listen to his words. He speaks the truth, I know it, but reconciling myself with Rosie's death was another thing.

'I bloody hate him, Daniel.'

'I know you do, Jenny. The things he did to you and your family were horrific. Coming to terms with what has happened to you will take a while,' his voice held a softness, that brought a sob to my throat.

'I shouldn't have got out of the car,' I whisper, pulling the throw tightly around me, 'Stuart and Henry told me not to get out, but I got out anyway.'

'Why did you? What made you get out?' he asks, calmly.

'I don't know,' I mutter, 'Henry was looking for Rose, I wanted to move things along, so I decided to get out to help him. Perhaps to distract Felix. I don't know. At the time my mind had seemed so clear. I'd made an open call to Stuart on Julie's phone, before getting out of the car, so he could hear everything that was happening.'

'I was too busy watching Henry, that I never noticed Felix moving closer to me until it was too late,' I mutter, 'I am so stupid sometimes. I should have been watching him. What is the matter with me?'

'You're human,' Daniel unfolds his legs and leans back in his chair. I'm not sure if this is a technique used to appear non-threatening and calming to his patients. If it is, it seems to be working.

For some reason, I feel calmer now that I've started talking. As though the build-up of emotion that hit me at the thought of coming here, talking about what happened, is over. He brushes his hands along his dark blue chinos, before letting them rest on the wooden arms of his chair.

'You're human. It's as simple as that,' he smiles for the first time, since we entered the room and it feels like the sun is breaking through a rainstorm, driving the clouds away. 'For what it's worth, from the little I know of you, Jenny. You are one of the strongest, bravest people I've met. And, I've met a lot of people.'

'Daniel,' I start to argue.

'No arguments, I'm the expert. Remember!' he chides, and I can't help but wonder if he's holding an invisible umbrella to protect me from storm. 'So, tell me,' he changes the subject, 'who do you think murdered Felix?'

I shake my head, 'I have no idea. One minute he's telling me he loves me, the next, there's a bullet in his head. Then he keels over with a knife in his back.'

'You must have been frightened?' he asks softly, 'Wait a minute. He told you he loved you?'

I nod, it's hard to speak. My tummy recoils in disgust. Why the hell did I say that? Bringing those memories back again, when I know I'm not ready to face that conversation, it doesn't sit well. My palms begin to sweat, I drop the throw and rub my hands together. Agitated. I remember my uncle's words, his confession of his love for me. An unhealthy confession. Warped. Wrong in every sense. It makes me feel dirty.

'It must have been extremely hard to hear those words from him,' Daniel rubs his stubbly cheek.

'Yes, his words seem to eclipse everything apart from Rose,' I explain, 'I just don't get how he could feel that way. It makes me feel dirty.'

'Because he had, and acted upon, unhealthy feelings for you?' he pushes.

'Yeah.' I mutter, as tears well in my eyes. I can't seem to stop them. Even as I tell myself that I'm letting Felix win by giving in to these feelings, one minute I'm all right, the next, I'm angry, weepy, disorientated. This is just not me.

For twenty minutes we chat, sometimes about last night or last week, occasionally about insignificant things. We talk about my actions, why some work, why some don't. What I can do to protect myself in future. It was surprisingly easy to talk to Daniel. He is a good listener.

At one point during our session, he asks me how Stuart is coping. I admit he was angry when he found me at the Summer House, he wasn't angry at me, he thought he'd let me down, hadn't protected me. He was sorely angry at me, when I got out of the car at the Clumps, though. He wanted me to keep myself safe and was beside himself with worry. I don't blame him. I couldn't help my actions though; I did what I thought was right at the time.

Above all else, Stuart has really stepped up and been there for me. Somehow, the horrific events of the past week have brought us closer.

The session ends and Daniel led me back to the waiting room where Stuart was waiting patiently for me, his face serious and full of concern.

'Hey,' he tries to smile, as he stands up and reaches for my hand.

'Hey,' I answer, taking his hand and holding his gaze.

'You're doing really well, Jenny. Remember those exercises I taught you, use them if you need to,' Daniel says, as he glances at Stuart, 'I'll see you next week.'

'Thanks,' I say, leaning into Stuart. I need his strength. The session with Daniel has all but wiped me out. My eyelids feel heavy and I just want to sleep. My feet were walking in the direction that Stu was guiding me, almost of their own volition. Thank God.

'You look wiped out, sweetheart,' Stu whispers in my ear, 'let's head back to the hotel so you can get some rest.'

I let him lead me along the corridor and out into the cloudy grey October morning. It's not overly cold for this time of year. Sometimes, if you're lucky, you even get the last dregs of summer sunshine.

As we reach Stuart's green Toyota, he takes his key fob from his trouser pocket to unlock the car, opens the passenger door and gestures for me to get in. I'm happy to let him make the decisions for the time being. Anything that allows my brain to take a break.

The purr of the car engine makes me close my eyes and I manoeuvre my arm so that I can rest against the window. I let the car lull me into a deep, almost hypnotic state. The car hits a speed ramp, jolting me awake.

My eyes stay closed, I'm not sleeping, just mulling things over, processing Daniel's words. They make a lot of sense. Deep down I know I'm not to blame for what happened to me and Rose. I didn't do anything wrong. Everything that happened was because of Felix and his obsession with me.

'You awake?' Stu's voice interrupts my thoughts.

'Yeah,' I acknowledge.

'Everything go all right with Daniel?' his voice is husky as he glances my way.

'Yeah,' I sigh, opening my eyes, 'we talked about what happened at the Clumps. We discussed the Summer House. Felix. Rose. He said it wasn't my fault. None of it was my fault.'

'He's right,' he stares ahead, one hand on the steering wheel, the other changing gear.

'I know. Believing it, and wondering if I could have done things differently, that's the hard part.'

'Yep,' he agrees, 'and it doesn't help when you put yourself in danger, by not taking advice when it's given. Such as getting out of a damn car when you're told not to.'

I look quickly at him, and even though, his tone is flat, the sides of his mouth tilt upwards. My lips twitch, offering a weird type of smile, and I shrug my shoulders nonchalantly.

'Comments noted,' I let my hand drop to his thigh, and rub my palm along his jeans.

'I was so mad at you,' he pushes, dropping his hand onto mine, 'I was tempted to throw you over my knee and spank your bottom to knock some sense into you.' I gulp, as his large, firm hand clenches over mine.

'Promises,' I laugh back, my voice sounding lighter. It felt good to just 'be' for a moment and not be reacting to the events that have already happened and that I cannot change. The car pulls into the hotel car park, and my heart drops as I see Henry's Land Rover. He's leaning against the bonnet of the car, face stern, arms folded, and legs crossed. A dark brown raincoat hangs from his tall frame, open slightly so that I can glimpse a brown jumper, white collar and his trademark blue trousers.

We park next to him. Stuart looks at me, his grin quickly replaced by furrowed brows, drawn eyes and a deep sadness.

'This is going to be hard,' he says, 'but it needs to be done.' He opens his door and I do the same.

'Henry,' I hear Stuart say as we walk to him. He's right, this is going to be hard.

And as Henry's arms fold in a defensive stance, in front of me, I fall apart sobbing, before throwing myself at him. 'I'm sorry. So sorry,' I mutter, as I hold his shoulders tight. Feeling the taut pressure within him, I keep my grip hard because I know he's holding everything in. He's been waiting for me, for this very moment.

He stands there, like a statue, with his arms still folded. *I'm not letting go Henry, so you might as well let it out.*

A minute or so later, I feel an inward breath, and a sob as he exhales, catches in his throat. His distress is deep, pained. Slumping forward, he unfolds his arms and somehow manoeuvres his arms around me. He's holding me in a vice-like grip.

‘Jenny,’ his husky voice whispers in my ear, ‘she’s gone. Rose is gone.’

‘I know, I know,’ is all I manage to croak out, before I lose my voice.

I’m not sure who’s crying more, Henry or me, but our faces are sodden with wet tears. Absolutely sodden. I can feel my nose running, and my head is beginning to hurt. No one ever tells you about the pain in your head after a bout of crying. I guess it depends on the tension, or anxiety involved with the emotion.

I shuffle to release myself from Henry’s arms.

Stuart clears his throat and breaks the silence, ‘How about we go inside? We can talk.’ He raises an arm to gesture to the hotel entrance and allows us to walk in front of him to the glass doors. It’s a big hotel and as we walk through the door, I catch a glimpse of myself in the wall mirror and wince.

When you see actors crying on the television, you see a carefully thought out, individualised, scripted performance. Somehow, they even manage to look dignified and realistic. Not me. I look a mess. From my blotchy face, red dribbling nose, to my red puffy eyes. Hideous.

Henry scans the lounge area with its red patterned carpet and scattered sofas and chairs, before finding a quiet area to sit and talk.

I drop onto a dark grey velvet sofa which is placed opposite two red wingback chairs, Stuart chooses to sit next to me. A faint hint of grapefruit and cedar comes my way, soothing me. I feel his hand reach out for mine, the sight of our fingers intwined, also soothes me. I know I’m not alone.

Henry looks across to us from his seat in one of the wingback chairs, his movements are stiff, rigid, every inch of his body seems to be in pain. He stares down at his hands that rest on his thighs.

'Have you heard anything from DCI Carter or DS Jones?' I ask, opening the painful conversation.

'Not yet,' his voice is gruff with emotion when he lifts his head to answer my question. 'I went back to the station with DS Jones last night and made my statement. Thankfully, everything that happened was confirmed by your call to Stuart,' he sent me a brief smile, before continuing, 'DCI Carter told me he'd be in touch this afternoon, to update me about the post-mortem.'

'I don't understand what happened,' Stuart states, 'I mean, Felix needed to keep Rose safe, to exchange her for Jenny. Why would he kill her?'

'I don't know,' I say quietly, 'maybe it was an accident.'

'I agree,' Henry answers, 'he had every reason to make sure that Rose lived. He knew Jenny would come to the Clumps, that she would want to help get Rose back. I think it was an accident.'

'Do you think he drugged her?' I ask, crossing my fingers, hoping he'll say no.

'Yes,' Henry says simply, and an icy chill makes its way through my tired body, until it reaches my shoulder in an uncontrollable shiver. Jesus. I push and push, trying to find exactly what has happened to myself and Rose, but sometimes, I just wish I could have my memory erased. It's like living in your own never-ending horror movie.

Stuart shakes his head and brushes a hand through his hair, 'Shit.'

Henry leans forward, resting his forearms on his knees, 'We'll need to wait for the post-mortem to find out what really happened to her.'

I take a deep breath and stare at the red carpeted floor. Thinking. About my small world. There are questions I need answered. I need to know what happened. To Felix.

Stuart's deep voice startles me out of my reverie, 'The people who killed Felix. Do we know anything about them? Were they working together?'

We look at Henry, hoping he can offer some answers about Felix's death. Memories of his last words haunt me. 'Jenny Gloverman,' he'd said. 'I love you.' Just thinking about them, sends a shiver down my spine and causes tingling sensations along my shoulder blades. What the hell am I supposed to do with those sick words? Some things you simply can't take back.

'It could be any number of people. I have no idea,' Henry says, breaking through my rambling thoughts. There's a harshness to his tone, anger in his words.

'He must have made some enemies over the years. I think he was into some sordid shit from what DCI Carter told us,' Stuart agrees, draping an arm over the back of the sofa.

'What about his PA, Amy?' Henry cuts in. 'Those goons knocked her about, and she was nearly six months pregnant. She lost Felix's baby,' he tells Stuart.

My heart stops, at this statement. I can't believe what I'm hearing. Felix was having a relationship with Amy Wilder? It seems too outrageous to believe. I don't know her well, but I hear she's a really nice person, calm, kind, efficient.

'Hold on there,' there's no denying the strain in my voice, 'what do you mean, she lost Felix's baby?'

A shadow falls over Stuart's face, before he raises his eyebrows to Henry.

‘Did you know?’ I ask Stuart, can’t keep the anger from my voice, ‘About her and Felix, and the baby?’

‘Sorry, Jen,’ Stuart answers quietly, his eyes holding mine, and all I can see is the deep sadness that he’s dealing with, ‘I found out a couple of nights ago, just before everything started to kick off at the house. The fire, hiding in Henry’s office, Felix in the house. Then Rose went missing. It completely left my mind.’

‘Don’t blame Stuart,’ Henry’s voice cuts in, ‘there was so much happening. I’m just saying that Felix has hurt a number of people.’

I understand, really, I do. I just can’t get my head around Felix and Amy having a relationship. Having sex. Making a baby. He is such a monster. He was such a monster. I just wish they hadn’t kept things from me. I touch Stuart’s thigh to reassure him and offer a small smile. ‘It’s OK,’ I tell him, ‘I get it.’

Henry looks at each of us in turn, before speaking, ‘I don’t mind saying, that I’d like to shake whoever did this, by the hand. After what he did to you and Rose, he deserved to die. Felix was nothing but a rabid animal, he needed to be put to sleep.’

Stuart nods in agreement, as the ringing of his phone peels through the air. It’s DS Jones. Henry and I look at each other and I can’t help but feel an overwhelming sense of guilt as I look into his weather-beaten face. Stuart asks if they can wait a few hours before taking my statement. He tells the DS, that I need to rest. What would I do without this man? He looks after me so well.

In a cathartic moment, I realise that I’m very lucky to have so many good people around me, helping me, giving me their strength, when mine has been taken or fails. In addition to Stuart, Henry and Lottie, the police officers and Daniel have been amazing. And Rose. There are no words.

***

I awake from a deep, calm sleep. No nightmares, no reliving the events that have taken place over the past week. No thoughts of Felix or Rose. And for that I am grateful.

Rubbing my eyes, I stare at the semi-dark plain ceiling and take a deep breath. It's now time to face reality. I move my pillows and shuffle up into a sitting position on the bed. A curtain is drawn across the window and Stu slumps in the blue leather chair, nearby. Asleep.

He looks so peaceful, my heart swells with emotion and a lump comes to my throat. Like me, he's had one hell of a week, and he must be exhausted. I put my hand to my mouth to hold back a sob. Emotion is getting the better of me. As if he senses that I'm awake, Stu's eyes shoot open, he stretches his arms and brushes his hands through his hair.

'Jen, sorry I must have nodded off,' he apologises in a rush.

'Don't worry,' I reassure him, getting out of bed and feeling the need for a hot drink. 'Fancy a cup of tea?' I grab the small kettle from its tray, check the water level and refill it, using the bathroom tap. My tummy rumbles and I look at my silver watch to check the time. Bloody hell, it's 1.30pm.

'What time will DS Jones be here?' I ask him, finishing off the tea.

'At 3pm. You hungry? I'm starving!' he says.

'Glad you said that, let's head downstairs after our drink. I'm absolutely famished.'

'Oh, I nearly forgot,' Stu takes a slurp of hot liquid from his cup, 'Lottie texted me earlier. She wants to see you. I said she could come over around 7pm and we could have dinner together. I need to pop back home to grab a few things. I'll do that after dinner, then you and she can have a good chat. Is that all right?'

I think for a moment. There wasn't much to do in the hotel, I couldn't go home to get my stuff yet, even if I wanted to. The idea of catching up with Lottie sounded good.

'That would be nice,' I smile, taking a sip of hot tea as I perch on the edge of the bed.

A sharp knock at the door, draws our attention. Stuart places his cup on the dresser, before going to open it. 'It's all right,' he says, 'it's probably Henry.' I watch with bated breath as the door is pulled open.

'How are you both?' Henry asks, walking into the room, with Mickey Shakespeare in tow.

'We're doing OK,' Stuart answers, 'you?'

'I'm OK. I keep thinking she'll walk in the door any moment,' he shakes his head, as though trying to rid himself of his anguish, 'DCI Carter called to say that blood samples have been sent to the lab to test for drugs and alcohol. We should know more tomorrow.'

I simply nod, there seems so little to say.

'Mickey and I are popping out for a few hours. Meeting up with a few old friends,' Henry tells us, as he turns to walk out the door.

'Look after him, Mickey,' Stuart says.

'Of course,' Mickey smiles, and responds by patting Henry on the back of his shoulder, 'I'll always have his back.'

I think of those words as I watch Stuart close the door to our room. 'I'll always have his back.' It's a big statement to make, even if you were former marine buddies. Who is Mickey

Shakespeare? We only met him yesterday. Just how far would he go to help his old friend, I wonder?

As if he can read my mind, Stuart says softly, ‘Who is Mickey Shakespeare? I was just thinking the same thing.’

I push off the bed and walk to him, ‘Would Mickey kill Felix for Henry? I know they’ve been through a lot, but.’

‘But,’ he finishes for me, ‘if Henry was so distraught about Rose, who knows what he might have asked Mickey to do.’ He takes my hand and moves across the room to the chair, where he drops down casually, and pulls me onto his lap. ‘To be honest, if it was you who had been taken or killed, and I had those resources and contacts, I think I’d do the same.’

I turn into his warm body and weave my arms around his neck, holding him firmly. ‘But, I’m fine,’ I tell him as I kiss his cheek. ‘I’m safe and I’m here with you,’ I kiss the other cheek and then his chin. I kiss his lips, ‘And, this is where I intend to stay.’ His mouth opens and I sweep my tongue along his lower lip.

I hear his brief intake of breath, as he deepens the kiss, and my body relaxes with a heavy sigh as his hands lightly caress my back and move lower to cup my jean-clad bottom. A delicious warmth spreads through my body, as though a match has been lit inside me, awakening feelings I’d forgotten I had. I want to spend my life with this man. He keeps me grounded, makes me feel as though we can overcome anything.

Slowly pulling away, he rests his forehead on mine, his breath caresses my cheek, ‘I think we need to take a rain check on this, or we’ll not have time to eat before DS Jones gets here.’

***

Hot water splashes off my body as I finish rubbing the hotel shampoo into my scalp. I close my eyes. Bliss. For the first time in what seems like forever, I hum to myself. I used to do this a lot before I was kidnapped. Hum and sing in the shower. It was 'my thing,' a way of relaxing. I continue humming the tune to The Mamas and the Papas, California Dreamin'.

'All the leaves are brown, and the sky is grey. I went for a walk, on a Winter's day,' Holy shit! I can't believe it. I am actually singing.

As the words soothe my head, I subconsciously think of the last few hours. Stu and I had booked a table for dinner at 7pm on our way to get food and eaten toasted sandwiches and shared a large bowl of fries in the hotel bar. We'd finished with steaming lattes and felt so much better after we'd eaten, and our tummies were full.

DS Jones and Julie had arrived at 3pm on the dot, to go over my statement for last night. I'd left Julie's phone on call, the moment I'd decided to leave the car, so that everything that I did could be heard. Which thankfully, collaborated my story. I confirmed that I had no idea who'd murdered Felix, and that due to the darkness, I didn't see anything, apart from the red dot that pointed to Felix's forehead. Everything had happened so quickly. Clearly someone had been watching my back, protecting me. Or maybe, simply determined to get rid of Felix. On both counts, I felt lucky.

What to do with Gateshead? I really didn't want to go back, not yet anyway. I don't know if I ever want to go back. Only time will tell. Knowing that the Summer House stood on its grounds didn't help. I felt ill, thinking about the place. My childhood home, which had once been a place of happy memories, was now my worst nightmare. Nothing was the same. It was where Felix kept his secret stash of photos of me. Where he went through my underwear drawer and took what he wanted. And, where he took Rose.

Still, Stuart and I can't stay here in this hotel forever. I need to access my parent's funds, so that I, or we can find a permanent place to live. These are discussions that we need to have soon; about us, and our relationship.

I rinse my hair and think of Stuart waiting for me, as we prepare to go to the restaurant for our meal with Lottie. I quickly dry myself and dress in my one remaining set of clothes. A pair of dark grey jeans, and a grey jumper that I was wearing the night we first arrived here. I use the fitted dryer in the bathroom to dry my long blonde hair, before pulling it back into a loose knot. Then, I take Stu's hand as we walk to meet Lottie.

Two hours, two lasagnes, garlic bread, and a chicken and bacon burger and fries later, Stuart left Lottie and me, to return home to collect clothes and stuff.

Lottie rests her arms on the mahogany table, one hand holds a small glass of red wine. The navy linen dress and white cardigan looks good on her slender figure. Red curls are casually tucked behind her ears and there are silver helicopters dangling from her ears.

'So,' she looks at me, tilting her glass, 'how are you really?'

My fingers play lightly with the white cotton napkin. I give it a couple of seconds before looking up at her, 'I'm all right. A bit up and down, you know.'

'I can imagine,' she holds my gaze, her warm brown eyes look serious, 'it's going to take time. Don't try to rush things.' She reaches across the table to stop my fidgeting hands, holding them tightly with her own, 'You can do this, Jen. You can absolutely do this.'

I looked at her dear face, the concern and determination clear. Her kind words hit me hard, and I try hard not to break down, but then my face begins to scrunch, my throat constricts, and the tears fall. Hard down my cheeks.

'Lottie, I hope so. I really hope so,' I tell her, pulling my hands away and wiping my cheeks. I promised myself that I wouldn't cry tonight, that I would enjoy a meal without letting my emotions get the better of me. Making promises can be dangerous, I'm beginning to realise. Lottie has been such a good friend over the past few years.

My mind plays back the memories of our first meeting.

***

'Where do you want these boxes?' Henry asks, pointing to several boxes on the luggage trolley that was provided for new students moving into halls of residence. We're in the room, which will be my new home for the next year. It's a student flat made up of six rooms, complete with their own bathrooms, and is situated on the second floor. There's a communal kitchen, living area and a hallway. I look at the shabby blue carpet on the floor, then at the bed.

'Maybe there's storage under the bed?' Rose asks, lifting the mattress to find a long moveable wooden tray, with a wooden hole. She bent, put her finger in the hole, lifted the tray and found the storage space under the bed. 'There we go,' she smiles, 'I'll sort the box with the pans, cutlery and food and put them in the kitchen. Does anything need to go in the fridge?'

'Milk, cheese, butter,' I tell her, pointing to a white carrier bag, propped precariously on the trolley. I felt uneasy, scared even and the butterflies in my tummy didn't help. Leaving home, was a big deal and I was going to miss Henry and Rose so much. I was looking forward to a new adventure though, new challenges, meeting fresh faces, new people.

Thirty minutes later, most of it is done and I was standing with a cotton bedsheet in hand and my duvet covered in my favourite purple cover. A movement came from the hallway, before someone knocked quietly at the door.

'Come in,' I say, looking at Henry and Rose. We stand, waiting as a pretty girl with a mass of curly red hair smiles kindly, and says in a soft voice.

'Hi, I'm Lottie. I'm next door to you.'

'Hey,' I say smiling, thankful that she didn't look like a mass murderer, 'I'm Jenny. Nice to meet you.'

***

'Jen?' a soft voice speaks, 'Jen? You there?'

I feel a light tap to my shoulder, and I look down to see that it belongs to slender fingers. It's Lottie. For the briefest time my mind is a whirl of emotions, before it settles and the fog lifts. 'Sorry,' I apologise to her. By way of explanation, I mutter, 'I was daydreaming. Seem to be doing a lot of that lately.'

'You don't have to apologise to me, Jen. There have been times in my life when I've been dreaming, mostly to forget. Reliving bad memories is hard. Takes its toll.'

Caught off guard, I glimpse a deep sorrow momentarily in her eyes. As though realising her error, she shrugs her shoulders and looks away. Too late Lottie, you can't hide anymore.

'Did someone hurt you, Lottie?' I finally ask the question that's been on my mind since our conversation yesterday. Bloody hell, that chat seems a lifetime ago. Her shoulders slump, she looks down at her hands, folded on the table. She looks so vulnerable, so sad. Maybe there's a reason she never told me about this. Perhaps it was her burden to carry alone. Her choice to keep silent. However, for me, burdens and friendships work both ways.

'Charlotte Peckham,' I say, in a stern voice, 'you know absolutely everything there is to know about me. Our friendship is precious to me. We need to share our worries, our failures and successes. Not keep them bottled up. This cannot be a one-sided friendship.'

'But Jen,' she looks up at me, her eyes are glistening with tears.

'No buts,' I interrupt, reaching out to pat her hand.

'But. I've never told anyone before,' she shakes her head sadly, as those glorious red curls follow her movements.

'Told anyone what?' I ask, pushing her to face whatever it is that's haunting her.

'If I say it, then it really happened and I don't want to admit that it did,' she says dully, still looking at her hands.

'I understand what you're saying, but the truth is, until you've processed what happened, you'll find it increasingly hard to move on. It will always have a claim on you,' I tell her, sounding stronger than I actually feel. Focusing on someone else's problems, means I don't think too much about my own, 'Let me share that burden. Let me help you.'

Silence fills the air. I look around the room. There are only three tables with guests eating, and they're at the far end of the dining room. We have privacy of sorts.

'Do you ever wish you could wipe out one single action? A momentary lapse of judgement, where one single action causes a tsunami of circumstances beyond your control?'

‘I think the answer to that, might be yes,’ I say softly, ‘what was your tsunami?’

‘It was a long time ago,’ she begins, her eyes focused on the wall behind me. ‘sometimes, I wonder if it really happened at all.’ Her shoulders sag, before taking a deep breath.

‘I was fifteen years old. I’d been invited to an older cousin’s eighteenth birthday party, at my aunt and uncle’s house. I assumed they’d be home later that night. I didn’t realise they had booked a hotel room. I took my friend, Katie with me, but we got separated.’

She sits quietly, as though remembering the events of that evening in slow motion. I stay silent. I think I know what is coming, feel the alarm of prickles on my forearms, but this is her tale to tell.

‘My cousin, he was confident, good-looking. He got me a drink. An open can of fruit cider. I didn’t know he’d spiked it, not until I found myself in an upstairs bedroom with him and two of his friends.’

I shake my head, swallowing down the bile that desperately wants to evacuate from my tummy. My eyes are so full of tears, I can hardly see. All I can see in my mind’s eye was Lottie being taken advantage of, so I reach out, take her hand and hold it tightly. I feel a white-hot rage and a fear of what she will tell me next, as her fingers squeeze mine back. I’ll never forget the look of absolute misery on her beautiful face, for as long as I live. Pale skin. Taut features. Dead eyes.

‘You are doing so well, Lottie. So well.’ I want her to know that, as I hold on firm to her warm skin, ‘I’m so proud of you for telling me, for letting me be here for you.’

‘I don’t remember much. I was in and out of consciousness for most of the night. I think they each used me. They used me while

I was drugged, can you believe that Jen?' tears swam down her face, 'Used a fifteen-year-old girl like a fucking whore? His own bloody cousin!'

I take a deep breath. This is hard to hear. My friend has been terribly abused by three young men who were three years her senior. Men, who should have known better. Date rape is a serious crime, it's about taking the control and the will away from a person, incapacitating them. I want to seek these vile people out and do bad things to them, on Lottie's behalf. The series of self-defence tips that Stuart had shown Rose and I, spring to mind.

With a calm strength, she continues her story, 'I must have blacked out, because when I next woke, I was downstairs on their sofa, covered in a blanket. Disorientated, sore, tired and fully clothed. I saw my personal things sitting on the floor beside me. My cousin had texted my parents to say that I was tired and had asked to stay over. I grabbed the blanket, my phone and my bag, that's when I saw him. My cousin, standing on the threshold of the open lounge door, that led to the kitchen. I walked over to him, still in shock.

'Cameron? What the hell? I was a virgin, how could you?' I said, almost spitting in his face, before I stormed out of his parent's house. He didn't say a word. Couldn't look me in the face. I never set foot in that house ever again. I never spoke to Cameron again. That day, I went to a pharmacy to buy the morning after pill.'

'And you never told anyone this? Not even your parents?' I ask, with a lump in my throat and tears streaming down my face.

I push my chair out and throw myself into her arms, 'Oh Lottie, I'm so sorry. So very sorry for what you've been through.' I hold her tightly, half sitting, half stooping. I can feel her tears beginning to soak through my jumper. 'I'm here. I'm here,' I coo soothingly, stroking her hair, 'shall we go to my room? It's more private.'

'Yes,' she half whispers, and I collect our things and steer her to the lift.

Part 22

Stuart

Unsurprisingly, it's been three days, and we're still at the hotel. Thank God they had availability, or I'd be googling hotel websites. They say, 'When life gives you lemons, make lemonade.' It sounds good in theory, but the reality is far from easy. How do you stand up and carry on, when you reach rock bottom? How do you live with the knowledge of unbelievable horrors that haunt your dreams?

When I'd returned to the hotel that evening, following the meal with Lottie and Jen, it was late,10.30pm. I'd topped up with petrol, grabbed more clothes and personal items from home, and drove around a little, to clear my head. I'd spoken to Steve, my line manager at the Tesco store in Didcot, where I did twilight shift work, refilling shelves each weekend, to organise a few more weekends leave, due to a family emergency.

I've been in touch with Bournemouth University, updated them about myself, Lottie and Jenny. They've given us an additional month to finish our dissertations for the Business and Management degree. We have all agreed that we've done too much work at this stage to let it go to waste. That would be like letting Felix Gloverman win. And that is something that won't happen, in any shape or form.

Jenny is fast asleep snuggled under the white duvet, when I am finally ready for bed. Absently, my right hand finds the ring box, that has been sitting in my jacket pocket for weeks. I'd been planning to ask Jenny to marry me on the evening of Rose and

Henry's twenty-fifth wedding anniversary. Well, we know how that night turned out. Or didn't. I'm not sure if Jenny would be ready for this kind of commitment after what has happened.

I slip into my pyjama bottoms and a short-sleeved jersey top, and slide into the bed next to her. Yes, we're sharing a bed again, but no, there's no sexual physical activity. This feels natural, right, as if it's meant to be. When she's ready, if she ever feels comfortable to explore a more physical relationship, I'll be waiting. She's becoming more relaxed touching me again. Take this afternoon, for example, I'd pulled her onto my lap, and she'd instigated our kiss. Wanting more.

In the darkness, I turn to face her back. She begins to move and shuffle until she is looking at me. I can feel her eyes on me, I try to stay as still as possible, as she moves closer. I don't know why I am shocked by her actions, I am flattered that she feels so comfortable with me, because that means we're making progress. I also know that I need to take things slowly with her. It is hard being the strong one all of the time, when I just want to sink into the comfort of her body and shut out the world.

'Stu?' her words are quiet, sounding sleepy.

'Yes, babe.' I reach for her cheek in the dark. 'Sorry, I disturbed you. Go back to sleep.' I tell her.

'I talked to Lottie,' she says with glistening eyes.

'Yeah? And?' I ask.

'Something bad happened to her, a long time again,' she says sadly, as my hand strokes her shoulder.

'Do you want to talk about it?' I offer, unsure whether she should be carrying more emotional baggage on her shoulders.

'Thanks, but no,' she answers, 'maybe tomorrow.'

'Goodnight sweetheart,' I tell her, shuffling forward and caressing the soft skin of her cheek.

'Goodnight Stu,' she whispers, 'thank you.' I gently kiss her lips and let her snuggle into me. I lay awake, listening to her soft breathing.

***

Henry and I had collected clothes and personal items from Gateshead yesterday. Jenny had listed things that she wanted me to collect. Passport, trinkets, photos of her parents, of Rose and Henry and of us together. We chatted a little, as we travelled in his Land Rover to the place that had been the family home for many years. It must have been harrowing for him to have to go back, without Rose.

The conversation in the car had been a little stilted at first. There were questions I needed answers to. 'Can I ask you something?' I'd said, glancing his way. There was a queasy feeling in my stomach. I wasn't sure if I was going to like where the conversation was going, but as I said, I needed answers.

'Yes,' he answered.

'Did you ask Mickey Shakespeare to shoot Felix?' I had rushed the words out, before I decided against asking.

I'd watched as Henry slowed the car down. 'No. I thought about it,' he began, 'it's not something I'm proud of. But, in the end, someone got to Felix before Mickey did.'

'Bloody hell, Henry!' I'd heard my voice getting louder and I'd wiped my sweaty palms, down my jeans.

'I had no choice. He'd taken Jenny, then he took Rose. I couldn't let him get away with it. Felix had to be stopped.'

We'd sat in silence, mulling over the situation. Who the hell had killed Felix? And, more worryingly, what if Henry was lying? Bloody hell, I'd felt like my head was going to explode!

After a while, Henry revealed that he had no intention of returning home to Gateshead. Mickey had planned to go home in a few days, and Henry was going to go with him. There was no evidence to say that Mickey was the shooter or the person who had stabbed Felix.

DCI Carter and Julie visited us after we got back from Gateshead, to update us on what was happening. We'd sat huddled, like a group of conspirators in the lounge, hot drinks steamed on the table in front of us. Jenny had held my hand as we'd sunk into the deep grey Chesterfield-style sofa. Henry's face was impassive, as though he just wanted to get through the meeting.

The last remnants of the summer sun tinted his weather-beaten face. He was only sixty, but he suddenly looked older, as though he'd given up on life. DCI Carter and Julie had sat in red wing-back chairs facing us. The hotel catering staff had kindly given us a plate of biscuits with the hot drinks. We really couldn't fault the hotel and its staff, who had been nothing but accommodating throughout our stay.

'The post-mortem on Rose has been completed,' DCI Carter began, looking up from his notebook. 'I'm sorry to say that Rose died as a result of temazepam and alcohol poisoning. It appears that Felix had crushed the tablets into vodka and fed it to her. We found a half-empty bottle of the spirit on the passenger seat. I'm pretty sure he never intended her to die. I think he just wanted to keep her quiet, until Jenny arrived,' he explained, glancing at Jenny, Henry and myself. Jenny had sat there staring at Carter, silent tears falling down her cheeks. She wiped them with the sleeve of her green cardigan. Rose's cardigan.

A member of the hotel reception team, a slim, dark-haired woman in a pale blue blouse, tight knee-length skirt and flat shoes, had shadowed the table and placed an open box of tissues next to the drinks. I'd smiled my thanks, and handed one to Jenny, before putting a reassuring arm around her shoulder.

'There are no leads on the knife,' Carter had continued working through his notes, 'and, we still have very little on the person who shot Felix. The area searches didn't find anything. We think the rifle is ex-armed forces. Although, we're exploring some theories, we have nothing concrete. Graham Foster gave Felix his Volvo to use, before he broke into your house, and took Rose.'

Henry spoke for the first time. There was a gruffness to his voice, 'Will he be arrested?'

'Yes,' Carter tells him, 'he's been arrested and charged on accounts of arson, and accessory to kidnapping and murder.'

'Good,' Jenny said with some passion, leaning forward to face Carter. I pulled my arm back, listening to her firm words, 'he deserves to be behind bars. Without the car, he may not have taken Rose. Who knows?'

'We'll never know,' Julie agreed sadly.

'When will Rose be released for burial?' Henry asked quietly.

'Sometime during the next seven days,' Carter answered, 'I've given them your number, they should be in touch. Meanwhile, you can start checking out funeral directors.'

Shit. This was really happening. She really was dead. It hadn't all been a bad dream.

'All right,' Henry told the DCI, 'Mickey is returning home to the New Forest in a couple of days, I'm going to go and stay with him for a while, at least until after the funeral. I just can't be here right now.'

'But Henry!' Jenny questioned him sadly, 'Please don't do this, stay with us. We're your family.'

'I'm sorry, Jenny,' he rubbed his hands over his whiskered face, 'I need to get away. I'll be in touch, to help sort out the funeral.'

Jenny nodded, and I grabbed her hand and held it in both of mine. Trying to give her what little strength I could. When you hit rock bottom, you wonder how you'll ever pick yourself up and carry on. You do the only thing you can do. You put one foot in front of the other, push yourself to your feet and force yourself to move forward, to not give up.

'It'll be all right, Jen. We'll get through this.' I'd stroked her hair and prayed that we would indeed 'get through this.'

'Henry,' Carter had looked directly at him, 'I'll need you to bring Mickey to the station at 9am tomorrow so that we can confirm his whereabouts for last night. We need to eliminate him from our enquiries into Felix's death.'

Henry nodded, his lips forming a grim line. He stared at the floor.

I'd studied the small group in front of me, Jenny and Henry were just about holding it together. One, almost grimacing in his attempt not to break down, the other, letting the silent tears fall as she came to terms with the consequences of Felix's actions.

I looked at Julie, with her short bob, freckles, plain black trousers, white blouse and V-neck blue jumper. She'd been a good friend to us throughout this ordeal. She was watching DCI Carter, as he spoke. Then, he looked up, as if he had sensed her looking at him, said something quietly to her that I couldn't hear, before offering him a small smile. Bloody hell! She liked him. I mean really liked him. And, by the look he'd just given her, he liked her too. Good luck to them both.

Julie had begun talking and I tuned back into the conversation, 'Gateshead has been secured, and SOCO have finished their investigation. You can return home, when you feel ready.'

'I don't want to go back there,' Jenny's soft voice travelled through the quiet lounge.

'Neither do I,' Henry agreed, 'I couldn't live there without Rose. Too many memories.'

'I'm going to put it on the market,' Jenny said firmly. I looked at her in shock, we'd not discussed this, and it made me wonder what other things she'd decided without telling me. My main worry was that she'd want to end our relationship, although deep down, I told myself not to be stupid, to trust my girlfriend. Jenny looked at me and mouthed the word 'sorry' before leaning back on the sofa and reaching her hand around my shoulders to stroke my neck. I had closed my eyes for a moment, blocking everything out, and enjoyed her touch.

There was a clearing of a throat and DCI Carter began to talk. 'There's one last thing,' he'd said, 'Felix had a burner phone, but he'd also taken photos on it. There are photos of you, Jenny, and a couple of photos of Rose after he'd taken her. I wanted to forewarn you all, that these may need to be used as evidence to convict Foster. I'll personally do everything I can to limit who has access to these photos.'

Jenny had nodded and hung her head as though she was embarrassed. With gentle fingers I'd tilted her face upwards, until our eyes were level. 'Don't,' I'd said quietly, 'you did nothing wrong. Don't feel bad.'

She'd offered a sad nod of the head. My beautiful woman, she was so strong, but so fragile and it hurt me to see her blaming herself and feeling ashamed. None of this was her fault.

***

‘Please try to eat something, Jen,’ I plead, as I watch her pushing roast chicken and mashed potato around her plate in the dining room. She allows her fork to clatter as she drops it on to her white dinner plate.

She told me about Lottie yesterday, after Julie and the DCI had left. I was blown away. And, not in a good way. To say I was shocked is an understatement when Jenny told me that Lottie had been drugged at a party by an older cousin. I was outraged, to find that her cousin and some of his friends had raped the poor girl. They’d taken it in turns to use her and it made my blood boil. Under the table, my foot kept tapping, as I fought down the anger that was building inside me. My heart breaks for her, for keeping her silence all these years and for finally having the courage to tell someone.

Jenny is due to see Daniel, the psychiatrist on Thursday. All things considered, she is doing well, but I am relieved and thankful that Daniel has set up a weekly appointment for her. Talking through her experiences with a professional, developing coping strategies and learning how to focus on her strengths and achievements, are key elements in how she can move forward. Jenny and Lottie were also talking about joining a victim support group together. I think their shared experiences will make them stronger.

Henry is resting in his room, said he didn’t feel like eating, drinking or talking. He said that he wanted to be alone. He seems to be withdrawing from us a little more each day, as though preparing for total separation.

‘Sorry, I’m not hungry,’ she tells me.

'I know,' I answer, putting my hand on her arm, 'but you need to keep your strength up.'

I didn't tell her, but I'd texted Julie and asked if she'd do a bit of digging on Lottie's cousin, Cameron. I'm not sure if anything will come of it, but I really need to do something positive, feel in control. And, I feel an urge to punch someone hard.

'Talk to me Jenny. What's going on in that head of yours?'

'I'm mulling around a few things, that's all,' she looks at me, and my heart sinks. She's going to finish with me, with us. After everything we've been through, she's going to call it a day. Shit. I take a deep breath. I stare at her. Eyes wide. Waiting.

'First, I'm sorry I didn't tell you about Gateshead. I knew Henry wouldn't want to live there, neither could I, not anymore. I thought I'd put it on the market and split the money between me and Henry. Then he can get a place of his own. What do you think?'

I exhale with relief. Is that all?

'That sounds like a good idea, but are you sure?' I ask, 'It holds memories of your parents and childhood.'

'I know, and yes, I'm sure,' Jenny replies with a steady voice. 'The bad memories outweigh every good memory I have. The sleepovers in the Summer House, learning to swim in the pool with Henry, baking in the kitchen with Rose. I can't face being there,' she explains, her eyes pleading for my support.

'Oh sweetheart,' my heart aches for her, as I listen to her words. Physically, she's fine, but emotionally her life over the last two weeks has been a rollercoaster of a ride. Swiftly pushing my chair away, I step across to her and kneel, letting my hand rest on her shoulder. 'Of course, I'm with you. It's your house to do with as you wish. I'll support you whatever you decide.'

I think for a moment, before her words flashed through my mind. She said two things. 'What's the second thing?'

Worried blue eyes hold mine. She hesitates, before speaking, 'I thought we could buy a house together.' Her eyebrows furrow and she gulps before continuing breathlessly, 'That's if you want to. Move in with me, I mean.'

Relief hits me like a giant rock hurtling at full speed into my body. She doesn't want us to part, she wants us to stay together, to be together. I've never felt this way about anyone before, we're like two halves of the same coin, a coin that fits together perfectly. Thank God! A smile starts to form on my lips, and I can't help but feel elated at the thought of having a place of our own, building a life together.

'You want us to live together? Have a home of our own?' I ask, my voice husky and emotional.

She nods, shyly and smiles. The world brightens a hundred-fold, restoring the balance of good against evil to the universe. A life worth living, with someone who loves me, who I love in return. I picture a life with Jenny, a good life, with feelings, love and warmth. If we're lucky, there will be children, if not, I'll still count myself as one of the most blessed people on this earth.

I stand up, pull her to her feet and gently place my hands on either side of her face. As the soft skin of our foreheads touch, I say quietly, 'It's a yes, Jen. There's no place else I would rather be, than with you.'

Part 23

DCI Carter

'You need to take it easy,' Mike gives me a concerned look as he stands in the open doorway of my office, his arms are casually folded, as are his legs. White shirt and blue chinos, his good-looking features, complete the television star look. He reminds me of Richard Armitage.

I roll my eyes at him, he doesn't know me very well, 'Time to take a breather, when this case is closed,' I retort, picking up Shep's report on Mickey Shakespeare's background history and his whereabouts last night.

Mickey Shakespeare, fifty-nine years old, a former Captain in the Royal Marines, tall and slender, brown cropped hair and a moustache, came into the station yesterday and willingly gave a statement on where he was on the night of the shooting. It took Shep only two hours to confirm Mickey's alibi with his former marine team-mate, Corporal Len Massey.

I stare at the black print on the white paper and mutter, 'I could have sworn that Mickey Shakespeare was our shooter.' There's a niggle of a headache starting at the front of my head.

'Me too,' Mike says, 'he's got the skills and has access to resources that would have made this hit job on Gloverman easy.'

I nod, and continue scanning the information again, hoping to find something that doesn't add up. Massey lives in Bridge Street, Abingdon. Mickey had arrived at 6.30pm, they'd chatted before walking to the nearby pub, The Nag's Head at 7pm for food and drink. He was there, with Massey surrounded by people until 11pm. The bar manager, Andrew Johnstone, confirmed this.

Mickey's had an interesting life. He was born to a farmer and his wife just outside Lyndhurst in the New Forest. He had two sisters and one brother. One sister is now deceased, cause of death, bone cancer when she was twenty years old.

Mickey left home to join the Royal Marines when he was seventeen years old and became an accomplished, and respected marine. He rose to the rank of Captain and applied to join the Royal Marine Commandos, there he met Sergeant Henry Dean, and the two became firm friends and respected colleagues.

In addition, both men received commendations for their service to the Crown during tours to Afghanistan and Kuwait. I understand that any sensitive information pertaining to their missions has been withheld, for national security reasons.

'Shakespeare and Henry both have one hell of a service record,' I absently rub my index finger in the centre of my forehead, trying to push away the pending headache, before leaning back in my chair and closing my eyes, 'where are we on the ballistics? And the knife?' It seems to be taking forever to get the reports back. I know the labs are busy, but we need this information. Mike nods and walks from the office.

'Shep?' he calls, as he walks to his desk, 'Anything back from the labs yet?'

She looks up, her red hair pulled back from her face, then gazes at the documents on her desk. 'No. I'll give them a call,' she answers before picking up the phone on her desk. I can hear Shep's low voice as she asks questions and makes notes. She mutters 'thanks' before grabbing the piece of paper with her notes and pushing out of her chair.

She walks to my door, in dark purple jeggings, black biker boots and a long blue tunic, Mike walks in step beside her. My phone pings, it's Julie. She's been to see Amy Wilder at her home near Didcot, to see how she is and to ask a few questions. She's on her way back to the office.

'Boss,' Shep studies the paper, 'news about the knife. It's part of a set, and commonly available on Amazon and in Argos. No prints.'

I shake my head, the lucky bastard. 'He or she were wearing gloves?' I know this to be true. I saw Gino with my own eyes, step into the dark road whilst taking off his gloves, on his return from stabbing Felix Gloverman. I let him go, closed my eyes to his crime and walked away.

'And the weapon?' I ask, forcing myself out of my chair, knowing that this will cause a dull ache in my shoulder. I grab my phone and push it into the pocket of my brown trousers, before walking to the incident board. Photos, documents and comments relating to timeframes are written in felt-tip.

Shep and Mike follow, and Shep's soft voice continues, as she reads from her notepaper, 'Ballistics report that the bullet taken from Felix's head, was fired using a standard British forces sniper rifle, Accuracy International PM, L96A1 which entered service in 1985. They're searching the firearms database, to find out if any rifles have been reported stolen or are missing, but nothing has turned up yet.'

'So, we've gone from a kidnapping, to a missing person, to another kidnapping and finally, to another murder. Bloody hell,' I push my fingers through my hair, in frustration, 'we need to wrap this one up. Did we find anything on the Gloverman Corporation finances? Or, the uncle's bank accounts?'

Papers are shuffled and Shep looks up, 'Nothing from Felix Gloverman has come to light. No large payments going in or out, regularly or not, over the last three-year period. The Corporation's accounts look healthy. I'm half-way through the last three years of their accounts. Can't see anything that looks suspicious. Yet.'

'Right.' I start to pace up and down the room, 'Someone must have seen something that night! Two people killed Felix Gloverman. Two people. And, they can't have just disappeared into thin air!'

Mike Jones studies the incident board and strokes his stubbled chin. He steps forward, studying the photo taken of Felix facing the ground with the knife in his back, 'You're right. What did the helicopter come up with?'

Shep steps forward, pointing to the map with the red triangulated area a five-mile radius from the Clumps. 'Thermal imaging detected no one around the area by the time they'd arrived. There were six cars on the road that night, first noted on the High Street of Long Wittenham, two cars turned left at Clifton Hampden traffic lights, towards Abingdon, four followed the Oxford Road to Berinsfield roundabout and headed to Oxford. Nothing untoward in their driving.'

'Bugger!'

I walk over to the kitchen area and fill the kettle. I need a coffee, a mug full of caffeine to get my brain cells working. There are still a few questions running around in my mind, in addition to who shot Felix Gloverman. Why had he drugged Rose? Was it, to keep her quiet? Was Felix involved in something more sinister?

Ten minutes later, the office door is pushed open and Julie walks through, breathing life into the room. She's wearing black jeans, black low-heeled boots, and a long dark green top. I watch with interest as she reaches down to lift her crossover handbag over her head and drop it on to her teak desk, along with the black jacket she's holding.

Her eyes search the office, for me. And, there's a warm feeling in my chest at the exact moment that our eyes connect. I see her smile and feel a smirk forming across my face. Bloody hell! I'm like a teenager.

'Hey, did I miss anything?' she asks, walking my way.

Shep looks up from her desk and smiles, 'Hey Julie, the kettle's not long boiled.'

'Coffee?' Mike offers, studying something on his iPad by the incident board, and looking briefly at Julie, 'How's Amy?'

'Please, and she's as you would expect. Heartbroken, frail, angry with the world. Her brother is staying with her for the rest of the week, before he has to return to base on Monday. He's in the marines.'

Julie takes the hot coffee mug from Mike, finds a wooden chair and drags it next to mine as I sit looking at the incident board with a heavy file of paperwork. We're missing something here, and I can't quite put my finger on it. One thing is certain though, Gino Camprinelli is bloody lucky that he didn't catch that bullet if he was standing behind Gloverman at the exact time the bullet was fired.

Shep and Mike bring their chairs, phones and paperwork to sit near us. I take out the post-mortem paperwork for Rose. I can't believe Felix crushed eight Restoril tablets, forced them into her open mouth and washed them down with half a bottle of vodka.

What the hell did he think would happen to her? That she'd simply sleep for a short while. Bastard. His only saving grace in my book is that he didn't rape her. That's no consolation to Henry, Jenny and Stuart, though, is it?

I return the papers to the folder and search for Gloverman's PM report, his entry and exit wounds. The pathology report states that the bullet entered at the centre of Felix's forehead, crashed through the frontal bone of his skull and lodged in the occipital bone, near the back of his head.

I push the diagram papers into the hands of the team. 'What do you think?' I ask them.

'Now, I'm no expert,' I state, 'but to me, this looks like someone who knew what they were doing. In Jenny's statement, she recalled seeing a 'red dot' on Felix's head, just before the bullet hit him.'

Shep looks up from taking notes, 'so he had one of those sight things that can shoot from a distance?'

'A sight and scope, yes,' Mike chips in, trying to hide a smile.

'Are you saying he's military?' Julie asks, her voice is quiet.

I sit forward and lean my arms on my knees, to look at her. 'Why?'

'Well, if the person is military, the only noted connection, apart from Mickey and Henry, to this case would be Amy Wilder's brother,' she seems agitated, as though she doesn't want to get Craig in trouble, just in case he's not our sniper.

I look at Mike and his eyebrows lift in possible agreement of Julie's comment. 'What's his name?' I ask Julie.

'Craig, Sergeant Craig Wilder. He's a Royal Marine, and is currently based at RM Norton Manor, in Taunton, Somerset.

'Did you meet him?' Mike asks, taking a slurp of coffee from his mug and looking at Julie.

'Briefly, he was on his way upstairs, when I arrived this afternoon. His sister told me about where he's based, she very proud of him. Do you think he could be our killer?'

'It's possible, but we need to check him out first.' Something in my gut tells me that Craig Wilder is the man we've been looking for. I can feel the excitement welling in the pit of my stomach. I look at Shep.

She nods, and walks to her desk to access her computer, her fingers flying over the keyboard in a mesmerising dance.

'Sergeant Craig Wilder, thirty-six years old. Born and raised in Bath Spa, Somerset. Has a younger sister, Amy Louise Wilder, aged twenty-seven. Parents were drink and drug addicts, until their deaths three years ago. Both of an overdose, at the same time. Like a suicide pact. Craig took Amy from the family home when she was eighteen and set up a home for them both in between joining the Royal Marines. There's a nine-year age difference between the siblings, and luckily for her, Craig took on the parental role.'

'That's bloody sad,' Mike says.

'I know,' I say, 'but we need to talk to him.' I look at my watch, it's 2pm. 'Mike, can you and Shep go back to Amy Wilder's house and talk to Craig? Bring him in if you need to?'

They nod and stand. Mike walks to his desk, grabs his jacket and car keys, before asking Julie: 'Can you text us the address?' Julie nods, heads to her desk and rummages in her bag for her notebook.

I watch Julie's movements casually, watch her flick the pages of her notebook to find the address details. When she finds the page she needs, she takes her phone from her jeans pocket and sends the information.

'Done,' she tells them, looking up with an easy smile. I can't help but smile in turn. I'm mesmerised.

'But we can't search the property?' Shep grabs her black padded jacket and bag, from the back of her chair.

'No,' I answer, getting to my feet, 'he's just a person of interest, at the moment. Talk to him, see if he has an alibi on the night of the shooting.'

It would be interesting to see what Amy had to say about her brother. Would she stand by him? Give him an alibi, look the other way? We never know what we are prepared to do unless we're faced with a situation that forces us to make heart-breaking choices, decisions that we would not normally make. The difference between right and wrong, good and bad, becomes a simple, extension of the primal need to look yourself in the mirror and know that you did what you felt was right.

'Sir?' Julie's voice breaks through my thoughts.

'Sorry, I was miles away,' I say, 'have they gone?'

'Yes,' she answers walking to her desk and sitting down, 'do you think it's him?'

'Possibly,' I reply, rubbing my hand over my chin absently. 'This case has baffled me from the beginning. Nothing has been straight forward,' I mutter before heading to my office. 'Listen,' I say, watching her turn her work screen on, 'how do you feel about dinner tonight? With me, I mean?' I catch the surprised look on her face, the shooting up of her eyebrows, the slightly open mouth, the hint of pink to her cheeks.

'Tonight?' she repeats.

'Yes, unless you're busy,' it's only fair to offer her a chance to back out.

Julie's face is serious, and I worry that she's having second thoughts about exploring a relationship with me. An age seems to pass as we stand firm and hold each other's gaze, magnetised, unable to move. The smile, when it comes, brings a lump to my throat, and a tingle down my spine.

'Italian,' she gives a throaty laugh, 'I like Italian.'

I smile like a teenager, who's just nabbed his first date, as I walk into my office. 'Italian, it is,' I call back, reaching for my phone, with the intention of finding a good Italian restaurant in Oxford.

Now, if I could just tie up this bloody case.

Part 24

Jenny: three months later

'Hi, my name is Lottie and when I was fifteen years old something bad happened to me.' the words tumble out of her mouth in a quiet rushed voice, that holds a note of determination.

I am so damn proud of Lottie. She is beginning to work through the traumatic events in her past, Dr Daniel Scott is helping. I was lucky, you see. And, I realised when the fog lifted from my brain that I had access to money, and I could help others.

So, I pay privately for Lottie and myself to see Daniel each week. Talking things through with him has made a huge difference. She's beginning to believe that being raped by her cousin and his friends, wasn't her fault. Damned right, it wasn't. Believing in yourself, believing that you are worthy and deserve to be treated with respect is a huge step to finding your true self again.

To finding the person you are meant to be, everyone deserves to be loved, to be treated with kindness and respect. Of course, there's an element of earning such things, that we can't demand to be loved and treated well but in essence these are our fundamental human rights, regardless of race, culture, age, gender, social standing.

I sit next to Lottie, her red curls rest on the shoulders of her grey cardigan which hangs over a midi black linen dress. Sturdy black boots, silver earrings that look suspiciously like elephants, dangle from her ears and a long grey beaded necklace with a silver elephant pendant, complete the look.

I smile at her, the love I feel for this woman is beyond anything, she is like a sister to me. She has always been there for me when I needed her. I'm pleased and honoured that I can do the same as I look at the faces of each of the six women sitting on chairs in a circle in a hired room of the local leisure centre.

Faces light up with compassion and pride, with empathy and understanding. These women have lived these events, they know what she's talking about. They can support each other. As I glance at Lottie, I know she was worried about disclosing her experience to the group, I see something new. There is a look of relief in her eyes, a slight tilt to her lips. The applause of the six support group members and myself is deafening.

As I clap, the white gold, sapphire ring glistens on the fourth finger of my left hand. My wedding ring finger. My heart swells with love for the man who kept me sane and helped to pull me through the nightmare of three and a half months ago. Stuart.

***

Stuart, the one person who held me tight and never let me go. Despite his anger at Felix and despite his pain about losing Rose. Even in the hospital, when he was struggling to cope with the full extent of Felix's assault on me, he stood up and faced his anger, faced his fears.

Stuart had booked a surprise weekend away to Chippenham, a month ago. We'd stayed in a lovely hotel in the old market town and we finally found the time to just be us. No drama, no threat or peril, no anger or fear. Just us.

The town had a great atmosphere and we decided to look for a property to buy in the area, to make a home and build a future together there. On Saturday evening we'd been eating in an

Italian restaurant, I'd dressed in a dark red linen dress and black jacket, Stuart had worn a burgundy shirt and black jeans.

Laughing at silly things, such as the way he always kinked his little finger when he drank from a teacup, made for a lovely light-hearted evening. A large chocolate cake arrived at the table while we were waiting for dessert. It held one candle. I was shocked because neither of us had a birthday looming.

I studied the cake with interest, and then I began to read aloud the words written on the top, in white icing. 'Marry Me.' A range of emotions whirled through my mind as I looked across the table at this man of mine. Surprise, excitement, happiness. In anticipation of his words, I played with the beads on my necklace and waited, a Stu cleared his throat. His brown eyes caught mine, and to my utmost embarrassment, he swiftly pushed his chair from the table, stepped in front of me and forced himself to the floor. Where he rested on one knee.

My hands flew to my warm cheeks, as he took a small blue box from his jacket pocket and used both hands to open in. He was so nervous his hands were trembling. I couldn't help but smile as he presented a beautiful white gold ring with a stunning square blue sapphire.

'I love you Jenny Gloverman. So damn much,' his voice was husky with emotion, when he looked at me, 'I will love you until we are both old and grey and are hobbling around on walking sticks. Through the good times and the bad, the sadness and the joy. Just you and me. Us.' He suddenly stopped, and I held my breath, wondering if he'd changed his mind.

A hesitant, but forced smile spread across his face. His eyebrows lifted in question, 'So, what do you say Jen? Put a man out of his misery.'

I'd leant down to him, took his hands and pulled him and the ring box to a standing position in front of me.

'Yes, Stuart,' I'd said in a low voice, my eyes full of tears, 'it's a definite yes. I love you.' With shaking hands, he'd taken the ring from the box and put it onto the fourth finger of my left hand. It's new home.

And, we'd kissed while staff and customers cheered and clapped. Offering us their best wishes.

***

'Jen?' Lottie's voice sounds worried. 'You OK?'

I shake my head, putting the happy memory safely in storage, so I can focus on tonight.

'Well done, Lottie,' I pull her in to a fierce hug, 'I'm so proud of you.'

This is our first session of the support group that we started a month ago. The lawyers have released some of the funds relating to my inheritance and, following Felix's death, David Dueller is no longer acting or Deputy CEO to the company, but permanent CEO to the Gloverman Corporation.

When I think of the Corporation, I think of Henry and that leads me to Rose. I miss her. It was hard enough losing my parents at fifteen, I loved them, but felt I wasn't really theirs. I know they loved me, but the Corporation always came first. With Henry and Rose, I always came first, and that makes the difference. It's supposed to be this way, with your children, right?

Rose's funeral had been a quiet affair. It had taken place in a beautiful church at Little Milton, not far from Stadhampton,

Oxfordshire, on a cold December morning. I'd arranged the flowers, while Stuart and Lottie had put the notice in the paper and sorted any major problems. Meanwhile, I'd arranged a small wake in one of the hotel's private dining rooms, for those who wanted to remember Rose after the funeral.

Henry had kept in contact via the phone, he had been trying to write a eulogy for Rose, and was struggling. He'd asked if I could take over and do it. Of course, I'd agreed. It was the least I could do. He'd managed to find a beautiful photo of Rose on his phone had it printed and put into a black frame. He'd continued to stay at Mickey Shakespeare's, despite the fact that I'd released £500,000 from the Corporation funds and gifted it to him to buy a new home. I think they both liked the company.

Taking into account everything that I'd been through, the kidnapping and the fear and panic of being imprisoned in a confined space. From discovering that Felix had raped me, and finding that he'd taken Rose, to when he'd chased me to the top of Wittenham Clumps to drag me back to his car, it still didn't matter so much. The saddest day of my life, thus far, was Rose's funeral.

Many people, some familiar and some unfamiliar came to pay their last respects to Rose. DCI Brian Carter and his team attended and made donations to Rose's favourite charity, Childline. David Dueller, Amy Wilder, her brother and Mickey Shakespeare were also there.

Memories of Stuart's warm hand softly tapping mine, when it was my turn to stand and read from my prepared script, made my heart ache. Henry flanked my other side, wiping tears from his face with a large white handkerchief. I'd patted his leg as I'd stood, tears threatening to fall as I 'd walked to the small steps that took me to the wooden pulpit.

The sea of faces before me looked sad and shocked. Henry, with his red, blotchy face suddenly seemed so old and fragile. Stuart had shuffled across and put his arm around him.

I'd cleared my throat and unfolded the piece of paper which contained my prepared handwritten notes. With my head held high, I'd spoke to the mourners in a clear voice, 'For those who knew Rose Dean, she was a caring, smiling woman who would do anything for you.

'She was involved with local charities and worked as the Housekeeper at Gateshead for many years, which was no mean feat. She was the glue that kept us together, the motherly figure that turned Gateshead into a home. She was Henry's loving wife and they shared many happy years together. But, to me,' I'd stopped reading the words, I knew by heart, but couldn't quite remember.

I'd looked at everyone, through eyes blurred with tears, and said on a sob, 'to me, Rose was the mother I never had. When my parents were too busy working, she was there for me, unconditionally.

'When I scraped my knee,' I rubbed the tears from my cheeks, 'she was there to pick me up. And, when I left home to go to university, it was Rose and Henry who helped me to settle in, with their firm hugs, and loving words. I will always be thankful to Rose and Henry, for allowing me into their life and for loving me as though, I were their own child. They say charity begins at home. It certainly did for me. May you rest in peace, darling Rose. You will be forever missed.'

I'd stepped down, unable to see through tear-filled eyes. Stuart came to take my arm. That day, I'd finally admitted to myself that Rose was gone.

***

Stuart, Lottie and I are on track for finishing our university degree. Currently, I visit the Ditton Park head office, once a week to see how things are going, to check in and ensure that people know who I am and that I will be taking a vested interest in the company. I will be attending board meetings and monitoring closely their management and financial reports.

I've not decided if I will become the CEO, despite what the paperwork says. Why change a finely tuned engine when there's nothing wrong with it?

Besides, my days are filled with attending counselling sessions, developing our new support group, searching for a property to buy in Chippenham and completing my Business and Management dissertation. I've put Gateshead up for sale. It's on the market for two and a half million. A fraction of what it's worth, because I just want to rid myself of it.

Stuart and I have been developing an exciting concept, based on something that is very close to our hearts. We're planning to add a new business venture to Gloverman's already impressive portfolio. This venture, unlike the others, is not to make money, but to give back to the community, to society, to offer a safe haven for women in need and to help rebuild lives.

I am lucky, I have people around me, and I have the finances and connections to ensure that I have the support that I need, following my ordeal. Not everyone has such opportunities. Statistics show that one in four women suffer domestic violence at some point in their lifetime.

Our business model will include two safe houses for women and children who are in need of refuge from violence in the home. Each house will have up to five bedrooms, with a manager who will live either onsite or next door. In addition, our venture will include access to solicitors, counsellors, hands-on support and, most of all, a family of people who will give unconditional love and support for life. The last is particularly for those who have no family, no network. Life should be about second chances.

From the moment I woke up in that dark, confined space of a box, to where I am now. This is what counts. This makes for a life uncommon.

Part 25

Henry: January

'Cheers mate,' I raise my pint of lager to the two men sitting around the table with me. We're in a quiet corner of a public house in Lymington, a vibrant town in the New Forest. It's 7pm on a Tuesday night, it's not tourist season, so the pub is fairly quiet.

'Cheers,' Craig's deep voice, holds a harshness to it. I watch as he takes a sip from the cold glass of lager, before his piercing dark blue eyes focus on me. And, in that moment he looks just like his uncle, Sergeant John Meadow, a Royal Marine Commando. Another close unit member, as I've said, we've built lifelong friendships. Sadly, John had lost his battle against bowel cancer last year.

Craig has a youthfulness about him, that I remember well. Toned, marine-trained, self-assured, with his short blonde hair and clean-shaven face. He's ready to take on the world. To be fair, after two tours of Afghanistan, I believe he has. He places his glass on the table and absently pulls down the sleeves of his emerald coloured woollen top. 'How are you doing Henry?'

I owe this man everything. I made a deal with the devil to sort out Felix. I involved Mickey and Craig and that's something that I'll have to live with. And, more importantly, something that they will have to live with. For, between us, we made sure that Felix wouldn't hurt anymore people. 'I'm doing all right, Craig. How's Amy?'

'She's getting there. Work keeps her busy. Not sure if she'll ever be the same, though,' Craig answers.

'I don't think any of us will be,' I shake my head sadly.

My phone rings, Neil Diamond begins to sing the first few words to 'Crackling Rose'. Bugger, it's DCI Brian Carter. Panic momentarily sets in and I can't move, I just sit staring at the singing phone sitting on the table. 'It's DCI Carter,' I say quietly to them before picking up the device and answering the call.

'DCI Carter. How are you?' I ask.

'I'm good,' he answers.

All the time I hold my breath, praying that he hasn't found anything to link me, Mickey or Craig to the shooting.

'How have you been, Henry?' he asks. And, I wonder if this is a leading question. Do I answer honestly? I decide to keep as near to the truth as I can.

'I'm fine. Mickey is keeping me busy with his gardening business.' I reply, 'Jenny and Stuart are doing well, they're busy putting together a new business project,' and then I add, on a chuckle, 'the Gloverman Corporation won't know what's hit them!'

Brian's laugh echoes down the phone line. 'Listen, Henry,' he says in a serious tone, 'I just wanted to let you know that we're closing the case on Felix Gloverman. No evidence has come forth. I'm annoyed, but that's how it goes sometimes.'

'Oh, well I guess that's that then,' I feel speechless, I was convinced he was calling to say he knows I'm involved in Felix's death. I close my eyes and rub my temple, before I speak. 'Best to move on I suppose. Rose would have wanted that. I appreciate you calling to update me.'

'You're welcome, I just wanted to let you know.'

I disconnect the call, put the phone on the table and stare at it. Oh my God! Did that just happen? Is it really over? I can hardly take it in.

Mickey looks at me, he shaved off his moustache yesterday and his face looks completely different. Younger. I'm sure I'll get used to it.

'We did the right thing,' Mickey says.

'Definitely,' Craig answers, 'DS Jones was quite nice when he came to get my statement. I told him I'd been visiting a marine mate's father who lives in an elderly residential apartment in Didcot, on the night of the shooting. I'd signed in at reception and stayed a couple of hours before signing out again.

'What he didn't know was that Ned's room was on the ground floor, next to the disabled access door. Ned lent me his key fob to get back in. He was happy to vouch that I'd been there for about two hours.'

'Jesus. You make it sound so easy!' I tell him, shaking my head in disbelief.

'It was the only way,' Craig said, 'I was hiding out on the other side of the car park, when I saw him drag Rose from the car and drag her out of sight behind that tree. She was unresponsive and I had my concerns, that's when I saw him grab Jenny, she fought back, and he chased her up the hill. I had to get up there double quick to get myself into position. Mickey sent me his text to confirm it was a 'go.' I took the shot. For Jenny, for my sister and especially for Rose and my sister's unborn baby.'

'To bloody right,' I mutter.

Craig slumps forward and drops his head. He stares into his glass, 'it was a little girl, you know. The baby,' he says, in a flat, quiet voice.

I look at Mickey and we pat him on the back to offer our condolences, ‘so sorry mate,’ I mutter.

We sit in silence for a moment, each in our own private world of pain, before Mickey changes the subject by asking, ‘where is the weapon now?’

‘It’s best you don’t know,’ Craig’s voice is low, ‘just be assured that it will never be found. The clothes I wore have been burnt. Everything has been sorted.’

Mickey and I nod in acknowledgement. ‘Thanks Craig,’ I say. ‘I appreciate everything you’ve done for me, for us. Your uncle would have been very proud of you.’ Craig simply nods. Sometimes actions speak louder than words.

‘I propose a toast,’ I raise my glass to them. ‘to Rose, and to moving on.’

‘To Rose, and to moving on,’ their glasses touch mine. And, for the first time that evening, we smile.

Epilogue

Jenny: June

The glass is cold on my forehead as I lean on the hard surface and stare out of the floor to ceiling window. A peacock walks gracefully over the wooden bridge, that covers a now dry riverbed and on to the treelined road that leads to the main building. A kaleidoscope of jewelled colours catches the mid-morning sunlight as the bird reaches the concrete walkway that serves as a bridge to the water-filled moat which surrounds the building. I wonder where his mate is, probably in the upper field trying to aggravate the bees in their beehives.

Behind me, feet shuffle into the boardroom and low voices mutter hellos and good mornings, before taking their seats at the grey meeting room table. More voices, more shuffling of feet and I pull away from the window but can't seem to take my eyes off the peacock. A movement catches my eyes and from behind a tree, a peahen with an emerald green neck and brown feathers appears and walks to her mate.

A gentle hand touches my lower back, a reminder that I am needed to lead the meeting. Stuart. My husband. The person who never gave up on me and the man who wouldn't let me give up on myself.

The room is filled with low voices and quiet conversation. The catering staff, I've organised from the restaurant on the first floor, bring in pots of coffee and tea. Plates of biscuits and cakes are carefully placed on to the table alongside, jugs of milk, bowls of sugar and drinking crockery.

I rub my hands down my dark blue linen dress, to smooth out any remaining creases, before interlinking my fingers. Absently, I stroke the metal band that sits on the fourth finger of my left hand, snugly against my sapphire engagement ring. I'm still getting used to wearing a wedding ring. I love the feeling of security it gives me, that Stuart is here with me and that he loves me. And, in this moment, it brings a tear to my eye.

***

My wedding had been a simple affair. Nothing showy, just a registrar in a hotel that used to be a prison in Oxford. Lottie, and a few friends from the support group, sat in smart wedding regalia alongside, Daniel Scott.

The DCI and Julie, who were now engaged, held hands as they offered us their congratulations. Julie had completed her detective training and had applied for a transfer to Newbury police station. It seemed the logical thing to do, in light of their engagement. It kept their private life separate. Sometimes, you just know when a relationship feels right, don't you? Why waste time?

Shep, Mike Jones and Mickey Shakespeare were also in attendance. A small group, by any measure. Henry gave me away, holding my arm with a fierce pride as I walked down the aisle in a plain ivory silk gown, with lace sleeves and a slashed neckline. Before he handed me over to Stuart, he'd whispered, 'Rose would have been so proud of you.' I held back the tears and swallowed the lump in my throat.

I needed to look forward. To my life with Stuart.

***

'Ready?' My husband's breath caresses the side of my cheek, bringing me back to the present. He looks good in his dark grey suit and crisp white shirt.

I step up to his warm body and my hand reaches out to cover his heart. His dark brown eyes brighten with pride as he whispers in my ear, 'You got this, babe.'

I smile and stretch to my full height, before placing a bright, confident smile on my face. Looking at the people seated at the table, this moment is pivotal, I need to stake my claim on this global company.

'Good morning, everybody,' I say, pulling my linen grey jacket down at the bottom, and walk to my chair at the head of the table. I place my hands on the top of the black padded chair, to steady myself, and smile. Out of the corner of my eye I see my husband take his place amongst the eleven men and women seated at the table.

'Thank you for coming this morning, to my first board meeting. I would like to introduce you to the Gloverman Corporation's latest project.'

I pause for a moment and take in the looks of surprise and panic on their faces. I force myself to work through my prepared speech, 'My husband and I have worked tirelessly.'

I stop talking and look across the table to Stuart's strong face. He is steadfast in his protection and support of me. He would die for me, and that's how I know he's the one. Stuart smiles, his eyes shining with pride, willing me on.

Inhaling deeply, I take a moment to look at the faces surrounding me, many of whom I don't know. I pick up the thread of my speech:

'Tirelessly to put together the proposals and plans for this project. It is a charity, very close to our hearts. We plan to offer safe and secure accommodation, with specialised and practical support to help vulnerable women and children who have suffered abuse in the home. Two refuge homes are initially planned as we build the business and put in place the necessary measures to comply with the law.

'We will work closely with local councils and already have a number of magistrates and council officials willing to work with us. The homes will offer vulnerable people the chance to re-build their confidence, skills and independence. In effect, to rebuild their lives.'

CEO, David Dueller's pale face contorts in anger as he raises a hand, to stop me talking. 'And where will the money come from to support this venture?' he asks in a high, squeaky voice.

I give David my most severe stare, I expected some resistance in the venture. It wouldn't be good business acumen to throw money away on every little thought or idea.

'Good question, Mr Dueller,' I can feel the confidence and passion building within me. This is my time to shine, and I'm going to damn well take it. This is why I survived, why I'm not going to live as a victim. I want to make a difference. I glance at Stuart's face, see the smile before he gives me the briefest of nods. *Go get them, Jen. Go bloody get them.* My words flow in confidence:

'My parents inherited this business from my paternal grandfather. They gave everything to it, toiled night and day to help make it what it is today. They even chose their own child over the business. They eventually died, on route to a meeting, for the business.

'I believe that a substantial amount of the money that the Gloverman Corporation makes, should be put back into the community, instead of finding its way into executive and trustee's pockets. We need to make a difference,' I lean forward and place my hands on the table, 'because, if we don't, we will lose whatever integrity we have left.'

‘Here, here,’ old James Forteskew slams his hand on the table, ‘you are your parents’ child.’

‘But,’ interrupts Dueller.

‘Let Mrs Greyson speak,’ Eliza Danes, the UK finance director addresses him in a sharp tone, ‘I for one, would like to hear what she has to say.’

I offer Eliza a thank you smile for her comment, before nodding to my husband. Stuart pushes from his seat and walks across the room to the light switch. As he presses the switch, the room darkens, and I can almost feel the air of anticipation in the room. It is so quiet that I can hear myself breathing.

There will be opposition to this project, to my interference within the company. There will be those who are too stuck in their ways to change, and there are those who want to move forward. I don’t particularly care what they think. The Gloverman Corporation is mine. I own eighty per cent of the company, and I will have my way.

I walk over to my laptop, which sits on a table next to the wall, and bring up the project proposal presentation on the homepage. The large display screen attached to the wall behind my seat comes to life, a brilliant array of colours, swirling around the central picture, a stunning blue and white lighthouse.

‘Ladies and gentlemen,’ I walk to the side of the screen, my heart is pounding, as my arm gestures to the screen. My voice is strong and confident, ‘I would like to introduce you to, The Lighthouse Charity.’

Acknowledgments

I wrote this book because I wanted to provide the back story for the two previous books of The Lighthouse series, The Lamp-post Shakers and The Ghost Chaser. It was important to make Jenny and Stuart into strong, believable characters that people could relate to. I think I did them justice.

Writing a book is a process. It begins as a seed of an idea and simmers slowly into the shape of the story I'm trying to write. Eventually, I reach something that resembles the novel you've just read, and when that time comes, I call in a variety of people for their input.

Thank you to the wonderful people who read and offered feedback on the first drafts. Julia, Tina, Denise, Wendy and Lisa, your feedback was essential in helping me to move the draft forward. I appreciate your honesty and friendship.

To Lisa, my editor, who saw the vision. Thank you. Your clear, constructive feedback helped to fine tune The Box to enable it to be publish-ready. You were a joy to work with, and I hope you'll be joining on my writing journey with book 4.

Thank you to my hubby, for his help in getting The Box onto Amazon. Although I'm learning all the time, his IT skills far outweigh mine!

Finally, thanks to everyone who buys and reads my books, for Amazon and Goodreads reviews and for supporting my FB page and website.

You are all very much appreciated.

AJ Warren x (Andrea)

Read on for several reviews and an excerpt of The Ghost Chaser

‘This is the second book in the Lighthouse series by this exciting new author. The storyline is absolutely riveting, I true 'page turner'. Looking forward to book 3!’

★★★★★ Amazon Customer

‘I thought this second book was excellent and can’t wait for the 3rd in the series.’

★★★★★ Mrs B Read

The Ghost Chaser

Chapter 1: Till death do us part

Steph

I look at the body and shudder. The corpse lies face up, the familiar mop of brown hair, cut shorter than I remember, and has gleaming scarlet blood sticking to parts of his fringe and head. Blood and brain matter seep from his violent head wound and drip slowly across the kitchen-diner laminate floor. His green eyes are open in that death stare that you never get used to. An iced chill runs through me. I take a deep breath, as a flood of memories swirl through my mind, moments of joy from our initial meeting. Of sunny days walking along the beach, hand in hand, laughing about the silliest things and licking our ice creams from their cones.

Memories filter through my mind, a rushed white wedding and an unplanned pregnancy. And then all I remember is heartache and pain. Dark days. Hard to forget.

Red marks cover his face, masking the handsome shape of his square jaw, straight nose and clear skin. He'd always been lucky with his skin I mused, and my heart fluttered in remembrance. This sallow, bloody lifeless face in front of me was the very one I used to dream about when we first began dating. Marks that look suspiciously like fingernail marks trailed across his skin. Had there been a struggle? I think of someone defending himself against him. He was strong, physically strong, and when caught in the moment, when his temper flared, he had the strength of an army of men. That, I could tell you from experience.

Eyes that had once looked at me with love and admiration, are now glazed and empty, in final slumber. A white linen shirt splattered in blood, hangs from his body and he's wearing trainer-style shoes.

I take a deep breath.

My name is Steph Rutland, and this is my first murder case since my fast track promotion four months ago to Detective Inspector, and for ease I'm usually known as DI Rutland.

Keep calm I tell myself. He can't hurt you, or another living person again. I bend down, as close as I dare without touching him, to study the angle of his body and search for clues to what happened to this man. This is the closest I've been to him, without him physically hurting me, in a long time. What does that tell you? This man, who was my first love, my husband and father to our fourteen-year-old son Ben – he became a monster with a short temper, who needed no excuse to use me as his punchbag. A temper that became his weapon, to use at his will if I didn't meet some impossible standard, that only he was allowed to set.

This was the devil himself.

I stand and walk around the kitchen area. The grey square wall clock says 1.15pm. There are two half empty wine glasses on the counter and a brown-handled screwdriver lies on the floor near the kitchen sink. I peer closely at it and see no obvious signs of blood. I'm sure the Scenes of Crime Officers, commonly known as SOCO, will use their equipment to glean any hidden blood particles and fingerprints. Questions rush through me. How the hell had he managed to move to the same county as us, without me knowing? Was this a coincidence? Why had he moved? Did he still own the car sales business in Basingstoke? Who was he with last night, and where was that person?

There's a brown wooden baseball bat lying on the kitchen floor near the sink unit. About a quarter of it is covered in blood. It's not rocket science to assume that this is the murder weapon. I'm feeling more confused every minute. How did this man, my ex-husband and someone who I've not seen in eleven years, find himself lying dead on his own kitchen floor? What the hell happened here? And why leave the bat here for us to find? Did the attacker run out of time, or panic? Something doesn't add up. I can't understand why the bat would be left like that. Thoughts run through my head, it's spinning, and for a moment I scrape my hand through my long curly jet-black hair and briefly press my fingers against my forehead. This cannot be happening.

Follow the evidence, that's what you're taught in the Major Investigation Team, follow the evidence and do the leg work. It's not like watching a TV crime show where everything is condensed into a sixty-minute solvable time slot. Solving a crime takes a lot of patience, time and perseverance. And also, quite a bit of luck.

"Is there a wallet to identify him?" asks my colleague, Detective Sergeant Chris Jackson, his clean-shaven oval face scrunched in concentration. A wisp of dark-blonde hair falls over his brown eyes and my fingers tingle with the sudden urge to push it behind his ear. Must be my maternal instinct kicking in.

"No," says the police constable who was the first person on the scene. "Nothing."

I stand and look at them as the duty forensic pathologist walks in, suitably dressed for a crime scene in a white protection suit and matching disposable shoe covers and gloves. Jesus, what a mess. I should have known that today would pan out this way. I mean, I'm not the luckiest of people. Soon, I'll have to own up to them that I know this man and that he was my ex-husband. I know I'm procrastinating, but I need a minute to process what has happened. I think I'm in shock, I never thought I'd see him again, but he's here. Now. Dead on the kitchen floor. I just need a minute to get my head together.

"Hey, Dr Soames. Good to see you," I say, giving her a quick nod. Dr Daisy Soames – thirty-something, petite, fitness freak with short blonde hair which has a streak of purple across her fringe. She's been a friend of mine from my Hendon training days. It's on days like this I wish I were back there at Hendon, working hard to complete the training, forming friendships and enjoying the social interaction.

A sudden vision comes to me of Daisy and I celebrating another Hendon trainee's 21st birthday, Andy I think his name was. The memory of Daisy throwing back a pitcher of cider for a twenty-pound bet still brings tears to my eyes. I spent most of my time with her in the bathroom, carefully holding her hair back to keep it away from her heaving mouth, the twenty-pound note peeping out of the top of her jeans pocket. I couldn't believe how rough we both felt the following day. Gosh, was that really seven years ago now?

When I think back to how low I'd been when I'd walked away from my marriage my tummy still churns and my heart beats a little faster. It brings a feeling of apprehension, a blackness to my soul. Anyone who's experienced that feeling of extreme exhaustion, the kind that sends you into a trance-like state of despondency, will understand the desolation of accepting a situation that you know deep down is simply not right.

Well, that was me a few years ago, accepting cruel words and a quick temper from my spouse that often resulted in me dragging my sore, bruised body through the motions of looking after Ben. Yes, when you hit rock bottom and there's no place left to go.

Struggling through each day as if in a dream. You will understand what I'm saying.

I am not that person anymore. I am the person I was before I met HIM.